"I'm a fanatical reader of thrillers and Stephen Hunter has always been one of my favorites."
—Malcolm Gladwell, Salon.com

NEW YORK TIMES BESTSELLING AUTHOR STEPHEN HUNTER DELIVERS "TOP-NOTCH ENTERTAINMENT" (*Wall Street Journal*)

"The best writer of straight-out thrillers working today."
—*Rocky Mountain News*

"Hunter passes almost everybody else in the thriller-writing trade as if they were standing still."
—*Daily News* (New York)

"There are few writers living today who can piece words together as well as Stephen Hunter."   —*Denver Daily News*

Hard-as-nails hero Bob Lee Swagger is

"ONE OF THE FINEST SERIES CHARACTERS EVER TO GRACE THE THRILLER GENRE, NOW AND FOREVER."
—*Providence Journal Bulletin*

"HUNTER IS BACK AT THE TOP OF HIS GAME"
(*Publishers Weekly,* starred review) with

I, SNIPER

"Pure reading bliss, a solid bull's-eye that places Hunter on the level of David Morrell, James Lee Burke, and Lee Child, as good a novelist as he is a storyteller."

—*Providence Journal-Bulletin*

"*I, Sniper* won me over. I don't pretend to share Swagger and Hunter's enthusiasm for gunpowder, but I've spent more than a dozen years being entertained by it."

—*The Oregonian*

"A masterful piece of writing by an old pro at the top of his game." —*Tucson Citizen*

"A thrilling page-turner." —*Denver Daily News*

"The first great thriller of 2010." —*Madison County Herald*

"In his guns-a-poppin' latest, Hunter pits his series hero against a nest of sharp-shooting vipers. . . . Dust off the OK Corral. Even the somewhat squeamish, and even certifiable gun-dummies, may once again find chivalric, heroic Bob Lee just about irresistible." —*Kirkus Reviews*

"A ramped-up, high-tech High Noon finale will leave even unsympathetic readers gasping. As always, Hunter makes it work with precise, detail-rich prose."

—*Booklist* (starred review)

"Hunter's thrillers are always taut, exciting, and well written, and his latest is no exception. Swagger fans will not be disappointed." —*Library Journal*

"Hunter has a unique writing style that thrills and captivates from the opening scene to deliver an exciting whodunit."

—*The Sun* (UK)

NIGHT OF THUNDER

"Few thriller writers out there can match Hunter's skill when it comes to writing about guns . . . in prose both lyrical and reverent. . . . The climactic set piece at the speedway is a real thrill ride, fueled by pure action-junkie adrenaline."

—*The Washington Post*

"Known for his cinematic language, action-packed suspense and multifaceted characters, Hunter delivers all three in his latest. . . . Add Hunter's sense of rhythm; his fast-paced, evocative language; and his talent for the just-right metaphor, and you get this can't-put-down tale."

—*The Baltimore Sun*

THE 47TH SAMURAI

"The novel Hunter's fans have been waiting for. . . . Genius."

—*Booklist*

"I have only one major problem with Mr. Hunter: He doesn't write often enough."

—Otto Penzler, *The New York Sun*

"Delivers chills and thrills. . . . Hunter is terrific with plot, action, and attention to detail."   —*The Denver Post*

"Hunter has a cinematic sense of story and combat, and *The 47th Samurai* kept me glued to the screen until the final credits."   —*The Oregonian* (Portland)

These titles are also available as eBooks

ALSO BY STEPHEN HUNTER

Night of Thunder

The 47th Samurai

American Gunfight (with John Bainbridge, Jr.)

Now Playing at the Valencia:
Pulitzer Prize–Winning Essays on Movies

Havana

Pale Horse Coming

Hot Springs

Time to Hunt

Black Light

Dirty White Boys

Point of Impact

Violent Screen:
A Critic's 13 Years on the Front Lines of Movie Mayhem

Target

The Day Before Midnight

The Spanish Gambit (Tapestry of Spies)

The Second Saladin

The Master Sniper

I, SNIPER

A BOB LEE SWAGGER NOVEL

STEPHEN HUNTER

Pocket Books

NEW YORK   LONDON   TORONTO   SYDNEY

Pocket Books
A Division of Simon & Schuster, Inc.
1230 Avenue of the Americas
New York, NY 10020

This book is a work of fiction. Names, characters, places, and incidents either are products of the author's imagination or are used fictitiously. Any resemblance to actual events or locales or persons, living or dead, is entirely coincidental.

First Pocket Books paperback edition October 2010

POCKET and colophon are registered trademarks of Simon & Schuster, Inc.

For information about special discounts for bulk purchases, please contact Simon & Schuster Special Sales at 1-866-506-1949 or business@simonandschuster.com.

The Simon & Schuster Speakers Bureau can bring authors to your live event. For more information or to book an event, contact the Simon & Schuster Speakers Bureau at 1-866-248-3049 or visit our website at www.simonspeakers.com.

Cover design by David Ter-Avanesyan
Cover photo by Shutterstock Images

Manufactured in the United States of America

10   9   8   7   6   5   4   3   2   1

ISBN 978-1-4165-6517-8
ISBN 978-1-4165-6616-8 (ebook)

Why, they couldn't hit an elephant at this distance!

MAJOR GENERAL JOHN SEDGWICK,
COMMANDER, UNION VI CORPS,
MOMENTS BEFORE HIS DEATH BY
RIFLE FIRE FROM CONFEDERATE
SHARPSHOOTERS, SPOTSYLVANIA,
VIRGINIA, MAY 9, 1864

The time has long passed in America when one can say of a sixty-eight-year-old woman that she is "still" beautiful, the snarky little modifier, all buzzy with irony, signifying some kind of miracle that one so elderly could be so attractive. Thus everyone agreed, without modification, that Joan Flanders was beautiful in the absolute—fully beautiful, extremely beautiful, totally beautiful, but never "still" beautiful. Botox? Possibly. Other work? Only Joan and her doctors knew. The best in dental work, an aggressive workout regimen, the most gifted cosmeticians and hairdressers available to the select? That much certainly was true.

But even without the high-end maintenance, she would have been beautiful, with pale smooth skin, a lioness's mane of thick reddish blond hair, piercing blue eyes set behind prominent cheekbones, a slender stalk of neck and a mere slip of body, unfettered by excess ounces, much less pounds. She was dressed in tweeds and white cashmere, expertly tailored, and wore immense sunglasses that looked as if flying saucers of prescription glass had landed on the planet of her face. She took tea with a great deal of grace and wit, with her Hollywood agent, a famous name but with a dull generic quality to him no one would recognize, and her gay personal assistant. The group sat on the patio of the Lemon Tree in downtown East Hampton, New York, on a bright fall day with just a brush of chill in the air as well as salt tang from the nearby Atlantic. There were two other stars on the patio, of the young, overmoussed generation, one female, one indeterminate, as well as a couple of agents with their best-selling writers, the wives of a couple of Fortune 500 CEOs, and at least three mistresses of other Fortune 500 CEOs, as well as the odd tourist couple and discreet celeb watchers, enjoying an unusually rich harvest of faces.

Joan and Phil were discussing—the market recovery? Paramount's new vice president of production? The lousy scripts that were being sent her after the failure of her comeback picture *Sally Tells All*? Ex-hubby Tom's strange new obsession with the kiddie shoot-'em-ups of his past? It doesn't matter. What matters is only that Joan was twice royalty: her father, Jack, had been one of the major stars bridging the pre- and postwar era and she had gotten his piercing eyes and bed-knob cheekbones. She was pure Hollywood blueblood, second generation. But as well, her second husband had been a prominent antiwar leader in the raging if far-off sixties, and her picture, aboard the gunner's chair on a North Vietnamese anti-aircraft battery, had made her instantly beloved and loathed by equal portions of her generation. That made her political royalty, a part of the hallowed crusade to end a futile war; or it made her a commie bitch traitor, but still royalty. The rest was detail, albeit interesting. She had won an Oscar. She had been married to the billionaire mogul T. T. Constable, in one of the most documented relationships in history. She had made one of her several fortunes as an exercise guru and still worked out three hours a day and was as fit as any thirty-five-year-old. All who saw her that day felt her charisma, her history, her beauty, her royal presence, including the tourists, the other stars, the wives and mistresses, and her executioner.

He spared her and America the disturbing phenomenon of a head shot. Instead, he fired from about 340 yards out and sent a 168-grain Sierra hollow point boat tail MatchKing on a slight downward angle at 2,300 feet per second to pierce her between her fourth and fifth ribs on the left-hand side, just outside the armpit; the missile flew unerringly through viscera without the slightest deviation and had only lost a few dozen pounds of energy when it hit her in the absolute center of the heart, exactly where all four chambers came together in a nexus of muscle. That organ was pulped in a fraction of a second. Death was instantaneous, a kind of mercy, one supposes, as Ms. Flanders quite literally could not have noticed her own extinction.

As in all cases of public violence, a moment of disbelief occurred when she toppled forward, accidentally broke her fall on the table for a second, but then torqued to the right and her body lost purchase and completed its journey with a graceless thud to the brick of the patio. Nearly everyone thought "She's fainted," because the rifle report was so far away and suppressed that no identifier with the information "gun" was associated with the star's fall to earth. It took a second more for the exit wound to begin copious blood outflow, and that product spread in a dark sheen from her body, at which point the human fear of blood—quite natural, after all—asserted itself and screams and panic and running around and jumping up and down and diving for cover commenced.

It wasn't long before the police arrived and set up crime scene operations, and not long at all after that when the first of what would become more than three hundred reporters and photographers arrived on scene and the whole two blocks of downtown East Hampton took on an aspect that resembled none of Joan Flanders's twenty-eight films but vividly recalled those made by an Italian gentleman named Federico Fellini. In all that, no one noticed a blue Ford van pulling out of an alley 340 yards away to begin a trip to another destination and another date with history.

The shooter did not spare his audience the theatrics of gore for his next two victims. He went for the head, hit it perfectly, and blew each one all over the insides of the Volvo in which they were just beginning their daily commute. The range this time was shorter, 230 yards, but the ordnance was identical and the accuracy just as superb. He hit the first target one inch below the crown of the skull, dead center. There had been no deviation through the rear window glass of the heavy Swedish car. Unlike in the Flanders hit, there was no immediate hubbub. Jack Strong merely slumped forward until his shattered skull hit the steering wheel and rested. His wife, Mitzi Reilly, pivoted her head at the ruckus, had a second's worth of abject horror—police found urine in her panties, a fact not publicized, thankfully—before the second bullet hit her above and a little forward of the left ear. In both cases the hollow point target bullet blossomed in its puncture of skull bone and spun sideways, whimsically, as it plowed through brain matter, then exited in a horrendous gusher of blood, gray stuff, and bone frags, above an eye in one case, below the other eye in the other, cracking the face bone like a pie plate.

The car, which was in gear and running, then eased forward under the pressure of Jack's dead foot and hit the wall of the garage, where its progress halted. No one heard the gunshots, and indeed, the sound of gunshots in that part of Chicago was not remarkable to begin with. Jack and Mitzi lay like that for over an hour until a FedEx truck came down the alley seeking a shortcut through Hyde Park. The driver had trouble getting by, noticed the exhaust tendrils still curling from the pipe, and got out to inquire of the drivers what was going on. He discovered the carnage, called 911, and within minutes the Fellini movie starring Chicago police, FBI, and media had commenced on this site too.

It would be said that Jack and Mitzi went out together as they had lived, fought, and loved together. They were famous, not as much as Joan Flanders, but in their own world stars as well. Both tracked their pedigrees back to the decade of madness against which Joan Flanders had stood out. But it had been so long ago.

Jack, high-born (né Golden) of Jewish factory owners, well educated, passionate, handsome, had grown up in the radical tradition in Hyde Park, taken his act to Harvard, then Columbia, had been a founder of Students for Social Reform, and for a good six years was the face of the movement. At a certain point he despaired of peaceful demonstration as a means of affecting policy, much less lowering body count, and in 1971 went underground, with guns and bombs.

It was there that he met the already famous Mitzi Reilly, working-class Boston Irish, fiery of temperament and demeanor, intellectually brilliant, who had already been photographed on the sites of several bombings and two bank robberies. Redheaded with green eyes and pale, freckly skin, she was the fey Irish lass turned radical underground guerrilla woman-warrior, beloved by media and loathed by blue-collar Americans. She reveled in her status, and when Jack came aboard—it was a matter of minutes before they were in the sack together, and the fireworks there were legendary!—the team really took off, both in fame and in importance. They quickly became the number one most wanted desperadoes on J. Edgar's famous list, and somehow, through sympathetic journalists, continued to give interviews, stand still for pictures—both had great hair, thick, luxuriant, and strong, artistic faces; they burned holes in film—and operate.

Their biggest hit was the bombing of the Pentagon. Actually, it was a three-pound bag of black powder going boom off a primitive clock fuse in a waste can that created more smoke than damage, but it was symbolic, worth more than a thousand bombs detonated at lesser targets. It closed down a concourse for a couple of hours, more because of the insane press coverage than for any actual threat to people or operations, but it made them stars of an even bigger magnitude.

Their career began to turn when they were building a bigger bomb for a bigger target, but this time the boom came in the bedroom, not the Capitol, and both fled, leaving behind a good sister who'd managed to blow herself up. They were hunted and running low on money, and a violent bank robbery may or may not have followed—the FBI said yes, it was them; the Nyackett, Massachusetts, police were split—that left two security guards dead, shot down from behind by a tail gunner. It was a bad career move, whoever did it, because the dead men had children and were nothing but working stiffs, not pigs or oppressors or goons, just two guys, one Irish, one Polish, trying to get by, with large families depending on their three jobs, and the hypocrisy of a movement dedicated to the people that shot down two of the people was not lost on the public. Jack and Mitzi were never formally tied to this event, because the bank surveillance film, recovered by the police, was stolen from a processing lab and never recovered. Otherwise, it was said, they'd be up on capital murder charges and have a one-way to the big chair with all the wires attached, as Massachusetts dispatched its bad ones in those days.

A few years passed; times changed; the war ended, or at least the American part of it. Jack and Mitzi hired a wired lawyer who brokered a deal, and then it came out that in its efforts to apprehend them, the police and federal agencies had broken nearly as many laws as the famous couple had. In the end, rather than expose their own excesses to the public, the various authorities agreed to let it all slip. They were "guilty as hell, free as a bird," as Jack had proclaimed on the event, and able to rejoin society.

The academy beckoned. Each, with a solid academic background, found employment and ultimately tenure in Chicago higher ed. Jack taught education and achieved a professorship at the University of Illinois Chicago Circle campus; Mitzi, who'd graduated from the University of Michigan law school, came to rest at Northwestern's law school. The two bought a house in Hyde Park and spent the next years preaching rather than practicing radicalism. It seemed an extraordinary American saga, yet it ended, just like Dillinger's, in a Chi-town alley in pools of blood.

"Someone," said Mitch Greene, holding up a copy of that day's *Plain Dealer* with its blaring head POLICE, FEDS HUNT CLUES IN PROTEST SLAYINGS, "please tell Mark Felt I don't wanna play anymore." He got some laughter from the few before him who knew that Mark Felt had been the FBI's black bag guy long before he became Woodward's Deep Throat, during the wild years when Mitch Greene was running hard and starring in his own one-man show, "Mitch Greene v. America: the Comedy." Among its brighter ideas: a wishathon by which America's kids would will the planes full of soldiers to return to California. And the bit where he petitioned the Disney Company to open a "Vietnamland," where you could chuck phosphorous grenades into tunnels and animatronic screaming yellow flamers would pop out and perish in the foliage? Wonderful stuff. Alas, more of his audience remained mute, these being the slack-faced, mouth-breathing tattoo and pin exhibits called "the kids" who now made up his crowds in larger and larger percentages. Forget Felt; did they even know who *Mitch* was? Doubtful. They just knew he wrote *Uncle Mitch Explains*, a series of lighthearted history essays that preached Mitch's crazed lefto-tilt version of American history with a great deal of the ex-rad's charm and wit and had become, astonishingly, consistent best sellers.

So here he was, another town, another gig. The town was Cleveland, the gig was *The Gilded Age: Peasants for Dinner Again, Amanda?* Rockefeller, Carnegie, Gould, those guys, the usual suspects, the data mined quickly for outrageous anecdotes, the dates at least right courtesy of a long-suffering research assistant. ("Mitch, you can't really say that." "Oh yeah, watch me.") Another mild best seller, though it annoyed him the *Times BR* no longer listed his books in the adult section but only in its monthly kid section.

"Mr. Felt," he ad-libbed, "please don't have me killed. I ain't a-marching anymore."

Again, the laughter was limited to those few who saw the allusion to the famous Phil Ochs anthem of the sixties protest generation. Still, it was a pretty good crowd for a weeknight in Cleveland, in a nice Borders out in the burbs. He saw faces and books and the blackness of the sheet glass window, and he had a nice hotel room, who knows, maybe he could get laid, judging by the number of women with undyed gray hair knotted into ponytails above their muumuus and their Birkenstocks, and his plane to Houston wasn't at a brain-dead early morning hour.

But then someone hollered, "Mark Felt is dead."

Mitch replied, "Tell *this* guy!" holding up the front page even higher.

That got a good laugh—even most of the kids caught it. He was quick, when he was on the road, to adapt the latest developments into his shtick. His real gift was for stand-up and he'd even tried it for a few years in the eighties, though with not much success. A typically lighthearted op-ed piece in the *Daily News* had attracted an editor at one of the big, classy midtown houses, and the next thing you know, he was a success again, in his second career, after the first, which consisted of overthrowing the government and stopping the war in Vietnam. The only problem with the writing, he often remarked, not originally, was the paperwork.

Was Mitch Greene funny because he looked funny, or did he look funny because he was funny? Good question, no answer, not even after all these years. He had one of those big faces—big eyes, big nose, big jaw, big bones all the way around, big ears, big Adam's apple—all of it set off by a big frizz of reddish-gold-turning-to-gray hair, a kind of Chia Pet gone berserk. When he smiled, he had big teeth and a big tongue.

"Anyhow, boys and girls," he said, "and that includes all you grandpas and grandmas, because if you haven't checked lately, you still are divided into boys and girls, not that it matters at our—oops, I mean, *your* age—this psycho thing we have going on now, with some berserk redneck dressed in camouflage and a 'Bring Back Bush' bumper sticker on his pickup, is a reminder of one thing: you may want to ignore history, but unfortunately history will not ignore you. Who said that originally? Ten points and I'll only charge you ten bucks for an autograph."

"Trotsky," came the call.

"Give the man a joint," said Mitch. "Anyhow, to be serious for just a second, we have a nutcase killer playing sniper wannabe shooting down some of my cohorts who gave it up to stop the war in Vietnam all those years ago. You little peasants weren't even born then, that's how long ago it was. Anyhow, these folks really gave it up for peace and to bring our boys—your dads—home in one piece. Since you're all here, you can see it worked. Now some guy is playing get even with the commies, because that's the way his mind works. No good deed goes unpunished, just like the man says. But history, guys and gals, it could kill you. And until it does, you may as well have a laugh or two at history's expense, which is why I worked for at least seven, no, maybe as many as eleven days on the book, which gives you a sense of where it started: with the wretched excesses of capital, of men with so much money they couldn't spend it, and after the fifth mansion, housing lost its charm, so they—"

The bullet hit him in the mouth. It actually flew between his two big sets of choppers and plowed through the rear of the throat to the spine, which it all but vaporized into thin pink mist on the exit. His head did not explode like Jack's and Mitzi's, as the cranio-ocular vault had not been compromised with an injection of velocity, energy, and hydraulic pressure. The bullet flew on through and hit a wall. But with the bisection of Mitch's spine, animal death was instantaneous, though Mitch's knees hadn't got the message and they fought to keep him upright, even fought through the collapse of all that weight, so instead of tumbling he sat down and happened to find his chair with a thud, almost as if he'd finally gotten sick of hearing his own voice. No one got it. Attention was also claimed by an oddity of sound— the nearly unspellable sound of something shearing through glass, a kind of grindy, high-pitched *scronk*

that announced that a gossamer of fracture, like a spi-
der's delicate web, had suddenly been flung across
the large front window a hundred feet beyond Mitch
at his lectern, and that at its asymmetrical center a
small, round, actual hole had been drilled in the glass,
which, though grievously damaged, held. As no loud
report was registered, no thought of "gun" or "bullet" occurred to anyone for at least three full seconds,
just the weird confluence of the bizarre: Mitch sitting down, shutting up, the window going all smeary.
Hmm, what could this mean? But then Mitch's head,
still intact, lolled forward and his mouth and nose
began to issue blood vomitus in nauseating amounts.

That's when the jumping, screaming, shouting,
hopping, and cell phone photoing began, and soon
enough the police-FBI Fellini movie would begin its
new run in Cleveland.

2

Politics, everything's politics. Even murder. There would be a tussle with Chicago PD upcoming; they'd want the glory, and in any case, under normal circumstances, murder was for a local jurisdiction and the FBI held no sway over it. But the FBI would win out as lead agency on the investigation, because of a statute holding that murder for hire when initiated over state lines was in the federal bailiwick. The utter professionalism of the shooting made the murder-for-hire inference inescapable, and thus the Bureau got the prize.

Nick Memphis was still the hot boy in the Bureau because of his triumph a year earlier in an ambitious, violent bank robbery in Bristol, Tennessee, which he'd tracked, penetrated, and taken apart with minimal loss to civilians. He was hovering on the edge of an assistant directorship. So though others lobbied intensively, it did no good and Nick got the agent-in-charge gig for "Task Force Sniper," once it was declared a major case, Bureau code for "Everybody is watching this one." Given the high publicity value of the investigation, the hugeness and brightness of the limelight, the grounds for endless speculation and fascination, it might get him the assistant directorship if he wrapped it up fast. He tried not to think of that. That had never been the point. The point had always been to use his talents, his work ethic, his intelligence, his courage to do some good in the world, make it a better place. So he tried to deny how fucking much he wanted that assistant directorship.

His first morning after getting the assignment—it happened the day Jack and Mitzi were taken down and the "pattern" emerged—he spent establishing liaison first with field offices in Chicago and New York (who of course resented suddenly having to report to a DC big shot, even if he was well-known and liked by reputation) and through them with the responding police departments. Since East Hampton's was small, the Long Islanders were happy to turn administrative control over to the feds, whom they despised less than the New York State Police; that was no problem. Chicago was bitter, but in a little time—Nick's diplomatic rep was well-known and amply justified—he'd gotten Chicago aboard and set up a working HQ in the Chicago Police Department (as opposed to the FBI's field office, which ticked off the field office AIC, but that couldn't be helped) and got down to the bolts and nuts. Evidence recovery teams were dispatched immediately to both localities, some of the Bureau's best forensic people taken off less urgent cases and reassigned here, firearms specialists invited over from BATF just to contribute what they could to the FBI's efforts, special agents moved in to monitor the local performance and offer gentle evaluations of what could be done better, what needed to be done over, and what was superb work. By 4 p.m., the feds had all but usurped the Chicagoans in the investigation.

But Nick had a first move to make before he even went to Chicago to take command. Just from press reports, he understood, as a onetime sniper himself, that the shooting was of very high quality, something rarely found in criminal cases. Neither his people in East Hampton nor those in Chicago could confirm exactly where the shots had come from, but the lack of rifle reports noted at each scene suggested they had come from a long way off or that the shooter had used some kind of suppressive device, and that con- clusion buttressed the operating assumption: a pro. A bullet recovered from the elbow of Joan Flanders's personal assistant—it had passed through Joan, hit her PA in the fleshy part of the shoulder and struck bone, though without energy to break bone, and lit- erally bounced off the hard stuff and rolled down the outer part of his arm, doing surprisingly little dam- age—proved to be, if mangled so that it appeared to resemble an especially lovely mushroom, the famous 168-grain boat tail hollow point unanimously used in its Federal or Black Hills loading by most SWAT sniper teams as well as nearly all Army, Marine Corps, Air Force, and Navy dedicated marksmen, combat or otherwise. It was the magic bean that terminated the lives of three Somali pirates in April '09 in one well- coordinated moment. So Nick had his own DC inves- tigators and through them via e-mail their reps in all fifty states began the hardest, dullest part of the hunt: the canvass.

All military units with sniper deployment had to be reached; the same was true of all law enforcement units with precision shooters as part of the team. Then there were all cadres and students, recent and other- wise, of the many sniper schools, not merely professional, such as the Marine Sniper School at Quantico, but also the literally dozens of private schools, because as of late sniping had taken on a kind of glamorous aura and many citizens wanted training in the art. But beyond sniper culture lay the broader shooting culture itself, and this generally involved the many dedicated high-power shooting teams affiliated with gun clubs and administered at some level by the NRA, which ran the national matches at Camp Perry, Ohio, every late summer. There were firearms schools that taught hunting techniques too, and there was a niche in the hunting community built around men who became proficient at taking out game animals at long range. There were varmint hunters, who also shot at long range and were truly superb shots, capable of, after much refining of their instruments and much investment in range and loading bench time, hitting twelve-inch-tall prairie dogs at ranges of over a thousand yards with regularity. There was a bench rest culture, in which men, again with highly customized rigs, shot for group size at over a thousand yards (the current thousand-yard champ had been able to put ten rounds into 4.5 inches from that distance). All had to be surveyed and the same questions answered.

Is someone messed up? Is someone bitter, irrational, nearly out of control? Is someone angry? Does someone talk a lot about how the lefties lost the war in Vietnam? Has someone's health declined suddenly? Is someone on drugs? Did a marriage break up, a child die, a job disappear? Has someone vanished? Is someone pissed off about something that happened in Iraq? Was there a flutter, a tremble, a twitch, a glitch, an anomaly in the community? The task was huge; there were a lot of people who could shoot well at long range in America, and it seemed for a while as if the investigators would have to shake out all of them.

Meanwhile, in the media, the immediate suspicion fell on *him*, as in the Great American Gun Nut.

That was the narrative, from the start. You know the guy; we all do. Something a little "weird" about him, no? Makes his office buddies a little uneasy, the women especially, with his dullness on all subjects save firearms, about which he lights up like a Christmas tree. Can be seen hunched at the keyboard not with secret Japanese teen nudes but with rifles on his screen. Goes a little nuts when the Second Amendment comes up, and in time people learn to stay away from the topic when he's around. Maybe he's got a house full of heads or a shelf full of trophies with small gold men holding weapons atop them. Ew, creepy. Maybe he knows the difference between .30-06 and .308 or that a "thirty caliber" can be a .30-06, a .308, a .300 Win Mag, a .300 Remington Ultra Mag, a .307, a 7.62X39, X51, X54, and so on. Maybe he spends time in the basement with his little mechanical devices and like some dark alchemist of medieval times is capable of fabricating his own cartridges. Maybe he's an amateur gunsmith who's got an eerie engagement with the clever mechanics that underlie the mesh of pins, levers, springs, valves, and tubes that constitute the interior of all firearms. All these things suddenly became suspect, and at a certain point, the reporters even started going through the Internet and calling gun stores for hints on recent bizarre behavior by otherwise nondescript customers.

It was the third death, poor Mitch Greene in mid-sentence, that narrowed the field. Anyone could have killed Joan Flanders, for she was hated as much as she was loved; hatred of her was too broad-based to be of any help at all. And anyone could have killed Jack Strong and Mitzi Reilly, for they were hated, perhaps even more passionately, by just as many, for their smugness, moral superiority, fancy education, contempt for authority, unconvincing contrition, reentry into society, low-watt fame, and so forth and so on. The fact that both Joan and the Jack-Mitzi crimes could be connected to the Vietnam War and the rages of the sixties was tantalizing but of itself not revelatory, not yet anyway.

But nobody really hated Mitch Greene, then or now. He was a clown, a comedian, a cornball; he made people laugh. He probably had never met the other three, for he was really several tiers below them in radical chic circles. He had more or less gone mainstream; he was the one-man answer to the question "Which one of these doesn't belong?"

He only belonged, if barely, by virtue of the Vietnam connection. Like the other three, he was famous in those years and got a lot of TV time. But was he a real radical, like the others, or was he just a guy riding history's currents as a way to a gig, getting laid, and doing a little self-expression at the same time? In fact, he'd never really *done* much for the movement except exploit it for his own ends. There were others, many others, who'd done a lot more, who could be held accountable for a lot more, if those were your politics and "punishment" or "vengeance" were your motive.

"He's a lightweight," said Ron Fields, Nick's number two, an institutionally famous Tommy Tactical type who'd won five gunfights but was known not for brains so much as loyalty and guts. "The only reason for whacking him would be unsophisticated. To a certain type of person upset with the Movement, he would be one of them, maybe even a face, although in reality he was never one of the key apparatchiks. He needed too much attention to do the hard work of revolution."

"Is that anything?" Nick asked. "Does it tell us anything? Are we learning anything?" He looked around the table, his staff of three or four stars like Ron who'd hitched themselves to him, hoping he'd rise, a New York State Police detective, repping the Hampton sector of the investigation, two smart guys each from Chicago and Shaker Heights, except one of the smart guys in each team was a smart girl. The group was clustered in a large, dreary room in the upper reaches of the Shaker Heights Police Station on the day after Mitch's death, sitting at a Formica table littered with dead cups of joe, half-eaten doughnuts, sugar grains everywhere, all of it rotting under the nurtureless light of an overhead fluorescent.

One of the women now said, "Here's what I'm getting: He's gifted technically but politically naive; he hasn't done his homework, he's just gone after the simplest, most obvious symbols of the Movement forty years ago, as he would know it or as he remembered it."

"So he's an old guy?" Nick asked.

"I think he *has* to be."

"I don't know," Nick said. "Shooting at that level is a young guy's game. Muscle, stamina, discipline, all young guy stuff. Then there's the moving around.

He's probably not flying, not with the rifle, and all the localities are within driving distance of the time differential. Lots of driving, lots of movement—again, that's all young guy stuff."

"Maybe he's a real good old guy," someone said. "I mean *really* good."

"Anybody know a really good old guy?"

Silence.

"Well, I do. The best. 'Nam sniper, operator, gunman. He'd be the logical candidate."

"Do you want us on it, Nick?"

"I already called him. First day, by landline, in Idaho, verifying for my own ears he was not in play but out on his ranch caring for his horses. He was. There was a one-in-a-jillion chance he snapped. It happens. He knew why I was calling. He was pissed. But I wanted a clear head to run this show, and that's what I got. So does anybody know of any other really good old guys?"

"We don't," Ron said, "but tomorrow a.m. I'll have people looking at Vietnam medal-winners, guys who killed a lot. Snipers, maybe aces, specialists."

"That's good," said Nick. "That'll give us a place to start winnowing. All right, what I'm seeing is someone paying 'them' back for their treason. To feel that all these years later, he had to be there all those years before. Kids today don't care much about Vietnam; most of them don't even know what it was. But whoever he is has borne a grudge for a long time. And now, maybe realizing that he himself has limited time left, he's decided to get the rifle out of mothballs, put on his camos, and go off into the boonies on one last stalk and kill."

"Makes sense," said one of the others and politely no one bothered to point out that this interpretation violated the premise by which the Bureau would run the investigation. That was because all of them were now attached to it, and all of them would prosper if it prospered.

"All right," said Nick, "then as Ron says, let's find our best people and jump-start this thing by testing the theory. Let's eliminate the large category of possibles for what we think is a smaller category of probables. I'm thinking former Vietnam snipers. Marines, Army, maybe CIA; they had a lot of paramilitary operators over there. I think it was called SOG, their little commando unit. Did the Air Force have snipers?"

"They would have had air policemen sniper-trained for perimeter security. Also, the Navy always has a designated marksman shipboard for mine disposal. Guy hits 'em at long range, makes 'em go boom. Those are two off-the-wall possibilities. I don't think the SEALs had a sniper program that early. They were more Delta cowboy gunfighters than precision takedown specialists." That was Ron, always good on sniper stuff and hoping to become head of Precision Marksmanship, the FBI sniper training unit, at Quantico.

"I'm sure by noon tomorrow everyone on this investigation will be an expert on the arcana of military sniping, circa 1965 to '75. Get 'em going. Stay with 'em. I'll be going to the autopsy tomorrow and I'm waiting to hear from forensics on the Greene bullet. I'm sure it'll be another 168."

Thus it was that the FBI, very early in the investigation, became aware of Carl Hitchcock.

*   *   *

Carl's name actually arose almost simultaneously from two sources. The first was the sergeant in charge of training and special operations for the North Carolina State Police, their SWAT guy, in other words. He'd been reached at home by a young special agent in the major case working room of Task Force Sniper in the headquarters building in Washington. She was making inquiries on the subject of good law enforcement shots who'd recently displayed instability. The sergeant abjured knowledge of such, and the phone call was brusque, abrupt, and professional, and almost short. But—

"I hate to do this, young lady, but there is one name that comes up."

"Yes sir," said the agent.

"Carl Hitchcock."

The young woman had no idea who that would be. She had no response.

"The name familiar?"

"No sir, can't say it is."

"How old are you?"

"Twenty-four."

"Okay, then. For a time, Carl Hitchcock was the most famous sniper in America. Someone wrote a book about him on account of all the kills he got in Vietnam. Marine sniper, you know, in the boonies, hunting bad guys one at a time."

"Yes sir," said the investigator, writing the name down.

"He was known as the leading sniper with something like ninety-three or -four kills. He had magazine articles written about him, he had a book published, and for years he went around to gun shows and sold autographs, just like an old baseball player. There was talk of a movie, and a lot of smaller products, you know, an authorized poster, a special brand of ammo, some rifles that bore his name. Carl got a little action off each one."

"He's now in your area?"

"He retired down here in Jacksonville, like a lot of old marines do. It's right outside Lejeune. He had a little house here. He liked to garden. His wife died a year or two back. But his health hasn't been too good lately."

"How do you know him?"

"He had a consulting business where he'd drop by and do some informal training days for police departments on their shooting programs. He helped our boys and was an exceptional coach. He made everyone shoot better and, more important, think better. He'd put a lot into snipercraft. He even had a license plate that read SNIPR-1."

He spelled it out for the young woman.

"And something's going on with him?"

"Well, it gets dicey here. This is why I'm reluctant to share. But yeah, something. *Something.* Don't know what. Carl's not the sort of man who talks a lot about how he feels. He prides himself on not feeling a thing. But I could tell. His voice was dead on the phone. He canceled his visits. Just something and it depressed the hell out of him. Classical. Maybe just old age, the realization there were a lot more leaves on the ground than on the tree. It hits different people different ways. I don't know."

"So when was the last time you saw Carl Hitchcock?"

"A month ago. I'm just talking a feeling. Seemed lonely, I suppose."

"Was he infirm?"

"He wasn't able to play basketball, no, but for a gent close to seventy, he was spry enough. Walked with a limp, had pain from some burns, that sort of thing, but he got around all right."

"Do you have an address?"

"Well, let me look it up for you. Would you want me to—"

"No sir," said the young woman, who knew that a local gumshoe suddenly asking questions might be just what the doctor didn't order. "I'm going to run this by my superiors and we will be back in touch soonest."

"Ma'am, I hear that all the time when I work with feds, and 'soonest' is shorthand for 'neverest.'"

"I apologize for that, sir, but I do mean 'soonest' this time."

The young woman, excited, raced in to see the legendary Nick, who waved her into a chair while he finished a call.

And the young woman heard him say, "You spell that H-I-T-C-H-C-O-C-K, just like the director?"

Source number two was the police department of Hendrix, Arizona, whose chief Nick had just been on the phone with. The chief had said the following:

"This old gal sat in our lobby for six hours and I will say she got the runaround. But finally a detective came by to take her complaint and it turned out that her sister was a former beauty queen named Mavis O'Neill Hitchcock, of Jacksonville, North Carolina, which is a town just outside the big marine base at Camp Lejeune. Mavis died, but her husband was a combat-injured retiree named Carl Hitchcock, who had been famous for a while as the marines' number one sniper in Vietnam. It was a good marriage. Both were old dogs, both had been around the block, and Mavis's first husband, Howard, had also been a marine sergeant, and he and Carl had been friends. Anyhow, for a long time Carl was a kind of a god to the marines and to lots of law-enforcement officers and the like. It was a life he liked very much and he enjoyed talking to the young snipers and so forth. But about the time Mavis took sick, something went sour. Belly-up. Don't know what. Now, the sister went out to Jacksonville as Mavis's condition worsened, and she could tell that something wasn't right with Carl. 'Carl, what's wrong?' Carl wouldn't say a word. Wasn't a talking type; all the lonely time he spent in Vietnam probably cured him of a need to talk. He tells her he was the champion. But now it turns out he wasn't the champion. There was another fellow, a few years earlier, killed more bad guys. 'Why would you let a thing like that upset you?' 'I feel like I've been living a lie,' Carl said. Anyhow, Mavis dies, Carl is all broken up, and the sister has to go back to Hendrix and her own life, but she tries to keep in touch. Several times she calls, he's too drunk to talk. Sometimes he himself calls, drunk. One day he breaks a hip and that takes a hell of a lot out of him. Then he just stopped answering the phone. Now this, and she wonders, could Carl . . . It's not like Carl . . . Carl was such a good, brave man, such a wonderful marine . . . but *could* Carl?"

"All right," Nick told them at the meeting he convened in about thirty seconds, "I don't want to commit to Carl Hitchcock, but we have to get more. I've been on the phone with the federal attorney for North Carolina and he's putting together a search warrant. I want our best team on this. Ron Fields will run the show, and Ron, you know what I expect. This is a tough situation, you don't want to brown off the locals with overzealous supervision, the marines are going to be very interested because he's very much a symbol of their branch, one of their heroes, but I've also got Joan Flanders's ex-husband T. T. Constable calling the director and demanding action, sometimes twice a day. Ron, you're up for this?"

"I am."

"Take the young woman here with you. She did good. What was your name, young lady?"

"Jean Chandler."

"Take Special Agent Chandler, Ron. Run her hard, treat her unfairly, call her by her last name, overwork her, don't let her call her husband—"

"No husband," Chandler said, blankly.

"—boyfriend, who's probably a linebacker for the Redskins, and see if she comes up smiling. Maybe she's a keeper, maybe not. We'll see."

Chandler smiled; Nick was famous for his needling, joshing style with the younger people.

Nick said, "You make sure—I know you know this, but they pay me to point out the obvious—you make sure the legal paperwork is *perfect* before you move; you don't ransack; you show utmost respect to this old duffer if he's around; you document everything, okay? Is this understood?"

"Yes, Nick."

"And you understand this one other thing: if, God forbid, he's the boy and if it gets dicey, you back off quick and look contrite. I know you're a gunfighter yourself, but you cannot engage Carl Hitchcock. Under no circumstances are you to engage Carl Hitchcock. If you want to see a lot of people dead in a hurry, you corner a former marine sniper with a rifle and a bagful of ammo with no way out, and I guarantee you, you'll have body bags all the way out to the trees and back in the first two minutes. And the survivors will *never* get a promotion."

They laughed, nervously.

"And you keep me in the loop and everybody else out of the loop. Everything goes through me, because I get paid to be the asshole. You let me be the asshole. If you do that, I'll fight to death for you. If you don't, I'll dump you and hang a do-not-promote-this-fool toe tag on your career. I will not be asked questions by the press I don't know the answer to. Okay, go, go, go. What, you're not out of here yet?"

3

The house was a one-story brick job under palms and pines in a leafy neighborhood full mostly of young marine noncom families. Jacksonville, it turned out, was one of those parasite towns that grew up on the outskirts of a large military installation, this time Camp Lejeune, North Carolina, the home of and training site for II Marine Expeditionary Force, the Second Marine Division, the 22nd, 23rd, and 24th Marine Expeditionary Units as well as the USMC infantry and engineering schools. The town was full of small retail for young marines—dry cleaners, tailors, shoe repair places, fast food—and of course a seamier array of afterduty amusements, mostly beer and strippers, as well as a bus station, a train station, and a surprisingly well developed taxi system, which ferried the boys and girls to and from duty and recreation if they were not advanced enough in their careers to afford autos.

Ron Fields and Jean Chandler met early that afternoon with the federal prosecutor for Shelby County, a USMC JAG staff rep, the local police chief, and a captain in the North Carolina State Police. Fields had a lot of explaining to do.

"I'm really a nice guy," Ron said, "and people love me. But I'm going to big-foot it now to save time and let you decide how wonderful I am six months from now. Sorry if I come on like a jerk, but that's the way it has to be. Jack," he said to the prosecutor, sliding into first-name familiarity, "I'm going to fax your office's legal work to DC for vetting by guys who went to Harvard. I don't think they're smarter, I just have to be sure."

"Of course," said Jack, "I only went to UNC, what do I know?"

"We have forensics and evidence recovery teams and SWAT people on standby. But we cannot approach this by kicking in doors. We go gentle. Slow and gentle. I want you, Major Connough"—the Marine Corps JAG rep—"to witness and sign off on all my decisions, and you tell me any time I act with disrespect; I don't want the Marine Corps mad at me."

"The Marine Corps is already mad. This guy is an institution. He's a god, a hero. If it turns out—well, it won't. Everyone who knows Carl Hitchcock says it won't."

Ron didn't like the sound of that. It was already out. That's the thing with these service cultures, he thought. They're hardwired for commo and something can't happen here without everyone knowing it in five seconds.

"I hope he's clean too. Makes my job easier. Okay, no police presence up front. I want it gathered at the school two blocks away; your SWAT people, your traffic control, your medical standby, your press liaison, whatever. How fast can you assemble?"

"We can have people in place by four p.m."

"Good, I'm hoping to get a yes from DC and that you can get to a nice friendly judge by then, all right?"

"We can work that time frame. The warrant's already at Judge O'Brian's. He'll sign. He always has before."

"Good move, Chief, that saves some time. Now at three, Chief, I want your people to begin a discreet evac of the neighborhood. Friendly cop style, ma'am, we're making a potentially dangerous arrest, and we'd like you to quietly gather your kids up and head over to the school, that kind of thing. These are marine people, they'll follow orders."

"Is that necessary?" asked the marine JAG rep. "Carl's nearly seventy. He's not going to go to guns."

"I'm sure you're right, Major Connough. But I can't take the risk. We cannot have civilian casualties. Furthermore, every public safety professional who has the potential of going in line of sight to the house will wear, I say again, *will* wear body armor."

"Won't stop a .308," said the marine.

"No, but it could deflect and we've found that the armor increases efficiency and confidence as well as survivability in critical incidents."

"We *do* have some critical incident experience in the Marine Corps," said the major. "Ever hear of Iwo Jima?"

"Yes sir, I meant no disrespect, I'm just covering all the bases in my dull, straight-ahead fashion. In the meantime, I'm going to take a cab ride over and just pass by the house a couple of times."

So next, while the various authorities moved their teams into place, Ron and Jean Chandler glided along Peacock Lane for the third time, with a Jacksonville cop in civies over body armor behind the wheel. The feds played elementary security games, maybe overkill, but coming from a second-guess culture bar none, they took no chances: first time they were in coat and tie and a formal blouse, the second in polo shirts and glasses under ball caps, and this time they had switched sunglasses and ball caps.

Each time, they'd seen nothing, though as they worked it, only one of them, in the off side, actually observed the house. The closer agent sat still, eyes dead ahead, utterly uninterested; it was his partner, leaning back just a bit, head cocked just a bit, who scanned for intelligence.

"Give me your read," said Ron.

"Nothing," she said. "It looks empty. The grass is trim, though it's been a while since the last cutting. The garden has been weeded, the lawn watered, nothing is lying around. It just looks dead. No sign of habitation, nothing out of the ordinary, nothing spontaneous or unexplainable, just the house of a neat older retiree who lives alone but is still spry enough to do his gardening. He's been gone a week, maybe two, but there's no sign of decay or instability. It'll run down in time, but not yet. It's still neat as a button. The car looks dusty but the dust covers a clean vehicle. It's been washed but not driven and it's sat for a week." That was Carl's Chrysler 300 with the North Carolina rear plate SNIPR-1.

Chandler's assessment did not deviate from Ron's; in fact, it confirmed Ron's in every detail.

Finally, at 4:09 p.m., Ron got the call he had been waiting for from Nick.

"All right, Ron, Justice has signed off on the legal and the judge down there has okayed the warrant. You can go. You get back to me soonest."

"Roger," he said, and turned to the gathering of officers. "It's a go. Agent Chandler and I will approach. I will have my mike open. Any sounds of shots or scuffles, you guys get there fast."

Nods all around.

"Okay, cowboy up."

The SWAT people climbed into their armored vehicles and turned the engines on. Ron and Jean put on body armor, then their coats. They hung their IDs on their chests by a chain necklace. A last quick check-off with the district attorney, the federal attorney, the police executives, the medical people, and so on made it clear that the moment was indeed here.

The two agents got into the black sedan, drove two blocks, and pulled into Carl Hitchcock's driveway.

Discreetly, the SWAT teams, locked and loaded, moved to holding points just out of line of sight of the house. All earphones were open to the same channel.

Ron and Jean exited the vehicle, took a look around, then Ron led the way to the front door. Both agents had unsnapped the safety strap on the holsters of their Glock .40s, which they now carried hot. Ron knocked, waited, knocked again, to no answer.

They edged their way around to each door, knocking. They peered through windows and saw nothing. Finally, circumnavigating the house and narrating their progress over the radio, they again reached the front door. Ron pushed it; it popped open, unlocked.

"Sergeant Hitchcock," he yelled. "My name is Ronald C. Fields, Special Agent, Federal Bureau of Investigation. I am here to serve a search warrant and to take you in for questioning. I have a marine JAG officer nearby if you wish to talk to him first. Please come out with hands raised. This is not an arrest; it's an interview and search. You will have ample time to acquire legal representation if necessary."

There was silence.

Finally Ron said, "Okay, we're going in." He withdrew his Glock. "Muzzle down. You do not fire unless you absolutely positively see a weapon or are physically assaulted, do you understand, Chandler?"

"Got it," said Chandler.

"You do not shoot Special Agent Fields in the ass, no matter how big a jerk he is, all right?"

"Ten-four that," said Chandler.

They entered, stepping into a living room.

It took a second to adjust to the darkness.

"Sergeant Hitchcock, FBI, please identify yourself."

Silence.

The living room was dominated by a wall of glory narrating a marine career, pictures from Lejeune and Pendleton and half the ships at sea, Rome, Paris, the war in Vietnam, a batch of magazine covers and a book cover all rendered into picture frames, medals in an oak display case, trophies boasting little golden shooters, all of it neat, all of it framed, all of it speaking of a man proud of his accomplishments and in control of his faculties.

They moved onward, Ron advancing, Jean covering, down the hall through a laundry room to a small but neat kitchen. Beyond was a bedroom, bed made, sheet tight as per barracks style (you could bounce a dime off the covers), nothing flung or discarded.

Finally there was only a last bedroom, closed.

In fact, locked from the outside, with a padlock screwed between door and frame.

"Kick it in," said Ron. "We'll pay for it later."

Jean Chandler gave it a kick and her foot bounced off.

"More time in the gym for Agent Jeannie," said Fields, with a snort.

"I can do it," Jean said, this time setting herself more correctly, aiming higher to bring more stress on the joinery of the screws to the wood of door and frame. She kicked, the door flew open, and they stepped in.

"Jesus Christ," said Ron.

4

A few hours later, in the press briefing auditorium of the FBI headquarters building in Washington DC, Nick stepped to the podium, almost blinded by the lights. He could sense the seething crowd in the darkness. He went to the lectern, cleared his voice, tested the microphone. Then he stood by to be introduced by Phil Price, the Bureau's public affairs officer, as "Nick Memphis, Special Agent in Charge of Task Force Sniper, with, as we said, important new information."

Nick leaned to the microphone.

"Thank you all for coming. Are we ready? Jimmy, hand out the circulars and the release; make sure everyone gets one. All right, as Phil said, I have information. I am here to announce that we have just obtained an arrest warrant in the deaths of Joan Flanders, Mitch Greene, Jack Strong, and Mitzi Reilly."

A wave of excitement radiated from the gathered reporters, as all squirmed forward on their seats.

"The warrant names Carl R. Hitchcock, sixty-seven, of Jacksonville, North Carolina, as prime suspect in the felonies. I should add that Hitchcock, a highly trained, experienced, and decorated marine sniper with a lot of combat experience, is to be approached with extreme caution, and I say this to law enforcement too. He is an exceedingly dangerous man, possibly the most dangerous man the Bureau has sought since Baby Face Nelson in 1934. He was credited with ninety-three kills in Vietnam in a 1969–1970 tour of duty and was one of the most accomplished of the marine snipers in that war. Here's his picture."

Nick stepped aside, and behind him, where the seal of the FBI had been projected, the image of a man swam into focus. It was a hard, lean face, dominated by hawklike eyes furious in their concentration, completely Scots-Irish, Appalachian-bred, from a hard-scrabble farm or vertical plantation. In older days, the cruel word "hillbilly" would have applied to such concentration knitting the brow, the bricklike chin, the eyes so close together. Nowadays, the snarky of the world would apply the word "redneck" or even "trailer trash." The planes of the face were all vertical slashes; the eyebrows thick, the nose meaty, the mouth a grim cipher. He wore the dress uniform of the United States Marine Corps with the saucer cap squared away atop his white sidewall, the brow low to his dark eyes. The tunic was immaculate, the chest festooned with medals and awards.

"This was taken in 1974, the week he retired as a master sergeant. He'd served the Corps for twenty-three years, did three tours in Vietnam, the last as a sniper and platoon sergeant with Scout/Sniper Company, Second Battalion, Third Marines near Huu Toc, just off the DMZ. He was in combat nearly every day for thirteen months. He was shot at a lot. In his other tours he was a military policeman and the platoon sergeant of a line infantry company. He has three Purple Hearts as well as the Silver Star, which was awarded him for removing men from a burning tracked vehicle at considerable risk and in considerable pain, as he had sustained forty percent first-degree burns. You can see that his service record is impeccable, the stuff of heroism and sacrifice at its highest level. That is why no one here is anything but saddened by this development."

A new face appeared. It was clearly the same, though the discipline had eased, the eyes were merry, there was more flesh. From the angle it was clear he'd been snuggling with someone, a wife probably, and the old warrior was happy.

"This is our most recent picture of Sergeant Hitchcock. It was taken three years ago before the death of his wife, Mavis. We've cropped her out of the picture. But this is the man we're hunting today."

"Can you outline the case?" came a call from the darkness.

"Briefly. Based on intelligence derived from a canvass of sniper and SWAT and other long-range shooting communities, we quickly obtained information that Sergeant Hitchcock had been depressed of late and hadn't been seen in two weeks. We obtained a search warrant, and at four this afternoon, a Bureau team with the help of local and state law enforcement agencies in Jacksonville, North Carolina, served it in his domicile. We found a room with photos on the wall of several of the victims as well as others in the antiwar movement of forty years ago. We found the number ninety-seven drawn on walls, pads of paper, on the photos themselves, all over the room. We found computer records suggesting a great deal of research into the lives and whereabouts of various antiwar movement figures, particularly Joan Flanders, but also Strong and Reilly. There was less on Mitch Greene, but he was included. We found gun oil, cleaning rods, ammunition cases, and a case of .308 Federal Match 168-grain hollow point boat tail cartridges, of the sort our forensics people have ID'd as used in the four shootings. Four boxes, eighty rounds, were missing. We found the paperwork for a Treasury Department stamp tax of two hundred dollars for a class III device, approved by ATF, called a suppressor, which you would call a silencer. We found packaging for that device from its manufacturer, SureFire Inc., as well as an invoice for the costs to thread the muzzle of a new Krieger barrel, by which method the suppressor could be effectively mated to the rifle, all dated from 2005. We found maps with routes marked out charting a trip that went from the Hamptons on Long Island to Chicago to Minneapolis. We believe he diverted from Minneapolis, where an ex-radical named Ivan Thorson is a controversial law professor, to Cleveland, where Mitch Greene was scheduled to appear at a book signing. We have determined that the time frame of the three shootings sustains the interpretation that he had sufficient allowance to drive to and away from each site. We have tracked his credit card records and have determined that he rented motel rooms in each locality the night before the shooting."

"Where is he now?"

"On the road."

"Do you—"

"No, but I assure you, all possibilities are being exhaustively examined at this point in time. We have a federal alert code blue, the highest category, and all police agencies in the continental U.S. were notified immediately prior to this press conference."

"What's the motive? Is he crazy? Did he flip? Some kind of combat stress disorder?"

"Combat stress disorder, almost certainly. His own declining health, yes, as records indicate a slow recovery from a broken hip some years ago, problems with alcoholism, two DWI arrests in the past six months, and other factors generally pointing to depression and disappointment. Loneliness, isolation, depression in the aftermath of the death of his wife. But there was something else.

"For close to thirty years, Carl Hitchcock had been known publicly as the United States Marine Corps' number one sniper in Vietnam. He had ninety-three kills, as I've said. A book was written about him, magazine articles and so forth. He was in a small world a king, a center of attraction and attention. I leave it to you all to discover the joys he took in that identity, as well as the benefits he reaped from it. He attended many gun shows, he sold autographs, he was kind of like an old ballplayer trading on his celebrity by attending public meets. He enjoyed small royalties from several products he endorsed, such as a rifle manufactured by Springfield, a lithograph that showed him in full combat regalia, a line of premium ammunition. I think this speaks to the point: he had a license plate that read SNIPR-1.

"But about two years ago, an article was published in *Soldier of Fortune* magazine mentioning offhandedly another marine sniper with ninety-six kills. It caused a storm in that small world. A researcher used the Freedom of Information Act to access Marine records and determined that, indeed, a Chuck McKenzie, a former lance corporal from Modoc, Oregon, had served for thirteen months in Vietnam in 1966 and achieved an officially credited ninety-six kills. It never occurred to him that he'd done anything remarkable, and he went on to a career in the United States Forestry Service, never mentioning his Vietnam service to anybody but other vets. As I understand it, he was never decorated, his kids didn't even know what their dad had done in the war, and he took no part in what might be called 'tactical culture,' a kind of celebration of various aggressive, firearms-centric methodologies that seems to enjoy some currency now and is supported by various magazines and Web sites and blogs. He never knew there was a Carl Hitchcock cult, so to speak, and that products and endorsements and magazines and the book had been written about Carl and his ninety-three kills. He only found out about it when *Soldier of Fortune* contacted him a few years ago. He had no comment then; I doubt he has any comment now. He's never done a thing to capitalize on his 'fame,' such as it was.

"But we now see that Carl was extremely upset. A taciturn man, he wouldn't have sought psychological help or counseling. He simply withdrew from the world, a process speeded up by the death of his wife at about the same time. Clearly he brooded on it; I'll let the psychologists tell you by what process he arrived at his conclusion, but from our reading of the materials in his house, it seems clear that he saw this week's shootings as a continuation of his Vietnam tour of duty. It was a last mission, and he identified as 'enemies' not Vietcong or North Vietnamese regulars but protesters who in his interpretation had helped the enemy. So he set out to eliminate them and, in some fashion, reclaim the title of the number one Vietnam sniper. Thus we find the number ninety-seven scrawled all over the headquarters room he'd dedicated in his house; it seems clear that he will go on hunting the supposed traitors until we stop him or he comes to his senses and turns himself in."

"What is the state of the manhunt at this time?"

"Well, even as we speak, this information is going to all law enforcement entities within the continental United States. We continue to receive information from hundreds of sources. Our last sighting places him in an Econo Lodge Motel on the outskirts of Shaker Heights, Ohio, two nights ago. We are concentrating our efforts in an area within two days' drive of that locality. Meanwhile, our forensic people, our evidence recovery teams, and their local equivalents examine the evidence for further information. We have established state police roadblocks on interstates in Michigan, Illinois, Pennsylvania, and New York State. If Carl Hitchcock is listening, we urge him to give himself up and end this madness. But I have to say again, he is armed and dangerous, highly trained, a superb shot, a combat veteran, a close-quarters combat expert, and he is capable of wreaking extreme havoc in a very little time. So he must be approached with caution."

"Do you have any opinion, Special Agent, on the use of 'trained killers' in the military and the risks such men pose for society when they return to the civilian world? I mean, this seems to dovetail neatly with the report released by the Homeland Security Agency some months ago that—"

"You must be from the *New York Times*."

"Yes sir," the young man said.

Then Nick saw movement, and his eyes flashed to it. In the back of the room Jack Hefner, assistant director and Nick's immediate supervisor, was winding the index finger of one hand around, helicopter rotor style, meaning "Wind it up, we have news."

"Okay, ladies and gentlemen, sorry I don't have time for more questions, but we've got to get back to the manhunt."

Trying to appear casual, Nick gathered up his papers, conferred briefly with the Bureau's public information officer, then slid out the door to the rear, avoiding the reporters who'd now clustered forward, wanting more, more, more.

Nick got into the off-limits sector of the floor and watched as Jack came toward him on the fly.

"We got him," he said.

"Where?"

"His credit card was just used to check into a hotel in Grand Rapids, Michigan. He's there now, in a room. Michigan State Police can have SWAT teams there in a few minutes. It's your call, Nick."

"No assault. Tell them to set up discreet surveillance. I don't want this guy opening up. One sniper team. I guess if he goes, we'll have to drop him. God, I'd hate to do that. But one sniper team in a truck across from the hotel. I'm leaving with my team now."

"Nick, I'd advise that you send the word to take

him down now. If it goes bad, Michigan will have to answer for it."

"Jack, if I'm incident commander, my best judgment is soft surveillance. I'm on my way, can be there in three hours." He looked at his watch. It was 9:35 p.m., 10:35 in the Midwest. "We'll let him fall asleep. We'll take him down at dawn."

5

Through the night-vision binoculars, the Econo Lodge just off 83 in Grand Rapids, Michigan, looked calm enough. It dozed under a clear if cold night sky. A few lights blazed greenly in the amped fields of vision, slightly pixelated in distortion, as if painted by a mad Dutchman who'd just cut off his ear. It was the kind of detail that shouldn't have come to Nick but did anyway, and he exiled it from his mind, just kept the lenses screwed on the first-floor window, sixth down from the office, which was dark.

"Any sign of movement?" Fields asked.

"Nothing. Captain, how are they coming?"

"I'm sure they're almost done, Special Agent," said the Michigan State Police SWAT commander, a burly guy in combat gear from head to toe, like some kind of medieval knight. He wore an MP5 submachine gun in a cinch sling tight to his body armor and a black watch cap.

He was referring to the slow evacuation of the Econo Lodge by state policemen. They were moving stealthily, almost creeping, knocking softly and emptying the motel, herding tired travelers to a nearby high school for safekeeping. Meanwhile several observation posts had been set up, one in a truck across the way in a Dunkin' Donuts parking lot, one in a civilian household behind the motel, and two others farther out with good angles to the motel. Three heavily armed and armored SWAT operators had taken over the room next to Carl Hitchcock's, inserted an optic tube through the duct system, and got a good look-see into his room, where they saw—nothing. Nick again checked the image as it was broadcast to a vid monitor in the command vehicle. He too, and all the men about him, saw nothing, just what appeared to be the shapes consistent with a generic motel room, low-end: a bed, a bureau, a TV on a TV stand, a small bathroom. No sound of breathing was picked up by the microphones.

"He either sleeps still or he's dead," said the SWAT captain.

"These guys are trained in stillness," said Nick. "He can control his breathing, hold it down to noth-ingness almost. We can't assume he's out."

A call came.

The captain took it, muttered into the phone.

"Okay," he said, "that's the last of 'em. The motel is empty, all the houses on the street beyond are evacked too. Just him and us."

"Okay," said Nick.

"You know, my people can blow the wall between the rooms and be on him in one second, behind a flashbang," said the captain. "Might be the safest, sur-est way."

Nick didn't like it. He knew the SWAT mental-ity. He knew the most aggressive officers applied, the ones who liked to shoot and had a little hero fantasy at play behind their eyes at all times. Dress 'em up like Delta commandos and give 'em fancy weapons and tools, and you all but tickled their trigger fingers. For some reason he couldn't understand, Nick wanted desperately to take Carl Hitchcock alive. The old guy deserved their best efforts.

"Negative, but thanks and noted. No, my team will apprehend. It's a small room, I don't want a lot of people in there rushing and crowding. Three's enough. Body armor, helmet, backup shotguns but primary personnel—that is, myself and Agents Fields and Chandler—will go in with handguns behind flashbangs. Okay? My call, that's how I'm calling it."

He went ahead with further tactical details: all SWAT teams cocked and locked at the holding point, the helicopters in orbit a mile out, roadblocks in place, medical teams on standby—everything was checked off until there was nothing more to do except the thing itself.

"Let's go," he said.

They scampered through the darkness, hit the hotel office, where a squad of cops waited breathlessly. They nodded, did a last checkoff, and slid down the hallway, passing cop sentries every few feet. The approach to Carl's room, however, was clear, and they slid to it.

Nick looked at his watch, saw that it was 5 a.m.

He nodded to his two colleagues. Ron Fields slipped by him. He had a Mossberg entry gun, a short-barreled pump-action shotgun with a breaching round in the chamber. Next to him young Chandler, her Glock holstered gunfighter style in a low rig strapped to her thigh under her body armor, had a flashbang in each fist. With the thumb of each hand, she pulled the pins, holding the levers down. Fields squirmed to the doorknob, braced the muzzle of the short-barrel against it, made a visual check with each teammate, pushed the safety off, and made a last visual check with Nick.

Nick nodded.

Fields took a deep breath and fired.

The breaching round detonated in the narrow space of the hallway, splintering the door at the knob. Fields gave it a kick, and it flew open brokenly, and then he stood aside as Chandler tossed in each distraction grenade. In three seconds, the two detonated with a stunning double thunderclap, filling the universe with painful vibration and a flash of illumination so powerful it cut like a knife, disorienting anyone looking into it instead of, like the raiders, away from it.

Nick went through the door hard, his Glock in a steady two-hand grip, trigger finger indexed above the trigger guard, a SureFire light mounted on rails beneath the barrel burning a hole in the smoky turmoil conjured by the flashbangs. His beam showed nothing, and he advanced quickly, screaming, "FBI, hands up, FBI, hands up, FBI, hands up!"

But there was nobody there with hands to raise. Penetrated by Nick's, then Fields's, then Chandler's beams, the darkness yielded no image of a man struggling to come awake and grope for a gun. The room was empty, the bed unmessed, nothing strewn about to signify human occupation, just the sterile neatness of an undisturbed motel room. The three rotated quickly to the bathroom, kicking the ajar door fully open and again revealing nothing. The shower curtain wasn't even drawn, so there was no concealment behind it. Other cops arrived, forming up in the hallway; outside, shadows moved, where SWAT teamers from stations beyond the motel got close and laid their muzzles on a window to prevent any escape. But no target emerged.

The lights came on, revealing what was now nothing more than a room of overexcited policemen with guns drawn.

One last door remained. It was to the closet, just this side of the bathroom, and a cluster of guns zeroed it. Someone dipped in, pulled it open.

The many weapons-mounted lights captured the still Carl. He was in his underwear, a plaid pair of shorts and an OD T-shirt. His legs were stretched out, pale and glowing, the dark hair on them standing up bristling in the merciless lights. He held his rifle, which Nick numbly noted was the inevitable Remington 700 with a heavy barrel; his hand lay relaxed upon his thigh, where it had fallen from its awkward stretch to reach the trigger. In fact, because of the extra length of the barrel with the eight inches of steel suppressor affixed, he'd had to push the trigger with a straightened-out hanger. The hanger had fallen to the floor. The weapon ran up the length of his body to his mouth, almost as if cradled, a loving thing till the end, but at the mouth, the muzzle of its suppressor had nested, though in recoil it appeared to have knocked a few teeth out. He'd fired his last shot through the roof of his mouth in the closed closet, and the bullet had tunneled upward through his brain, plowed through the roof of the closet and perhaps lodged itself in the motel structure, where it could be recovered. Carl's eyes were closed and his brains and blood painted the upper third of the closet, more abstract art for the clinically inclined. In all the circling light beams, the blood itself, red-orange, seemed to dance or pulsate, as if it still welled from the crater that had been the top of the man's skull.

"He must have done it right away," said Chandler. "There's rigor in the limbs, so he's been gone a long time. Maybe right after he checked in."

"He knew it was all over," said Ron. "He had no place to run. Besides, he completed his mission, he got to ninety-seven. He's the champ again."

6

As in Vietnam, the rains came. It was the season. They fell almost horizontally, sopping everything, turning the earth to gruel, squeezing mud up and over shoes. It was a penetrating rain, and nobody got away from it or didn't feel its chill.

Swagger stood apart from the others and watched the box that contained what remained of Carl Hitchcock go into the ground. He hadn't known Carl, as Carl had finished his sniper's tour before Bob started his; afterwards, in the melancholy aftermath of a lost war, things turned and stayed strange for the longest time, and the two never came upon each other, though they cut trail often enough.

Then, the odd thing: in slow, steady increments, Carl got big. Being number one, at anything, still mattered in this country, and a book came along, some articles, and soon enough Carl was adding to his pension by standing still for autographs at gun shows and being beloved as the avuncular "Gunny," a pop-cult stereotype with a background in real bloodletting that made certain no one ever laughed in his face and, stamping him a member of the killer elite or a knight of a round table, depending on your politics, would only permit other snipers or shooters in his presence; those who had not shot for blood felt quietly driven out and shunned.

Then, another thing, wholly unpredictable: what

might be called "tactical culture." Because of Carl or in spite of him or completely apart from him—who knew? but for some reason—a fascination with the designated life takers, the sanctioned force appliers, took root. The new man was the sniper, the commando, the CQB professional, the pistol jockey, the long-range hitter. Magazines like *Soldier of Fortune* and *SWAT* and *Combat Handguns* came alive, and serious men consumed reams and reams of paper debating such issues as "9mm v. .45 ACP" or "Instinct Shooting: Lifesaver or Fool's Folly?" The fascination took hold of a certain demographic, some professional, some dreamers, but all obsessed with a kind of ideal warrior in an ideal gunfight. The core of the culture was equipment fetish, and soon enough boutique providers were turning out dedicated sniper rifles, pouches, straps, gizmos of all shapes and purposes, whole lines of tactical clothing, headgear, watches (always black), boots, vests, holsters with elaborately engineered snaps for security on the one hand and quickness of draw on the other. Carl was somehow the professor emeritus of this world, its guru, its revered elder. And it fed him, as he rode sniper chic to a nice enough income with his seminars for law enforcement marksmen, which he put on all over the country. He became at the same time a kind of sniper social worker and spent more than one night talking to someone who'd blown a shot or frozen at the ultimate moment. He counted again. He loved it. Who could blame him? Human nature being what it was, it was more fun to spend a retirement beloved than ignored.

But it had come to this: a civilian graveyard on the outskirts of Jacksonville, North Carolina, a wet fall day, a few disconsolate loners standing about in what appeared to be a crowd but was not, really, as no one pressed close; it was just a group of individuals standing in an almost-crowd. Some generic holy fellow read from the book but added nothing other than God's pro forma respect for the dead. No one from the United States Marine Corps attended.

How could they? Carl was DERANGED MARINE SNIPER, Carl was COMBAT-SHOCKED VET, Carl was CRAZED GUNMAN, Carl was DISAPPOINTED, DEPRESSED SOLDIER, in the words of a prominent newspaper in New York that thought it was all right to call marines soldiers. So the Corps sent no one officially, despite all that Carl had given the Corps. That seemed wrong to Bob, but what did he know of such things and the way they turned out.

> Again, like a Faulknerian blood curse, an original sin of violence and oppression, the hideous adventure that was this country's misguided path in Vietnam in the late 1960s reaches out to claim yet more lives. Let it be written, that the tragic marine sniper Carl Hitchcock, once a hero and now an alleged murderer, is the last casualty of that war and that it can kill no more. Let us hope we are at last safe from it.

> But let the Vietnam War stand also as a warning to further enticements in far-off lands; there have been a few since. The temptation to solve with violence that which cannot be solved with diplomacy is powerful, yet always wrong. Victory or

defeat make little difference in the end. War turns heroes into Carl Hitchcocks with kills 94, 95, 96 and 97 the civilians who were only trying to save him. They are victims, but Carl Hitchcock was the tragedy, constructed by a culture that seeks its answers in high-velocity bullets.

That was the *New York Times* editorial page.

Bob hadn't read any others online; he didn't have the heart to, and it was another of his resentments that Carl had somehow become the platform for the eastern asshole press, and he doubted there was a man in an eastern press editorial room who'd been in Vietnam at all, much less as a marine, and yet somehow they were the ones who felt entitled to sound the words and play the bugle.

He tried to shake it off.

Getting old, all beat and cut to hell.

He still walked with a limp from a bad cut picked up a few years back. His hair was gray, his face bleak, his body old and achy. He'd been shot at a lot, hit a few times, and one of his hips was cold steel, five degrees icier than the weather every single day, always a reminder of how things can go wrong. But all that said, it was true too that he had it made.

He was sort of rich. He owned seven lay-up barns throughout the West and drew a good percentage from each with not a lot of overhead; his wife ran them beautifully. He had pensions from the marines as well as disability pay, so there'd always be enough money. He lived in a beautiful house outside Boise that looked across meadows to mountains. He had a few good horses, a few good rifles, a few good handguns, and a damned comfortable rocking chair on the porch. He had an all-terrain vehicle and a Ford F-150 and a Kawasaki 350. But he was richest in daughters: his oldest had just moved up in her chosen profession to a big newspaper, which made him happy; his other daughter had just won the girls' Idaho twelve-and-under pony slalom crown at the junior NCAA rodeo in Casper and was only seven. The kid was a true samurai on horseback. That was a day of happiness so pure he thought he'd die of it, but then this terrible week happened that left four people dead and Carl with his brains blown out and everybody and his brother saying terrible things about marine snipers.

In time, the reverend Mr. Minister was done and backed off. One by one, the men filed by, just to see the box close up, perhaps reflect on the boxes he had put men into or the boxes they had put men into or the boxes they had almost gone into themselves. No one said a word. It wasn't a crowd that would throw a drunken wake and end up in the hoosegow with black eyes, broken teeth, and memories of a great bar fight. In many ways, they were all Carls and all Swaggers: scrawny men with lots of fast-twitch muscles, hair crew cut yet thick, thousand-yard stares, the dignity of the professional military or police, no sense of emotional excess anywhere, no moans or tears. They weren't quite buying into the CRAZED MARINE narrative and felt an urge to pay solemn last respects to a guy who'd done his duty always to the end.

When it was finished, the minister came to Bob.

"Was that what you had in mind, Mr. Swagger?"

"It was fine, Reverend. What do I owe you?"

"Sir, I hate to put a figure on such a melancholy occasion. Whatever's in your heart."

It wasn't in Swagger's heart; it was in Swagger's hand, a crumple of hundreds, three of them, and he discreetly passed them to the minister.

"I'll go to the office now and pay the cemetery people," he said.

"You're a Christian soul, sir."

"Not really," said Swagger.

"You knew him . . . before."

"Knew *of* him. Not in his league. Sorry it came to this."

"We all are."

Bob said his good-bye to the man and walked to the road, where the few cars were parked. He drove the rental quickly to the cemetery headquarters, went inside, and took care of business. It was a matter of $4,000, and he wrote the check quickly, without thinking about it.

"Very good, Mr. Swagger. I must say, decent of you. I don't know what would have happened to the body otherwise. No survivors. The estate will be tied up for weeks, maybe months. It's so sad. He deserved so much better. I just don't know what—"

Swagger didn't want to hear it. The mortuary director was unctuous, as they tend to be, and trying to say the right things, but Swagger tuned him out, smiled, and when he heard a break in the man's patter, slipped away.

He was walking to the car, thinking, Get to the airport by six, be back to Boise by ten, get to the house by midnight. Glad it didn't run long. It'll be—

"Say, wouldn't you be the famed paid killer Bob Lee Swagger?"

The voice took him unawares because he'd been so deep into his own internals, he'd lost contact with the real world, always a bad mistake. Now what the hell was this? Some asshole?

He turned, faced another soaked man about his own age, swaddled in rain gear and melted boonie cap but with fewer lines and deeper tan, and something mischievous in his eyes, cluing Bob to the fact that the comment, in a tone of jest and needling, hadn't been meant in hostility but as evidence of membership in the brotherhood of life takers.

"Who would you be?" Bob asked.

"Gunny, my name's Chuck McKenzie. Lance corporal, retired. I was in the same line of work for a year plus a month."

Swagger felt something pulse in his cold, dead heart and realized he was still a little alive.

"Chuck! Damn! Sure, Chuck. You're the big Mr. Ninety-six, right?"

"That's what they say. Myself, I never counted. Just figured if it had an AK-47, it was worth shooting."

"Chuck, I'll shake your hand gladly. You and me, brother, that's us out there looking for AKs with targets attached. Glad you made it through your thirteen, glad you made it here."

"You paid for this, right?"

"I guess so. Somebody had to, and I have a few bucks scraped up. That's all."

"Gunny, can we talk? Can I buy you a cup of coffee, a drink?"

Bob thought: there goes the flight plan.

"Sure," he said. "Let's find a place. Coffee's fine. I have a drinking problem just barely beat, and if I take a slug of bourbon, you won't see me until the next monsoon."

Chuck turned out to be something rare: the funny sniper. They sat in some imitation Starbucks in a suburb of a suburb, a nondescript warren full of interchangeable boys and girls, two old guys laughing and cackling, like the dry drunks they were, over topics so arcane no man but a sniper could have stayed with them or found it funny.

"It wasn't the killing I minded," Chuck said, "it was the *paperwork*. All them after-action reports. My trigger finger got cramps. I said, 'Sir, you want me out shootin', you gotta cut digit number one some slack, that old boy's gittin' all tuckered.' I thought he's going to say, 'Corporal, put it on ice, like a pitcher. It's too valuable to treat lightly. You, go on KP, but that finger, it's got to be taken care of.' Really, we wasn't men, we's trigger fingers that was unfortunately connected to men.

"What I liked," he continued, "was the way some officers looked at you like you were Murder Inc. Mankiller, psycho nutcase, piece of dog turd on the shoe. That is, until they's pinned down by a little guy in the bushes with a ninety-year-old Russian bolt gun, a three-buck scope, and a hunger to kill something big and white, with bars on its collars. Then you're the man's best friend! 'Brother Chuck, so damn glad to see you. Chuck, Chuck, Chuckity-chuck, my closest compadre! Where you been, how's the wife 'n' kids, how'd you like a nice promotion, say, do you mind dusting that little feller in the bushes trying to put a squirt of lead up my ass?' "

Bob laughed. It was pretty funny and oh so true.

"Ran into that a dozen times," he said. "What was it? 'Killer elite,' something like that. We were more like dip-sucking redneck boneheads too dumb to know we were on the bull's-eye ourselves, doing what they told us to do. Turned out they didn't mean 'Kill all those little bastards.' What they meant was 'Kill all those little bastards but don't tell us about it, because we don't want to have to think about it.'"

"Exactly." Chuck laughed. "Gunny, that's it. *They* didn't want to think about it, but they didn't care if *we* thought about it. Like the man said about whores, it ain't the sex you're paying them for, it's the leaving after the sex. It wasn't the killing they's paying us for, it's the remembering, so that they didn't have to and could go home and enjoy Christmas with the kids and feel all clean and moral and heroic."

"Well," said Bob, "we made a lot of them feel heroic then. Still, with all the shit, we lived lives few men could imagine."

"Amen, Gunny. Look at all them poodles: they don't have clue one about the real world, and we lived and fought and died in a world so real they couldn't imagine it."

"Here's to the United States Marine Corps, which gave us three hots, a cot, a rifle, and a target-rich environment."

"I'll drink to the target-rich environment, even if

the hots wasn't hot that often and the cot not that comfortable that often. Sure was good shooting, though. Never saw anything like it, and I wish I could feel ashamed like I'm supposed to, but I figure every little yellow guy I sent to Buddha-R-Us didn't put a 7.62 through PFC Jones, and he got to go home to Passel O'Toads, Tennessee, and go to work in the paint factory."

"Damn straight," said Bob, "here's to all them paint factory personnel departments we helped meet the quota!"

Too bad it was overpriced coffee they were drinking instead of some hard slop-chute poison that would have mellowed them out and made them feel no pain. But it was just caffeine, and in a while, Chuck got around to the real reason he'd struck up chatter with Swagger, as Swagger knew he would.

"Gunny—"

"It's Bob. All that Gunny shit's long gone."

"Bob. I have to tell you, this whole thing doesn't sit right."

"No, it don't."

"Did you know Carl?"

"Never met him. Knew many who knew him; all said he was the bravest, the straightest, the best marine. I never had any reason to doubt that. You meet him?"

"Well, yes and no. All this stuff about number one and number two? It wasn't a thing I gave a goddamn about, but when it come out, it did gnaw on me some. Suddenly I have newspaper assholes wanting 'feature stories' and I just knew who they wanted me to play and I didn't want to play that guy. I just wanted to be with my family. My daughter's in the honors program at University of Oregon and my son just signed a minor league contract with the Mariners organization. I put in twenty-five years in the forestry service, had a nice pension, and I wanted to have some good time with my kids and watch them develop. There's also a great many smallmouths out there signed up to go on my hook and I don't want to disappoint 'em. Nothing more than that. All this 'You're number one' crap didn't mean a thing to me. It don't put fish on the hook. But it got me worrying that it might have meant something to Carl. It just seemed wrong and I worried he'd be upset. If he was. I mean, who knew, really? The numbers was made-up to begin with. The official tags was only seen and confirmed by line squad members or officers and reported. There were hundreds more probables, and you know as well as I do, if you can call your shots, you *know* that there wasn't nothing probable about most probables."

Bob knew. The kills were a lot more than the official tally. A lot more.

"So anyway, I thought the right thing to do after the news came out was try to reach Carl. I wanted him to know that nothing of this had anything to do with me. I wasn't behind any of it. I'm just minding my business, takin' care of my kids and wife, that's all. Someone else thought it was a big deal, not me. Of course I didn't know how to reach him, so I sent him a letter care of Ballantine Books, which had printed *Marine Sniper*, that biography of him that fellow wrote. Didn't think there's a chance in hell it'd reach him. I suppose I did it for myself. Anyhow, I just said, 'Hey, look, Sarge, just so you know, it wasn't me behind "Who's number one" that everybody's talking about, it means nothing to me, I haven't thought about it in thirty years. You were a great marine sniper, the greatest. I just got a little luckier because a few more assholes saw me pull the trigger, that's all.' I felt a little better after sending the letter."

"You got a response?"

"Well, yeah. It took a while. It took close to two years, but goddamn if I didn't get a letter just a couple of days before all this craziness started. That's why all this is so strange."

Bob knew he'd be offered a chance to read the letter. He also knew he shouldn't.

It was over, it was finished, it was gone. Put it behind you. Walk away from it. It means nothing. It's the dead past. You have a life, a family, kids, the world. You have everything. No man has more than you, plus you got to be a marine sniper and you saw a lifetime of stuff no other man ever saw, much less survived, and you've got the scars and steel bones to prove how close the calls were over the years.

Chuck got the letter out, unfolded it.

"It just don't make no sense to me. Here, read it."

Bob took the letter, and read.

Of course. How could he not? He had to read. He owed it to Chuck, he owed it to Carl, he owed it to all the boys under the ground. You can't walk away from certain obligations.

"Dear Chuck McKenzie," the letter read, in Carl Hitchcock's big, looping penmanship, not the slick handwriting of a man who wrote a lot.

Thanks so much for your letter and I'd heard you were no part of this deal, so it's no problem for me at all. Don't you worry about it. You were a hell of a marine and it's a shame you didn't get the medals and the rank you deserved, but then that was the way the thinking went in those days. But like me and all the other snipers I know, I figure you realize your true reward is all the boys walking around today who wouldn't be if you hadn't done your duty. I suppose I had a rough time for a while, because I'm as dumb a bastard as there is. And the "number one" thing put beer in the fridge and bait on the hook. I thought that might be over. Funny thing is, ever since the news came, I been busier than ever. I thought it would go away and instead it got louder. In fact, I have more bookings at more shows this year than any of the past five. And I told the promoters I'd have to up my fee because the cost of gas was so high, and that turned out to be fine with them. So as I sit here, damned if it don't seem to be working out. It's really the attention, more than the actual meaning. Being number two makes me somehow more interesting than being number one and I don't know why. Civilians! But I do know a good thing when I see it and I will run with it all the way to the bank, or at least the bait shop. Semper Fi, marine, and best to you and yours,

Carl Hitchcock

"Hmm," Bob said, a sound he made involuntarily which seemed to have the meaning, That's interesting but I will have to think harder about it.

Then he said, "He sounded pretty healthy."

"That's it, Gunny. He doesn't sound like a depressed fellow about to go off on some kind of killing rampage, obsessed with getting his number one ranking back."

Bob looked at the date. It was dated two weeks before the killing of the movie actress in Long Island.

It teased him.

"You show this to anybody?"

"No. The FBI asked questions about me, I hear, but no one ever contacted me directly and I never had a sit-down face-to-face, so I didn't have a chance to bring it up."

"Yeah, they asked questions about me too," said Bob, remembering a call from Nick before it was clear what all this was about.

"Now," said Chuck, "I'm not sure what to do. Should I call the FBI? I'm hoping to get some advice. Is this anything? I just don't see how Carl could write this and just a few weeks later blow a hole in Hanoi Joan's rib cage. It doesn't add up."

"No," said Bob. "It don't."

"Yet the FBI, they say categorically, over and over, it's been in all the papers, that yep, Carl did it, all the proof is in, they going to release a final report with all the evidence, case closed, and that's it, that's what the history books'll say."

"Yeah," said Bob. "They've clearly committed to that interpretation and it'll take something to get them off it. I know a little about how this stuff works. Once the big guys make up their mind, you can't change it. Just like a sniper program. Took years for the brass to see the value and sanction a school, and meantime every unit on the line put one together ad hoc, because it was so obvious and necessary."

"Should I contact the FBI?"

Bob honestly didn't know. He had no policy.

Then Chuck said, "Here's why I'm really here. A guy hears things, you know. And one of the things I hear is that you never really left the life. You're a sniper still, through and through. You've done stuff, survived stuff; lots of people say you're way at the top of the pyramid in terms of getting certain kinds of work done. I remember years ago you were wanted for the murder of that archbishop. Then that all went away, magically, so something not too many people know about was going on."

"I've had some crazy stuff happen," said Bob. "But I'm retired now."

"But it's said you have a gift. I mean, more than the shooting, but understanding the shooting. You can look at circumstances and you have some kind of feel for what happened. You can infer in ways other people can't. You're Sherlock Holmes, you're *CSI, Gunfight*, that sort of thing."

"Chuck, you're way overstating it."

"I'm just saying what I've heard."

"It's true that men of my family are natural-born people of the gun. Don't know why. But I had it, my daddy had it in spades, and his dad—who I hear was otherwise a monster—his dad was quite the gun man as well. It goes back, off and on, through generations, since somehow a mysterious fellow called Swagger appeared in the territory that would become Arkansas in 1783, from God knows where. His son had the gift and it's why so many of us died in wars or other violence. We're drawn to it, fatally, our character, our fate, one side of the law or the other, I don't know why."

"Well, I had a favor to ask."

"Ask it, brother Chuck."

"It's this. Maybe Carl did go all nuts like they say, and maybe he did all that killing, and maybe, somehow, I'm a little part responsible. If that's the case, then I'll just have to learn to live with it, and it's okay, it's what happens in the world. But suppose it's not. Suppose it didn't happen the way they said it did. Suppose, suppose, I don't know what, just suppose. Anyhow, what I'd like is for someone who is sympathetic to the marine side of the story and not under pressure to issue a report to make the newspapers happy to go and look hard at it. Go to the sites, reconstruct it in your mind, see what you see without prejudice. Look at it fair and square. If all the facts point to Carl, then that's where we are, that's it. At least there's no worry in it, nothing to keep you up nights."

"Chuck, I—"

"Now, I have a check here for five thousand dollars. That's not a payment. But you shouldn't have to gin up the expense money on your own. I'd like you to take it for travel, for hotels, for this and that, anything that might come up. Just take a week and satisfy yourself that everything's on the up and up."

"Chuck, save your money. I'm sixty-three, a little old to be tramping around strange cities with a range finder, hoping to find something the most sophisticated ballistic forensics techs in the world missed. It's just not going to happen. I'm too old, they're too good. It's not for me and it's a waste."

"Gunny, I—"

"I just can't do it. I don't want you mad at me and I'm sorry for Carl, but I can't go off again. I'm old. It'll kill me, I know."

"Okay, Gunny," said Chuck. "I get it. No problem. Hey, I had to give it a try."

"You're a good man, Chuck."

"Look, just do me the favor of saying you'll keep a mind open to it. No pressure, but if you change your thinking, the check is still there. And if you need help of any sort, here's my card, I'll be there in a second. I'm still a lance corporal at heart."

Swagger still made his plane, but just barely. He flew across America charged with melancholy at the way it had worked out. But he put it out of mind for a while, tried to get to sleep. Finally, after all the connections, he made it to Boise and went to his car in the lot. Another hour or so and then the day would be finished, at least.

He thought to call his wife to tell her he'd be home in a bit but was astonished to see his message light blinking.

Couldn't hardly work the damned thing, but managed to figure out how to call up the "missed call" menu after a bit, and was stunned to see a Washington area code on the caller. Who in that town gave a damn about him? But then he realized there was one person, and he recognized the number from last year: it was Nick Memphis's.

7

When the Seventh Floor calls, you have to go. It was J. Edgar's rule, back when the floor was the fifth and the building was across and down Pennsylvania, but it still held. Nick was glad he'd worn a tie that day. He dipped into the washroom and gave his face a scrub, but the lines driven into his flesh by a week of twenty-hour days and a lot of flight and airport time weren't helpful. He ran some water through his hair, toweled off, went out and found his jacket, and took the elevator up to seven for the director's office.

He was waved through by the Big Guy's secretary and two uniformed Joes who formed a security perimeter even this deep in the heart of the federal beast. He'd been in this office before, with its altar of flags, its glory wall summing up the director's—this director's—career, its shelves of unread books, its mementos and naval flourishes (the brass telescope!) and so forth. And he'd seen this view, which looked to the southeast over Pennsylvania and the Archives' Grecian pretensions toward the dome of the Capitol, giving the room an absurd fake-movie quality, on the presumption that all offices in Washington had views of the Capitol, with its red-white-blue bunting flopping in wind jets.

But the director sat with two men, by dint of haberdashery alone—well-fitted blue suits with subtle striping; dark, shiny mahogany loafers affixed with the je-ne-sais-quoi languor of tassels; fresh, un-dry-cleaned red power ties—of a higher professional political ranking. Each face was smooth and ruddy (Botox? only a coroner would know for sure), each head of hair lush and vibrant, each profile taut, each body toned (hours per diem in the gym). It took a while, but Nick recognized the heartier of the men as a congressman from out west somewhere; the other guy had lawyer or prominent lobbyist written in his flesh.

"Nick, sorry to interrupt," said the director, "but I wanted to get these two interested parties a little shot of face time with our lead guy on Sniper."

"Nick," said the congressman, rising, hand out, "Jack Ridings, Wyoming, thanks so much for giving us a few," and the other quickly fell into line, IDing himself behind the well-turned-out presentation as Bill Fedders, no affiliation but by implication powerful affiliation.

"Nick's one of our heroes," the director said. "He still limps a little because he was wounded in a gunfight while busting up that armored car robbery in Bristol, Tennessee, last year. How's the leg, Nick?"

"Well, my basketball days are over, but I can still jog and ride a bike, so it's a fair trade. I never could hit a jumper anyway."

"Nick, can you catch the guys up? Jack's Wyoming's single congressman and Bill's T. T.'s private attorney, and Mr. Constable—"

"'Tom' is what we all call him," said the slicker of the two, with a conspiratorial warmth, as if he were letting them in on some inside skinny. "He just came up with the 'T. T.' for publicity purposes. The man is *insatiable*."

"Tom, then," said the director. "Tom is very concerned with the progress in his ex-wife's death."

"Sure," said Nick. "No problem. Most of it's been in the papers."

So, this was a private confab with the forces of Constable? Constable, wealthy beyond measure, the famous star's equally famous hubby for eight years, fingers in all the pies there were—Constable was big-footing it. He needed private assurances that this thing was getting full attention from the Bureau—as if something this insanely high-profile wouldn't of its own accord—and insisting on a little inside dope. That was fine, that was okay, that was the way the town worked, and if you were going to have a career in the town, you had to play by its rules.

The rules were: Information is power. But power is also power. Power must be not so much obeyed as acquiesced to, massaged, assured. The key to all transactions was the congressman, who got his big donors and supporters private audiences with linchpin feds. It had always been that way, it would always be that way. Now Tom Constable—T. T. in the papers, Tom only to friends and intimates—wanted to be in the loop. In a way, Nick was surprised it had taken so long. Constable had a yen for attention himself, which may be why he married Joan in the first place, and he'd been front and center on all the Sunday talkers about the tragedy of his second wife, how much she'd given, what a crime it was that this tragedy took her, how it was as if she hadn't survived the war she had tried so hard to stop. Of course Jack and Mitzi and the poor funnyman Mitch more or less disappeared during this orgy of calamity, but again, that was the way of the big foot. Nobody ever said it was fair. It wasn't supposed to be fair. The process, in fact, in the language of engineers, was operating as designed.

Nick quickly ran through the actions his investigation had taken and tried not to overplay his hand. The director supplied that ingredient.

"See how fast Nick cut to the heart of it. He knew exactly where to go to smoke this guy out and it took, what, Nick, less than three days?"

"We didn't begin to look at the pattern until after the second incident," said Nick, "and we became lead agency. But we had the name one day after the third incident, went public with it the second day, and had our man early in the morning on the third, though for all of us involved, there was no breakdown by days. Nobody went home, we worked straight. It was great staff work. My people really did it. I just tried to stay out of the way."

"I'm sure Nick is being modest," said the congressman.

"I think I speak for Tom when I say the Bureau's actions have been extraordinary," said Bill. "Really fine work. Now what happens?"

"Well," said Nick, "as the defendant is dead, obviously there won't be any trial. What we do, we assemble the case just as if he'd survived, and we'll issue a report. When we do that, we'll officially declare the case closed. Chicago, New York, and Ohio will then declare their cases closed. And then—well, that's it."

"What happens if someone comes along," asked the congressman, "and says, 'Hey, you got it wrong, it was actually Freemasons from the Vatican and the Uzbeki mafia that did it'? That could happen. And then it's all dragged out again. I think Tom's a little worried about Joan's life becoming some kind of cash cow for cranks."

"You know," added the smoother Bill, "unlike, say, 'sixty-three, we have the Internet, we have bloggers, we have anybody with or without a thought in his head having instant worldwide contact with billions of others of questionable competence. The result, I'm sure you're aware, is a kind of festival of the bizarre, of the mendacious and the frankly exploitative. Good God, some are saying that Tom killed Joan because she was going to tell the world Tom dresses up in women's clothes! Or he never forgave her for not having his child. Or she cheated on him with a key grip on the set of *Justine's Revenge*. Others are saying Mitch Greene was a Russian agent and was about to turn himself in and reveal Tom as a spymaster. I mean, can you imagine? I can't even repeat some of the viler stuff."

"Well, there's a kind of systemic guard against that," said Nick. He was smart enough to lean a little forward, as if he were divulging some real inside dope, when what he was about to say was clearly known by everyone above the precinct level. "See, once law enforcement closes the case, it goes into the records as 'case closed.' That's a percentage, and every department, especially big-city departments or state police agencies and the political bureaucracies behind them, want their percentage as high as possible every year. I don't think the director will fire me if I tell you we do too. So the reality is that *nobody* wants to reopen a closed case that's on the good side of the ledger. Practically speaking, that means when the guy with the psycho best seller idea comes to us, we just say case closed and refer him to our document. Which, of course, he's already seen on the Internet. When that final doc comes out, it really does, in our experience, pull down a curtain that never comes up."

"Nick, may I call you Nick?" asked Bill.

"Sure, everybody does."

"Nick, is there a time frame here you could share?"

"Well, this one is unique, given the celebrity of the victims and the killer, the media attention and so forth, so of course we don't want to rush anything or make any mistakes that can later be attacked or reinterpreted. So I'm thinking another week at the least."

"Ah." If Bill was disappointed, no hint of it showed on his pampered, sleek, confident face, but in time he did make a further comment.

"I'm wondering," he said, "if we can't hasten it just a bit. Tom is extremely disturbed by Joan's death, and it's unnerving the way it's just hanging there in the open right now. This is painful for everyone, and Tom is also speaking for the heirs and families of the other survivors as well, and that poor, crazed sergeant. So I'm wondering if we can't speed the process somewhat. Get it out, get it done with, get it put to bed and closed, and we can return to our lives and begin the healing."

"I understand that," said Nick, "and we are working extremely hard. But, sir, it is a complex investigation, given the disparity of the four victims and the geographical spread, and my fear is that if we do somehow misstate or miss something, that'll just be fodder for these goblins. Look at the Kennedy thing, how that went on for years and ultimately compromised a generation's belief in the United States government."

"I see, I see," said Bill. "Then possibly here's a way

we could go. Could we leak something to, say, NBC News or the *Times*? I happen to know a young guy at the *Times* who could be very helpful. And that paper almost speaks with the authority of the state, and an early peek at the findings of the investigation would do a lot to calm this grotesque speculation."

"Well," said Nick, knowing it to be a bad idea. You couldn't trust those guys anymore, and some hotshot egoist reporter with a desperate need to advance his own career could completely mess things up.

"I appreciate Tom's interest," said the director, "but I don't think we've got anything comprehensive to leak yet. I'd be very happy to keep you gentlemen, and Mr. Constable, in the loop, and when we have something near an end product, we'll get back in touch and then maybe we can work something out. In the meantime, Nick, consider yourself officially interfered with by the Seventh Floor and pressurized to bring it to a boil faster, because there are so many interested parties. It's wrong, it's unfair, it sucks, but it's Washington."

Everybody laughed at the director's skillful jest, which nevertheless carried the weight of authority behind the humor.

"Now, if you'll excuse me, I'm going to walk Nick back to the task force real estate; it was good of you to drop by and express your concerns."

Everybody rose, shook, palavered inconsequentially for a bit, and then the director herded Nick back to the hallway and shoved him down it toward the elevators.

"Sorry, but Constable has juice with the administration, and when he leans, I have to pretend to give a little."

"Yes sir," said Nick.

"For some reason, they want this thing moved ahead. I know you're working your ass off, but it's so much better for all of us if you can release sooner rather than later and if you can slip something to the *Times*."

"As soon as I can, sir, believe me, I'll—"

"Just let me ask you, what's the hang-up? Do you need more people? Is it a manpower issue or a technology thing? Whatever support you need, I'll give it to you one hundred fifty percent. I want this thing over too."

"Yes sir. No, it's not really manpower, it's—"

He paused.

"'Memo to Special Agents: Never pause thoughtfully in the presence of the director. Thoughtful doesn't get you to the Seventh Floor, only results do.'"

"Yes sir. It's this, then. I'll lay it out. Not a major issue, I think, but it is something I've—*we've*—never encountered before. It's weird; it's got us somewhat baffled."

"An anomaly?"

"A huge anomaly. I've never seen an anomaly this big."

"What is it?"

"Here's the anomaly: there are no anomalies."

The director grunted.

"This is real life," Nick said, "there's always an anomaly, some little random fact that doesn't make sense or seems stuck in there and is connected to nothing. Someone gets somewhere too fast or not out of breath; someone's looking out a window and sees something and misinterprets it; a fingerprint from seven years ago turns up on a scene and screws up everybody. That's the universe we work in: squalid, messy, human, full of the unexplained or the untidy. The unusual is to be expected; it's even banal. But in this case, *nothing*. It all fits. There's nothing left over, nothing unexplained. Everything is perfect, from the ballistics to the forensics to the arterial spray patterns to the fiber samples to the fingerprints to the paper trail to the witness accounts to the time line to the coroner's report to the DNA testing. It's not messy enough. It's too neat and it makes me very nervous."

"But you can't put your finger on any one thing, is that it?"

"Exactly. We go over it and over it and we're stymied. Every day we get something new and it always fits just right, like a puzzle."

"Well, let me just caution you that you don't want to get too overwhelmed by what is, after all, well and truly *nothing*. I mean the prime craziness of the conspiracy gooney birds is the notion that the less the evidence, the more proof the authorities saw of conspiracy. Less was never less, it was always more. The absence of evidence was seen as more significant than evidence itself."

"Good point," Nick conceded. "Still, there's a thing I want to do. Let me run it by you."

"Go ahead."

"A wild card."

"Hmm," said the director.

"Meaning somebody from outside our culture, not in our boxes, with our prejudices, who would look at it with a fresh eye."

"A neutral observer."

"Actually, someone inclined to disbelieve our explanation. Someone who'd fight us. Someone with an instinct for our weaknesses. Someone who's very good on guns, particularly the dynamics of shooting, because he's won a batch of fights with big iron. Someone whose life experience inclines him to revere the marine sniper and who would never make an axiomatic assumption about a marine sniper's guilt. His mind doesn't work that way. Then, he was himself a marine sni—"

"Swagger."

"Yes."

"Christ, Nick, no doubt he's quite the operator, but can he be controlled? I mean, we spun his adventures in Bristol to our advantage, no doubt about it, but he was just that far from being out of control. Nick, suppose that fifty he fired at that helicopter had missed and hit a busful of orphan piano prodigies on their way to prayer camp."

"I'd be a crossing guard in Mississippi," said Nick.

"And I'd be your supervisor, making twenty-five cents more an hour. Nick—"

"He's smart," Nick said. "Almost nobody knows more about this stuff than he does. And he's honest. He'll call it as he reads it, no bullshit, no PC, no spin. He's straight nineteenth-century lawman in that regard."

"Matt Dillon!" said the director. "Here we go again. You ride him hard, you control him heavy, you have three more days. We need that report sooner, if not faster than sooner."

8

He beheld the thing itself. It was Carl's "teaching rifle," a patiently constructed replica of the Remington M40A1 .308 USMC sniper rifle of the nineties. Carl, of course, had done his great shooting in Vietnam with one of the old marine special services target rifles, a heavy-barreled Model 70 in .30-06, and a two-foot-long Unertl 8x scope. But that system was hopelessly outmoded, and as a "teacher" at sniper schools and an adviser to police SWAT teams and a gun show celeb, he'd had to acquire something more up-to-date, and thus in 1997 had purchased 5965321.

It seemed that 5965321 was Swagger's fate, no matter how he tried to avoid it. Nick had pushed all the right buttons: responsibility to the Corps, responsibility to the sniper program and to sniper culture, the one-in-a-million shot this was a game some assholes were running that only he, Swagger, could see into, the old cowboy thing about setting things right in the world. Against such arguments, "I'm old, I'm tired, I'm used up, I need a nap, my leg hurts" didn't cut much. So here he was with Carl's rifle, in the city he hated above all others, surrounded by people of whom he trusted only one.

The rifle: Carl had gotten 5965321 through the PX system at Camp Lejeune, a system which as a retiree he was still allowed to use, writing a check (also recovered) for $345.89, as opposed to a civilian retail of about $700, a very good deal. The agents had found the bill of sale in his papers, and Bob looked at it now: a Remington police rifle, in the model PPS, with a heavy 24-inch barrel and a tuned action. Carl bought it, Carl used it, Carl knew it, Carl loved it, no doubt about that.

Carl also, as sophisticated shooters will, improved it. He'd bought a McMillan Hunter stock, in the sand-and-spinach camo pattern that was state of the art in the nineties, before all this desert digital came in. Either he or a marine armorer buddy had bedded the action to the stock and hung a 1903 leather Springfield sling on it. He bought a Leupold 3.5–10x tactical scope with mil-dots in the reticle for ranging, a good alternative to the Marine Unertl 10xs not commonly available on the open market. He mounted the scope in Badger Ordnance tactical rings on a Badger Picatinny rail bolted and red Loctited to the action. He'd changed out the Remington trigger for a Jewell that gave 5965321 a five-ounce pull without creep or overtravel. He'd fired nothing but match 168-grainers in it and had shot out the original barrel and replaced it with two Hart barrels, keeping a detailed log of each shot fired. A few years ago, realizing that his clients would mostly be law enforcement and that many would be shooting suppressed systems, he'd gone through the ATF/Treasury Department rigamarole to legally purchase an otherwise illegal Class III device, i.e., a suppressor from SureFire, the tac light, laser, and suppressor giant, and had paid the SureFire armorers to machine threads to his new Krieger barrel on which to screw the noise-dampening steel tube. When the trigger was pulled, the gun didn't go bang, it went *ulch* or *groff* or something like that, a lot less loud but more importantly dissipated to other points on the horizon and thus a lot less identifiable as a firearm report. The SureFire armorers were so good that they could mount the can, as suppressors are called, without affecting the accuracy of the weapon, and FBI shooters had already proved the efficacy of the construction: they'd gotten consistent minute-of-angle groups, averaging .675 at a hundred yards, 1.866 at two hundred, and 2.84 at three hundred yards, the scope well zeroed at the hundred-yard marker.

It was a formidable piece of weaponry, easily capable of killing each of the targets that had been fired at during Carl's last mad week, and given his expertise in the art, the kills were clearly within his capabilities; moreover, the suppressor disguised the origin of the shots and guaranteed his getaway. Ballistics matched, casings matched, fingerprints matched; all the shots were makeable by a man with Carl's extensive training and field experience, and all the movements seemed within his capacity even as a sixty-eight-year-old man.

The rifle, slightly out of balance because of the eight-inch suppressor, lay on a long table set up in the Major Case working room on the third floor of the J. Edgar Hoover Building in Washington DC. It was part of the melancholy accretion of data by which the agents and technicians had proved that Carl and Carl alone had been responsible for the four murders in the seven-day time line of his killing spree. Their arguments and their evidence were contained in the draft known as "the report," meant to be issued through PIO as soon as possible, in tandem with the case being officially closed by the Bureau, and the police agencies involved would

certainly, even eagerly, follow suit. And that would be
that. Swagger had read the report many times, and even
though rough and unfinished, it was an extremely convincing document.

In Carl's home, address given, agents had located
a "mission room" in which detailed accounts of the
lives of nine "famous" antiwar activists from the late
sixties and early seventies, among them "Hanoi Joan"
Flanders, Jack Strong and Mitzi Reilly, and, a much
lesser presence admittedly, Mitch Greene. Moreover,
the number ninety-seven, representing the number
of kills it would take for Carl to take over as "number one marine sniper" from the war, was scrawled in
thirty-nine separate localities in the room, on scraps
of paper, on the wall, though again admittedly, it was
difficult to get a convincing handwriting interpretation based only on two numerals.

That number spoke to motive, perhaps seemingly
irrational to many but certainly arguable in the context of advancing physical decline, signs of dementia
or depression, alcohol problems, loneliness, and isolation.

The means were equally convincing. A paper
trail documented the former marine's travels in his
last week, from his purchase of the blue Ford van
for $16,900 from Woody's Fords on the outskirts of
Jacksonville to Bank of America Visa card records
for fill-ups, which traced an odyssey that ran from
Jacksonville to Long Island to Chicago to Cleveland
to finally near Ann Arbor. Motel bills told the same
story.

There was the van itself, smeared with Carl's fingerprints and DNA traces, as well as dirt samples

essentially linkable to two of the three shooting sites, clearly brought into the cab by Carl's boots. Witnesses corroborated it all, more or less. Yeah, that's the guy, yeah, old guy, kind of thorny, looked like that guy. The witnesses were the least impressive, of course, because they were people in the hospitality industry who saw hundreds of faces a day, but they basically agreed that yes, that's the guy.

He was there. He'd done it. Face it, Bob said to himself.

The motive? Well, who knew about that? It seemed to make sense in the way killers' motives made sense in the movies. Yeah, sure, he learned he wasn't number one no more and the freakin' redneck hillbilly cracked and went wacko/psycho. It didn't sound like any marine NCO Bob had ever known, because those gentlemen—himself included—tended to be the kind that stuffed it way inside and let it sit there. Even at the worst of times, with lead flying in and hitting everywhere, everything, everybody, tossing up stinging clouds of jet-spray debris, their faces remained, on long discipline, phlegmatic and almost uninterested. It wasn't that they were fearless, it's that they were responsible, and they had boys under them on the verge of panic and flight, and that dull, unimpressed face was their greatest weapon. It was cultivated, a sergeant mug—flat, smooth, unworried, kind of irritated maybe, but hardly really noticing all the shit in the air.

Would a man with a face like that crack the way this theory held, and then—here was the strange part— fragment into two beings, one still stoic and capable of intelligence gathering and analysis, complex escape planning, and execution in the form of great shooting followed by fallback through an unfamiliar area, without a single slipup, and the other clear-out crazy as a burning duck in a tornado? It didn't sit with any theory of human behavior Bob had ever seen or heard of, and he'd been around a bit. He'd heard of great warriors who suddenly were torn down by black dogs of depression—hell, he'd been one of those, in another lifetime, a solitary, furious loser off in the woods by himself, with nothing but mean for any and all—but those guys usually just ate the .45 one night. They had too much respect for what guns can do to go serial killer on anybody. They might end up lonely, bitter drunks, wife beaters, terrible fathers, serial adulterers, bar fighters, but it wasn't in the mind to go out and kill. Still, evidently some docs somewhere said it was possible. It was a symptom of post-combat stress syndrome, or whatever they were calling it these days. These guys in white coats were much smarter than him, so maybe they knew something. They said that it worked as a motive, and so the reality was, it worked as a motive. That would not go away. Carl got what little glory RVN bestowed, rode it hard, saw it turn to nothing, and he cracked. So be it.

So Bob set aside motive and turned at last to his most dreaded and melancholy task, feeling no progress had been made and none was on the horizon.

This was the actual product of the killer's enterprise: four corpses. Bob had seen corpses his whole life and had donated more than could be counted to the cause of universal extinction for meaningless reasons. He knew what bullets did to flesh and bone. He himself had been hit at least seven times and had in his hip a stainless steel ball joint to keep his old thigh-bone functional where a .30 caliber had torn through and shredded everything it hit. He knew what grotesqueness the collision of supersonic bits of copper-covered lead and human matter was likely to produce, and there'd been little grotesqueness of that sort he hadn't seen.

Nevertheless he was pleased to ease into his virtual trip to the morgue via the first of the victims, the movie star, who alone had been shot in the body. The crime scene photos were of little use; they simply displayed a woman handsomely dressed, petite, lithe, lying facedown on the bricks in a sleepy, relaxed, yet dignified position: her knees were together, and nothing untoward could be glimpsed (and police photographers were notoriously inclined to denude the body of any vestige of dignity by going for the looker-upper to panty). A pool of blood lay beneath her, and one expensive shoe had dislodged itself from her foot. She had pretty painted toenails, and nothing that he could see suggested that she was older than he was by a few years: taut legs, thin wrists, a thin neck. She looked a toned thirty-five. A little sherbet stain marked the entrance wound, but most of the gore was from another angle, and when he turned to that photo, he saw nothing but a delta of black liquid soaking her clothes. A hand at the end of a splayed arm hung limp; blood ran down it, inside her sleeve, and it slid down her curled fingers and deposited itself in little splotches on the bricks beneath.

The morgue shots showed even less, really. A neat puncture of an entrance wound, an exit wound (now cleaned) about the size of a fist, traversing her from left front to opposite rear right, that is to say, breast to shoulder blade. Alas, between them had lain her heart, and it had been neatly exploded by the velocity; a separate photo showed the shredded organ, and he shuddered, thinking of the millions who'd loved and hated this woman, who'd been moved by her art or sickened by her politics, who'd worked out with her on her exercise tapes or loved her famous father and brother, who'd followed her in the gossips or on the tube. What would they say of this pulverized piece of meat that stood for her soul?

He put down the case of Joan Flanders and turned to the far more devastating photos and diagrams of Jack Strong and Mitzi Reilly. He tried to be professional, objective, distanced, but couldn't quite bring that off, as indeed what he saw was an atrocity.

The integrity of the head, after all, is the surest of biological assumptions. The head is a vault, a treasure chest, a reliquary, the container of all our sacraments, of all that makes us human. When you blow it up, the sight disturbs anyone.

It disturbed Bob. Jack Strong's face was gone. It simply wasn't there. The bullet had tilted sideways— its entry was small enough, a little bitty thirty-caliber hole hard to find under Jack's thick hair—as it coursed through and churned up stuff and had built up enormous energy in just nanoseconds so that like a typhoon of brain matter, it literally exploded, tearing out everything that had been the upper left quarter of his face. What remained was an immense crater of red curd, squashed bean, broken potato chip, and vomited banana, sustained in a bowl of shattered skull; stared at long enough, the image fuzzed and became a volcano photo-reconned from above.

If anything, Mitzi's photos were even worse. Because she was thin-boned and thin-skulled, the bullet had actually broken her face into three plates as it exited her head sideways and bent. The three plates had been propelled by hot gas and hydraulic pressure to expand, almost as if inflated, and when the trauma of that moment passed, they reassembled themselves on her skull, though not quite precisely. The result was a terrible sense of the broken: each part of the face was recognizably Mitzi Reilly, famed guerrilla warrior of the sixties turned law school professor, but each was askew from the other, and the fissures that separated them deeply were evident. The face so diverged from assumption that it had a truly nightmarish reality. Even Bob, no stranger to the horrors of war, couldn't stomach it for long, and turned away to the autopsy diagram stapled to the report, which displayed nothing but a nude, generic body upon which the doctor had Xed the entrance and exit wounds in the frontal and rear skull and concluded that they were "consistent with death by high-velocity bullet trauma." No shit, Sherlock. The trauma was also located cartographically, by centimeter. "The epicenter of the entrance wound is located longitudinally 133 centimeters beneath the highest point of the crown and 133 centimeters from the lowest point of the jaw. It is located latitudinally 62 centimeters from the left and right occipital bones."

It was here that it first hit him. A strangeness, a

premonition, his subconscious telling him to pay attention. He didn't like it. He didn't want to make a discovery, see a clue, a trace of some other hand. It made his own and everybody else's life so complicated. He wasn't sure he could face it.

But still, that feeling would not go away: what am I missing? He could feel he was missing something. Something was not right. It was so obvious that no one had seen it; he could feel it, sense it, almost touch it in the empty space of the Major Case working room. It was in the Xs. Each diagram of each body bore an X to designate an entry wound and an exit, four Xs doubled for a total of eight Xs, carrying the inadvertent meaning of pornography, but something else too, X the unknown, X the mystery. He stared at the Xs, advancing even to Mitch's, and looked for a pattern in all eight . . . but then it was gone.

Feeling frustrated, he turned to poor Mitch Greene, least important of the four comrades in arms. Mitch would have called them "comrades in *holes*, see?" Always the joker, Mitch, even in death; from the first photo, he looked like he'd passed out and puked, sort of lolling on the chair behind the podium of the Cleveland-area Borders, with a spew of blackness from his slack jaw. You could look at it and almost laugh, calling up the memory of the man and his antics.

The back view, dead-on, told the truth, however. The lower part of his skull, directly behind the mouth, had been blown out, including, perfectly, the joinery between spine and brain. His head looked like a cantaloupe, with a broad scoop where the seeds and pulp had been dug free. Another great shot—didn't disturb teeth or tongue but simply plowed through the back of the mouth into the lower cranial vault.

Bob shook his head and turned quickly to the remaining morgue photos and the autopsy report, finding nothing particularly illuminating about them. They showed the crater, scrubbed, and the doctor had colored in a little patch on the generic diagram to document the missing skull and brain matter, at the center of which, of course, was the X signifying exit. In that case too, the bullet had been recovered, this time from beyond the wall behind Mitch, where it had bored through into the Borders' staff break room, touching no one and extinguishing its flight in the padding of an old sofa. Slightly deformed by its journey, it had turned out to be yet another Sierra 168-grain boat tail match hollow point, like the others, straight out of the Federal casing found in Carl's van in the motel parking lot. Four shots, four kills, just like the book said. It was sniper warfare at its best.

Bob sat back. Pain in his head, pain in his hip, pain everywhere. Lord, he needed a drink; too bad that wasn't in the cards. He'd essentially finished and he had nothing, not a goddamn thing. It was all as the experts from the Bureau said it was, tight as a drum. Carl had—

He hated it, but there it was. Carl had—

Well, Carl certainly hadn't forgotten how to shoot. As pure warcraft, you had to say, great shooting.

He sat back in his chair even further, wishing to be far away. He ought to run through it again and again, just to make sure he hadn't missed a thing. He didn't think he had, but sometimes you do, and he wasn't as sharp as he'd once been.

He snatched a sheet of paper from the yellow legal pad on which he'd been writing notes—there weren't many, the only interesting one being "No beveling in Strong-Reilly; why BTHP bullets go through glass without beveling? Did shooter move gun? Why?"—which had led nowhere. He crumpled it, thought he'd go to the hotel early this evening, maybe take in a movie, have a nice booze-free meal, something like that. He pivoted in the chair and spotted a wastebasket fifteen feet away, and like nine out of ten American men would, he immediately brought the crumpled puff up in two hands, riding the line up the lapel of his jacket while he fumbled for the right touch, found it, and as his arms flowed upward, he arrived at the point of release, so he launched toward the basket, which had become an orange hoop ten feet above an arena's wooden floor as the last shot had come to Bob Lee Swagger, shooting guard, with but a second left on the clock as the Razorbacks, down two (91–89) in the NCAA final against, who, oh yeah, Duke, they're always good—

The gods of small, airborne, crumpled paper balls were kind. The thing rode a perfect parabola, floated on nurturing air currents and eddies, and at the apex began its descent. He swished it. Perfect. Three. The buzzer sounded, the crowd cheered, Arkansas wins. Dead center, didn't even rustle the net.

His little guy drama come to an end, Bob turned back to—

Say now. Perfect shot. Couldn't do that again in a million years. Or could he?

He quickly crumpled another paper ball, turned, and went through the same ritual. Arkansas still won, 92–91, and guard Bob Lee Swagger was still the nation's hero, but this time on the descent the paper ball caught on the rim of the basket before falling in. He shot three more times, made two of them, but came nowhere near the freak dead-center perfection of the first shot.

What does that tell you? What does that tell you?

9

They were adults and professionals, so it was ridiculous that on those very few occasions when the director, jacket off, sleeves rolled up, tie askew, entered a room, everyone tensed. Yet it happened, always.

So when the great man strode into the Major Case working room, instant silence fell upon the workaday chatter, where Chandler—now called "Starling" after the Jodie Foster character in *Silence of the Lambs* because she was young, blond, and extremely attractive—sat with Ron Fields and a couple of other senior special agents assigned to Task Force Sniper, grousing good-naturedly about the "situation."

The "situation" was that nothing much was happening except re-checks, double checks, and then triple checks. It was Starling's responsibility to maintain the time line, to chronicle the input of the investigation, to make certain every piece of evidence was logged, its source, chain of custody, and disposition kept pristine, all lab reports properly annotated and summarized, all physical evidence cataloged. She had written the first, rough draft of the report that, polished and expanded, would announce the end of Task Force Sniper and the closing of its case.

But of late, even the hyperbusy Starling was not overworked; she'd even taken a full half hour for lunch, not the usual twelve minutes, and got home to her fiancé, a star photo analyst at a notable but unnameable government entity located in Langley, Virginia, before ten.

"It's eerie," she was saying. "I keep checking and checking—"

"Now, Starling," said Fields, "this is the rhythm of a major investigation. It goes and goes and goes and then, poof, it goes away. You just have to get used to it. And you have to understand that one of the things the Bureau pays you for is to wait until a genius consultant speaks his piece."

"Say, who is this guy anyway?" asked Bob Martin, assigned to the case as the best investigator from the Shaker Heights Police Department.

"He's supposedly some big gun guy. Not just in theory but in operational terms too. It's whispered by I-don't-know-who that Nick may have put him undercover in Bristol and that's how he brought down the Grumley crew."

"He looks like Buddy Ebsen as that old detective," said Bob. "What was it, MacGyver?"

"No, that was the young guy. Barney Fife?"

"No," said Starling, who'd watched every law and order show ever broadcast, as she was from a total police-culture family, with a father in command of and two brothers supervisors in the Arizona Highway Patrol, "Barnaby Jones."

"Score one for Jodie," said Martin.

"Come on, Bob, you can't call her that. It's Starling."

"You guys," she said, and then she went silent as His Eminence walked by.

The director knocked on the door of Nick's office and opened when he got the "Yo," from inside. He left the door open, presumably so the troops could hear and get the word before Nick himself put it out. He was known to be a guy very clever in managerial skills.

"Nick, hey, don't get up."

Nick, half rising, sat back down.

"Yes sir. Can I have someone get some coffee?"

"I heard your coffee down here sucked. I much prefer Organized Crime's coffee. Now *that's* coffee."

"Yes, Mr. Director."

"Nick, talk to me." He hadn't bothered to sit, which indicated in bureaucratic language that this was a quick chat type visit, a buck-up-the-troops initiative, rather than a serious policy discussion.

"I'm just passing by, I don't want to be one of those asshole micromanagers, you know the type, but do we have an arrival time yet on your consultant?"

"Sir, I've told him over and over that time is not on our side. But he's a cautious, deliberate guy. That's how he's stayed alive all these years."

"I'm getting all kinds of crap on this one. I think the *New York Times* is working for Tom Constable, as well as his lobbyist and that congressman. I'm hearing from Chicago and New York, and I know Cleveland will be on me soon. They all want action and we've got people literally living downstairs in Public Information."

"I see 'em every morning."

"Okay, what I'm thinking, is there some kind of interim report we could put out? Something we haven't given out before. Maybe it could be confirmed that we've matched Hitchcock's movements to the shootings? We have, haven't we?"

"That part's real solid."

"It doesn't commit us, but it makes us look good. Leak it to the *Times*. Got anyone here who could make a creditable leaker?"

Nick stood, looked beyond the director's shoulder.

"Starling, come here, will you?"

The young woman got up instantly, came in.

"Sorry. I shouldn't have called you that, Agent Chandler. Have you met the director? Sir, this is Special Agent Jean Chandler, whom I've appointed our case monitor. She's very good, works like a dog."

"Starling, eh? I get it. Well, I hope you're as good as Starling, Starling."

"So do I, sir," said Starling, for whom the original Starling was a complete goddess and the primary reason she'd decided on the Bureau for a career.

"I think I know your dad. Arizona? Great cop."

"He's the best."

"Starling, I'm sorry, *Agent Chandler.*"

"I'm used to it, Mr. Director."

"Anyhow, any experience with the press?"

"My father and brothers were not disposed to share things with the press."

"Well, that's sound principle, most of the time. But sometimes it buys us some time if we can feed the dogs a little something so they fight among themselves and leave us alone for a bit. Hmm, I'm wondering if—"

The phone rang.

"Go ahead, Nick, answer it, this can wait."

"Yes sir."

Nick snatched the phone up, glad for the interruption. He knew that having a thing with the press was tricky; you could never outsmart them, and Starling, even if she was working under the director's guidance, could get tagged as a snitch, never trusted, and it might hurt her career. He didn't wish that on anybody so young, so bright, so hardworking.

"Memphis."

"Swagger. I think I've got a little something. Should I come over? I don't know how you want to play it."

"My idea is, I'd bring the upper management of the investigative team over, plus some of the forensic and ATF loaners. Is that okay? You can talk to the group."

"Sure, in for a penny, in for a pound."

"And since he's here, I might bring the director along."

"Why not?" said Bob.

"Tell me you have good news."

"I have news," Bob said, "and it's up to you whether it's good or bad."

"That doesn't sound promising."

"Your people did a great job. Amazing, really, in the time. They only got one little thing wrong."

"And that is?"

"They got the wrong guy."

10

He stood at the head of a table with his notes written on a yellow legal pad. Immediately to his right, some very pretty young woman had her own pad, presumably to take what he said down. The others in the room were the executive special agents of the Task Force Sniper investigation, two loaners from ATF, a Bureau ballistics lab guy, one or two junior analysts, an Ohio detective, a Chicago detective, a New York State Police detective, also loaners to represent local interests, Nick as the task force commander, and the director, who had allegedly "been in the area" and wandered in. All basked in the dead institutional light of the overhead fluorescent, which turned them a kind of pale gray-green.

They knew. It was a sullen crew, hostile, not furious but disappointed and ready to fight. No smiles, no eye contact, nothing but sluggish body language, whispers with attitude launching them too loudly into colleagues' ears, a whole "We're not impressed" vibration throbbing in the room.

"Folks," said Nick when the shifting and shuffling and whispering had settled down, "as I've told all of you, I wanted to get an outsider's opinion on our findings, and I asked Mr. Swagger here because he's a former marine sniper himself. I'm sure he'll admit that he began with the honest bias to come to a different finding, to exonerate a fellow marine, but I knew that if we convinced him, we were doing pretty good. I guess we haven't. But I also know that he is the most experienced shooter I've ever met, an authentically honorable and dependable man, and I believe he has a certain kind of, uh, 'gift' for seeing into shooting dynamics. Not that he's a court-approved firearms expert, but he's just got some extra gene for seeing things that other people don't see. So let's listen to what he has to say. Bob, why don't you get started?"

"I should add," said the director, "and excuse me Nick, I don't mean to take over your task force, but last year as a consultant to Nick in Tennessee, Mr. Swagger performed with heroic distinction in an undercover capacity. He's earned the right to muss a few feathers around here, so I expect complete professional respect from everybody. I will be very disappointed if this turns into a yelling match."

"I won't do no yelling, I promise," said Bob. "I can tell there's disappointment here. I'm not here to criticize or to suggest somebody missed something. I don't want nobody's career hurt. I don't want nothing but the truth. You can also tell from the way I mix them verbs and subjects up, I'm not particularly well educated, and I apologize for that also. If I try to sound like I am, I will just sound even dumber, so generally I won't make no attempt to speak 'smart,' like you'd expect. If I lapse into it and my verbs and subjects start agreeing, give me a kick in the butt."

That brought a laugh, a respite, however brief, in the hostility.

"But it don't matter how I talk. I'm here to bring experience none of you has, which is as a sniper, a man who's taken lives in the field and who's spent too much time thinking about this sort of thing. So let me thank you in advance for your attention, and let me sum up and put cards on the table. Yeah, I'm here to tell you you're wrong and that Carl Hitchcock didn't do nothing. He spent the last week of his life, I'm guessing, in a drug-induced coma, and right away you say, 'How come there's no drugs in his bloodstream?' and the reason is, the drug they used was bourbon. There was plenty of that in there. He was an alcoholic and he was pickled forcefully via an arm drip—okay, I don't know the medicine, maybe it was just pure alcohol—after he was kidnapped. By who? I can't give you no name. But when I'm done you'll have a pretty good picture of who the guy is, where he is, and what it'll take to catch him. So shall we start?"

A few mumbles seemed to acknowledge reluctant assent.

"I begin with the shooting. You noted the shooter was a fellow of some experience. This boy knew what he was doing. Twice he made brain shots through heavy back window auto glass from what looks to be two-hundred-plus yards out. He drilled the actress between the ribs and into her heart. He shot Mitch Greene through the open mouth from a hundred yards out through glass. Carl Hitchcock clearly had the capacity to make those shots. So did his rifle. So did his ammunition. With that rifle and that ammunition and that skill, y'all are thinking, as I did at first, it's a piece of cake. Cold-bore kill shot. Yes, you could have made the cold-bore kill shot, Nick could have made the kill shot, I could have made the kill shot. But these shots weren't no cold-bore kill shots. These weren't bull's-eyes. These weren't center-target hits. These, all four of them, were abnormally perfect shots."

He let that sink in.

"He didn't hit the target. He didn't hit the bull's-eye. He didn't hit the center of the bull's-eye. He didn't hit the X at the center of the bull's-eye. Four times running, he hit exactly the spot where the two slashes cross to form the X in the center of the bull's-eye. He hit the exact mathematical center of the target, and you can verify that by checking the locations as figured by the coroners who measured. All four shots are centered right on the goddamned button by measurement."

Instantly, a hand shot up.

"I'm sorry to interrupt," said the New York State Police detective, "but that isn't what I see at all. What I see is a hole in the ribs to the left of the left breast, a hole in the center of the back of the skull, a hole in the left side of the head two inches above and a little ahead of the left ear, and a hole in the back of the mouth. I give you, *maybe*, the hole in the center of the back of the head and the mouth shot, *possibly*, but the other two are way off-center. They're not bull's-eyes at all."

"Good point. However, you're thinking of the targets as if they's lying still. You're thinking of them as two dimensions on a mount and looking for equal measurements top and bottom, right and left. But these was human and they's in motion. They are dead center, dead bang Fourth of July center, to the body at the angle it was at the time of the shooting. It's easiest to see on Reilly. Her husband got blasted, right next to her. She turns her head to look at it, pivoting to the left. As she turns longitudinally, her head gets longer. The shooter shoots exactly for the center of the head and at that angle, with the head cranked around forty-five or so degrees to the left, the exact mathematical center is four inches up and one inch in front of the left ear."

He looked at his notes.

"At a forty-five-degree angle, her head would have been 425 millimeters wide. I called a fellow to run it through the computer. Our asshole put the bullet exactly at 212 millimeters from the extreme furthest point of the skull and 133 millimeters from the crown and 133 millimeters from the jawline. Do you need the figures on Flanders? It's the same. Dead center side to side and top to bottom, given the angle of the bullet to the target. If he were shooting groups, he would have put those four bullets from varying distances in varying conditions into one hole of about .312 inches. Moreover, the group size, measured from center to center of the four bullet holes, would have been less than one-tenth of an inch. Ain't no man alive can shoot like that. Only God could."

He tried to let it sink in but in most cases saw confusion.

"How did he do it?"

He waited for an answer.

"Here's the funny thing. If you asked him, he wouldn't know. He wasn't trying to do it. It was a mistake. If he'd figured it out in advance, he'd have shot less well, just for kills, not for the center of the center. He actually did it by mistake. How?"

No answer.

"The answer is the scope. Don't you see? Carl had—and the rifle was found with—a Leupold 2.5–10x Mark 4 mil-dot sight, state of the art to the year he had his rifle built, which was 2005. It could hit head, heart, mouth, sure, but it would put its bullets in a random pattern across a couple of inches over three hundred yards. The group is maybe an inch per hundred, two inches for two hundred, three for three, called 'minute of angle.' It ain't refined enough, no *way* is it refined enough to make shots that accurate into a group less than a quarter of an inch. The killer did it because that's what the scope let him do."

"He used a target scope?" somebody asked.

"No sir. The wars have pushed the technology of scopes hard since 2005. There's military money in it now, because we're fighting in sniper campaigns, we have to tag people way out there before they can tag us. Our shooter had access to this stuff. Our guy used some new generation software-driven piece of equipment that allows amazing cold-bore first shot accuracy. The manufacturers are Horus, Holland through Leupold, Tubb through Schmidt & Bender, Nightforce, the BORS system from Barrett, and an outfit calling itself iSniper. Whoever did this job took Carl's scope off, mounted one of these babies, did the shooting, then replaced the Leupold Mark 4. He sat there in the dark in that truck, he figured the distance, the temperature, the wind, all went into an equation, which he then ran through the software program preinstalled and precalibrated to bullet weight, powder amount, primer influence, and his little baby computer give him a solution. It said something like seven down, four-three to the right. He looked in the scope, and instead of one crosshair like you think you know, it has a kind of Christmas tree of points of aim—reticles, in the trade—descending from the scope center, and he found the one that was seven down and four point three to the right and pressed the trigger. Instant super bull's-eye. Okay, let me tell you, first thing, Carl was an old guy, and there was no way that technology meant a goddamned thing to him. He couldn't have begun to have used that thing to make those shots. I doubt he used a cell. I called seven folks who knew him to verify that."

Of course, silence. He was beyond them. Then Nick said, "But maybe he just made those shots out of luck. I mean there's no physical reason he couldn't have had a very good day. Four times in a row. It happens. Nothing evidentiary sustains your presumption. In other words, there's just no proof except your reading of the bull's-eyes, your subjective interpretation."

"No," said Ron Fields, ever the bull in the porcelain museum, "I have to agree with him. I shot designated marksman on the St. Louis SWAT team for six years. I got very, very good, but I could never *ever* shoot like that. I could hit anybody, bring 'em down dead in a second, and thank God I never had to, but my shots were all in what he called minute of angle. This guy is shooting second of angle. Tenth of second of angle."

"Mr. Director?" asked Nick.

"Nick, I'm just listening. Go on, Mr. Swagger, do you have anything else?"

"Well, let's think about who'd use a sight like this.

There's basically two sniping communities, military and police, with some interchange. But for a fact, most police teams never shoot beyond a hundred yards."

"That's right," said someone. "Our Quantico people put out a report last year that found the average police marksman shot takes place at seventy-seven yards."

"It's only the military that needs to take people out way beyond a hundred yards. That's what they're doing in the sandbox right now with calibers like .338 Lapua Mag, .300 Winchester Magnum, .408 CheyTac, .416 Barrett, and of course the .50 BMG. They're dumping bad actors out to a mile, maybe even farther."

"So he's military. Carl was military. That seems to prove our point, not yours," Ron said.

"No sir. Carl started military, Carl was great military, one of the best marines that ever lived, but in the last twenty years, Carl has been putting on seminars for police all over the country."

"That's how Chandler found him," said Nick.

Chandler seemed to be the young woman taking notes; she smiled but didn't look up.

"So Carl had to learn the ins and outs of your kind of shooting as well as his own. That's why he didn't have no .408 CheyTac, 'cause he wasn't working with young snipers headed out to the sand to pop ragheads at fifteen hundred long ones, he was working with police sergeants who might have to take down a crazy husband who has a knife to his baby's head. That's why he stayed with the .308. Y'all go through his logbook and see that he's been working almost entirely in a police environment for about ten years now. That's another reason why he wouldn't know and couldn't have learned fast enough to master that high-tech, software-driven thing. But there's another thing. You, sir, you were a police marksman. You were called out, I'm guessing, even if you never pulled down on anyone. You recall lying there in the dark, worrying. What were you worrying about? What was your biggest problem?"

"Well," Ron started, his eyes going troublesomely vague as he looked back through hazy memory, "as I recall it was . . . well, glass."

"That's it," said Bob. "What's the situation of a man with a knife at a baby's throat? What's the situation of a bank robber with hostages? What's the situation of a gangbanger who won't come out? What's the situation of a kidnapper with a gun to his victim's head after a car chase? The answer ain't 'indoors.' The answer is 'behind glass.'"

Again, the pause.

"That's something Carl had to know if he was going to help law enforcement boys with their rifle shooting. That's something that military snipers pay no attention to. They're almost always dropping people outdoors. They never have hostage situations. They scan, they locate, they calculate, they drop, and if it's in town, most of the windows have been blown out, if they was there at all. The guy with the AK or the RPG. The guy with the cell phone, whatever. Glass ain't in their plans. Sir, how do you shoot through glass?"

Ron nodded. It was as if he was conceding a clever checkmate that he hadn't seen coming.

"Yeah," he said, "I get it. To shoot through glass, every police marksman knows, you don't shoot that Federal 168-grain match hollow point. You shoot a hunting round, a 165-grain Federal Trophy Bear Claw, it's called. It's a much stronger bullet structurally, which means it won't break, shatter, or deviate on glass, particularly the heavy glass in an automobile. But this guy didn't know that."

"Carl would have. But this guy didn't," said Bob. "But he wasn't no dummy. He had an uninformed idea on glass and his solution was improvised, as a military sniper would impro out in bad-guy land. His solution was to minimize the angle of deflection by actually *moving* the gun in the Reilly shooting. He was, what, over two-hundred-odd yards out, the next block over, and he knew that he didn't want to try and go through the back window of that Volvo at an angle, because there's no predicting how the bullet would deviate. It might not even penetrate, it might skid off. So he— he had to have help, I'm guessing—he just *pushed* his sandbags or shooting pedestal eighteen inches to the right so his angle to the glass would be zero degrees. That's why there was no beveling on the second shot. Both were straight-throughs."

The room was quiet.

Bob finally said, "A sophisticated team set this up. They watched Carl, they knew Carl's weaknesses, his strengths, his tendencies. One night, when they had their intelligence set up, they took Carl down, injected him with something strong; he probably never came awake again, as they kept him stewed under a fast alcohol drip for the next week. They had someone who resembled him in some vague way take over his identity, buy the van, rent the rooms, establish his bona fides, drive to the shooting site. Their shooter did the killing, while some people rigged that room in his house. When the ID was made, they hauled poor Carl to that room and blew his brains out. Then they vanished. It was set up so you couldn't help but think it was Carl. They's running a game on you and they almost got away with it. Only thing is, their sniper didn't think rigorously about the hits he was making. Too bad for him."

"So who are we looking for?" Nick asked.

"Lots of military experience, no civilian experience. Superb technician. He's got to be a grad of some service sniper school, lots of kills in the war. Thinks he's pretty damn good."

"What do you recommend we do now, Mr. Swagger?"

"Just one thing: you want to catch a sniper, there's only one way. Get another sniper."

11

In the town of Cold Water, there lived an outlaw by the name of Texas Red. He kicked open the swinging slatted door to the Spotted Dog saloon and slid through as it rode its hinges back and forth. The piano man stopped his tinkling, and cowboys cleared away from the bar. He stood, tense, as the crowd cleared, leaving but three, who seemed not in the least perturbed.

They were the Mendoza brothers, Mexicans. They had greasy mustaches, bandoliers crossed on their chest, guns worn low, gunfighter style.

Red appraised them. He was thin and wiry with a straw mustache. He had hard black eyes. He wore a tall, round-topped Stetson, pale gray, a lot of hat. He wore a faded red placket shirt, a pair of suspenders to sustain the weight of his tight wheat-colored jeans, a pair of well-beaten boots with silver, jingly spurs. Across his waist, in a Mexican flap holster, engraved beautifully in a floral motif by the folks in El Paso after the artist-gunman Bob Meldrum, he wore a first-generation Colt Peacemaker in .44-40 with yellowed, ancient ivory grips. It contained five cartridges because he had carefully loaded by pattern so that the hammer of the old revolver, with its fierce prong of firing pin, now rested on an empty cylinder. It was a safety measure. You wouldn't think at nut-cutting time with the Mendozas a fella would think about gun safety. But Red had.

"Bastards," said Red under his breath.

The Mendozas said nothing, not because they were tongue-tied but because they were black metal plates.

He heard the buzz of a timer, signifying *go!*

Texas Red drew, and he was smooth and that meant he was fast, and he cocked as the gun came up, fired from instinct honed on practice, and sent a wad of lead to bang hard off and knock down José Mendoza's black-plate chest, another to gut the black-plate belly of Frank Mendoza, and—dammit—a third which just missed Jimmy Mendoza in the black plate. Then Texas Red thumbed back the hammer fast— this had taken months to learn—and in the same motion tried to ride the gun up to his eyes and fired a fourth time, hitting Jimmy in the center of the black plate. The black plate fell. Cottony swirls of old-time black powder smoke rolled in the air.

"Goddamn," he said. "Goddamn, goddamn."

"I think Jimmy might have toasted you, Mr. Constable," said Clell Rush, the legendary Hollywood gun coach. "I saw you go to sights on the fourth shot. Because you missed the third shot. And the reason you missed the third shot was the gun didn't set up in your hand correctly on the recoil after the second shot. And the reason that happened is that after each shot, the gun was a little higher in your hand. The first two shots were good, though. But if you go to sights, you're thinking, and all the time you're thinking, that black plate is shooting back."

Texas Red turned.

"I can't seem to get to three," he said. "I'm fine through two, I can do two, but I get tangled up and it makes me cautious on the third."

"Are you drawing each night like I said?"

"I do my homework, Clell, you know that."

"Well then, you're momentarily plateaued out. Same thing happened to Bob Mitchum on *El Dorado*. He got good and then he stopped developing. I didn't think he'd ever get it. But he was a pro, like you, Mr. Constable, he did the work, and when he had the saloon scene, he was smooth as butter. Sometimes you get a natural—Dino was a natural, he just took to it with super hand speed and coordination—but if you didn't get the gene for gunwork, you have to practice."

"I guess I'll just have to work harder," said Texas Red–Tom Constable. "The real Cold Water is next month and I do mean to win."

Tom Constable was fond of winning, and pretty good at it too. He'd won a fortune in his twenties by pushing his inherited advertising agency (it specialized in roadway signage) into other forms of media, and he got into cable early, rode it hard, and made his first billion. Then the sailing bug caught him and he put two years into that and won an America's Cup. Then sports, then news, buying or creating teams and networks. Then he married a movie star, decided to become a rancher, bought more land than anybody in America, reinvented buffalo herds, started a restaurant chain, and now he was into a new obsession called cowboy action shooting.

It was an interesting diversion. It played with his old Wild West fantasies, which had first been cultivated in front of the TV in the golden decade of the fifties, when Paladin, Marshal Dillon, Chris Colt, Cheyenne, and the boys from *Laramie* and *Bonanza* had dominated the American popular imagination. The way it worked: you got yourself all dressed up like one of the old boys, you called yourself by a nickname, you packed four guns—two handguns, a rifle, a shotgun, all of them of a design preceding 1898— and you shot real bullets and buckshot (black powder loaded) in low-key fun house scenarios adapted from the TV shows of yore.

Most folks did it because it was a nice baby boom wallow; it was relaxed and social and all men met as equals. But Tom, as always, wanted to win; it was a part of his unmalleable personality, the least pleasant thing about him, the way he got fixed on something and all life ceased to exist except that issue. That's why he'd had so many wives, was so estranged from his children, drove so hard in business, and could not stand to be bested in anything. Who'd have guessed such a handsome man had such fiery pathologies hidden beneath?

And in Texas Red, he'd stumbled upon a creation that pleased him immensely. In the sport you could cook up your own character, and for some reason Constable had instantly conjured Red, twenty-four, of South Texas, a kind of Billy the Kid knockoff, young, fast, loose, dangerous. Red was the dysfunctional deviant boy that Tom's well-disciplined business life and public image could never acknowledge, but who lived somewhere inside him, hiding under layers of polish, tailoring, grooming, and flossing. He was all id, he was a killer, he was a fast-draw piece of work, and when he saw wrong or threat by his own standards, not society's, he faced it and gunned it down. One and nineteen men had tried to take him in his fantasy, and one and nineteen were dead. The next man who faced him, whoever he was, wherever he was, soon would be dead.

Meanwhile, on the dreary planet called reality, he'd immediately commissioned a famed Peacemaker gunsmith to build him the most refined and accurate six-gun possible, ditto the rifle and shotgun, and he paid the legendary Clell Rush an outrageous fee for private coaching. He'd gotten good too. Tom worked every damn day on it, shooting privately reloaded .44-40s by the bucketful on his vast western ranch. There too he'd had the scenarios from last year's Cold Water Cowboy Action Shoot in Cold Water, Colorado, re-created. He wanted desperately to place well in the upcoming matches, because like so many other things, a victory wouldn't be from who he was but from what he'd done.

He reloaded the Colt, sliding the big cartridges through the loading gate, just as generations of cowboys had in this land two centuries ago. Around him, the mountains of southwest Montana towered, glistening peaks lit by snow at their higher altitudes, under a sky so blue it made your teeth ache and wads of cirrocumulus clouds piled high. Of course, he noticed none of that.

"I don't know why I can't get it to set right on that third shot," he said. "Maybe that one had a little extra powder in it and it kicked a little harder."

"Could be. Most likely you held it too tight and

didn't give with the recoil, and it acted up on its own. You can't be fast fast. You can only be fast slow."

"You know, Clell, you tell me that every damn time, and one of these weeks I'm actually going to understand what you mean."

"Well, sir, what it means is, you can't fight it. You can't conquer the gun. You can't beat it down, make it do what it don't want to. You got to do it with love. You got to meet it gentle, let it have its way, and in that way you get your way. It's like a horse. Or a woman."

"It isn't like any of the women I was married to, I'll tell you," Tom said with a laugh. "They like to broke *me*, the bitches. Anyhow, I will—"

"Mr. Constable?"

It was his secretary, Susan Jantz, standing next to him in her pantsuit, an extremely plain but unbelievably capable woman.

"Susan?"

"A call from DC. Mr. Fedders. He says it's urgent."

Tom made a little comic face for the benefit of Clell, took the phone, and stepped away.

"Yes, Bill."

"Tom, I've got some news. Not good, I'm afraid. I've heard through a source that the FBI's going to postpone releasing its report for a little bit."

"I thought you—"

"Tom, Jack Ridings and I went and had a one-on-one with the director himself. We met the head guy on the investigatory team. It looked to be in the bag. It seems there's a new direction they want to pursue."

"Lord, I don't want this dragging on all year. I

don't want books, I don't want TV specials, I don't want any who-killed-Joan bullshit selling product and little weasels getting rich off Joan's death."

"Yes, Tom, I understand. It's the chief of the task force. He's somehow reluctant to sign off on the narrative they've established, so there's some dicking around, I'm not sure exactly what and I'm not sure how long it will take. He seemed like a guy who was reading the wind, and I just don't know what's happening with him now."

"Bill, I'm paying you a great deal of dough. If this FBI guy is suddenly getting cute, then find some way to get him out of the picture. Have him shipped to Toledo, dig up something about him and plant it in the papers, just get him the hell out of there."

"Tom, of course, I just wanted you in the loop. I actually know a young *Times* reporter who can be very helpful to us in this case."

"Please handle it, Bill."

12

"You're a little ahead of us," said Nick. "We don't even know where to begin."

"Someone here knows where to begin. That fellow, there," said Bob, pointing to a man.

"I wondered when you'd remember," said a mild-looking older man, hair gone thin but still combable, sitting at the far end of the table. He looked like the professor at the frat party, among all the young go-getters.

"How are you, Mr. Jacobs? Are you the lab boss yet?"

"I'm fine, Mr. Swagger, and yes, actually, I am the lab director. I remember how I tried to send you away; it was like this, all the evidence pointed to you. But you'd figured it out and pulled the rug out from under me."

Years ago, in a different lifetime, Walter Jacobs, then a young technician from the lab, had testified for the government in a case in which Swagger had been accused of the murder of a prominent man by long-range rifle fire. It was a complicated thing, and it almost got him killed, but it also got him out of the bitter woods, lifted the anger that had weighed like a yoke across his shoulders, got him married to a fine woman, and got him two of the best daughters a man could dream of.

"That old lawyer was spectacular, Mr. Swagger.

I've never forgotten it. But before I answer your question, do you mind if I ask *you* a question?"

"Was waiting for it when I saw you."

"I'm aware that once again, or so it appears, someone extremely knowledgeable has apparently manipulated ballistic evidence to frame a Marine Corps sniper. Though in the first case the sniper survived—you—and in this one he died—Hitchcock. But you're playing the same role, aren't you? You're still the man who sees through it and on his own goes into the wilderness and puts a conspiracy under the ground, so that justice, in some form, pays out. But it also seems you could be reinventing your biggest triumph. Maybe subconsciously you're trying to re-create that episode in your life, like Captain Queeg and his strawberries aboard the *Caine*. Maybe it's all a delusionary structure that the much older and perhaps less rational Bob Lee Swagger is subconsciously forcing on all of us. Are you Swagger or Queeg?"

"Has anyone here read Mr. Herman Wouk's *The Caine Mutiny*?" Bob asked. No hands went up.

"See, Mr. Jacobs, I have, so I'm with you. And I'll let you decide. But before you decide, let me ask you *my* question. And I bet when you hear it, you withdraw yours."

"Well, isn't this interesting," said the director. "Nick, you do give a good meeting, very dramatic, even if your coffee sucks. Go ahead, Mr. Swagger."

"All right," Bob said. "Yeah, maybe I am a foolish old coot who's playing tricks on myself and on you to have a taste of old triumphs. But let's just examine the technical stuff a little. I'm betting that when that rifle came to your lab, you went over it at a microscopic level. It ain't got no secrets, not even among the atoms, you don't know about, is that right?"

"That is right, Mr. Swagger. Even to the point of measuring the firing pin to make certain that it was up to spec, even to the last two or three thousandths of an inch, so that nobody could have cut it and soldered it back so that it wouldn't fire. We learned that one the hard way."

"Yes sir. Now, is it not true that any object in the world picks up microscopic debris of some sort? A record at the smallest level possible of where it's been, what it's done."

"Yes sir, just like on the *CSI* shows."

"Never seen one. Figured it out on my own. Now, a sniper rifle would be particularly rich in such a micro record, wouldn't it? I mean, mostly it's kept cased or in a safe, so it's not picking up a lot of random crap. It's rarely used, and when it's used, it's used in some dramatic enterprise. So the stuff aboard ought to tell a straightforward story, yes?"

"True again."

"And a rifle is a particular kind of vacuum then, right? I mean, it's always slightly lubricated, and lubrication has an attraction factor on its own. It's like glue. Lot of tiny fragments and stuff sticks. Some can be identified, some can't."

"That's right."

"If it were paint or carpet fibers, you'd have a huge database to compare anything you found against. You could do it by computer in a few seconds. Right?"

"Right."

"But if I'm reading correctly, you came up with an amount of 'unknown baked paint debris.'"

"That's what it says. That's what I wrote."

"And it's unknown because you ain't got no 'baked paint debris' database, nothing to compare it to."

"Right again."

"Now," said Swagger, "here's where I am. That baked paint debris—my thought is that it's some kind of peelings, fragments, dust, motes, whatever you call it—"

"We call it 'microscopic shit,' Mr. Swagger," Jacobs said, and everyone laughed, even Bob. Good one for Mr. Jacobs, and the laugh let a little tension out of the room.

"My read is that some of it came from the scopes. In other words, whenever you tighten the rings on a scope to mate it to the rifle, you leave microscopic trace amounts, 'shit'"—another laugh—"off the finish of the scope. You do it a lot, you have a lot of shit. You do it rarely, you don't have much. But it's always there, right? However, since rifles with scopes are so seldom used in crimes, no one's bothered to accumulate a database, when of course paint samples from cars and carpet fibers are always found at crime scenes."

"Yes."

"Okay," said Swagger. "Here I am. Here's what the old man is driving at. This kind of scope I described— as I said, there's only six makers in the world. Well, in America. They are Horus; the Tubb DTAC, which is made by Schmidt & Bender; Nightforce, an American outfit actually manufactured in Australia; Holland, which has a contract through both Leupold and Schmidt & Bender to manufacture a scope with a ranging reticle and a series of aiming points; the BORS from Barrett, which fits on and adjusts the scope itself; and finally a company out west called iSniper, which makes a top-dollar variant called the iSniper911, said to be the best of the bunch. One of those brands of scopes this joker used. Therefore, you have to go to a big firearms wholesaler who has all these scopes in stock, you have to obtain one of each and test them. And one of them will yield baked paint debris identical to the microscopic baked paint debris you found on Carl's rifle. And that's the kind of scope this sniper used, while Carl was all alcohol-stupored up. Then his old scope was remounted and zeroed. So my question is, if you find it and make that match, would you withdraw your question about this thing being a Swagger fantasy? In other words, ain't that your, whatchyoucallit, *objective* evidence?"

"Once again, Mr. Swagger, you're the smartest boy in the class."

Nick said, "We can track the sales records of the scope. Someone on that list—and I'm guessing there can't be many because it's new and it costs a lot of money—someone who's bought one of these things, he'd be our person of interest."

"So why again do we need to send an undercover, Mr. Swagger?" asked Ron Fields.

"This is why," said Swagger. "The flaw in this system is that it's tricky. That's why an old guy like Carl never could have mastered it, and that's why these things will always be primarily for the government, because they demand basically a professional, highly trained shooter to get them to do what you're paying all that money for them to do, which is head-shoot Taliban field commanders at sixteen hundred meters cold-bore. You got to be good with numbers, good with small machinery, confident with higher logarithms and minicomputers, familiar with software, all that tech-weenie stuff, plus be able to use it all in the dark or the cold or the jungle or after three days of sitting in a hole in the ground under a net on a mountain slope in someplace that ends in 'stan.' It's a highly refined skill. So most of these companies run schools to teach potential shooters—mostly special ops people, or high-contact military like Rangers or some government SWAT outfits, highly trained contract operators like Blackwater or Graywolf, people who need to know, your elite professionals—to teach them how to run the stuff under pressure and in field conditions. Our man will have gone through that training."

"We get the records—"

"You have to subpoena the records. The records can be diddled or destroyed. You don't know who or what is behind this, what the point is, where the trail leads. You need to send a man who can play in that league to the shooting school to see what he can come up with. You need to do it fast. I have a recommendation."

He couldn't believe he was about to say this, but there it was. In for a penny, in for a pound. Last mission of a long-dead war. And as in all wars, who else was there to send?

"I recommend me. Let me hunt this bastard."

13

He didn't introduce himself. He simply strode to the front of the small group of shooters assembled in the bleachers next to the benches under the bright Wyoming sun and said, "Your insert was at 2200, you got to the target zone at 0500 in the dark after a long uphill, over-rock belly crawl, so you've no time to range the target area by light. You're in a hole. You're bleeding everywhere. The scorpions are crawling over your backside, looking for the breakfast you yourself ain't had. It's cold. There are Taliban all over the place. The light comes up, and that's when you see the Cherokee. It putters along and finally stops at a hut in the valley, and out pops the tall fellow for his dialysis. You've maybe two to three seconds clear shooting when he stops to talk to a kid. You'd also like to go home afterwards and have tea with the boyos, right? Oh, you fellows would have a Bud and a steak, but you take my point. How do you do it?"

He stood in front of them, burly, with a bristle of dark hair and a taut NCO's face from any army in the world, his seemingly an Irish one. He was muscular, powerful, built for war or football, little else. His small eyes burned darkly and it was clear he was high clergy in the church of the sniper. He wore the uniform of the trade—the tac pants, a military-cut shirt and jacket, assault boots—and his eyes ran from man to man. His cadre stood to the right at parade rest, same uniforms, same burly men, or at least two were, the third being scrawny and dark and feral, all fast-twitch muscle.

"You, Blondie? How do you make that shot?"

Blondie was actually redheaded, about thirty, with his own set of sniper's hard eyes. He was one-seventh of this quarter's iSniper five-day tutorial, out here in the wastes to learn how to run the tech. Like his six colleagues, and like the speaker, and like the three other silent members of the teaching cadre, he was sunburned, tattooed, thick-armed, and he knew the drill as to kit, appearing in the de rigueurs of the tactical trade, complete to assault boots from Danner, khaki cargo pants from 5.11, polos from Blackhawk, scrunched boonie hats or weatherbeaten LaRue Tactical dusky green baseball caps, and a whole sales rack of tear-shaped, mucho-dinero sunglasses including Wiley Xs, Gargoyles, and Maui Jims.

The site was a thousand-yard rifle range twenty miles outside Casper, Wyoming, a featureless blank of land that could have been the backdrop for a play by Beckett, just nothingness under a bright sky, with a lean-to sun shade on a cattle ranch hunted for prairie dogs and mule deer in other months but in the cool fall fallow. Six of the students came from unnameable military units. If they told you which one, they had to kill you, but they'd do it fast so it wouldn't hurt so much, and they'd smile so you wouldn't feel disliked. The seventh looked like a gentleman cowboy.

"I'd pass," said Blondie. "Without the range, there's no shot. How the hell am I going to range, then go to Kestral for temp, altitude, wind, and humidity numbers, then figure in the ballistics, then run the algorithms on my Palm Pilot, then go *clickety-clickety-click* dialing the scope this way and that, hoping I get 'em right? In three seconds? No way. By the time I'm done, he's inside. Meanwhile, there're more and more people around till the area's thick with 'em. So when he leaves, even if I'm suppressed when I take the shot, they can gauge where I am and put a lot of shit in that area, and that makes me bacon. If I got a big kill out of it, maybe I'd pay that price. But I'd have to think on it, and all the time I'm thinking, he's getting smaller, and by the time I've got it all thought out, he's gone. Mama didn't raise me to be no dead hero. Ain't no virgins waiting for me where I'm headed."

"Exactly," said the lecturer. "Now, possibly Mr. Swagger here"—he pointed to the gentleman cow-boy—"possibly Mr. Swagger could make that shot cold-bore. But he's not human, he's mythical. I'm simply human, so I couldn't make it. Could you make that shot, Mr. Swagger, as I've described it? You made so many others."

"Doubtful," said Bob. "Not now, at any rate, I've lost too much. When I was as young as these fellows, there's a possibility. I never worried about humidity because where I was it was consistent, and there wasn't much wind, except during monsoon. I don't know, though. Some men have a knack for distance. I never did."

"But you had a knack for knowing the hold. Genius possibly more than 'knack.' A feel for it, something subconscious. All of you Vietnamers who scored in the nineties or better had to have that subliminal gift."

"Well, maybe we did. I never talked with any of the others about it, because both Chuck and poor Carl were long gone before I started my third tour, and I never ran into 'em here neither. So, if the question is, would I take that shot, the answer is probably no. Turns out I ain't so mythical after all."

Bob was a crash attendee at the tutorial under his own name because there was no time to put a legend together, and unless you immerse yourself in the details of your fictional narrative, you'll make a mistake sooner or later. So he was here, publicly, as Bob Lee Swagger, of Boise, Idaho, Gny. Sgt. USMC (Ret.), on government contract as a consultant for the Department of Energy security sector. It was all Nick could come up with quickly, once the forensics people had determined that the baked paint debris had come from an iSniper911 unit and nothing else, and quickness was important, for the iSniper911 was produced in such small numbers that the tutorial that taught it ran but once every two or three months, depending. So Nick called in a favor at Energy; Energy ran the paperwork top speed and got the special exception to iSniper's usual procedures on the basis of Swagger's well-known name in the community. The premise was Energy's security teams, known as very well trained operators in charge of guarding vulnerable, volatile Energy Department sites the nation over, were going to upgrade their sniper capabilities to make shooting out to military ranges possible in the new age of terrorism and were looking for an optics system to handle the task. They'd hired the ex-sniper Swagger to run an R and D on what was available and to make a recommendation; the story would stand up to any kind of vigorous examination, unless Bob let it slip he'd never seen a Department of Energy installation and wasn't too sure what the Department of Energy did, anyway.

"Anyhow," Bob allowed, "if you want I could bore all these young guys with stories about how different it was for us, how much more primitive the equipment was, how the landscape favored snipers in a way high desert don't, but it would be just an old man's gas. I'm here like them to see if you can do this stuff way out there without a head for numbers."

Some laughter, even from the Irishman.

"Grand, fellows," he said, "I'm here to teach you how to make that shot, and any others that may come your way. The name's Grogan, but you can call me 'Anto,' as we of the Irish tribe shorten 'Anthony.' I've done this work too, with a well-known British unit, and then I saw the way to endless riches by jumping to Graywolf Security, where it was my pleasure to handle caravan and bodyguard gigs in many other sandy places. Now I teach for iSniper, and enough with intros, shall we turn to the toy?"

More laughter. The black Irishman Grogan had a wit to him.

"Fellows, here's the why as to your presence here. The scope which don't need no wizard work to get on target. Why, if a sod like Anto Grogan can do it, you smarter fellows will have no trouble. But you question, can it possibly be worth the seven thousand dollars the bosses are charging for it now, plus five days when you could be with loved ones instead of cooking out here in the cowboy sun?"

He opened the rifle case before him, removing a British L96A1, the Accuracy International job, tricked up all very SAS, dun-colored, bi-pod mounted, barrel an inch thick, with what looked like an oar for a stock with a hole in it where your hand set to reach trigger and bolt, all of it crazily adjustable, and then up top two pounds of optical magic secured in Badger Ordnance tactical rings, thick as a giant's wedding band. Turrets, nodules, knobs, tabs, dials, even a small TV set, a cube with screen above the eyepiece and decorated up top with a keyboard of buttons, the whole damned kitchen sink crunched into one piece.

"It looks hard. It ain't. That's its point. As Sergeant Blondie has said, and since I've seen the records, I know you all know and have done this work, but to shoot well far out in the field, you must have three instruments besides a rifle and a scope. You must have a range finder to lase the distance to target, a Kestral 4000 wind indicator to read wind and other atmospheric conditions, and a small computer or Palm Pilot or whatever to feed the distance and weather data into where you've already stored your ballistics data so that you can drive it all through an algorithmic equation and come up with your solution, which you must then hand-transfer to the scope itself. If any of those all-tricky and confused things goes wrong, it's a miss. You give up your hide. You probably buy it. All that training gone to waste. Some camel bunger with a red and white tea cozy wrapped around his noggin has inherited your expensive whiz-bang rifle. No, that ain't why we're over there, now is it?"

He paused, waiting for the little eddy of giggles to die down.

"Not with iSniper911. With iSniper911, you prang the tall fellow in his heart and he's dead before his tongue is in the loam. Everyone jumps around and goes jibberty-jabby. They start shooting wildly. Then they realize it's they themselves on the target black and off they go, not ready for the virgins yet. You wait till dark, crawl back up the damned hill, and wait for extract. Twenty minutes and a loud helo ride later, you're in base camp with your mates. 'Shoulda seen the look on Osama's face,' you say, and the colonel opens you another can."

He let this satisfying scenario play in their minds for a few seconds.

"Rather thought you'd like that one. All right, then, here's the genius of iSniper911. It combines all the functions of ranging, weather analysis, algorithmic computation, ballistic prediction, and scope correction into but one instrument. There's little devils inside move all them knobs, smart little leprechauns who can do the calc in their cute little heads in supertime. You simply lase the target and wait for the answer in the TV set up top, and in less than a second you're on target. I mean completely and wholly on target. Here's how."

He turned and threw a cover off a portable blackboard next to him, to show a chart that diagramed the 911 reticle design. Busy, busy, one might say, and all the young snipers involuntarily groaned at the density of it, all the knowing and learning that it demanded and the stress of doing all that while possibly being shot at. The iSniper reticle wasn't just the old standby crosshair, not even the crosshair with its mil-dot ranging diodes on the hairs; it displayed indeed the central crosshair, its nexus a kind of anchor point. From that spot, a veil of lighter netting seemed to descend, in the shape of a Christmas tree, a sort of delta of interfering imagery. Upon closer inspection by all it became evident that the netting itself consisted of rows and rows of smaller crosses. It looked like a cemetery on a hillside.

"See all them markers?" said Grogan. "Sure, they're the tombstones of men who've stood against iSniper. In a manner of speaking. They're all points of aim.

"You press the lase button to initiate the targeting sequence. In one tenth of a second, you have distance, while at the same time this little unit"—he tapped a collection of dials mounted behind the bell of the scope—"reads temp, wind, atmospheric density, and humidity and automatically inputs to the minicomputer, where some kind of mysterioso chip runs it through the mathematical universe, also taking into consideration the ballistic template of the weight, speed, design, and trajectory of your chosen round, and when it's all done, a little voice pipes out, 'Honey, let's fuck.'"

Laughter, of course, as the boys were used to the metaphorically imagined sexual dynamics of sniping and had heard and issued the cry "Get some," which had once meant "Get some pussy" and now, in the War Against Global Terror, meant "Get some kills."

"It does not, of course; even the head university boys at iSniper aren't that clever. No, instead what happens is that once the solution is produced, automatically again and again in supertime, that data is crunched as target coordinates are impulsed up here on the screen of the monitor, so you get a readout. 'D thirteen, seven R,' it'll say, something like that. You go back to the scope, count thirteen hashmarks down, seven tiny cross-hashes to the right, and that's your aiming point. You put that little cross, that reticle, that pip, on Johnny Taliban and use your good shooter's discipline, enjoying all the fundamentals you've worked so hard to master, and when you shoot, the thing you shoot dies. Not usually. Not sometimes. Not if luck is with you or God is your copilot and the wind be mild, but *always*."

A hand came up, from a thick-necked young man who looked like a linebacker. But then, they all looked like linebackers.

"Yes, mate?"

"Sir, I—"

"Mate, I'm just a sergeant rating, like all you boys are, and 'sir' makes me hair stand up. You could call me Colour Sergeant if you can get your tongue around something so Waterloo-sounding, but I'll settle for Anto."

"Anto, like all of us here, I ain't no Bob the Nailer, but I know enough to know that there's nothing made that don't get beat to hell in combat in three days or less. I look at that little thing and it looks like an iPod or something. I just get worried that after that long crawl, I turn it on and I get 'does not compute' or some such and there ain't no IT to call and bitch at where I'm hunkered down."

"Excellent, chum. Most excellent. I imagine you're all worried, no? Mr. Swagger, yourself same, sir?"

"It's a concern," said Bob, trying to wear his designated celebrity status gracefully and not come across to these young men as a pompous asshole. "Busted more than my share of glass in the boonies and they didn't have no batteries in 'em."

Anto Grogan smiled at the fellas, all confident and pleased, then at his cadre of three other boys, and then he hoisted the rifle and threw it hard upon the ground.

An involuntary groan arose from the little audience, for all were shooters and knew to cherish the weapon as long habit, and if rough stuff happened to it, you hoped it stayed true, but under no account did you abuse it yourself.

"Let's give it a right and proper licking," Anto said, picking it up, turning it wrong side out in his strong hands so that he gripped it like a batsman by the barrel, and whacking its stock three times hard against the beam that supported the roof over the shooting benches, the collisions sending a buzz of vibration through the ramshackle structure.

Then he held it up and began to spin the windage and elevation knobs randomly in one direction, then the other.

"Gentlemen, if you could see your own faces now you'd be laughing yourselves. Ever see a man treat a fine rifle so poorly? No, and I don't recommend it neither, but let's see what we've done. I'll take two volunteers please, that would be you and you. Jimmy, get the boys the ATV."

Jimmy detached himself from the line of cadre and went to a parked ATV, keyed it to life, and brought the three-wheel rough-ground bike up to the bleachers. In its cargo tray behind the second seat, everyone could see three bright round objects, red, yellow, and blue, beachballs actually.

"Now here's the drill. You two boys are going to go on a little drive out into the field, and whenever the spirit moves you, though I hope it's beyond five hundred yards, you'll kick a beachball out, with the last one way far out there. Maybe the wind will come along and move 'em even further about. I, meanwhile, will sit here and continue to talk to the other lads, with the somewhat odd situation being that I've been tightly blindfolded"—he pulled a red bandana out of his back pocket—"by Mr. Swagger; that is, after Mr. Swagger has checked the bandana to make certain it's up and fine. The point is, I can have no idea at what ranges the beach balls have been placed. When all is done, I will turn, Mr. Swagger will pop off my blindfold, and using iSniper, I'll shoot cold-bore offhand and bang all three in under five seconds. I'll range, compute, acquire, and fire on three unknown-range targets and hit 'em dead-on. Sure, I've practiced some, and sure, I'm deft with the thing, but not at a level any man here willing to work and follow instructions can't himself achieve over the next five days. And when you see that, imagine your same selves in that hole, only it ain't beachballs, it's boys with RPGs moving against your site, and enjoy watching me pop them. And mind, this is after all the abuse you've just seen."

"Anto?"

"I am."

"Anto, seems like you're taking the sport out of it," someone said.

"True, I am, but for sport I butt heads in Irish football and chase a chesty whore now and then, or curl up for a nice read with a book by Agatha Christie. For shooting infidels, by that I mean 'non-Irish,' I want no sport at all, just piles of dead Johnny Muhammads feeding flies and scorpions fast as possible. Gentlemen, shall we?"

There was no point in "examining" the bandana; it was just a bandana, and Bob folded it in thirds, looped it about the Irishman's eyes, and tied it tightly, Grogan going, "Say, that fella's going to squish me head; easy, old man," to much laughter, while two of the young operators took their ride on the ATV, this also ginning up laughter because like all young men with too much IQ and too much testosterone all stirred up in a lethal mix and driving them forward, the man piloting the bike took it to the limits, while his bud hung off it, waiting till he was way out there, and then gave each beachball a wicked toss until it came to rest at the farthest reaches of the range. Then they sped back, just barely in control, and came up short in a slithering, too-much-damn-brake powerslide that kicked dust and grass a hundred feet.

"Did anyone die?" asked Anto from behind his blindfold.

"Colour Sergeant, all will live to fight again," said Jimmy.

"Excellent. We lose a man now and then that way. If someone will guide me to the rifle, please."

Bob and an operator brought Grogan to his rifle. Bob lifted it and handed it to the man.

"Mr. Swagger, the ammunition, if you please."

Bob went to a red box of fresh Black Hills .308 match loaded with the 168-grain Sierra boat tail hollow point, that sniper's preferred number one, slid three out, and said, "Want me to load it?"

"No sir," said Grogan, "and the loading can count in the five seconds."

Everyone watched.

"Gentlemen, ears on, glasses on. Me too, Jimmy," and Grogan's boy slipped earmuffs over his head. All the muffs, of course, were miked up to allow normal conversation, yet were engineered to close down instantly when the decibel count spiked upon a shot.

"Now, Mr. Swagger, pull off the bandana, and you other fellows count to five in your head and see where you are."

Bob put his hands on the bandana and—

"Oh, wait," said Grogan.

He paused, milking the theater of the moment.

"Won't it be more fun with some stress? Let's do a game. Since Mr. Swagger is a champion, let's let him shoot against me. Blondie, you're his spotter. You go ahead now, work your range finder, tinker the Kestral, run the numbers and the proper ballistics through the Palm Pilot, get coordinates and click 'em into Mr. Swagger's scope. Then when the bell goes up, Anto goes up against Bob the Nailer, not man on man—no doubt who's the better man—but system on system, so we may learn which is the better system."

"It ain't necessary," said Bob.

"Mr. Swagger, sir, them smart boys who run iSniper have instructed me to do all I can to sell 911 to the Energy teams, and this is part of my initiative, begging the gentleman's pardon. I'm after showing the toy in game against the best."

"Well, that ain't me now, if it ever was. And outshooting an old goat like me ain't going to get you much in this world," Bob said, "but if it's what you want." He turned to Blondie.

"Okay by you, son?"

"Be an honor, Mr. Swagger."

"You good on the numbers?"

"I can run 'em fast as anyone and have done a fair amount of it under incoming."

"Then you're the hero here. You run the brainy stuff and diddle the scope and I'll just pull the trigger."

Bob took a seat, wedged himself close to the bench, as Blondie placed his own M40A1, by which Bob knew him to be a fellow marine, and watched as the young man swiftly loaded and locked three 168s. Bob squinched behind the rifle, and it was all familiar. He settled in, feeling the tension in the trigger, finding his stockweld, sliding to the eyepiece, and seeing the world through the mil-dot-rich reticle of the Unertl 10X Marine Corps–issue scope, a unit overbuilt so powerfully you could use it to break down doors. He diddled with the focus ring, waiting for it to declare the world pristine and hard-edged at five to eight hundred yards, and when it did, he nodded to Blondie.

"I'm gittin' bored, me just standing here like a fella on a pier, watching ships," said Anto, drawing laughter.

"Almost ready, Sergeant Anto," said Blondie, and then went all serious pro on them, first laser-ranging the three distant brightly colored dots in the thousand yards of green beyond them with his small Leica unit, then pulling out his Kestral 4000 weather station and noting the wind, humidity, and temperature. Then he ran the data through his Palm Pilot and came up with three solutions. He dialed the first into the scope of the rifle, clicking mostly elevation but some windage, for there was a drift of light wind that rustled undulations in the grass.

He whispered to Bob, "Okay, you're set up on the first target, which is 492 yards out, in a quarter value left to right wind. When you take that shot, I'm quickly turning you eighteen clicks up for the next one, which is at 622 yards, and then up fifteen for the last one, at 814 with a wind correction of five clicks. Are you ready?"

"Good work, son," said Bob. He was firing off a bench on sandbags while Grogan stood to do his offhand.

"Sure you don't care to sit, Colour Sergeant Anto?"

"Nah, I'm fine this way. Some other fellow come up and pull the bandana when you're ready."

Bob realized that Anto would pass the first target because he himself was already set up to that range and Anto would have no advantage. Instead he'd lase and shoot the second, then the third, while Blondie worked the clicks up for Bob's second. He had a rogue impulse toward anarchistic victory: he'd shoot the second one first, taking away Anto's advantage, then shoot the farthest, them come down to pick up the closest. That would be the way to win.

But what would that prove? That he was smarter at a stupid game? That he was an asshole? That he couldn't go with the agenda out of some petty vanity?

Don't do it, he told himself. Don't be an asshole.

"Someone start us off," said Anto.

Someone did.

"Pull on one, ready now, three, two, o—"

Bob was alone in the world of the scope. He was home, really; it was all familiar, the feel of the rifle, the smell of the cleaning fluid, the touch of hand to comb, cheek to fiberglass, finger to trigger, the rifle firm, the breathing stopped, the body nothing but steel except for the littlest tip of the trigger finger, and he saw the bright, tiny dot nesting at the confluence of the cross-hairs and, as usual, some inner voice commanded his finger's twitch and so deep was his concentration that he neither heard the shot nor felt the recoil, just watched the tiny blot of color leap.

With his practiced hand, he got the bolt thrown and felt the vibrations of clickage as, hunched close, the young man called Blondie rocketed through his eighteen clicks. Bob put the hairs on the even smaller dot just in time to see it scoot into the air as Anto nailed it dead solid perfect.

No need to cock then, but some impulse came to him from a trick bag of shooter's savvy that just seemed to be there when you needed it, and he waved off Blondie and went for the shot on intuition, his gift for hold, knowing that Blondie couldn't click fast enough. His mind was a blur of numbers. He rea-soned that at 800 yards, each mil-dot below the cross-hair represented an increment of 35 yards off the last zero at 622, which meant that the 92 yards further out to the third target represented about 2.7 mil-dots, and at a speed that has no place in time, he found the seg-ment of line between second and third mil-dots that represented the 2.7 hold and involuntarily fired, just as did Grogan.

The ball leaped up, then jagged hard right.

"Whoa!"

"Jesus Christ!"

"Damn!"

Grogan's shot, dead-on, had knocked the ball upwards as it deflated, but Bob's, arriving a nanosecond later and off-center, had banged it hard to the right, and it squirted off and bled its atmosphere out in the grass, signifying death.

"Well shot, Bob the Nailer," cried Grogan. "Damn, sir, that's shooting!"

Applause arose, and Bob was shamed at the vanity of his wanting to win, but at the same time pleased he'd done all right and impressed all the young guys who'd done it for real much more recently than he had, and would be Out There again soon, beyond the point of the spear.

Grogan was all lit up.

"Lord God, many's the time I've done my little trick, yes sir, and no one has ever come even half so close. You was what, a hundredth of a second behind me, and here I am with all the techno gizmos and you just shot on pure instinct. What a shot, what a bloody damned shot."

For just a second there, it seemed like the point of the whole exercise was to congratulate the old lion on his near-win in a game that proved nothing. But Anto was the leader in this development; he led the celebration.

"Tell me, Mr. Nailer, how you done it. I never could, not in a thousand years, no matter the rifle."

"He waved me off," Blondie was saying to anyone who would listen, not that anyone was. "Jesus Christ, can you believe that?"

"When the Marine Corps went to mil-dots in the late seventies with the Unertl, it was something I had to know. Don't know why. So I learned mil-dots, just beat it all into my head. It's no good as a system, really, too much dependent on figuring, and so you've got to be a mathematician as much as a shooter and a stalker. I just learned it by rote memorization and practice, don't know why. It kept me off the booze a whole year, I suppose, and maybe the mil-dots saved me from my own black dogs. Anyhow, when Blondie told me the range of the targets, I figured the difference between the two and realized what the subtend value was for the dots at that range. So I was able to come to the point of aim faster using the dots cold off the middle-range zero than I could have with Blondie adjusting the elevation knob. It was 2.7 mil-dots down from the 622-yard zero, so that's where I held and shot."

"There's a professional for all you younger fellows, and I hope in the land of the scorpions you've got as much sense."

"But I was shooting known distance, where you wasn't. So it don't really come to much 'cept my vanity. Seems like we lost the point here: the point is, that goddamn thing works like a charm, and I am a believer. Now I will sit back and just watch while you teach these young guys how to use it. They will need that, where they're going. They will send many bad boys to wherever them kind of people go when they're sent, and on account of that a lot of good boys will be coming home. If iSniper can up the count on home-comings, then by God, I am a true believer in iSniper and its, whatever you call it, that 911 thing."

14

Sally was working on some big case with a team from Treasury involving fraud in the financial meltdown, so she wasn't around much, which meant that Nick found himself with more spare time to kill than he ever expected. Task Force Sniper was nowhere, just going over more leads, tracking down some of the wilder ideas, all of it more or less make-work, waiting for Nick's decision to release the report and release the task force's assets, and he was holding out to see if Swagger came up with something truly interesting. Meanwhile, the reps from the three local departments had all been sent home with nothing to do.

Nick decided, late that night, to have a nice dinner, since he hadn't eaten real food since this thing had begun. He left the ominous Hoover Building, stepping around the line of cement revetments arranged to keep the mad terrorist car bombers at bay, and dawdled aimlessly around Southeast DC, looking for a spot to eat.

It was getting glamorous around here. In the nineties and early in the following decade, Southeast had been a dump, a crappy zone of once-prosperous retail and apartment buildings gone shabby with neglect, a little too far from the federal triangle to attract the lunchtimers who drove more central city food culture, unserviced by movie houses, bookstores, boutiques, that sort of thing. Then it changed when the Verizon Center opened, a new big cathedral to the religions known as NBA and NHL; with it, restaurants opened, a big multiplex of theaters, a busy and hustling main street of sorts, Seventh Street, and all kinds of snazzy little places. It seemed to fill up overnight with that disturbing tribe of unrecognizable barbarians called "the young," and as Nick moseyed through the streets, he was astounded by their numbers, their energy, their clothes, their heat, their hubbub, their urge to fill the world with their own centrality. It gave him a headache. Ugh, how'd he get so old, over forty, with a big house in Fairfax he hardly ever saw and a wife who had turned out to be such a hotshot he hardly ever saw her either.

He drew his overcoat a little tighter, as deep fall, threatening winter, had come to the East. He took his ID card on its chain off and stuffed it in his pocket, as he didn't want to be ID'd as a bureaucratic geek out on a late-night prowl. He felt the Glock .40 against his hip, well back in a Safariland holster, and the counterweight of two mags with twelve apiece on his other hip; he bought his coats a little big so that the gun wouldn't print, even if it meant he had to have the sleeves taken up.

Fish. He decided it would be a fish night, because he was a long way from a reputable steak joint, the nearest, Morton's, being over on Connecticut at K. It was a cab ride away. Nearby there was a place called Oceanaire he'd always heard good things about; he'd hit that, have a nice dinner, walk back to the Hoover underground, and be home in Fairfax by midnight.

He got to Oceanaire, which was on L, and liked what he saw: it seemed to have a kind of forties look to it, and it made him think of movies about G-men, where everyone wore a tough fedora with a tilt to the brim and a trench coat and carried a Colt Dick Special. Oh, and smoked, they all smoked, and he remembered the movie that had set him off on this path in life, which he'd seen on television in the seventies lying on his belly at fourteen in his parents' split-level, gray in the light of the tube; it was called *The Street with No Name* and told the story of a heroic G-man named Gene Cordell who had infiltrated some mob in the tacky slumtown of "Center City," and it ended in a blazing shootout, with tommy guns spitting flashes and spurts of spent gas and long columns of tumbling brass into the night air, while slugs chewed the shit out of a guy named Shivvy, sparing Cordell's life at the last moment. Cordell was played by—what was that guy's name? Some guy who never made it big, but boy, he'd seemed big in that movie. Steve Jackson? Jack Smith? Bill Stevenson, some name like that, some—*Mark Stevens*, that was it, and for that movie at least, no matter what happened before or after, Mark Stevens was so cool, so smart, so tough, so brave, so everything a kid could want to be, that's when Nick knew he had to be a G-man or his life would come to nothing.

Nostalgic for the good old days of G-manning he'd only experienced in the movies, no matter twenty-odd years of service as a special agent, Nick slipped in, saw the place was half full, caught the maître d's attention, and was taken to a nice out-of-the-way table. He sat, turned down a drink, listened to the specials, chose grilled rockfish with mashed potatoes after a salad, oil and vinegar, and began to work on a little plate of on-the-house munchies in sour cream the waiter had brought before he'd taken the order.

Meanwhile big-band music filled the air, and Nick waited for the announcement that the Japanese had bombed Pearl Harbor, but it never came. Instead, a bottle of champagne did.

"I didn't order that," he said to Chad, the waiter.

"I know, sir, but a fellow at that table sent it over. It's the very best. Not cheap."

Nick looked across the room and saw that man Bill Fedders, waving pleasantly at him.

Nick smiled back, then turned to the waiter.

"Take this back, thank Mr. Fedders for me, if you don't mind, but tell him I'm on duty. I'm an FBI special agent and I'm carrying a firearm, so it's against regulations for me to drink tonight. He'll understand."

"Yes sir," said the waiter, and sped off. But if Nick thought that would be the end of it, he was sadly mistaken. He had the salad, the rock, nicely done, and was enjoying a cup of decaf when a shadow crossed the table, and he knew who it was.

"Nick, hi. Bill Fedders—"

"Sure, Bill, I remember, in the director's office a couple of weeks ago. You're working for Constable, right?"

"I am indeed. Doing the boss's dirty work, as usual. Sorry you couldn't take the champagne. It's a really light one, very good with fish. But I understand. Something happens, you have to pop a bad guy, and the fizz-juice comes up and it's a lot of trouble."

"Even I admit the chances of me popping a bad guy tonight are pretty remote, but if you get into a way of living, it's tough to get out of it. Thanks for the offer. I'm not a prude. It just wouldn't have been a good idea."

"Got it. Nick, do you mind if I join you for a sec?" Fedders had a smooth way of ingratiating himself, that professional Washington player's sense of entitlement to attention everywhere, welcome assumed. He was a radiantly handsome man, wearing the power attorney's immaculately fitted blue pinstripe, with a glisten in his gray-black hair and the fresh look of just having stepped out of the barber's chair.

"Mr. Fedders—"

"Bill."

"Bill, it's probably not a good idea. I do official business at the office, in the open, where everybody can see and hear. If you want to schedule an appointment, we'll certainly do our best to accommodate you. Or if—"

"It's not really official, Nick. Not really."

"Well, sure then, but bear in mind I have a walk back to my car and a long drive back to Fairfax tonight. And I want to be in early tomorrow. I always try to be the first guy in the office. It goes with all that big money they pay me."

Fedders smiled, eyes sparkling, as he eased into the empty chair. He put a half-full glass of scotch down before him.

"Nick, it's my job, you know. I have to ask around, I have to find things out, I have to know how things work. That's what Tom pays me for. I guess I'm sort of his 'special agent.'"

"Sure."

"So I hear things. I hear, for example, the investigation has suddenly gone off on another route."

"We're trying to be diligent, that's all."

"Sure, sure. I hear that too. I hear from people, 'That Nick Memphis, sure to be an assistant director before the year's out, just gone from triumph to triumph.' I understand that thing in Bristol was hairy."

"I caught a piece of lead, but I'm okay except for the funny walk."

"Well, a hero. Very good guy. And that's what I hear, that's the summary judgment on Nick Memphis, FBI. 'Very good guy.' 'The best.' 'One of the incorruptibles,' 'really a comer,' 'going places.'"

"Bill, going places isn't the point. I've had a wonderful career and I'm happy at the small contributions I've made. That's enough. If I make it to the next floor, won't that be swell. If I don't, that's the way the cards fall. My ambition doesn't include myself. I want to make sure we get it right; that's my ambition."

"Well said. You're a noble man in a town full of assholes, professional and amateur. Okay, Nick, but let me just be square with you. This guy Tom Constable is your classic big foot and he's not afraid to hurt people who get in his way. I try to get him to exercise some constraint, but these made-it-themselves celebrity billionaires are tough cookies when it comes to getting their own way. I'm just here to say, if there's no point in antagonizing him, don't do it. He can and will bring hurt, and I've seen it. Nick, I'd hate to see a guy good as you get buried under the big guy's big foot over nothing. He wants the investigation closed; he wants his ex-wife's name out of the papers; he wants the whole thing to go away. I'm only telling you this out of respect for your accomplishments."

"Oh, I see," said Nick. "You're doing me a *favor*. See, I thought you were threatening an FBI agent."

"Nick—"

"Mr. Fedders, I'd like this conversation to end now, before you get in trouble. Yeah, you have to serve the big man, and yeah, I have to tread softly around the big man, we both know how it works in this bad old town. Okay, you've made your point. Power talks, bullshit walks, welcome to the City on the Hill."

"Nick, be pissed if you want, but think of it from another angle. This guy could really help you. I mean why do the assholes like me make it big and the good boys like you never quite do? It's because us assholes aren't afraid to suck up to a big foot, flatter him end-lessly, do his dirty little jobs, and get the big payoff. You could say that's the life I chose, and I'm not going to pretend otherwise. But a good guy like you, if you do this one little favor for the big man, you have no *idea* how it can help a career. It could get a good guy like you to the Seventh Floor, and think of the good you could do there, and the pride you'd take in it. You'd be ahead of your wife too, and I know that's got to play into it"—so Fedders had actually looked into Sally's thriving career at Justice and knew that she was fast-track to the upper floors—"and think how good that would feel. Nick, that's all I have, thanks for lis-tening, you have my card, and if you ever, and I mean *ever*, need a favor in this town, call me."

He smiled warmly and without a trace of shame, then got up and gracefully left.

Nick watched him go, thinking, Oh Christ, where is this going?

15

It turned out to be almost too much fun. Bob had to watch himself; he could be seduced by the pleasure of the three days into forgetting why he was here, which was to recon iSniper and see if he could get some kind of look at the student log and learn who had purchased and been taught to use the thing. But he almost had to force himself into that: most of the time was spent on the range among guns and gunners, men like himself, who'd been and done, except they'd be and do again. So he more or less slipped aside and watched as Anto and his boys helped the younger Americans master the toy.

It was almost as advertised. It could put you on target without a doubt in the world faster than anything going, and in the sand it would be a major boon to American sniper teams, if it held up. There were some ergonomic issues, and the iSniper cadre, led by the irrepressible Anto Grogan, took careful notes to feed back to the iSniper geniuses for the next generation. For one thing, the ranging button atop the monitor to the left of the nodule was difficult to access quickly, unless you were well used to it and had done it ten thousand times and had burned it into muscle memory. It was the key to initiating the target sequence; it was also the same size and height as the enter button and the reset button, and the young snipers sometimes groped for it or hit something else. A slightly roughened surface to distinguish it from the other buttons would help. Then there was a problem with the battery housing, which worked well enough in the day on the range with access to tools but might be a bitch in some frozen third world bog with bad actors on the prowl all over the joint, even if the batteries were said to last for a thousand hours. The housing latch was too small for men with big, blunt fingers and no fingernails; it had to be redesigned more generously for the big-size boys marine and special forces snipers tended to be.

But the real issue was the necessity of taking the info off the readout screen; it meant you had to come out of your hold, out of your cheek weld, out of your proper eye relief, out of your focus, out of, in short, your shooting world, read a set of numbers, then mentally retain the figures and work them out in the delta of aiming points under the crosshairs. It worked well enough, though when you came up, you always lost your scope vision, your pupils dilated, and it cost you seconds when you came back to the eyepiece to reach max efficiency.

"Aye, it could be better on that score," admitted Anto. "It's not perfect, not quite, maybe in the next generation. We told 'em it would be something if you just pushed the ranging button, the leprechauns inside did the heavy lifting, and then instead of presenting a number for you to look at on a screen, the proper aiming point just lit up, you never having to leave the scope. You put it on Johnny, and bingo-bango, time to paint a new swastika on your fuselage. Maybe they'll get there some time."

"It's still the best," Bob lied, as if he were familiar with the other items from anything other than a Google experience. "Horus is too much time off the scope, though I like its reticle design. DTAC has too busy a reticle with all those other graphs there, and the same with the Holland. Y'all had any luck with Horus out there?"

"Yes sir," said Blondie, "it gets you on target, but like you say, it's too slow, too much Palm Pilot and Kestral stuff. I like this here too; it cuts the time way down from figuring to shooting, not quite perfect but perfect enough."

"Have we made that sale yet, Mr. Swagger?" Anto asked.

"You're damned close," Bob said. "I just want to see how the things hold up over the extensive shooting you put them through these five days."

"We'll beat 'em to hell and gone and they'll keep on ticking, you'll see, sir. I'm here to serve, oh great and mighty and shining one."

"Anto, I'm just another—"

"Anything I can do I will, which is why they're paying me the big buckeroos."

But that all went away at nights, off the range, where the snipers took over a bar called the Mustang across from the Red Rooster where iSniper had booked all. Then it was just men of the gun, lots of beer, war stories, a sense of the smallest, most exclusive community in the world, men who'd shot for blood and lived to tell about it. Bob went too, under the pretext that he might learn something off Anto in a moment of weakness, but Anto never had any, and anyway the love that came to Bob was something he was unprepared for and had never encountered before.

"Mr. Swagger—"

"Please call me Bob, young guy."

"Bob, I'm not supposed to let this out, but me and Chip are Delta snipers, headed now to Afghanistan for my third, his second, tour with Fifth Special Forces."

"My hat's off to you fellows. You're doing a hell of a job out there."

"Nothing like you, sir. We've heard the An Loc story; it's a legend. You stopped an NVA battalion, a fucking *battalion*, that was headed into an A-camp under siege. I just wanted to say, it's a fine moment for us to be here with you."

"Y'all make me out to be more than I am. I didn't stop no battalion. I slowed 'em down, that's all. Took some of their officers. The rain helped, but what helped most of all was the young man with me, who I am so sad to say didn't make it home. Anyhow, it was the Phantoms that did most of the killing. They got there with the dawn just as the weather broke, and I have to say those were brave men in those planes; they got so low to the deck to put the burning jelly where it hurt the most, I'm betting most came back with grass in their scoops. I just watched it."

"He's a modest man, our Bob," said Anto, leaning in, "but the story as I heard it has him racing through Indian territory by his lonesome and squeezing down on that battalion for two solid days. Officially it was eighty-seven, was it not, and I'm betting it was eighty-seven that day alone, with no officer there to check. That's a soldier of the king, I'm telling you, and it shows the power of the fella with the rifle."

"It was so long ago I can hardly remember," said Bob, "and I won't talk no more about myself because you're doing it better and harder than I ever did, no matter what this drunken IRA bastard says, but I will raise a drink, even if it's a Diet Coke, to the fella with the rifle."

When he got back on the second night, the message light on his cell was blinking. He called, knowing it would be Nick, but instead it was the young special agent Chandler and she asked him first off how it was going.

"Going fine. Having a hoot. Ain't found out much, though. I see Anto's got some kind of book with him, and he's a well organized man, so I'm betting he's got notes taken on all the tutorials he's run. I'd like to get a look-see at that and let you know if it's worth subpoenaing."

"You have to be careful. If you peek and it comes out you're working for us and we used any information you obtained, a defense attorney can use it against us in court, along the lines of a highly problematic warrantless search, and no matter what, the whole thing could go away. You're much better off just looking and learning what's in the open, taking careful notes, and we'll see where we go from there."

He sighed. It was clear she had no feel or imagination for undercover work. Her tendency was to push him toward the strictly legal, can't-get-in-trouble line. But he knew that sometimes you had to push it, just a little, poke it, dance around it. Either that or walk away.

"Yes ma'am. Did you get the info I requested on this fellow Anto Grogan?"

"Yes, we did. He seems straightforward, nothing to indicate tendencies."

"That's good to know. Seems like a nice fellow."

"Here's the dope. Born Killarney, Ireland, 1964, down there in the south far away from all the crap in Belfast. His dad and his dad's dad were British Army in their time, and he was drawn to it from the start. Highly decorated service record, lots of deployments in famous actions and not-so-famous actions. He was one of their best guys."

"Royal Commando?"

"No. He's Twenty-two all the way."

"What's that?"

"That's Twenty-second Regiment SAS, kind of their Delta Force. He was a colour sergeant, I guess that's staff sergeant, in Blue Troop, which is what they designate their sniper element. He was a long-time Sabre Squadron guy, which is what they call their operators as opposed to their staff people, as I understand it. He was in what they called the Counter Revolutionary Warfare wing. He deployed in ninety-one to the Gulf with SAS, had a long stay in Afghanistan in oh-two to oh-three, where I'm told he racked up quite a score. He then spent some time back in Credenhill, where SAS is headquartered, where he bugged so many people he got himself sent to Basra in oh-five, where he ran sniper elements again. He seems to have had some trouble there. You would know more about this than I would, Mr. Swagger, but our military liaison picked this up from his contact with the British military liaison; apparently Anto Grogan was rather too enthusiastic in getting his kills. He evidently got a lot of them in Basra, ran his own intelligence-gathering operation, took a lot of people down, and the British Army was a little, um, embarrassed, I guess. That's why he left and went to work for Graywolf, where he also ran intelligence, organized security on caravans and dignitary visits. Did you know that Graywolf owns iSniper? So he's still working for them."

"Hmm," said Bob. "You better fill me in on Graywolf."

"Oh, you know. Famous, big security firm, put together by some ex-SEALs. Teaches shooting and survival skills, manufactures products and clothes for the security sector, puts people in the field on contract. There were some problems in Baghdad when these contractor guys got a little trigger-happy and blew away anything that moved; you might remember the fuss in the papers."

"Now I do. Give a guy an M4 and a pair of cool sunglasses and a ball cap, and he's Mr. Murder Inc. in no time."

"He's a very experienced man, sir. A great soldier, a great sniper, now working for a big international contractor's firm that is mixed up in a lot of shaky stuff."

Bob felt a little indecent having requested the dope on Anto. The problem was, he liked Anto Grogan, as did all the boys, and surely Graywolf realized how personable he was, which is why it took him out of the field and made him the public face of the iSniper division. Now Bob had to use him to get a list of names of the men he'd trained, so each could be vetted by the Bureau and checked against any connection to the four sniper killings.

"How's Nick holding up?" he asked.

"Oh, it seems the pressure is building on us to issue that report. He gets called into the director's office three times a day and yelled at by Tom Constable's people. He ran into one of Constable's brown-nosers last night at dinner and was even offered a little friendly career advice. Mr. Swagger, can I talk frankly with you?"

"Sure."

"He's way out on a limb, and what's got him out there is his belief in you. Sir, if you don't get anything, pull the plug fast. A lot of us around here don't want to see the great Nick cut off at the knees by this monster Constable because he wouldn't play ball for believing in you and you didn't turn anything up."

He realized: the girl is in love with Nick.

"I hear you. It'd be a crime if Nick got his career wrecked for old goat Swagger, and it turned out old goat Swagger was just blowing smoke on some dream business. Okay, point taken."

"This can be a tough town."

"I get you and I will hurry this thing along, so Nick isn't out there much longer. But do you mind if I say one thing?"

"Go ahead."

"I ain't telling you your business, but to me one of the things you investigators ought to be doing is checking to see if there's any contact between Graywolf and Tom Constable. Are they players in this thing? Or are they just like everyone else, guys who got sucked up by the sniper killings?"

"I'll run it by Nick."

"You do that. Out here."

"What?"

"Out here."

"What does that mean?"

"Oh, sorry, that's the way we talk in the field. Sounds all gung ho movie bullshit to you, I guess. Maybe it is. 'Out here' means I'm out of stuff to say, good-bye, and so long."

"Ah. Sorry to be so dumb. It's a girl thing, I guess. Good luck, Mr. Swagger."

The problem was, there wasn't a place to penetrate or break into. There was no school, not really. The iSniper tutorial was simply the four-man cadre— Anto, Jimmy, and two other fellows, Ginger and Raymond, who seemed decent enough; they had their teaching props, their charts, their own weapons, crates of ammo, and a world's worth of know-how, but that was it. There was no *there* there, like an administrative center, just the four iSniper Irishmen, Bob, and the six young elite-corps snipers whose units had purchased the gizmo and thereby qualified them to attend the week's schooling. Maybe back at Graywolf corporate headquarters in North Carolina, at the big training center, there was an administrative center, and maybe that's where you'd have to go to get the dope on iSniper's schoolees, but that was no one-man job; rather the Justice Department would have to descend, full-strength, on Graywolf, and Graywolf wouldn't like that, since a lot of its work was classified, as was its client list, and it clearly had big connections in Defense and wouldn't be prone to giving up its secrets without a fight.

So it came down to one little absurd thing: Anto's book.

How am I going to get ahold of Anto's book?

There was no answer. He went to bed depressed.

The next day at the range, as usual Bob stood aside and let Anto and his cadre work mostly with the young snipers, who'd learned the mechanics of the thing really quickly, being both motivated and highly intelligent, as well as highly dextrous. They could spot an object at unknown distance and take it down very fast, letting the microchip inside 911's housing do the brainwork, themselves just making sure to master the method of taking the readout info and applying it to the scopeful of aiming points.

Swagger, though, shot enough with it to see its superiority, and a part of him wished he'd had the thing in 'Nam all those years ago. He, Carl, and Chuck McKenzie with iSniper911 on their rifles, what a unit that would have been; we would have won the goddamn thing instead of . . .

The last night, late, a knock sounded.

"Who is it?"

"Mr. Swagger, sir, me, Anto, here. Can I come in?"

Bob opened up.

"Hope you don't mind if I'm after bending your ear a bit, do you? Wish you'd let me buy you a drink."

"Anto, you know I can't drink. If I do, I'm waking up in Kathmandu on Tuesday with a new wife, four new kids, and some very odd tattoos." It was an old joke he'd told many times before.

"How about this: if it's not to be whiskey, let Anto buy you an ice cream. Can't be thinking of no better place for mankillers of our ranking to have a chat than that ice cream shop across the pathway. They mix a high and mighty bowl of flavor. I always overeat when I come to the teaching, I do."

So Bob and Anto walked across the highway— more dangerous than anything Swagger had done since Bristol—where indeed the ice cream shop was still open, and the two snipers went in, waited among sluggish teenagers with needles in their noses and fathers with squawking babies and a lone truck driver, all travelers consumed with late-night ice cream blue munchies, and got themselves a cone each. Who wouldn't have cracked a smile if they'd known that these two were professional dealers in death, and now they sat like old fools nibbling at mint chocolate and raspberry and chocolate-chip cones?

"Bob, may I call you Bob?"

"Wish you would, Colour Sergeant."

"And I'd be Anto. So let's proceed on to business. Am I asking too much to ask where we stand? The toy, I mean."

"My report to Energy security will be very positive. I'm extremely impressed by iSniper; the mechanism is first-class; the training is superb. The guys you run through here go to their units five times more effective. That translates to more boys on the planes home, and I like that a lot."

"Is there anything—"

"Not in my report."

"But you know we're owned by Graywolf, and Graywolf isn't as beloved under this president as it was under the last one, and we've got a lot of pressies peeved at us."

"I know. I can't account for which way the winds blow in Washington. You may field the best piece of equipment and still lose out, just because that's the way it is in that town. I'm not a Washington guy."

"You are not. You've nothing of the headquarters rat to you. Them I hated. Always sniffing about HQ on the lookout for the next appointment."

"You and I share more than a skill set. I hate them mealy climbers too. Not many in the Corps, but a few. I hate the stink of headquarters. Always corrupt, that's the rule."

"It is. Well now, here's where I am. I know we have the best stuff, because I've tested the other rigs too, like you. I know we can save lives; it's not just a matter of business. So I've thought long and hard: what can I do, me, just Anto, what can Anto do to help Mr. Swagger make the right decision? And I've come up with something." He licked his ice cream cone.

"Sure."

"I'll give you our records. Every man or team we've sold a unit to, his record in the tutorial—and we keep very close records even if it appears we don't— his subsequent actions, how successfully he's used 911 or before it iSniper 411, his most recent address and number. With the full expectation that you'll contact some or all of these folks, and you'll get a view of 911 in the sand or the mountains or wherever, of what it does, of how it stood up, of whether they stayed with it or went to something else. All of that, I will give you. You use it as you see fit, no strings attached, except that I trust you, sniper to sniper, to burn-bag or shred when you're finished. That's how much I believe in 911, sir. It's quite an offer."

It was. How could anyone refuse it?

16

"I don't know how he did it," Nick said, "but somehow he talked the head boy at iSniper into turning over their entire distribution and disposition record on a disk."

The director said, "Tell me you ran this by Justice."

"I did. Their ruling is that since Swagger didn't ask for or put pressure on the iSniper rep for the disk, and the iSniper rep specifically enjoined Swagger to use at his own discretion, without consequence, any info on the disk is legally ours to use."

"But he did turn it over under subterfuge. He thought Bob repped the Energy security people."

"True. But Swagger *did* rep the Energy security people, we have the paperwork to prove it, and I had Swagger dictate a report which was duly forwarded to them. What their security people do with it—probably nothing—isn't the point; the point is that it was all done by the book. Moreover, Bob was given total freedom to dispose of it as he saw fit."

"Okay," said the director, leaning back in his chair. "Maybe it'll come up, maybe it won't. It's always best to dot the *t*'s and cross the *i*'s before you move on."

"I agree, sir."

Outside, in late-fall Washington, a pewter sky encased a pewter Capitol dome; a view like that was what the Seventh Floor got you, plus terrible anxieties that you could be taken down at any time. But today the director seemed in a good mood, well pleased that the Swagger ploy had brought some new energy to Task Force Sniper and that he'd have something to tell the people who were on him.

"So what's the haul, where does it lead us, what's the time frame, what are we doing now? Oh, and what's Swagger's final read on the iSniper device?"

Nick checked his notes.

"It turns out 346 people had gone through the iSniper tutorial, and another 78 had purchased units without attending the tutorial, some private citizens with big bucks, hunters, wealthy gun people, that sort of thing. It's not a Class III weapon, after all, just a scope with a computer chip. But mostly it's government or military people, snipers or members of the professional sniper community. Of that total, 424, we had already vetted 309 by other means, encountering them in the initial canvass of, you know, shooting schools, high-power rifle competitors, firearms manufacturers or reps, custom rifle shops that specialize in tactical work, that sort of thing. I have two people rechecking them, of course, to see if anything was missed the first time."

"So that gives you—"

"One hundred fifteen new guys. Many are military, and we were quickly able to eliminate twenty-three of them as having been out of the country and in deployment during the event. So that leaves—"

"Are you going to quiz me on my arithmetic?"

"No, sir, I took the liberty of using a calculator. That leaves us with ninety-two new players. That is, ninety-two men with access to and training on iSniper, unexamined in our first canvass of the field.

I've got teams working them hard now, and we're going at it twenty-four/seven to see if we can come up with anything. Oh, and put in the four iSniper cadre guys, Anthony 'Anto' Grogan, and three guys named Jimmy South, Roger 'Ginger' Speed, and Raymond Richardson-Brown, British nationals, who may have been in-country at the time. And then I've also got a team probing iSniper and its ownership, Graywolf Global Security, but I will tell you, those guys are barricaded behind some powerful legal talent."

"What's Swagger say?"

"He says Hitchcock's rifle with Hitchcock's ammo and an iSniper was indeed capable of making those four shots, and that's all. Other than that, he's not saying a thing."

"Where is he?"

"In a motel room in Arlington. I wanted to get your idea on what to do."

"Send our two best assassins"—he waited for the shock to register on Nick's face—"no, no, Nick, a *joke!* No, I think it's best to pay him his money and thank him for his brilliance and make him happy and send him home. He has rogue tendencies, and you don't want him mucking things up, especially since we're under so much time pressure."

"He wants to stay with it, I'd bet."

"He did a hell of a job, I have to say. Pointing our lab to the baked paint debris from the iSniper on the Hitchcock rifle. That's genius-level stuff. You said he was smart and you were right. But he's too hard to control. He did his sniper versus sniper undercover op and it worked brilliantly. We'll get him a bonus and a commendation. But that's it. He's got to be farmed out now."

"Yes sir."

"Meanwhile, back in the real world, do you need more investigators? Is that where this is going?"

"I'm afraid so. We lost our loaner investigators from Chicago and the other towns, and getting dumped with ninety-two—ninety-six with the Irishmen—new persons of interest is taxing. The more experienced bodies I have, the faster we'll get through this, the faster we'll come to a conclusion, and the sooner we can all start keeping regular hours again."

"Okay, you've got 'em. Don't know where I'm getting them from, but I'm going to give 'em to you somehow. Nick, get me something I can go to the papers on, will you? We are getting chewed to pieces on the old 'inaction' meme. Sluggish bureaucracy, gutless lifers, daily naptimes when we're not screwing our secretaries. They think we're up here twiddling our thumbs. I've got Chicago and Cleveland PDs beefing that we haven't called it yet, and they're being leaned on by their politicos because everybody wants the highest crime solution rate possible by end of year."

"Yes sir. Constable, is he still on you?"

"His fine, dead hand may be involved in this, yes, wouldn't surprise me a bit. Run into your new buddy Bill Fedders recently?"

"No sir, but if he shows up in the men's room, I won't be surprised."

"Okay, Nick, good job, tough case, now bust it for me or put it to sleep, okay?"

"My best, sir."

"Oh, and Nick, I'm told you owe Phil Price in PIO a callback."

"Just been busy, sir."

"Well, make an old fool like me happy and call him, will you?"

17

Now what?

Now nothing.

Now the rest of your life.

You did everything for Carl Hitchcock, for the United States Marine Corps and its medieval notions of honor and duty, despite what you said to Chuck McKenzie. If you owed him and that ever-smaller membership of the generation of men who'd put scopes on things and killed them in the Land of Bad Things, you've paid that debt. You turned up significant new information, new leads, turned it over, and now the professionals will run it to ground. If it turned out Tom Constable had hired Anto Grogan of Graywolf to kill his wife because she'd slept with Johnny Carson or Warren Whateverthatguy's name was, then that would come out. Or maybe Mitzi Reilly had hired Anto Grogan to kill her husband and Anto got carried away. Or maybe someone in South America hired Graywolf to kill Mitch Greene because they didn't like his young adult books. Or maybe—

Or maybe whatever.

Swagger sat way out in the weird, isolated departure terminal at Dulles. It was a strange, glassed-in island of mall commerce in the middle of an airfield. Great aircraft rolled by out the windows, but in here was nothing but TGIFs and Benettons and Starbucks as far as the eye could see. His flight to Boise was in another hour, but he always got to these places early because the metal ball-and-socket joint meant riga-marole in security as often as not. Here it had not. So he sat at the gate area on a terrible plastic chair, wait-ing for the flight to be called, watching the place fill up, ignoring the persistent pain in the hip where the ball-and-socket construction had taken a full-power cut a few years back and the flesh never healed quite right, tried not to look too enviously at a bar down the way, with its rows and rows of ever-beckoning bot-tles, then ordered himself not to imagine the pleasure it offered, and waited for time to pass so that the old man could get back to his rocking chair and watch the weather chemistry manufacture clouds the size of cas-tles and more complicated structures over the blue-green meadow that fell back for miles until it broke apart on a sawtooth snarl of mountains.

I'll count my money, see what to do with that nice bonus check. I'll read a book or a gun magazine. I'll think about building a tactical rifle in something weirdly off-center and interesting like .260 Reming-ton, 6.5 Creedmoor, or Grendel or XC. I'll hit the Dillon for a day and crank out a thousand .45 ACP 200-grainers. Then I'll count my money again and be nice to my wife, whom I don't deserve, and maybe help my younger daughter with her homework, though it's rapidly reaching a level I don't understand, because Miko has turned out to be sublimely smart and even at seven is attracting attention, not only for her unbe-lievable test scores but for her medal-winning riding ability. Then I'll call my daughter Nikki and see how she likes that big paper where she now works.

You couldn't have a better life. Did anyone? Land,

daughters, love, guns, a little money, a sense of having done what you could to bring boys home alive, settle old business, stand for something even when the lead or the blades were flying. That was okay, that was a life, it was the best but—

But he couldn't leave it alone.

It wasn't enough to wait for that big joker Ron Fields and that girl they called Starling and that Walter Jacobs and even Nick himself to figure it out and bring it off. It wasn't that he was better than they were, or smarter, it was just . . . what? Vanity, craziness, old-guy bullshit, he just thought he should be there, doing what had to be done, contributing.

Leave it alone.

I can't.

Subversive thoughts kept churning up from his unconscious. There was a ramification, exiled almost purposefully from the FBI's perspective. The FBI would not impose meanings; it would follow clues. They had new clues, new persons of interest, and they would methodically follow that course, letting meanings emerge. They had the resources for such an approach.

He, Swagger, had no resources. Thus such a broad-front approach was ruled out. He had to rely on intuition and strike in terms of specific interpretations. He had to have a working theory and had therefore to examine, test, or abandon that working theory.

Thus he was where he was, stuck with a buzz in his head that would not go away. And that was: if Carl Hitchcock's irrational motive was not behind the killings, if Carl was in fact the setup with the phony motive, then the motive was rational. It meant to get something: money, revenge, threat elimination, satisfaction, something real. Therefore the killings were coldly plotted and executed by extremely high-end operators, based on a brilliant conception, brought off with near-perfection. No amateurs had been involved; it was elite-unit, state-level craft.

If that were so, then there was but one starting point: the target could not have been Joan Flanders, movie star and radical and ex-wife to T. T. Constable. Joan's point in the proceedings was to unleash, as a function of her complex and well-chronicled life, her litany of "interesting" husbands, a chafe of covering information. Her murder would automatically flood the investigation with possibility, too much possibility, too much attention, too much information, all of which would hopelessly bog, clot, and overwhelm any investigation while at the same time pressurizing it for fast solution.

Therefore, sitting in the Dulles terminal in the middle of sunny Virginia, Swagger committed to his first principle: this is not about Joan Flanders. She is camouflage. This is about one of the others. It is about Jack Strong and Mitzi Reilly or it is about Mitch Greene, and from what he knew, it was probably not about Mitch Greene, who was, after all, a comedian. So he committed to his second principle: it was about Jack Strong and Mitzi Reilly.

But even that was a daunting task. They too, though on a smaller scale, had lived extraordinary lives, much chronicled, much documented. Political lives, social lives, intellectual lives, professional lives, writing lives, teaching lives (endless students, twenty-five years' worth of students alone!). How on earth could anyone investigate them—that is, anyone short of an FBI task force with its nearly unlimited manpower?

He had to limit it. Limit it. How do you limit it? How do you find one thing to focus on, the right thing to focus on? What's your principle of operation?

His head ached. He really wanted that drink. And who did he think he was? The feds in time would get to Jack and Mitzi, and they'd do their usual thorough, patient, professional examination, and if there was something to be found, they would find it. Maybe not this week or this year or . . .

What was different about Jack and Mitzi? Really, from a technical point of view, only one thing: Joan and Mitch had been killed in public. Their deaths became immediately the property of dozens of witnesses, then the law enforcement staffs, and then the maggots of the press. They were immediately public deaths.

But Jack and Mitzi had been slain in an alley and lay undisturbed for almost an hour. Well, there were easy explanations: they were, in fact, vulnerable and accessible in that moment when they were pulling out of their garage and the shooting team, in that van in the next block with only a bit of door opening, was itself well protected and generally impervious to discovery. Hmm, on the other hand, Hyde Park was notoriously well policed by a more than capable University of Chicago police force, and the lack of street traffic, the lack of public hubbub, could itself turn quickly enough into a deficit; there'd be no crowd cover for the escape route. It was, or rather it could be seen as, a somewhat fragile operation, a chancy enough thing, the greatest dare of the operation. That put it out of the modus operandi to a significant degree. So it was . . . provocative.

What would be the meaning of that kind of kill? What did it permit? What advantages would it generate and to what ends, and why would those ends be worth what might easily become a risk?

He sat crunched in concentration. He didn't notice that they'd called the Boise flight. He didn't even hear his name being called by the gate attendant. He was a lanky man in jeans, a polo shirt, an outdoorsy coat, and a Razorbacks baseball hat, sitting there, his scuffed Nocona boots announcing to the world he was a cowboy of sorts, but his face taut and distant.

He missed the plane.

He felt he had something, almost.

He could feel it there, and even as he struggled to articulate it, it went away.

And then he had it.

Another problem: over the last years, he'd used the personnel department of the United States Marine Corps as his private intelligence agency. When he'd needed a contact or an expert, he'd called an old colleague and they'd dug up, quickly, a name for him that always fit a specific category. They got him in the game fast.

But that was changing. His generation was all but gone; new men came and took things over and they had no living memory of Bob the Nailer and were not by nature inclined to help him. So he had to do some thinking and some calling before he was finally able to set up the right linkage: a retired NCO in Personnel who was friendly with a current NCO in Personnel who would do the favor for the friend of the friend.

But finally, close to six, he got a name, a number, the sufficient in-between calls had been made, and he was talking to his man.

"First Sergeant Jackson."

"First Sergeant, I'm Swagger, Gunnery Sergeant retired, I think Bill Martens may have—"

"Sure, sure, Gunny. After I got Bill's e-mail, I ran you, and you were some marine, I'll say. You were the best. Before my time, but the best."

"Son, I was before everyone's time."

First Sergeant Jackson laughed.

"What can I do for you?"

"It's this. I'm looking into Carl Hitchcock's last week and death—"

"Gunny, this ain't some crazy T. T. Constable did it thing like I'm seeing on the Internet, is it?"

"No, and I don't think aliens took over Carl's brain neither. No, I'm just trying to get a grip on it."

"I'd love it if Carl turned out to be innocent. So would all of us. But I don't see how."

"I don't see how either, but I told some folks I'd give it my best shot. Semper Fi, gung ho, ding how, and all that good shit. So here's where I am: I'm thinking a lot of our people go into law enforcement after they retire. It's a natural progression. So I'm guessing there's a guy for real like the one I've imagined in my head. He would be ex-marine, now working Chicago police, maybe even homicide. He was part of the team that investigated the Strong-Reilly shooting. He was there, he was noticing, he had ideas, he heard what the other cops said. All that before the FBI took over as lead agency and concluded Carl was the boy. Once that happens, it's all different, because they're all looking at it only in the way it links to Carl. I want to hear what this guy might have to say about what he noticed *before* the news on Carl arrived. Can you help find me such a guy, if he exists?"

"I will make a big try. Can I reach you on this number?"

"Roger."

"Okay, and I'm guessing time counts."

"Yes sir."

The call came at eleven, long after he'd checked into the motel in Alexandria, long after he'd had a chat with his wife, explaining that no, he wasn't on his way home, he had a few things to check out first, that was all. Her silence expressed her mood. She believed he had a crusade pathology and was always looking for excuses to veer off on strange, violent adventures; she finally accepted it, but at the same time, her silence made it clear that she still hated it. But he repeated that this was nothing, this was just some low-level inquiries, and there was no danger whatsoever involved. Still, he told her, don't tell anyone about this call. If anyone asks, I'm on my way home.

When the call came, he picked up the cell and said, "Swagger."

"Gunnery Sergeant Swagger, retired, USMC sniper, all that, number two in Vietnam?"

"Yes, that's me. Except it was number three."

"Gunny, I got a call from my ex–battalion commander, who evidently got a bunch of calls, the long and the short of it being you wanted to talk to a Chicago detective who'd been on the Strong-Reilly crime scene."

"I'm very glad you called."

"My name's Dennis Washington, I was an infantry officer, USMC, from '88 through '94, loved the Corps. Did the Gulf, got hurt a little, and had to give it up. Went to Illinois State Police, then came to Chicago. I'm a detective sergeant, Nineteenth Precinct, the Woodlawn area of Chicago. I do murder. It's usually some gang boy popping another gang boy, sometimes a kid gets in the way, or it's a Korean in a market, or a cabbie. It ain't no *CSI* kind of thing. I'm not a master detective, if you think I am, Gunny, sorry to say. I'm a little reluctant here. I've never done nothing like this and I know I'm in violation of policy."

"This ain't official, Sergeant Washington. But I know you want to hear this, so I'll say it. I ain't asking for no violation of ethics on your part; I sure ain't part of the press; I ain't a Net crazy who thinks Tom killed Joan because she slept with Warren or any shit like that. I ain't publishing, I ain't talking, I ain't telling. If you ask around about me, you'll see that most folks think I'm a stand-up guy. What this is about is my hope for Carl's innocence, and since I know a guy in the FBI, I got to go through the Bureau's case."

"It's solid, I hear."

Bob didn't feel like explaining.

"Well, we'll see about that. Maybe there's a little thing or two off."

"I hate to see it come down on an old marine, especially a guy who gave as much as Hitchcock."

"Roger that."

"So, I'll try to help you. I don't have a lot. The FBI took over within a few hours, and although they made a good attempt to keep us in the loop, once they got the call on lead agency it became totally their investigation. If you've seen their stuff, you may know more than I do."

"It's not their findings I'm strictly interested in. I know enough to know that findings are usually what people want to find. That's the nature of the damn animal. See, I'm looking for stuff that *wasn't* in no findings, wasn't in no report, something that you, an experienced homicide detective, might have *felt*, even if you didn't know you felt it at the time. You might call it hunch or buzz or vibe, some soft, unofficial word like that. I have a specific idea on this but I ain't going to give it to you because it'll tarnish your thinking. So I guess what I'm asking—sorry it ain't more specific—is, did you get any funny feelings? Was anything wrong? Did anything unusual happen?"

"I'd have to have an actual imagination to answer that, Gunny."

"Well, do your best."

"I went over my notebook, trying to re-create it carefully. No, there wasn't much there, except a thing so tiny I'm kind of embarrassed to mention it. It ain't the sort of thing that's admissible in court. It ain't evidence, it ain't forensics, it ain't factual. Like you say, a funny feeling."

"Detective, I am so ready to hear this."

"You know what a homicide dick is? I mean, really is? Forget all the *CSI* TV bullshit. From a practical point of view, he's what you call a professional interrupter."

"I ain't reading."

"Nobody ever plans on getting murdered. It's the last thing on everybody's mind. Even dope dealers with another gang out to get them, they don't think today's going to be their last day. They always live life like there's going to be a lot of tomorrows."

"Okay, I'm with you."

"As that translates practically, I'm the guy who interrupts. I bust into their life on a day they never in a million years thought would be their last, and I see exactly how they lived, without scrubbing or cleaning or getting ready for company. And here's what I've learned: everyone's a secret pig."

"I know I am. And my daughters! Wow!"

"Mine too. Those damned girls couldn't pick up sock one if their mom didn't yell at them. Anyhow, what this means is you go into a lot of messy homes. Mr. Brown got popped, so you go to the Brown home, and it's the way it was exactly at the moment Mrs. Brown heard Mr. Brown checked out. She's in shock. It's like the house is frozen in Jell-O. Newspapers on the floor, socks on the floor, garbage cans full to overflow, the litter in the cat's box ain't been changed, a coupla glasses from last night's cocktail hour are still out, maybe there's some plates in the sink, or someone forgot to put the cereal away. You know, that's how life is lived. To do stuff you have to take stuff out; then you have to put it away. But between the taking out and the putting back, sometimes a lot of time passes, and after having gone into a thousand houses in the past ten years with the worst possible news to deliver and then asking the worst possible questions, I'm here to tell you that most lives are lived, minute by minute and hour by hour and day by day, at some weird place between taking stuff out and putting stuff back. Stuff is everywhere. Daily life is about stuff. You follow me?"

"Sure do. You're saying—"

"If it had been tossed hard and fast, it would have been a mess. You ever see what IRS does to a house when they toss it? Looks like a cyclone hit it. Our guys ain't much better, and I don't bet the Bureau's are much better than that."

"Got it. So the Strong house didn't appear to have been searched."

"That's what you might think. But I'm concentrating here on his office, and what I saw was a room that had been searched and then *overcorrected*. Do you get what I'm saying? It's subtle. All the stacks were neat. People don't stack neat. They just throw things on top of each other. The computer monitor had been dusted, even on that pedestal and on the casing in back of the screen. Nobody dusts the pedestal, but this pedestal was dusted. The books were all neatly shelved, the stacks of—I don't know, he was a professor, right?—articles, books, whatever research stuff a professor would have, it was all neat on the big table and it was centered on the table. It didn't have the spontaneity of real life. It looked like a museum display. I noted it, maybe didn't think much of it, but it was especially weird in retrospect because I went out to his office in the Circle Campus the next day with one of the Bureau's people, and his office, well, it wasn't a mess, but it was an office. It was kind of messy, not wildly messy, not a shit hole, no, but it had the usual human mess in it. The rest of their house: usual human mess. Glasses in the sink, unmade beds, laundry on the floor, not in the basket. No pigsty, but just the random crap of life. But that one room, it had the look of having been freshly tidied, as if a) he knew he'd be murdered in his alley and wanted his investigators to think, 'My, what a tidy fellow this man was,' or b) someone tossed it, but tossed it very carefully, and tidied it up so that no one could tell it had been searched. They just overtidied by a tiny degree, and only a guy like me, Mr. Interrupter with Bad News, would pick up on it."

"Does the time line work out that someone could have been in the house between the killing and the arrival of the first units? You seem to be implying someone tossed the house, then straightened it out. Was there time enough?"

"Yeah. I checked, and that's maybe why I'm glad to hear from you, because my thoughts on this were kind of subversive to the general thrust and momentum of the investigation. But of course once our lab people arrived, the FBI people arrived, the media, that sort of condition of his office was destroyed. I didn't think to have crime scene photo work it, because it wasn't the crime scene, the car was the crime scene. My bad. But yeah, in terms of time, it was about ninety minutes as far as we can say."

Bob thought, that's why he took them in the alley. To give the team time to penetrate, search, tidy, and disappear. No one would notice the search team, because of course it wasn't a crime scene yet, charged with that special energy of such a place, that charisma. He kills them, the team enters and finds and—

Or maybe it doesn't find.

Or maybe it finds but it leaves traces of what it found.

"Is this of any help?"

"It's a great help, Detective Washington. Listen, I see now I'm going to have to come to Chicago. Can I call you? Can you help me?"

"When will you get here?"

"I'm already late."

18

Nick groaned. "What's the policy on this?"

"You can meet him or not meet him. It's up to you. I should be there to ride herd."

"You're sure it's necessary?"

"You tell me. He said one word. He said if I said the one word to you," Phil Price continued, "you would want to meet with him."

"And the one word was 'Tulsa'?"

"Yeah. I checked the records. I know what it means."

Nick sat in Price's office, nicely appointed, on the third floor. Price was Special Agent in Charge of Public Information, but unlike most "public information" hacks in fancy offices all through DC, Price was more agent than reporter suck-up. He'd done street time in New York, LA, and San Francisco, had taken a round in his hip on a raid (a friendly round, no less, from a poorly trained SWAT moron), and now finished out his time in Public Information, cordially hating the reporters who bedeviled him even as they cordially hated him. The subject was a proposed meeting with a *New York Times* reporter named David Banjax, who was the *Times*'s man on the still-hot sniper story.

"I hate these guys," said Nick.

"I hate 'em too," said Price. "But that's neither here nor there. What's here and now is this guy is levering for a meet, off the record. He's angling for a scoop, and the *Times* always feels entitled to scoops, so he wants his so he can get sent to the London Bureau or something."

"Agh," Nick said again, his gorge full of bile.

"Nick, in case you're wondering, let me tell you he didn't get this out of Public Information. We do not release background on special agents, not ever, certainly not in the age of terror. So I don't know how he got it."

"I do," said Nick. "It seems I've displeased Joan Flanders's big-foot ex-hubbo Tom Constable, that is, 'T. T.' Constable. His guy tried to nudge me in a certain direction, and I wouldn't play. So this is their first move, and this guy, this David Banjax, he's just a rube, a pawn, being run by a guy named Bill Fedders. Banjax doesn't know how he's being used."

"Don't tell him that. He's Harvard, Harvard Law; he thinks he's important."

"Ugh," Nick said. "Now I *really* hate him."

"But they do hold cards, Nick. I can't tell him to fuck off. I'd love to, then raid his crib for the 'ludes and pot he probably has stored in a waterproof baggie in the toilet, convict him, and send him to some hard ugly federal hotel where he and his new fiancé LeRoy could live happily ever after in anal cowboy bliss, guess who's the gal? But I can't do that. I have to play nice. And you can see how it might look. It could look bad or at least questionable. It could reflect poorly on the Bureau. And that's what they pay me to watch."

Nick shook his head. "Tulsa," he said again.

He remembered being in an office window in Tulsa, Oklahoma, in 1992, his second year on the street. He was crouched behind and held securely a then state-of-the-art Remington 700 sniper rifle in .308, on a Harris bipod. He watched reality through a ten-power Leupold scope as a crackhead skank bank robber named Nathan Bowie rode down an empty street in the back seat of a convertible. Unfortunately, surrounding him were three women, cashiers in the Tulsa State Bank and Trust Morgan Avenue branch, while the bank manager drove slowly. Nathan was tripping wilder and wilder, waving his pistol around, addressing God, the whole evil white race, the Martians who spoke to him through his dental fillings, the various bitches who'd left him before he was done kicking the shit out of them. He was going to go firecracker at any second and it was Nick's duty to put a 168-grainer into his cranial vault before that happened.

But Nick also had an FBI agent in charge in his earphones, a guy, now long gone, named Howard Utey, and Howard was one of the worst combinations: he wanted you to do exactly what he told you, except he didn't know what that was, and if he told you one thing, he could very easily change his mind, and it was your fault you didn't quite get that he hadn't meant "Shoot" when he screamed *"Shoot,"* he'd really meant "Don't shoot." Any idiot would know that.

Howard was as flippy as Nathan Bowie, as the tapes later revealed, not that it mattered, because Howard had contacts on the Seventh Floor and was supposedly headed up there.

"Are you ready, are you ready, get ready, Nick, I can't hear you, tell me are you ready are you ready, do you have him, do you have him, wait till he stops moving, *now* no not now, no, no the one on the left she moved, she's crying, why the hell won't she shut up, what is—"

Nick should have thrown the earphones with their little microphone on the pedestal, all cool SWAT TV-like, across the room and just buckled down, cinched in, made the fucking shot. But he didn't; that wasn't Nick. Howard was authority, and Nick had been drawn to, had respected and believed in the church of authority. Howard was boss, he was agent in charge, he was day-to-day a very decent guy, if a little moody when he thought he wasn't moving fast enough, but he got good results out of his people and he was well liked, if thought a bit callow and overambitious. But he was—and this was well known—absolutely no good in an action situation.

"Do you have him, I can see him, Nick, acknowledge please, I have to—"

"Howard, the girl on the left, she's—"

"Take him down, take him down!"

"No shot, Howard, goddamn, it's not clear."

It had to be clear. No other SWAT people were on call, the state police team couldn't get set up in time, the city people were in their usual sullen fit about being overruled (by Howard) in their own town, so it was a mess, and behind him, nobody was quiet, there was a lot of moving around and chatting.

"You have to shoot!" Howard screamed.

But Nick couldn't. There wasn't gap enough between the two girls, one of whom kept leaning over, as if she was losing bodily control, so great was her fear, and her head kept swimming into Nick's sight picture and the car would be turning in a second and he knew, he knew he had to shoot.

"Shoot, shoot, don't shoot, don't shoot, shoo—"

Nick thought he had it. The crosshair quadra-sected Nathan's head just behind the ear and it was clear. His finger did what it had been trained to do. He fired, the buck of the rifle, the largeness of the shot, it felt good, and when the scope came down—

"Oh God oh God you missed oh God he's shooting stop him!"

—Nick saw one of the girls twisted left, blood on her back, her body in a heartbreakingly broken pos-ture. Nathan Bowie shot the girl on the right, then shot the girl in the front, then put the gun in his mouth and blew the roof of his head off.

That was it. Med techs and cops with guns drawn raced to the vehicle, and from his perch Nick watched as the med team worked the fallen. He wanted to puke. He felt a surge of depression melt the strength out of his bones and fill his brain with self-loathing and remorse. Howard was there yelling, "Nick, Nick, my God, why did you shoot, didn't you hear me? I told you *not* to shoot, God, it's such a tragedy."

God, what a fuck-up. What a total disaster. Nick had thought he'd be the guy with the strength and the coolness and the good decision. But no. He had to play the goat, the mistake, Quantico's shame.

Poor Myra. He'd hit her in the spine, the bullet actually passing through her arm first, bouncing lat-erally off the metal of the car and clipping her spine. It paralyzed her in an instant. She never walked again and spent the next few years in her motorized wheel-chair. She had deserved so much better than Nick and the FBI had given her that day, and he tried to give it to her, to somehow make amends, by marrying her.

He discovered her to be a wonderful person, bright, funny, without a shred of self-pity. Once her father had gotten drunk and accused Nick.

"Why? Why did you do that to my baby girl? Oh, Nick, why, she didn't—"

"Daddy, you stop that. I've said many a time that if the only way I could have met Nick Memphis was to get shot by him and lose my mobility, I'd take it even with that foreknowledge, because Nick is the best man I've ever met, kind and generous and gentle and honest and moral. You cannot blame Nick. You blame Nathan Bowie or the man who sold him the crack, but do not blame Nick. He was only doing his duty."

Of the other two girls, one died, the other recovered and moved away. The bank manager recovered but died the next year, early, of a heart attack. Really, what had it proved? You take the shot and the shot goes off. It's so amazing how much pain can be released into the world by the little six-ounce press of the trigger, how it changes everything, totally and forever.

Nick sat back.

"You can see how it would play," said Price. "'Sniper investigator had bad sniper shooting in background,' that's how it'll read, and the implication is that maybe someone who had been a sniper, who'd had bad luck—"

"—Who'd fucked up."

"—who'd fucked up, maybe he shouldn't be in charge of an investigation involving a sniper. Maybe his judgment was clouded, maybe he was prejudiced. Maybe *that's* why the investigation, which was going so well, has now bounced off in a strange new direction."

"So is he threatening me, is that it?"

"They don't work like that. He wants to meet you, develop a relationship. Tulsa will come up, sure. But just give him the idea of working with him, play him a little, buy us some time. That's what the Bureau needs. Meet him for lunch. It's just lunch."

"Arggggh," said Nick.

19

It was in the middle of the block on Fifty-third off Blackstone, what was called a row house from an earlier century, strange to the eyes of a man who thought of houses as being miles apart from each other. But it was still magnificent, with a broad stairway leading to a broad porch and vast oak door, its windows wide and deep, its gables peaked. It had the look of a castle, something from Olde England, built with refined money in a neighborhood full of refined money, where everything old had been made new again, with the best in modern design, plumbing, lighting fixtures, and the best in burnished old wood and brick. Hyde Park, in southeast Chicago, in the shadow of the Museum of Science and Industry, all that remained of a White City where a hundred-odd years ago they had celebrated science, industry, and progress. A steady wind rushed in off the cold lake, throwing torrents of fallen leaves about.

"What do you expect to find?" Detective Washington asked Bob, who sat in the front seat of Washington's unmarked Impala a couple of doors down from the Strong-Reilly house, now darkened in the falling light.

"I don't know," said Bob. "Evidence of penetration, I suppose."

Washington, in his forties, 240, exceptionally black and full of unconscious tough-guy mannerisms with a sheen of graying hair that looked like gunmetal, said, "You sure you want to do this? You could get yourself in a peck of trouble, me too, and for something you ain't even sure exists. Don't sound like a good play to me. You could do it official and save us both time in jail."

"I'm just looking at options," said Bob. "If we go the route the law requires, I have to talk your department or the FBI into doing something nobody's ready to do. Time passes. Then even if they say yeah, they got to get warrants, assemble a team, dot the i's and cross the t's, and that's more time. Time is not on our side. My position is the guys we're investigating right now—"

"If they exist."

"Yeah, if they exist, they would have been the ones to toss the house that you picked up on, so at some level *you* think they exist. The point is now, they think they got away clean. They're not taking any precautions, they think they're so smart; this is when we have to go aggressively against them. If they sniff our interest, they'll go into a much harder defensive position, double-check, begin to erase clues or witnesses, move against us. This is the sneaking-up part snipers are famous for."

Washington shook his immense, wise head. "Gunny, okay, but answer me this one, then. Say, for example, you're right. These guys had to get something, something physical, out of that house. So why do they need to go to the trouble of killing not only Strong and Reilly but also Joan Flanders and Mitch Greene? If they're professional enough to put something like that together, they'd certainly be professional enough to hire some burglar who could take the house down, locate, and remove whatever it was."

"Well," said Bob, "he wants them dead. But in a certain way. If they sell everybody on the idea that crazed sniper Carl Hitchcock, fucked up from Vietnam, killed these four people, and all of that seems to add up, then that's as far as you go, right? You got it all there—motive, opportunity, means, time frame. It's so *tempting*. Everyone wants this thing solved, and there's the solution, plain as the nose on your face. What you don't do then is look into the lives of the victims. You don't see what they were up to, what they had going on, who they were, what connections they had, what moves they were making. All that stuff's off the board. So I'm putting it back on the board. My read is that something Strong and Reilly did or were planning to do got them whacked hard. The other two went down as smokescreen. Strong and Reilly were the target. If whoever he is kills just them, he knows their lives will be investigated, and such an investigation would lead to him. He needs a way to kill them in which their deaths are seen as unimportant, marginal, an afterthought, while all the focus goes on Joan. So if there's an answer, it's somewhere in Jack and Mitzi's lives in the last few weeks, so I'm going to take a look-see. I'm going to shake the tree and see what falls out."

"I got no argument except to say it doesn't happen that way. Not hardly. Nothing's ever that clever, that well planned, that secret in the real world. It's just drunks getting pissed or going nuts, whacking the innocent. That's what I see time and time again. Or some hothead kid fighting for his corner of Blackstone when Willie done took it, so he pops Willie with his nine-em and thinks he's a hero. That's the reality, man; you in James Bond land."

"Even if you don't buy it, and maybe I wouldn't either if I'd seen all the people murdered with beer bottles and ball-peen hammers and twenty-five Brycos that you have, I hope you'll indulge me a little, Washington. I can't do this alone."

"I wouldn't do this for a guy without USMC tattooed on his arm, Gunny," said Washington. "Okay, we'll drive around back, and you peel out right behind the garage; there's no crime scene tape anymore. Can you get through the back gate latch?"

"Yeah."

"Okay, how about into the house?"

"Well, if my theory is right, one of the basement windows has already been opened. That's how they got in. Hell, the team may have even been in the house before Jack and Mitzi left; they got in at night. That would save them time and exposure. They work the house, that office particularly, while the bodies are outside. When the cops come, guess what our team is dressed as? Cops. In ten minutes the place is jammed with cops. They emerge from wherever, join the crowd, mill, then slip away. Who's to know? Did you recognize everyone there on the crime scene?"

"A big murder draws more gawkers than a new *Star Wars* movie. You always see strangers there, at least in the beginning. You got people from all different agencies, all different departments; you got brass, you got brownnosers and suck-ups, you got press assholes, the more the merrier. Yeah, I recognized about fifteen percent of the faces."

"Well, there you go."

"All right, Gunny, let's play the game. When you're done, you slip out the same way, call me on the cell, and begin to walk down the alley and I'll pick you up."

"Got it."

"When do you think that will be?"

"About three a.m."

"Three a.m.?"

"Three a.m. Wednesday."

"Three a.m. Wednesday! This is *Monday*!"

"I need to go through the house carefully. I need to get a read on their life. I have to find out who they were, what they were into, what they were planning, why this happened to them. You don't learn that in an hour."

"Just don't get caught."

Bob slapped the backpack he carried.

"Infrared gear. I can see in the dark. No lights will show on the outside. If anyone comes into the house, I'll go to ground. Nobody'll see me. I can be real still. The sniper thing again. I'll call you when I'm done."

It was a different America. He hadn't seen this America. He'd been in the America of the United States Marine Corps, in mud and jungle and slatternly, jerry-built outposts and tempos, under monsoon weather or baking heat, and only glimpsed this America on the TV in the squad room, if there was a squad room. But everywhere in this house the late sixties and early seventies still lived, like some sort of Camelot, some sort of holy time when we were young and green and firm and the world was filled with possibility. Mr. and Mrs. Strong were narcissists for sure, in that they had dozens of photographs of themselves and their actions on the walls, as well as souvenir front pages—PENTAGON BOMBED, THOUSANDS DISRUPT DOWNTOWN, CAMPUS ADMIN BUILDING OCCUPIED, COPS USE TEARGAS ON DEMOS, TWO KILLED IN BANK ROBBERY, and finally WANTED COUPLE FREED—as well as political campaign buttons, flyers, gas masks, anything that spoke of the realities, and maybe the fun, of the Movement.

A whole section was devoted to their day of freedom; Bob ran his infrared over the framed newspaper front page, with its famous picture of Jack and Mitzi in midleap, full of the joy of freedom, as the famous radical lawyer Milton Tigermann had just checkmated the Justice Department into dropping all charges against them because the means used by pursuing detectives over the years, from FBI to Massachusetts State Police, were so flagrantly illegal. "Guilty as hell, free as a bird," Jack's comment; it made the two even more famous. Swagger's eyes ran through the coverage, including the bitter sidebar interview with a Mrs. Samuel Bronkowsky, mother of four, identified as the widow of one of the two bank guards slain by robbers—robbers thought to be Jack and Mitzi but uncaught and made more unindictable when the bank's surveillance film was stolen from the evidence closet of the Nyackett Police. And thus Mrs. Bronkowsky left history, her cause unmourned, her husband forgotten, her economic situation unsettled.

History turned on the next wall to great men, big men, giant men. These were the portraits Bob didn't recognize, but they were helpfully identified as if in a hall of fame, people with names like Frantz Fanon, Régis Debray, Che and Fidel of course, W. E. B.

Du Bois, Emma Goldman, Eugene V. Debs, Gavrilo Princip, and of course Marx, Engels, Lenin, Stalin, and some other big commie boys. Ho was there, and so were Chou and Mao, and someone called La Pasionaria.

The infrared gave the history a special green hue, as brought to life in the AN/PVS-7 goggles. He was a frogman swimming the bottom of the murky bay of radical America, 1969 to 1975.

Bill and Mitzi were everywhere in those days. Beautiful radical children, with wild piles and tendrils of hair and eyes wide as pie plates, elves, stars, charismatics, leprechauns of mischief. A hundred shots showed them with megaphone or loudspeaker, leading or addressing the masses. They were always sexy, in raffish war surplus cast-offs, with Indian bands about their heads, gaudy scarves, tight jeans that showed off their leanness, combat boots, sharp cheekbones, and everywhere they appeared they fronted rows and rows of hand-painted signs, like medieval kings leading an army of banners: STOP THE WAR NOW, STOP THE BOMBING, NO MORE NAPALM, GET OUT NOW, BRING THE BOYS HOME, LEGALIZE POT, LSD NOW AND FOREVER, and he realized that while they were painting, he'd been crawling through the bush, hoping not to get his belly blown open.

He checked for signs of search and came up with ambiguous possibilities. Yes, the cabinet locks in Jack's office appeared uniformly scarred. But that could have been Jack's own clumsiness with keys as easily as a professional burglar's pick. There had indeed been an open window that allowed him to squeeze into the basement, and that lock too bore signs of picking—or of a careless window washer banging it with a squeegee.

He himself picked each cabinet, and inside, besides Jack's secret stash of porno (he was a *Penthouse* guy), a pound of very nice hash, some prescription meds, there seemed to be nothing suspicious, certainly no obvious sign of something having been removed. But what would that be? A blank space on a shelf? An opening in a row of books? There wasn't much.

He went over the office top to bottom, opening each cabinet, riffling through each book, looking in each drawer, searching for computer code words (and finding none). He'd wait to turn the machine on in the light, so that its glow wouldn't radiate through the windows into the night. He thumped the walls for evidence of a safe hiding behind the bookshelves, but no safe seemed to present itself.

Nothing, nothing at least on a first pass.

He tried all the obvious hiding places, feeling under the drawers for tape strands that might indicate something had been secretly affixed in an out-of-the-way site, opening the battery casings of all the portable tape recorders, the cameras, the iPods that lay around, finally, laboriously—it took hours—opening each CD jacket, running from jazz to classics to heavy metal to songs of the Spanish Civil War, and in each finding nothing but a CD. He went to the bathroom, took the lid off the toilet for a waterproof bag—yep, but full of grass, not diamonds or other contraband—opened all the folded towels and washcloths in the closet. Went through the laundry hampers, the pile of folded clothes, the kitchen with its abundance of spices and herbs and exotic condiments from overseas; Mitzi was evidently quite the chef. Again, nothing, just life, lived by aging baby-boomer haute bourgeoisie with fading memories of the glory of the struggle, so long ago, when they were young and bold. It was a kind of counterbiography: for each demonstration they'd led, he'd been on a deep jungle mission; for each cop they'd confronted, he'd dropped a man with an AK-47; for each time they'd fled gas, he'd fled napalm or heavy bomber ordnance or some such. Same coin, different sides, and now the years have passed and what's gone around has come around, and who's the only one who cares why you assholes got your brains blown out but me, the guy you thought was a war criminal, a psycho kid killer. Ain't it a strange fucking world, though?

He went upstairs and spent the rest of the night in the bedroom, the slow, methodical search, unfolding each item of clothing, paging through each volume—the house was stacked, crammed, jammed with books—emptying the wastebaskets and uncrumpling each wad of paper. Nothing, just the detritus of an involved professional life—notes on meetings, calendars, appointment books, nothing at all out of the ordinary. One of them spoke French and one spoke Spanish; there were many, many books in either language, and he went through them too, page by page, looking for notes either written in the margins (frequent and meaningless) or tucked between the pages. Nothing.

He worked through the morning, going to his low crawl during the daylight hours so that nobody walking by might catch a glimpse of shadowy movement and call the police.

He slept for two hours in the spare bedroom, then

got up with enough light remaining, turned on Jack's computer terminal, and didn't get much beyond the desktop full of icons, because a code was required. He'd found no code; obviously Jack had committed it to memory. He tried number sequences based on obvious dates—Jack and Mitzi's birthdays, the dates of big demonstrations, the date they almost got blown up in the house in New York, the date of the Pentagon bombing, the date they were freed from prosecution, that sort of thing. Nothing.

When it got dark, he reverted to the photos on the wall. He took each one down, carefully probed it for hidden documents folded between the photos and the matte backing, and that was more tedious than anything. He looked at each one for scrawled notes or something. This went on and on, as the Strongs literally had hundreds of photos. It seemed their every second was subject to a photo, some with celebs, most on the glorious ramparts. He even found one of the two of them with fists upraised after some sort of dinner with T. T. Constable and his then-wife, the beautiful Joan Flanders, four extremely beautiful human beings caught in a circle of love and adoration, all celebrating the smugness of the moral righteousness that made them so perfect for each other, maybe early nineties, when everyone was in from the cold.

He felt a momentary spasm of rage and had an urge to smash the picture, but what would that prove? Really, what would that prove? He hung it back up and continued with the thankless task, picture after picture, again coming up with nothing.

What am I missing? What is here that I don't see? I'm too stupid to see, of course, because I'm the redneck marine from Arkansas and these people are so much smarter, so much more insightful, so much more penetrating. Bob Lee, Earl's son, was just a grunt who followed orders, almost got killed, and killed too much. They knew better. They were above that. With their airs, their sophistication—the wine cellar was amazing, and clearly Jack knew his vintages, while Mitzi's kitchen was the most complex room in the house, still full of life from the dinners she'd cooked for their many friends, the many joyous nights of camaraderie here in the old castle in Hyde Park. He'd seen the pictures, for many had been taken; Jack more or less holding court, lots of young, beautiful kids, lots of earnest intellectual types with the bushy hair, the wire-frame glasses, the women all with straight, undyed hair, in tight jeans, all of them so goddamned happy.

It was like they were some kind of European royalty, Bob thought. It had nothing to do with—

European.

That was something, yeah. Yeah, they really didn't see themselves as American, did they? There was nothing anywhere in the house that was, strictly speaking, American. No pictures of landscape, nothing celebratory of American themes like farms, mountains, plains, no flag; instead it was all European in tone and texture. From the food to the books to the photos on the white walls, to the slick, hardwood floors, to tapestries of multitextured, usually African or Afro-Cuban tonalities, all of it belonged in a house in Paris.

What does this mean? Practically, not philosophically. They don't shower enough. They have affairs, Jack a mistress? They drink espresso? They have wine with dinner? They won't eat sliced bread? Hmm, among other things, it meant they put little lines through the letter *Z* and the number 7, after the European fashion, an idiosyncrasy that he'd noted that meant absolutely nothing.

But it did mean something. It meant they were European.

He tried to think of other ways that—

And for some reason he thought of the computer, how he'd tried to run the famous dates of the glorious Strong-Reilly history as a way through the code. But Americans wrote dates month/day/year, as in March 25, 1946, 03/25/46. But Europeans wrote them day first, as in day/month/year, and put periods between them, so that March 25, 1946, came out 25.03.46.

Bob first drew shades so that its dead glare wouldn't leak into the night, then flicked the computer on, watching it stir lazily to life, clicking mysteriously.

The blinking demand for an access code stared at him. He was an expert; he'd read *Radical Romantics: The True Story of Jack Strong and Mitzi Reilly*, by O. Z. Harris.

He remembered the date they got married.

He remembered the date of the bank robbery in Nyackett.

He remembered the date they got pardoned.

He remembered the date they blew up the Pentagon.

He remembered the date they blew up a judge's house in Connecticut, during a Black Panther trial.

He remembered the date the bomb had gone off accidentally in their Greenwich Village townhouse, killing its poor builder and sending Jack and Mitzi into the streets.

No, nothing.

Then he remembered the date Saigon fell. He'd never forget that one; it had sent him off on a three-day drunk and he ended up in a jail in Alabama with his real estate business totally trashed and his first wife filing a missing persons report.

He typed it in, European style: 30.04.75.

And thus he entered the secret world of Jack Strong and Mitzi Reilly.

20

They met at Soleil, a tapas restaurant popular with the lunch crowd in the redeveloped sector of SE. It was a gaudy, mock-peasant place, full of young government workers and journalists and others who considered themselves quite fascinating. David Banjax was evidently well known enough here to command a table in the window, and Nick and Phil Price were escorted into the great man's presence.

Banjax, about thirty-five, with a goatee and otherwise short hair, in a suit without a tie and a pair of Italian architect glasses, rose and put out a hand as Price handled the intros. Then they sat, and it turned out that thankfully Banjax was not one for small talk, didn't offer an opinion on the Redskins or the new president or the war in Afghanistan or any other topic of the day. He commenced immediately with his sucking up.

"So, Agent Memphis, I hear you're quite the hero. You shot it out with those bad guys in Tennessee last year or so. Is that why you limp?"

"That is why I limp, Mr. Banjax. But I wasn't quite the hero. I was with a very skilled undercover officer who handled the gunfight. My only contribution was that I stopped a bullet that might have hit him, and I did manage to shoot a car twice in the right rear fender, which cost the Bureau over seven thousand in repair costs. But I think we're countersuing now. Don't mess with the Bureau."

"Nick is known for his modesty," Phil said smoothly, showing some minimal gift for the job. "Nick ran the team that broke up what could have been an eight-million-dollar heist and put seven men in prison for the rest of their lives."

"Wow," said Banjax. "No wonder everyone I talk to thinks so highly of you."

"They're a resilient mob. I'm sure they'll have escaped and be drinking Jax beer and sporting with the gals this time next year. You can't keep the Grumley boys down," Nick said.

Banjax laughed, as if he got Bureau humor, or knew who the Grumleys were.

"Nick's a kidder," said Phil. "He has a lot of fans in the Bureau. Nick's integrity and honesty are treasured in the Bureau, but it's his sense of humor that makes him beloved."

"I guess it's not a laff-riot kind of place," Banjax said.

"Not much shtick, no," said Nick. "In fact there hasn't been a good pie fight in years. But I'm not that beloved. Phil exaggerates, which is his job. I'm loved and I'm hated and I try to do my job and I wish I were smarter and I'm glad I'm not dumber. So, I know why we're here, Mr. Banjax. Would you do me the favor of fast-forwarding to the hard part of the conversation? I have heard the word 'Tulsa' mentioned."

"Oh, that," said Banjax, smiling easily. "It was just something that came up. You know, what you do and what I do, it's similar. You're investigating a killer. I'm investigating a man investigating a killer. An agency, I should say, but that agency happens to be represented by a man. I'm very sorry for what happened in Tulsa, and I'm not here to make noises about it. It's just that I'm in a very competitive news situation, and in my bureau there's a lot of pressure to produce. There's an awful lot of smart people there and we all want to do well. So I ask as many questions as I can and I throw out a very broad net, and somehow, this stuff about Tulsa came in."

"Phil, help me, I'm not clear on the rules here. Is it fair for me to ask him how he found out about it? I mean it wasn't part of any official release, so he had to hear about it from someone. Can I ask him who?"

"Probably not a good idea, Nick. The press values its right of confidentiality and feels that if it gives up sources to law enforcement inquiries, it becomes an arm of the Bureau. Nobody wants that."

"Agent Memphis, if you must know, and I hope you'll appreciate my candor here, it was a guy I know, one of those gray elder types; he knows everybody and everything. I'd prefer not to give you his name, but he said he heard about this from someone he knew."

"You don't have to give me Bill Fedders's name, Mr. Banjax. I already know it quite well."

"Well, there you go. Anyway, 'someone' forwarded through 'my friend' an envelope with a set of Tulsa front pages and the unidentified FBI sniper marked heavily in highlighter, with question marks. Crude, but effective. Anyhow, I called the reporter who wrote the story fifteen years ago and he knew your name, even if he didn't release it then. I don't think he was sworn to any confidentiality agreement, and I don't think I've skirted any confidentiality issues. I got it fair and square, nothing dubious. I take it you're not denying it."

"Is this off the record?"

"Of course. Sorry, I should have said that earlier. I'll let you know when we go on."

"Well, obviously, I can't deny it. Yeah, I took that shot and missed and all sorts of terrible things happened. And some good things: I got seven years with Myra."

"I heard that part too. Extraordinary."

"Anyhow, it's not going to do the Bureau any good to get this all mixed in with the ongoing investigation. It'll cloud matters. I'll tell you, man to man, that I have no beef with snipers, as the implication seems to be, based on my unfortunate tour as one. My job is not to find the sniper innocent by some trick, it's to find out who's guilty and put him away or prove the case so totally that even if he's dead, there can be no doubt he was the guilty party, sniper or not. But it's more complex than it seems. We have to be diligent. We can't be nervous about media pressures or outside political pressures. If you look at the Kennedy thing, you'll see that Warren was rushed, made mistakes, and there was hell to pay for it. I don't want that happening here. That's my only concern, not my career in the Bureau, my next promotion, the book contract I'll get when I go, how *60 Minutes* will handle it. If I have to leave the Bureau because doubts are raised about me, then that's what I'll do. It happens in Washington all the time."

"I haven't published yet. I don't know that I will."

"What is it that you want? I mean, exactly."

"Well, look, we're not kids here. We're all professionals and we're all under great pressure from management to produce. Now, I have to come up with something. I have to publish something. I can't go in and say, 'Oh, I spent three weeks and I came up with nothing.' That's just not good. So if I have to, I suppose I could go with the Tulsa episode. It does seem like legitimate information that the public needs to have. There is a great deal of interest in this case, and you folks did such a good job and worked so fast and got there in time to prevent any other killings, but it seems to have come off the tracks since then. We thought we'd get that report in a couple of weeks. Now I hear that as of last week, you came up with a whole new area of investigation and that you've sent a lot more people into the field. If that's true, maybe we could put it on the record, explain it, put it in some kind of context, and get it into the paper. Get it into the paper the way you want it, not picked up third-hand from a variety of other sources."

"See," said Nick, "from a PR point of view and a career point of view, that would be the right thing to do. But the direction and thrust of our investigation has to remain confidential. In fact, details may alert some people we have to look at. They act differently when they know they're being looked at, and it clouds the issue. We have to make preliminary inquiries confidentially to see if this is even worth pursuing. I'm not saying there are other persons of interest than Carl Hitchcock, but I have a duty to be diligent. Is that all right, Phil, what I said to him?"

"It's your call, Nick. I won't tell you how to operate."

"Okay," said Banjax. "I hear you. That's fine. But I don't have much wiggle room myself. I can only say,

I'll try and keep Tulsa out of the paper, but if I get in a jam, I may have to go with you. I'd have to put it in the record and come at you with hard questions."

"I will be very happy to discuss Tulsa with you, Mr. Banjax. Here, I'll give you my direct number, call me anytime you want. If I have some development, maybe I'll give you a heads-up. That's all I can say."

21

Bob finally slipped out of the house Wednesday morning at 2 a.m. and Denny Washington was waiting for him.

He climbed into the car.

"Man, am I hungry," he said. "Any place still open?"

"You look like a homeless guy," Washington said. "I'd bust you for looking like that in the old days. Today I have to call you sir and ask you if you need assistance."

"Welcome to modern times."

"Ain't it the fucking truth, bro? Okay, I know an all-night eatery, a cop place. You don't mind eating with cops?"

"If they don't mind eating with me."

They headed to a joint called Johnny's, outside of which a lot of blue-and-white cruisers idled. The place was bright, first from the lights, and second from the more than a few white faces among the black, unusual in this part of town. Everywhere Swagger looked, he saw the blue-and-white checkered hatbands that were the unique signature of the Chicago officer's cap. He was in a blue-and-white universe. Washington made his way down the aisles to a booth in the rear, nodding to the other pilgrims as he led Swagger through but making no intros, and Swagger recognized the faces, all tough urban warrior mugs, under hair either short and frizzy or a little vain. Why did some cops have such elaborate hair? Anyway, he and Linebacker Washington sat in the booth, ordered coffee, eggs, bacon, toast, enough for a battalion, and waited for the food to come.

"So are you going to tell me anything, Gunny? Or is it need to know?"

"It is need to know, but you're on the team, so you need to know," said Swagger. "First off, guess what? Mr. and Mrs. Crusader for Peace and Freedom were broke."

"Broke?"

"Broke, as in 'broke.' Broke, as in, We can't make no payments. He'd had an inheritance—that's what they'd been living on—but they'd been into the capital for years and now it was down to nothing. They lived big, did you know? Always a houseful of guests, always the hosts, spent a fortune on wine and food and big dinners out. You'd think he was rich; wasn't that part of the joke, the rich protesters, them rich people who believed in the rights of the poor? But they way overspent their salaries, which weren't great, and his book royalties and speaking fees were down. He spent six years working on a book for a big New York outfit, and in the end they turned it down and sued him to get their money back."

"Boo fucking hoo. You're breaking my heart."

"Yeah," said Bob, "and here this was the land of opportunity. So they were desperate, or so it seemed."

"I guess being a revolutionary isn't that high-paying a job."

"Oh, and he had to pay a girl three hundred thousand a few years back because he fucked her after promising he'd leave Mitzi. Then he changed his mind. They didn't want it getting out, didn't want any publicity, so that ate up a big chunk. So much for bringing higher morality to the world."

"How did you find this out?"

"I cracked the computer code, and he had a combination on file. I didn't know there was a safe the first time I went through the house, but it was in the corner of his office, under the floorboards. If you know there's a safe, you can find it. All this stuff was in there, the letters to the lawyers about the three hundred K payment, all that. In the safe."

"Hmm. So to hit the house without the combination, you'd need a safecracker, right?"

"Yeah," said Bob. "Yeah, *yeah*," seeing how Washington's insight seemed to lead to another development, a safecracker who could maybe be convinced to talk. "So there'd be a safecracker who—"

"Not so fast, bro. There was a guy in this town named Willie Beazel. Very good fingers. Could open anything."

"Past tense?"

"That's where he lives now, in the past tense. He was found floating in the Chicago River with a twenty-two through the ear three days after the hit on the Strongs. I'm thinking they paid him big upfront, brought him into the house, and he popped the box for them. They knew whatever it was they needed was in that safe. Of course, once he's done his job, he's a liability. He's a loose end. Tidy motherfuckers."

"These people ain't messing around. If they want you dead, you get dead, fast."

"And of course nobody would ever think to link Willie to the Strongs, no reason to. But he had colleagues, pals. I can run 'em down. Maybe he said something before he went for a float. You left the records in the safe?"

"Yeah. If we can get a warrant, we can get all that stuff into play legally, I'm thinking. But that might be for later."

"So back to the Strongs: they were poor?"

"Running out of dough. But, but, but there's a big *but* coming up."

"I'm listening."

"Just a month before they were hit, they opened a Swiss bank account. It sounds like a movie, but it was an actual Swiss bank account, number 309988762554. They were expecting some big money coming in. They didn't want to pay taxes on it, they didn't want to pay their creditors with it, they just wanted to spend it on themselves. They wanted the big life somewhere off in Europe. They were nuts about Europe. They thought they belonged in Europe. I think—well, no matter what I think, it's clear they were getting ready to go underground again."

"On the lam?"

"Yeah, but in a different way. Not on the run but under new identities. They had spent money they didn't have, that they owed various relatives and friends, to get new identities. They had phony passports in that safe, under the names William and Mary Ives, of Dayton, Ohio. Very good phonies, and I'm thinking they used some old radical contact to get into underground culture to come up with that sort of high-end merchandise. I mean, you just don't go to a phony passport shop in the mall; you've got to know somebody, you've got to be wired into the organization, you've got to have your bona fides up front to get stuff at that level."

"Don't it seem they was anticipating a big payoff of some sort, a getaway, a new life of ease and luxury somewhere?"

"It does."

"Any idea what the scam was?"

"I only know that all this started around September first. There was a big flurry of activity the first week in September. That's when they got the passports, that's when they opened the Swiss bank account. I found an invoice from Amazon for a batch of books they'd ordered: *Europe on $5,000 a Day*, *Castles of the Rhine*, *Luxury Tours of Europe*, dated September third, then another one for September fourth. With all his money problems, Jack bought some kind of Italian Armani suit for six thousand bucks September eighth. Can you believe that? Jack Strong in a six-thousand-dollar suit."

"Maybe he was turning her out for trickin', and he was making his pimp hand strong."

Swagger laughed. Washington was cool. Big, black, dead face, fists that should have been nicknamed "Thunder and Thunder," but he had a street wit to him.

"I hadn't thought of that. But anyway he didn't have the money in his account, but he bought it. He's to pick it up from the tailor next week, after the alterations. He expected to have the dough by then."

"You ought to pick it up, Gunny. Shame to see it go to waste."

"I could. Man, my daughters would have a laugh at the old goat in a fancy suit!"

The food came, and Bob shoveled it down, though he stayed off the coffee, because he was dangerously blurred with fatigue and needed sleep next.

"Don't leave any for the poor people in China, Gunny," Washington said. "They don't need it."

"I am a hungry guy," Bob said, beginning to feel more or less whole again. "Sarge, can you drive me back to my hotel? I need to sleep."

He glanced at his watch. It was nearly four.

"Sure. You sleep. I go to mass, I take my kids to school, I go be a policeman for twelve hours, then what?"

"Tomorrow I call my guy at the FBI and I lay my stuff out for him, the Willie Beazel connect, where I think we should concentrate, what I think should happen next. He argues, we yell, eventually it comes around. I fly out to DC and lay it out for them people, and suddenly there's a new lay to the land. And now we have a really good chance of getting Carl Hitchcock out of the murderer's box. Maybe even putting the real shooter in it. That ain't a bad night's work."

"Swagger is the man," said Washington.

The big detective got him efficiently enough back to the hotel room, and he fell into bed and felt the rush as unconsciousness overtook him. He slept and slept and slept, and when he woke it was near three. How could he have slept so long?

He rose, rushed through a shower and the other ablutions, then picked up his cell and pushed Nick's number.

No answer.

He tried three or four more times, never connecting. Finally he called the other number, the task force working number that he had, got some earnest intern, asked for Nick, waited, and finally a young woman's voice came on.

"Agent Chandler, can I help you?" she said.

The one called Starling.

"Agent Chandler, it's Swagger, you remember me?"

"Of course."

"I have to reach Nick. I can't seem to raise him."

The pause told him bad news was incoming.

Finally she responded.

"Where have you been the last ten hours?"

"I was asleep. I was working three days without rest and I had to catch up, and now I have some things I—"

"Oh. Well, there's been a shake-up. You didn't see the *Times* this morning?"

"I'm in Chicago."

"Well, it's national news. Anyhow, some *Times* reporter broke a big story on something in Nick's background. Some botched shooting twenty years ago."

Swagger knew the story; the shot that hit the woman, not the robber, and paralyzed her. He thought it was all over, forgotten. Whose business was it?

"What does that have to do with anything?"

"It's caused a big stew. Some congressman is threatening hearings on how the Bureau is handling this. Nick's been upstairs all day."

"He's all right, isn't he? Jeez, he's their best guy."

"He is. But we don't know what's happening. There hasn't been any news. There's a rumor he's resigned—"

"Resigned!"

"For the good of the Bureau. It's all a mess, a typical Washington thing—politics, influence, lost time, anger, recriminations—and the press is eating it up."

"Oh, Christ," said Bob.

"Do you want to talk to anybody else? Ron is here."

"Oh—No, I'll wait and see how it shakes out. If you see Nick, give him my best and tell him, well, that I called."

"I will," she promised.

22

Bill Fedders hit the putt, watched it ride the undulations of the green and break right just where he thought it would. But he hadn't quite hit it hard enough, and it quit short six inches.

"Great putt," said the congressman. "I wish I could read a green like that."

"My one true talent," said Fedders with a glowing smile, and the smile was really his one true talent. He went to the ball, insouciantly leaned over it, and knocked it casually into the cup with one hand. Par, another par, and the congressman's handicap kept him close so he wouldn't go home embittered.

Bill could par any course in Washington. He was a superb gin, bridge, and poker player. He could drink ten Navy boatswains under the table. He had an aristocrat's thick silver hair (you had to have had a relative at the original Round Table to get hair like that, he often joked), a keen, original wit, and a gift for strategy. His suits were Italian but subdued; he had an excellent collection of Aldens, in both wing tips and, for casual wear, the tasseled loafers. He had a good racquet sense, excelling at both squash and tennis. He could ride a horse or a motorcycle or pilot a sailboat or speedboat. He was a licensed flier. He was a Yale grad, from a grand old family. Skull and Bones, University of Virginia Law, Navy JAG during Vietnam, then a partner with Occam Dobalt Hunsucker until he established his own practice. He made three million a year and had put four kids through Ivy League schools and law school. He was on wife number three and mistress number twenty-five. He lived in a really big house in Potomac. He went to all the right parties, knew all the right people. He hated his life.

The cell rang.

"Oh, I know who that is," said the congressman. "His master's voice."

Bill rolled his eyes and turned to wander to the edge of the green, while caddy and foursome gave him privacy, as all knew he was Tom Constable's number one guy in Washington, and even here, on the fabled thirteenth green at Burning Tree, under soaring poplars wearing their fall russets and golds, when Tom Constable called, Tom Constable expected an answer.

"Yes, Tom. Did you see it?"

"I saw it," said Tom Constable, from wherever he happened to be, in Wyoming or Atlanta or China, for Christ's sake, Tom was always on the go; he might have even been on the twelfth or the fourteenth here at Burning Tree.

"Was it what you expected?"

"I liked the information. The tone was more sympathetic than I imagined."

"Evidently Banjax got to know Memphis and liked him quite a bit. It seems everybody likes Memphis. *I* like Memphis."

"I'm sure I'd like him too," said Constable. "That's not the point. The point is, he's in the way, he has to be removed. That's the point, the only point. Tell me what I want to hear. He's gone as of now. Some obedient number two guy is about to release the report. I don't see how they can keep him aboard with all this shit in the air."

"No changes have been announced, but it's still early. There'll be a period when clarity isn't available," said Fedders. "It'll be murky. Nothing will seem to be happening. What's going on is that everybody is figuring out how the game has changed and how the situation now sits, where the power is, who's got the momentum. That'll take a bit of time. Then on to the next move."

"I know, I know. If I ran a goddamn business like that, I'd be in the goddamn poorhouse by now."

"That's why I've always told you to stay out of Washington, Tom. You don't have the temperament, and all you'd do is give yourself an ulcer. You pay me to have your ulcer for you."

"Pay you goddamn well, Bill, as I recollect. So, the story ran, the Bureau is locked up behind closed doors, media pressure is building, there's a lot of scrutiny. Has the White House said anything?"

"No, but Jack Ridings has gotten the Leader to threaten to hold hearings. The FBI does not want to go to the Hill and discuss dirty laundry, believe me. They want all this to go away."

"Don't they see? Dump Memphis, issue the report, watch the case-closed signs go up, and everything is fine. No more books on poor Joan, no more Internet shit about me. Have you seen the latest? Joan had pictures of me in a feather boa dancing with J. Edgar. We look like Alice B. Toklas and Gertrude Stein. I had her murdered to get the negatives."

"Tom, there are lots of people who hate you. You know that. It's not worth acknowledging their existence. They would love nothing better than to be sued by you."

"Okay, okay. Don't let this slide, Bill. Stay on Jack, stay on the Bureau, keep me informed. I want to be in the loop. I want this goddamn thing closed."

"Yes, Tom."

"By the way," said Tom, "you shouldn't have hit the seven on the approach."

23

Give it to Chicago homicide. In the four hours between the discovery of the Strong and Reilly bodies and the arrival of the FBI on the scene, not as advisers but as lead agency on the determination that a murderer-for-hire had crossed state lines (even though it seemed not to have gone that way) and the formation of Task Force Sniper, the usual processes had already begun to proceed. Given that Strong and Reilly were well-known and that their deaths were unusual enough to merit consideration as major cases, two teams of detectives were dispatched and spent the day interviewing witnesses and acquaintances under the common-place theory that the vics' death was rooted in their own behavior, not their membership in some larger, national pattern.

Thus detectives interviewed neighbors, colleagues, some journalists (Jack was a favorite of theirs, always good for a radical quote to get readers' blood boiling), and so forth. That campaign was formally halted around 3 p.m. and the detectives then reported to the FBI, which was not interested in their findings and reassigned them to crime scene inventory and other of the bureaucratic jobs important at a major investigative site. The feds already had their man, even if only a theoretical man, and local investigations were unnecessary.

But no cop ever throws out a notebook. So a few

weeks later, casually and informally, Sgt. Denny Washington, under his own initiative, canvassed the dicks involved and recovered five of the six notebooks, with promises to return them. He turned them over to Bob, who alone had the patience, the time, the interest, and possibly the context to examine them carefully.

Bob was alone in his hotel room, sitting at a desk under a cheap HoJo lamp. It was near midnight, and today felt like a lost day, as he'd slept late, been disappointed to learn of Nick's troubles and the way the case was now bollixed up in some sort of political situation. He'd watched the national news, where Nick's face was prominently displayed, and anchor haircuts, without saying a word, communicated by eyebrow and turn of face their disappointment that the Bureau had chosen such a compromised candidate to head up this important investigation, and that the investigation, which had begun so promisingly, had seemed now to come off the tracks and was evidently barking up wrong trees or chasing wild geese hither and yon. What was wrong with the FBI? You'd think a case this big, they'd make sure not to screw up, huh?

Some reporter named Banjax was all over cable, documenting his disclosures, trying desperately to separate himself from the implication of his words. He of course had no opinion on the appropriateness of Nick to head the investigation, no investment, emotional or professional; his job was to report the facts and let others draw the conclusions. He just felt the public had a right to know that the FBI's chief sleuth had been himself involved as a participant in issues similar to the ones here—tragically so, sadly so—and the question of why was a logical one to ask.

The Bureau had no comment; Nick, of course, had no comment. Bob saw a glimpse of the girl Starling, her head down, racing past the assembled cameras outside the Hoover Building in DC; he thought she looked upset.

Then the shows all cut to an interview with Joan Flanders's ex-husband, the rich oddball T. T. Constable. He was all cowboyed up, because now he lived in the West, had essentially given up his eastern identity, and by now everybody was used to seeing him in a cowboy hat and open-necked red shirt with a red bandana about his neck.

As usual, he was ornery and colorful, and the cameras ate up his rugged, tanned face and grizzle of day-old beard, as if he'd spent the day ropin' and brandin' instead of sellin' short and firin' low producers.

"Well, damn," he said, "I do expect more from the FBI. We all know who did this, and the sooner we reach that legal determination, the sooner we can put it behind us and celebrate Joan's great life instead of her unfortunate death at the hands of some screwball marine who thought he was still in the war or something. It's so straightforward, it's a mystery to me how they could get it so knotted up."

Then the Wyoming congressman—the shows didn't point out that he represented the district in which much of Tom Constable's vast ranch, one of several, was located, nor did they mention that his party affiliation was the same as Tom's and that Tom had donated generously to his campaign—this Jack Ridings took over, and promised hearings on FBI hiring and promotional practices, and wondered how a situation like this could come about. Essentially you had a sniper investigating a sniper, and was it not fair to wonder where his allegiance lay? Did he have some sort of psychological investment in the act of sniping? Did he think it was noble to eliminate a human being at long range; would that cloud his professional judgment, cause him to refuse to accept certain realities?

Bob turned it off then. Enough. And shortly thereafter Washington called, at the end of the duty day, saying yeah, he knew what was going on, but he did have these notebooks for Bob, if Bob wanted them. Bob wanted them.

So Bob sat there, trying to make this or that out of the notes. Each guy or gal had his own scheme, his own method, his own set of abbreviations, so it wasn't easy going, and a lot of it was guesswork or inference. Eventually, he got to know the two simplest styles of penmanship, so he could read those books easily enough, even if some of the initials remained mysterious, and another guy had gone back over his notes with a red pencil, starring each entry that he thought might lead to further inquiries.

Essentially what he found confirmed his own investigations. In the past few months or so, both Jack and Mitzi had been morose, uncommunicative, seemingly depressed. Friends wondered about the health of the marriage or the long-term depression the rejection of Jack's book might cause. A perhaps too bitchy interviewee made the point that it had been so important to him to have a big New York publisher take it, but nobody would, and that had been a devastating blow to Jack's dream of literary glory and a return to centrality. Plus, he now owed the publisher the money he'd been living on for five years.

But then everyone agreed that there'd been a miraculous recovery. Suddenly the old Jack, the old Mitzi were back: they always had a swagger to them, a charisma, and a happiness, an ebullience. Most people seemed to put this as happening somewhere early in September; it was as if that ship, which seemed to have vanished, had arrived at long last.

What could have happened? Bob wondered.

He wished he could get back into the house, maybe look more carefully at appointment books or calendars for that time period. Once he'd penetrated the safe, that's all he'd cared about and he'd concentrated on it at the expense of everything else.

Fool! Idiot! Making mistakes! Sloppy, old, stupid, eyes not working, brain asleep.

He tried to think what to do with the information. He could go over the information from the safe again, for the fiftieth time; he could go over the notebooks again, thinking perhaps he'd missed something; he could log on to the Internet and call up newspapers from the first week in September on the possibility that it was something out there, in the real world, that had left a mark that he could understand and link to them for a clearer picture; he could go through the biography a journalist had written about them and check to see if something in their past happened around the first and they were celebrating—but that one was dumbest.

He was so tired. It was time to go to bed. His mind was blurring; he was getting nowhere.

But he couldn't tear himself away. Silly as it seemed, he had to run it out. He got out his laptop, logged on to Google. He thought he'd just Google randomly for a bit, *Jack Strong/Mitzi Reilly/September*, and see what he'd get. He got nonsense. Nothing, crazy, insane, lots of refrains of some song or pieces of doggerel poetry like "Try to remember, it was the kind of September, when we were mellllllowwww," whatever that was. He jumped through the listings, and then something caught his eye on about the seventh screen under the listing O. Z. Harris, an obituary, from the *Chicago Tribune*, page D15, with the lines blackened ". . . and was the author of four books, including *Radical Romantics: The True Story of Jack Strong and Mitzy Reilly*, a 1997 biography."

He called it up.

The headline read RADICAL JOURNALIST O. Z. HARRIS, 81.

He read,

> Oscar Zebulon Harris, a Pultizer Prize–winning journalist who challenged the system and earned renown for his integrity and intrepidity, particularly in the '60s and '70s, died Wednesday after a long illness.
>
> Harris, 81, better known as "O. Z. Harris" and "Ozzie" to the many young writers who admired and loved him, covered the American left over many years and worked for, among others, *The New Republic*, *The Nation*, *Mother Jones*, *Rolling Stone*, and finally his own newsletter, called *Ozzie's Oz*, a famous muckraking journal that took on the powers that be.
>
> Frequently called an agitator and, in a different age, an activist, Ozzie was as

prickly to his enemies—usually the Justice Department, four Republican administrations, the Department of Defense, and the Department of the Army—as he was loving to his friends, which included a generation of progressive journalists and activists.

His reporting on war crimes in Vietnam won the Pulitzer Prize in 1967 and he was the author of four books, including *Radical Romantics: The True Story of Jack Strong and Mitzi Reilly,* a 1997 biography.

He died September 3.

According to his own wishes, no services will be held and his body was cremated. Donations on his behalf may be made to the American Civil Liberties Union.

The Cook County Department of Public Administration warehouse was west of the city, even beyond Oak Park, in a town near O'Hare called Franklin Park, full of tidy bungalows and Italian, Mexican, and Korean restaurants, tracing the demographic tides that had flowed outward from the big town. It was flat, out here, and so far gone the skyscrapers that contributed to America's second-greatest skyline were unseen. Trees filled the little crosshatched streets off the main drags, but the drags themselves were the usual run of strip malls, chain restaurants, the odd old free-standing restaurant, even a racetrack with an imposing stadium abutting it.

Washington and Swagger found the nondescript old factory building on Mannheim Road, in an area zoned for light manufacturing, each building separated from the others by Cyclone fences with barbed wire discouragement up top. They turned off the busy Mannheim, pulled through a gate, earning admittance on the power of Washington's police ID, found parking, and went through a green door to a grimy office with a counter.

What brought them there was Bob's call to Dennis Washington, Washington's to the coroner's office to learn the hospital in which Harris had died, followed by Washington's visit to that establishment. The hospital kept careful records, and it became clear that over the last months of his life, Ozzie Harris was regularly visited by his friends and comrades Jack Strong and Mitzi Reilly and nobody else. Washington did some quick, casual interviews, found a few people who remembered and all agreed that the old radical really came to rely on Jack and Mitzi, who in turn had treated him with respect and love. He remained "Mr. Harris" to them, never "Ozzie," as everyone else called him.

The clerk eventually noticed Bob and the imposing Washington and ambled over with a melancholy weight to his movements. It wasn't much fun, Bob thought, working among the aisles and aisles of unclaimed property of the dead; most of it, according to statute, would remain in escrow against claims by long-lost relatives for six months; then it was auctioned, and what remained went to the burner.

Washington flashed ID, laid the death certificate out, and the clerk toddled away, returning with a key attached to a necklace that wore a metal disk upon which H-1498 was stamped.

"Go on in, Detective. It's pretty self-explanatory; you just follow the rows to H, then go down the shelves till you get to unit 1498. The key opens the padlock. I'd take a mask; it's pretty dusty in there."

"Thanks," said Washington, and he and Swagger headed through the big double doors into a kind of cathedral of American stuff, a huge, darkened brick room that was crosshatched by a wooden latticework that supported Cyclone wire dividers.

Ozzie Harris didn't have much, as his life had clearly not been about stuff. There was furniture, surprisingly Victorian, bags of old clothes, Oriental lamps, rolled-up woven rugs, an ironing board, a small TV that was probably black-and-white, various cheesy appliances like a microwave and a toaster, an old Mixmaster, a juicer, a crate of cereal and laundry products, surely burner-bound, an old bike, a Barcalounger, a state-of-the-art 2003 computer and printer from some clone outfit, tons of books and magazines, six filing cabinets, a ratty set of golf clubs from happier days, the inevitable framed photos of world events Ozzie had witnessed or written about, speeches he'd given, conventions he'd covered, great men he'd loved or despised.

They worked. On hands and knees, bent over the material in poor light in a cocoon of drifting dust in an airless room, they patiently processed all that was before them. The books took the longest, and many of them had notes or underlined passages that had to be examined and determined to be text-related, not secret messages. The photographs had to be probed for things folded and hidden, the files had to be gently exhumed, each sheet quickly examined.

Many were articles, razored out, dumped in manila folders indexed by various outrages: Racism, militarism, sometimes whole drawers like Vietnam '64–'67, Vietnam '67–'70, Vietnam '71–'75. There was a file of erotica, surprisingly mild, mostly drawings of women in tight latex lingerie that pushed their breasts and buttocks out plumply and had highlights from unseen illumination glowing on them; many were tied, all were made up, with bright red cupid lips. Then too there were files of acceptance letters and rejection slips, fan notes from kids, letters from lawyers threatening libel suits or political opponents expressing disappointment or outrage or sucking up. A whole file was full of mash notes from celebs, mostly second-tier movie lefties. There was a file of letters from students wanting Ozzie essentially to write their papers for them or at least do the research or—

"Hey, Sniper," said Denny, "hey, come lookee here."

He was lying under the box spring, a tough fit for such a big fellow, and his suit coat spilled open, showing the Sig 229 holstered to his belt.

Bob scootched and knelt and wedged, and saw where Denny's rubberized finger pointed: inside the box spring frame, toward the end of the structure, four yellowing strands of Scotch tape peeled away from the wood, drying out in the arid atmosphere. Each one showed one end that suggested being torn or twisted loose.

"It looks like he had something taped here. And judging from the yellow color of the tape, for a long time. Then recently someone pulled whatever was there loose, breaking and twisting the tape. I make it to be four by four, about."

"Yeah," said Bob. "I wonder if there's prints on the tape."

"Well," said Denny, "I will mark it down, and if we find something corroborating, maybe I'll get an actual search warrant and come in with technicians, and we can check the tape for prints. Be interesting if Jack Strong's prints showed. There'd be your proof he took something. I don't know where that would lead you, but you'd know Jack had dug through all this, at least."

Bob looked at his watch. They'd been at it over three hours. He had a couple of drawers to go.

Bob went back and tried to find renewed vigor as he plowed through the details of the old lefty's life, but it had never been new to start with and stayed old all the way through, although a file of letters from angry readers showed some life: "You fucking commie bastard, they ought to hang you from a lamppost. All you Reds will get your day of the rope, you just wait." But even the craziness grew boring, and none of the letters—the signed ones, as most bore the signature A Patriot or I Gave to My Country—displayed a name that suggested anything or led anywhere.

Agh, he thought. What did you expect? You can't do this sort of thing on the quick with a buddy helping out. This is what the FBI is for, to go through this stuff, run it down, track it, read it for fingerprints, analyze the forensics, do the dozens of tests, the magic stuff they do. You are stuck in the year 1948, and this is an obsolete black-and-white movie where the detective finds the Big Clue in some dusty old file.

But he didn't find the Big Clue.

"Well, I guess we crashed and burned."

"I guess we did."

"Okay," Bob said. "Nothing here. Nothing here at all. I'll call the feds and see where we are. You were great, really."

"No big deal. Semper Fi, all that shit."

"All that shit."

Washington rose and then said, "It is kind of funny though, a guy as red as this guy, so kill-the-rich and power-to-the-people and all that bullshit, of course he saves a letter from his broker. His broker! Can you imagine?"

"They're all like that," said Bob. "Look at Strong. He's secretly trying to get a roll together, not to pay off his debts but to take off and live big like the millionaires he'd execute if he became, God help us, the big boss."

But then he thought, why wasn't the letter in the files with all the other crazy shit?

"Where did you find it?"

"Oh, it was folded up in *Das Kapital*. I don't know why it was there."

Bob thought, that is odd. That is unexpected.

"What did it say?"

"Nothing. It was just a recommendation of stocks for him to buy, sometime in 1972."

Bob thought, nowhere else in all this shit is there any expression of interest in the stock market, any interest in capitalism except how to destroy it, any relationship with a broker, any connection to anything that isn't somehow political—for Ozzie, whoever he was, was like Jack and Mitzi: a total creature of politics.

"You didn't find any other letters like that?"

"Nah. Some guy in New York."

A New York broker.

That set off a tiny alarm in Bob's brain, from somewhere in his own past.

"You have the letter?"

Washington went to the case, bent, found the thick spine of the book, pulled it out, pulled out the envelope, and began to hand it to Bob.

"No, no, just look at it," Bob said. "The guy who sent it. Was his name Ward Bonson?"

Washington looked.

"Give the man a prize. He's a mind reader."

"Jesus," said Bob.

"Why? Who the hell is Ward Bonson?"

"At one time he was the highest-ranking Soviet penetration agent in the Central Intelligence Agency. In 1972, after he'd left Naval Intelligence and before he went to work in the CIA, he was a very successful Wall Street broker, just waiting for the Agency to come and lap him up, which of course it did soon enough."

"You knew him?" asked Washington.

"I killed him," said Bob.

Nick resigned every day at 8:30 a.m., and every day at 8:30 a.m. the director turned him down.

"I am not going to let those bastards tell me how to run the Bureau," he said. "Get back to work. *Bust* this thing for me, Nick. Now. Soon. Fast."

"We're trying."

Nick gave him a daily summary after the resignation ritual, on any given day reporting the task force's progress along its new lines of inquiry: of the ninety-six new suspects, Task Force Sniper, with its additional manpower, had eliminated over forty-one. But there were sixteen of that first already-vetted group who demanded more careful attention—reinterviews, records checks, travel and time line indexing, overseas liaison—and there were still over fifty to go who hadn't been looked at at all.

Meanwhile, the scandal refused to go away. Usually things in Washington blow over as new news cycles demand new material, but the reporter David Banjax was clearly on a hot streak as he chronicled the life and times of Special Agent Nicholas Memphis, the hero and goat of Tulsa, Oklahoma, who now ran the Bureau's sniper investigation. Banjax was given a quarter of the *Times*'s front page to tell the story of Nick and his first wife, Myra, whom he'd paralyzed and married. While some saw it as a human interest story that made Nick look like a prince, many others saw it as another example of Nick's misjudgment, of his emotional cloudiness on the issue of snipers and sniper victims and the discipline and potential tragedy of the figure of the law enforcement marksman.

Then there was the issue of Nick's "breaking" of the Bristol, Tennessee, speedway armored car robbery a year ago, in which, allegedly, the special agent had penetrated a violent mob, interdicted and destroyed a robbery attempt in progress, kept civilian casualties to a minimum, and apprehended the bad guys, all of whom now languished either in prison or in the graveyard (six had been killed).

But even that heroism, in Banjax's telling, had its downside. Some sources gave all the credit to an unidentified FBI undercover operative who had done the actual penetrating and gunfighting. Nick had come along late and taken that man's credit—so unfair to the unknown hero, who couldn't be ID'd even now as, quite possibly, he was undercover in another caper. And looked at carefully, the episode itself had a sloppiness to it that made its ultimately happy disposition seem somewhat arbitrary, if not out-and-out lucky. If the conspiracy had been penetrated, why did the feds wait until the robbery itself to spring the trap? There were hundreds of shots fired at the jam-packed Motor Speedway venue, and only by the grace of God did they not kill or maim anyone. The public safety emergency also cost local law enforcement millions of dollars (to say nothing of the trauma of the wounds to several of its officers, plus the cost in medical and recovery expenses); couldn't that have been avoided? It was also alleged by some, bitter at the Bureau's high-handed treatment of the locals, that the real object of the Bureau's enterprise, a professional killer who used the automobile as his weapon of choice, had escaped and still roamed the world, free as a bird. And finally there was the issue of a helicopter, shot down by an FBI sniper under Nick's command. Again, only luck, or so it was charged, prevented a catastrophe; that crippled aircraft could have fallen from the sky onto a home or a bus or a school or a hospital just as easily as it fell upon the empty seats of the Bristol Motor Speedway, resulting in the capture of the pilot and all the personnel of the Grumley gang. Why didn't Nick have to answer to that?

Still another day, Banjax reached and interviewed one Howard D. Utey, former agent in charge of the Bureau's New Orleans office, who'd also been Nick's supervisor during the bungled attempt in Tulsa. Utey, now a professor of public safety and police science at a community college in Ohio, told how Nick's poor judgment resulted in the botched shot in Tulsa and the escape of a wanted fugitive later in New Orleans during the furor over the assassination of a Salvadoran bishop, an event never really satisfactorily explained and occasionally brought up by enterprising reporters in search of an easy, sensational feature.

In short, Nick was emerging as the kind of bad-penny agent who had had a hand in a lot of disasters and yet, somehow, kept his career marching ahead, as if supported by men in high places with a secret agenda.

It was on just such a day when Ron Fields, Nick's ever-more-grumpy number two, sat alone in the Cosi's on I Street, just down from the Hoover fortress, nibbling disconsolately at some garish salad concoction, when he looked up to see someone vectoring in on him with a raptor's hunger. It was the girl agent, Jean Chandler, his partner in the raid on Carl Hitchcock's abode that had broken the case wide open, or so they'd thought, weeks ago. He didn't want to talk to her. He was depressed, he had a headache and a long afternoon ahead, and Nick had seemed even more uncommunicative that morning. Plus, spontaneous meetings between old stars like him and newbies like her were to be avoided, for a lot of reasons: he didn't want it said he was mentoring her, which would mean he was ignoring the other juniors; still worse, he didn't want rumors of an extra-hours connection, much less a sexual liaison, which scuttled careers fast in the Bureau's puritanical halls. But at the same time he couldn't be rude.

"Starling," he said, nodding, "imagine seeing you here."

"Isn't this a little low-rent for a hotshot like the great Fields?" she said, somewhat insouciantly, for the AIC/SA relationship was an extremely tricky one, part colonel/lieutenant, part Hemingway/Mailer, part Jeter/Cabrera, part Conan/Andy.

He smiled tightly.

"I usually eat in the cafeteria," he said. "It keeps me humble, which is hard given my natural state of magnificence."

"Look, Special—"

"You can call me Ron, Starling, at least out of the office. We raided together, we've sat twenty-five feet apart in the same office for the past six weeks, despite the glass wall between, and I mean that literally not metaphorically, as I'm sure I'll be working for you shortly, and we've worked the same endless hours. So I won't wreck my career if I'm seen talking to you."

She slid in.

"It's said you've already wrecked it by hanging on with Nick. You could have gone to the director and unloaded on Nick. You could have watched as they sacked him and, if you played your cards right, replaced him."

"Anyone can succeed by betrayal," said Fields. "It's time-honored, a beloved Washington tradition. I'm trying to do it the old-fashioned way, through ass kissing and dumb obedience. I do tricks. I'm the Lassie of the FBI, haven't you heard? Now, I have to say, I have a suspicion you didn't follow me for the classy banter; you're here for a purpose. I'm a detective; even I could figure that out."

"I wanted to talk about Nick."

"You mean 'Poor Nick.'"

"He is getting royally screwed. They say he's finished and he'll take you with him. Maybe me. Now, I don't matter, because nobody's shot at me yet, but you and he have been shot at a lot, and it's no good that you guys get taken down in some political influence shitstorm."

Fields made a show of being not impressed by her passion.

"That's the way it goes in this town. He's fighting the power: you got lobbyists for big rich, you got three departments who want to hang a 'case closed' sign on it and walk away, and you got the press. Those are tough odds. And in the end, we serve at the whim of the director. So far, he's holding fast, but yeah, the pressure is mounting. If he decides to cut us free, wave good-bye as we drift out to the horizon, that's the town. You have to get used to it."

"I wish I could."

"Seriously, you've done good work. Let me look around and see if I can place you somewhere. Oh, I know—in Fairbanks, going after Sarah Palin's daughter for breaking curfew. How about the pirate porno squad, you know, enforcing those 'fines up to $250,000' for illegal showings of *Debbie Does Dallas 32*?"

"No, I don't want to leave. I want to get this guy, whoever he is, Carl Hitchcock or not. I want to put him away. Or kill him. Maybe he's one of the names in the notebook we haven't cleared yet. I'd like to be there when he goes down."

"Me too. That's why I'm sticking."

"Here's what I'm asking: why can't we *do* something? Do we just have to take it? Can't we find *our* reporter? Who'll tell our side and make Nick look good?"

"You're so young, Starling. You must actually believe in justice or something fantastic like that."

"I do."

"Let me tell you what's going on, and why this one is so touchy. We are fighting the narrative. You do not fight the narrative. The narrative will destroy you. The narrative is all-powerful. The narrative rules. It rules us, it rules Washington, it rules everything. Now ask me, 'What is the narrative?'"

"What is the narrative?"

"The narrative is the set of assumptions the press believes in, possibly without even knowing that it believes in them. It's so powerful because it's uncon-

scious. It's not like they get together every morning and decide 'These are the lies we tell today.' No,
that would be too crude and honest. Rather, it's a
set of casual, nonrigorous assumptions about a reality they've never really experienced that's arranged in
such a way as to reinforce their best and most ideal
presumptions about themselves and their importance
to the system and the way they've chosen to live their
lives. It's a way of arranging things a certain way that
they all believe in without ever really addressing carefully. It permeates their whole culture. They *know*, for
example, that Bush is a moron and Obama a saint.
They *know* communism was a phony threat cooked
up by right-wing cranks as a way to leverage power to
the executive. They *know* Saddam didn't have weapons of mass destruction, the response to Katrina was
fucked up, torture never works, and mad Vietnam
sniper Carl Hitchcock killed the saintly peace dem-
onstrators. Cheney's a devil, Biden's a genius. Soft
power good, hard power bad. Forgiveness excellent,
punishment counterproductive, capital punishment
a sin. See, Nick's fighting the narrative. He's going
against the story, and the story was somewhat suspi-
ciously concocted exactly to their prejudices, just as
Jayson Blair's made-up stories and Dan Rather's Air
National Guard documents were. And the narrative
is the bedrock of their culture, the keystone of their
faith, the altar of their church. They don't even know
they're true believers, because in theory they despise
the true believer in anything. But they will absolutely
de-frackin'-stroy anybody who makes them question
all that, and Nick had the temerity to do so, even if

he didn't quite realize it at the time. That's why, led by brother Banjax and whoever is slipping him data, they have to destroy Nick. I don't know who or what's behind it, but I do know this: they have all the cards, and if you play in that game, they will destroy you too."

"Why can't we simply destroy the narrative?"

"Starling, it's everywhere. It's all things. It's permanent. It's beyond. It's beneath. It's above. It's in the air, the music, the furniture, the DNA, the blood, if these assholes had blood."

"I say, 'Destroy the narrative.'"

"I say, 'You will yourself be destroyed.'"

She achieved a particularly cute and fetchingly petulant look, so totally charming that he fell in love with her until he remembered he had a wife and three kids.

"So you think it's hopeless?" she asked.

"Starling—Agent Chandler, Jean, *Jean*, that's it, right? Jean, listen, you do not want to get involved with these birds. They are smart and in their way they are ruthless; they will smile at you and charm you and look you in the eye, and for something they believe is the Truth, they will cut your heart out and let you bleed out in the sun. You do not need that. You have a bright future in a job you were meant to do, and if Nick gets the ax and if I get the second ax, that's the way the ax falls. You go on with your career and put a lot of bad guys away and don't get hung up in this stinking town. Nick's gone, sad to say; I guess I am too, sad to say. You do not owe us a thing; you owe that cornball lady with the blindfold and the weighing pans in her mitt. She's the one you owe, not us. I say again, old goat to young babe, do not get involved in this. It can only destroy you."

"If we could somehow find its weaknesses. It must have weaknesses. In its very arrogance, there have to be weaknesses. We can't just—"

"It can only destroy you. This is Dead Man Talking: it can only destroy you."

25

From the Franklin Park warehouse, they took Mannheim to the Eisenhower and headed east in light, late traffic toward downtown, which loomed ahead like some glittery city of the future, idealized by darkness and dramatic lighting. On either side of the highway, the dreary flats of west Chicago told a different story.

Then Washington left the expressway, taking the South Pulaski exit, heading toward the precinct house on the South Side. He cut diagonally across the grimmer parts of the city, stop-and-go all the way, through old neighborhoods, under the el tracks, down old Chicago boulevards, because like all cops he knew the secret, speedy rivers in the city's traffic map. Finally he settled on South Kedzie as he found less traffic and gunned toward the South Side, which lay beyond the Adlai Stevenson Expressway ahead.

As they drove through the night streets of Chicago, Bob told Denny Washington the strange and twisted story of Ward Bonson, naval intelligence star, brokerage king, CIA executive, and Russian mole, and how he, Bob, had tracked him through the deaths of Donnie Fenn, his wife's first husband, and Trig Carter, prince of peace. How it had finally, so many years later, become time to hunt for Donnie and Trig's killer; how he had tracked Bonson and left him smeared on a wall in a Baltimore warehouse.

"Whoa, Jesus. Man, you are a *player*. I had no idea you were anything but a broken-down NCO," said Denny. "That is *all right*, Jack. Swagger, sniper, operator, counterintel genius, world-class detective, outsmarting the professionals."

"I ain't no genius. I just had the motivation. In his way, he killed Donnie. So Donnie didn't die in the Vietnam war, he died in some spy game that this motherfucker and his clown brothers dreamed up. I tracked down Donnie's killer and turned him to splatters. Justice don't come often, but now and then it shows up for a second or two, helped along by a good trigger finger."

"Okay, Gunny. You tell me now what to do. We'll get this thing figured out and between the two of us, we'll run these fucks to earth, I swear. I'm on your team from here on in."

"You're a good man, Denny. Few enough of you guys left, sad to say. Nick's another and they're trying to ruin him. Anyhow, here's what I see. This letter"— still untouched by anything except fingers clothed in rubber gloves, now bagged and marked as Chicago Police evidence exhibit no. 114 and riding inside Bob's pocket—"is a coded message. It's an instruction from a Soviet agent, Ward Bonson, to Ozzie Harris, who was either a subagent or some kind of sympathetic freelancer or agent of influence under Bonson's area of responsibility. I guess they got to know each other in Washington in the late sixties, when both were involved heavily in the antiwar movement, though from different sides. But it turned out they were on the same team. So somehow in 1972, Bonson sends

Ozzie this letter, possibly in response to a letter from Harris. I'm guessing it's the book code, which means it's indexed to something easy to come by but impossible to penetrate if you don't have the key. It has to be the New York Stock Exchange results for the date of the letter. They ran in every newspaper in America, and Harris would have no trouble getting them. So we have to find them, and run each of Bonson's recommended stocks down. Maybe it's as simple as first letter, maybe it's a progression of letters, maybe it's last letter; anyway, it has to be fairly simple. So we decode it. Maybe it refers to this thing, maybe it refers to someone like Jack and Mitzi. Then we'll see where we are."

"That's good," said Denny, "but we have to keep it in evidence. I've already risked chain of custody with it by removing it, but I want to get to the station, log it in to evidence in the minimum amount of time—since we logged out of Unclaimed Property at 11:04, I can get it logged in by midnight; I think that'll stand up to any court scrutiny—then you can work on it at the police station in the duty room. There's a computer terminal—"

"I'm sure I can dig up the stock listings from that date somehow, even if I have to buy an old copy of a newspaper—"

"Oh, I'm liking it."

"Then, if it's something we can use, I can call Nick and we bring in the Bureau."

"And if you can't reach Nick, tell you what. I'm friends with a real good county prosecutor. This is a Chicago homicide, after all. These are Chicago people they gunned down. We'll run it by Jerry and maybe he'll take on the case. It sounds like it could go big if it's played right, and he'd know how to play it right."

Up ahead, Bob saw the brown mercury vapor light of the entrance to the Stevenson Expressway, a little Jetsons architecture here in the derelict section of Chicago, a construction built of concrete and machine corruption. A green sign pointed to Gary and Indianapolis, but Washington hummed ahead. The car slid under the overpass, then found itself in traffic, and came to another overhead, the ancient trusses and rivets of an el station. Rain had begun to fall lightly, scattering the light points ahead into glittery red-green stars.

"Good thinking," said Bob.

"Oh, and one other thing," said Washington, slowing as a light went suddenly to yellow and he knew he wouldn't make it, while another car suddenly slid by on the left, also halting. "There's also a possibility—"

The first bullet, passing through windshield, smeared a quicksilver maze of fractures and hit Washington in the eye, destroying it, blowing his head backward and filling the air with arterial spray.

26

Tino was the driver, Rat the shooter. Both were good at their jobs. In their midtwenties, handsome, amply tattooed, muscular, scarred, well dressed, with beautiful teeth and glossy rolls of oiled black hair, they'd come up through the Almighty Latin Kings, South Lawndale division, at one time ruling the gang's heaviest hitters, known as the Chi-town Two Fours for their locality, which was Twenty-fourth and Drake. But the two were ambitious, without scruple, cunning and hungry, a dangerous combination. Their reputations approaching legend in gang-related street violence, they knew that the gang universe had its limits; they made contact with a guy who knew a guy who knew a guy in the outfit, and they segued into the occasional mob hit.

It was quick, clean stuff. Tino tracked the vic, cut him off, and Rat put him down, car to car, usually a subgun, sometimes a shorty twelve. Tino was good with cars, had a genius-level reflex time, while Rat had that hand-eye thing in spades, which meant if he saw it, he put lead in it, fast. They didn't make mistakes, they didn't leave witnesses, and the payoffs were surprisingly generous. They hit debtors, they hit strong-arm boys, they hit witnesses, they hit Insane Maniac Disciples who'd crossed the line, they even hit a cop or two. They rapidly became known as the best in Windy, and were thinking about taking their talents nationwide, maybe flying around for guest-starring spots in wired towns like Miami, Cleveland, Detroit, even New York, though of course LA was the real center of the world as far as they were concerned, but they'd have to work out something with MS-13 before they went partying in that town. They knew you do not fuck around on MS-13 turf without MS-13 permission up front, or those crazy fucking Salvadorans will stick pliers up your anus and pull your entrails out through it an inch at a time for a very, very long weekend's worth of dying.

This one looked almost too easy. The vics were a cop and some out-of-town cowboy guy, whatever, and they didn't have a thought in the world that today would be their last. They were just cruising without security or even much in the way of attention paying, and the very good intelligence came from Tino's man Vito, who repped the outfit on the South Side and had go-betweened for Tino many a time. Vito was good, solid, dependable; he owned a restaurant and wasn't no pimp or drug lord but just a courier from the shadowy higher organization that made the big decisions and set the big policies and negotiated the rules with the various players.

Tino stole a car and picked Rat up and they met Vito behind Vito's pizzeria at eleven that morning. Vito handed Rat a grocery bag, heavier for its size than it should have been, and Rat felt something dense and mechanical and tubular and awkward slipping around inside. It felt like something for a plumbing job. Were they going to fix a toilet?

"Swedish K, they call 'em," Vito said. "You can run a chopper, right?"

"If it shoots, I can run it, Vito," said Rat. "Remember, I am an artist with a Mac-10. I paint pictures with a Mac."

"Artist my ass. This fuckin' thing is bigger than a Mac-10. Client provided, client insisted, to be returned to client. It's got a silencer, which is why it's so big. Untraceable. It's some kind of spook shit. Let me tell you, do not fuck this one up, as these customers know their business and seem to have the kind of connections that turn your mouth dry and I don't want to have to give them bad news."

"They scare you, Vito? They must be some heavy motherfuckers. Nothing rattles them."

"The heaviest."

He gave them the drill. They were to get out on the Eisenhower to Franklin Park, off Mannheim, to the Cook County unclaimed property warehouse.

"I know it," said Tino. "My mamacita bought me a bike at auction there."

"You ain't looking for bikes," said Vito. "It's a cop Impala, gray-black, plate number K599121, you got that?"

"Got it," said Tino, who had a talent for numbers and could remember anything.

"You follow them back into the city. It's best to wait till they get to the South Side, which is where they'll head. You drive careful, Tino. Stay far back, don't rush or do anything stupid. I'm told these guys, or at least the cowboy, is tricky as hell. He's done this kind of work, on both sides. You up for this?"

"Man," said Rat, who'd peeked into the bag and liked what he'd seen, "I am up for anything with this cockroach killer."

"Don't force it. Be grown-up. You follow 'em from a long way off, you wait till they're in traffic down here, 'cause the cop is a South Side precinct guy, and you set up next to them and you just go buzz with the buzz gun. Then you get out, you buzz each body. That gun shoots fast, watch that it don't run out of ammo. It's so quiet, it won't scare the squares away. But it won't draw cops to you either, that's the point. You buzz each guy, put a few in the head to make sure. Then Tino uses all that magical driving power he is known for and makes you invisible in two seconds."

"What's paydown?"

"Oh, that's the best part. You get ten long apiece."

"Ten!"

Even on a cop, that was very nice.

"I told 'em, you were the best. These guys are hard but fair. You don't need to know nothing now, and I ain't giving you no advance because you'll spend it on whores and Ripple, but you do this job clean and you will make many friends and set yourselves up nicely."

"It sounds easy," said Tino.

It was easy. They made the car in the lot and parked across Mannheim and down the block a bit. There was even a temptation to go in, hit them in the warehouse, the last place they'd be expecting it. But Tino argued no, because then what was his part in it?

When the vics emerged it was after dark, so Tino and Rat got no good look at either. They were just shapes, blurs, targets. It was better that way.

Tino watched as the Impala took Mannheim south after a daring cross-lane left turn from the lot, highly illegal but something a cop would think nothing of. That maneuver accomplished, the Impala built moderate speed, and Tino fell in two hundred yards behind, no problemo. The traffic was light and he had no trouble maintaining the distance until the vics hit the Eisenhower and took it toward downtown, again through moderate traffic at reasonable speed. The Eisenhower could be a bitch at rush hour, jamming up for miles and miles so that the fabled skyline never seemed to advance at all and it was hard to predict the way the traffic would break and squirt in segments, so you could have some trouble keeping a tail. But that never happened and the cop held in the second right lane at fifty-five, never deviating, never jumping lanes, just droning along two hundred yards or so ahead.

He even, so helpfully, signaled about a mile in advance of the turnoff at Pulaski; he signaled again when he turned left off Pulaski and then still again in another mile when he turned right down Kedzie, running through gang neighborhood after gang neighborhood, running through territory Tino and Rat knew well.

"When he passes the Stevenson," Rat said, "another three blocks there's that el station overhead, it's always a choke point. He'll stay in the right lane, we'll breeze by and drive him into the el supports, and I'll put the heat to 'em. Then you left and right, hit Granada, and it's just a shot back to the Stevenson. We'll be home before eleven."

"It sounds good," said Tino.

Rat slid over the seat into the rear, arranging himself against the door behind Tino. He wanted maneuvering room. "When I say, you punch down the window. Try it."

Tino hit the button and the right back seat window hummed down, admitting a blast of fresh air. Then Tino raised it.

"Good," said Rat.

He slipped the gun out of the grocery bag, beholding it for the first time. It looked like it felt, like some enterprise of plumbing, a joinery of pipes and tubes at right angles. It was, moreover, a kind of powdery green. A bolt riding a spring pronged from the right-hand side of the main tube, just behind a cartridge ejection port; what made the thing look funny was that the tube didn't diminish into a barrel, as on most guns, but continued, thick and long, for another full foot out, giving the whole apparatus a front-heavy look. Beyond the ejection port, that long run of tube, that was the "can," as the silencer was called, Rat knew. This was a high-class, well-engineered professional tool, dedicated to exactly one purpose—the silent, fast extermination of the designated. He picked it up and realized that its wire stock was folded alongside. He peeled it backward by the leather-encased top strut through spring pressure, finally prying it loose, and it snapped into place, the stock fully extended. He reached back into the bag and came out with three mags, each dense for the size because each was loaded with thirty-odd 9mm cartridges, and at the top of each mag, a single cartridge was imprisoned and displayed in the lips of the magazine. Making certain it was oriented correctly, Rat eased a magazine into the housing, gently lifted it toward its destination, and felt it lock in place. He turned the gun sideways in his hand and drew back the bolt, feeling the slide of lubricated machined metal against lubricated machined

metal and the increasing tension of the spring until a
click signaled the bolt was set. He knew the gun was
of an older type like a tommy called an "open bolt
gun," meaning you simply locked the bolt back to fire
it, and when you fired, the bolt rocked in its groove,
and when you let the trigger up, it collected itself at
the end of the groove, ready to go again. He bent close
to it, found no safety lever anywhere on the primitive
firing mechanism of trigger and rear grip, and realized
that a notch cut above the bolt groove, where the bolt
could be lodged, was the safety. Man, they built 'em
simple-simon in those days.

The gun cradled in his arms, his right hand
locked around the wooden panels of the pistol
grip, his right thumb resting in the nexus between
magazine housing and barrel, his trigger finger
indexed along the receiver over the guard, Rat
mentally rehearsed his moves. Tino pulls up by
the still car in the right lane and cranks hard to the
right, pinning it, at the same time hitting the down
button on the right rear window. Rat scootches over,
favoring the left half of the window to give him
an angle into the car. He never bothers with eye
contact or target marking; not enough time, he's too
close, these guys are too good. He raises the piece
and stitches the first burst right to left, driver to
passenger, across the windshield. He tried to imagine
the details so they wouldn't be shocking to him and
disorient him when they occurred: the spitting of the
spent brass, the *chug-a-chug* hydraulic sensation of
the bolt reciprocating at killing speed in the receiver,
the muzzle flash blowing holes in his night vision,
the stitchwork of punctures as the burst ate its way

across the windshield, turning the glass to lace and frags, all this at a time much faster in the happening than in the telling of it. Then quick out, put a burst into the driver's head, then step aside to get an angle and put a burst into the passenger's head. Then back into the car and Tino drives him off.

His reverie was interrupted.

"Okay," Tino said, his lips dry, his tongue dry, his breath dry and shallow, "just passed under the Stevenson. I see the el tracks ahead, I'm accelerating to catch up, they seem to be slowing down in the traffic, the light is changing."

Expertly, he maneuvered the stolen vehicle through traffic, cutting a guy off, peeling through a gap, spurting into the oncoming lane, then back again, closing the distance on the unsuspecting Impala, which was itself slowing for the yellow-to-red light that impeded its progress.

"They've stopped, don't have to hit them," said Tino.

Rat held calm, felt good, had no trouble breathing, marveled at Tino's grace behind the wheel, and the seconds rushed by. Suddenly they were even with the vehicle, then a little past it as Tino jammed to a halt just exactly where he should, and as Rat slithered forward on the seat, the window magically sank into the door, and he raised the gun to find a perfect angle on the driver and he thought, Eat *this*, motherfuckers, as he pulled the trigger.

27

Banjax reached Bill Fedders at nine, as Fedders had become his ex-officio counselor, his Deep Throat, if you will, but also his adviser, his mentor, his confessor, his priest. Banjax explained what was happening and sought Bill's advice on whether to fish or cut bait. Go for it—Bill knew in a second—but he was smooth, he knew well enough to keep the greed out of his voice, and so he did a number on the young reporter, all wisdom and gravitas and admonitions to the ethical side of the equation, but in the end, he felt confident he'd made the sale, and he sent Banjax off on his mission with enthusiasm high.

Then Fedders poured himself a stiff Knob Creek in a crystal highball glass, let the bite of the bourbon blur a little as the ice melted, yelled upstairs to his wife that he'd be up in a second, went to his Barcalounger in front of the fire, and placed a call to Tom Constable's private number.

"Can this wait?" said Tom, clearly in the midst of something energetic and interesting.

Bill took great pleasure in responding. "No," he said. "Not really. You'll want to hear it."

"Okay," said Tom, and the phone was set down at his end as various arrangements were made, until finally he returned.

"This better be good. She was worth every penny

of the thirty-five hundred dollars and I don't know if I can get back to where I almost was."

"You will, Tom. Trust me. You might even surpass yourself."

"Let's hear it."

"Well, it seems that brother Banjax, ace reporter that he is, has just gotten a very interesting tip. It could be the end of our problems with Special Agent in Charge Memphis."

"He has hung in there a long time."

"The director likes him. Everybody likes him. But not after this."

"Go ahead."

Fedders savored his drink, letting the mellow glow spread.

"It seems that maybe Memphis isn't the boy scout everybody thinks he is."

"Interesting," said Tom.

"He may be dirty."

"Very interesting," said Tom.

"Now the one thing the FBI needs is sniper rifles. They're in the lengthy proces of acquiring three hundred new ones. These rifles are traditionally built by the custom shop at Remington; they're something called a Remington 700. A special barrel is mounted on them, a special scope, special ammo is used, all that stuff, and they're guaranteed to shoot, hmm, I think it's angle of minute—"

"Minute of angle," corrected Tom, the world-renowned hunter. "It means very accurate."

"Yeah, well, although the contract isn't big in monetary terms—less than a million—within the gun industry it's considered a big prestige thing. Remington has had it for years, and on account of the FBI's belief in the product, they've become the preeminent sniper rifle supplier to police forces and military units the world over. That million-dollar contract is really worth twenty million annually; it also feeds civilian purchases, because so many of these gung ho gun guys want the rifle the FBI uses, for their hunting and targeting and whatever. Maybe to play sniper themselves, who knows."

"So?"

"Well, there's a European firm called FN. It's part of the Belgian government, actually; FN just means 'National Factory,' and it has been making guns for a hundred years, and now they make a lot of our machine guns and stuff. But recently they bought up what was left of the old American firm Winchester, which produces a gun called the Model 70."

"I have a dozen. Very fine guns, the old ones at any rate."

"Yes, well FN has started manufacturing Model 70s again at a plant it built in South Carolina. Now if FN could get the FBI sniper rifle contract from Remington to replace the 700 with the 70, it would be an incredible coup."

"What does this—"

"Nick Memphis, an ex-sniper, is on a committee to pick the next rifle. It seems there's some internal feeling that it's time to shake things up by going to the FN product, and according to Banjax's source, Nick is in the forefront of that move. Now, it turns out he accepted an all-expenses-paid trip to South Carolina—"

"Good God, I can see selling out for a trip to Brussels, but *South Carolina!*"

"Hard to believe. But they flew him down there to talk to the big shots at FN, which is a big no-no without prior executive permission. It seems also that there's a long track of 'gifts' made to Agent Memphis from his good friends at FN that may well be in violation of FBI guidelines. There's lots of receipts for dinners at a local Ruth's Chris and some mysterious checks for a place called the Carousel. And here's the best part: there may be—and Banjax has a line on it—a photo of Nick at the FN range in South Carolina, with the new FN rifle; there's even a date visible in the picture, if you blow it up, because he's holding a target where he's just fired a .321-sized group, or whatever, and signed and dated the target."

"Where did all this come from?"

"In my opinion, it came from Remington. These guys play rough and they are very worried about losing this contract. So they hired a security firm to monitor the process, and one of their guys evidently came up with it."

"So, Memphis is dirty. The Bureau can't stay with him then, right? He's out, he's gone, he's history."

"He's definitely history."

"And the *Times* will run this story?"

"They're way out ahead of everyone, and in that business, that's the greatest thing. They can feel it so close it's driving them nuts with desire. A scoop. A big, government-humiliating, career-wrecking scoop. That's how Pulitzers are won. Corruption and misjudgment, sniffed out by a vigilant press—it's the cocaine that makes them insane. You're damn right they'll run it."

"So that's the straw that broke the camel's back. Or the rifle that shot out the camel's spine."

"That's right, Tom. When Banjax gets the photo and it's vetted by the photo experts the *Times* hires, we'll have him. Memphis has to go. And I'll make sure the next guy is more cooperative."

28

Swagger hit the floor hard amid a spray of glass sleet from the windshield as the burst atomized the glass, a bullet flying so close by his neck he felt the breeze. He wedged himself low into the cave under the dash, thanking God he'd forgotten to buckle up for safety, hearing the bullets bang hard off the hood, the engine block, back again to the windshield as the gunner dumped his mag into the vehicle. He blinked hard to force himself to face the reality of what was happening, knowing that if he stayed there in the fetal curl on the floor, the gun boy would come out, stick the snout of his subgun through the window, and dump the next mag entirely into Mr. B. L. Swagger, late of planet Earth.

Inspiration came from—well, who knows? God? Intelligent design? A hundred previous gunfights? The obviousness of what was before his nose, which was Denny's gigantic foot resting on the gas pedal? Swagger craned upward, spun the wheel against Denny's dead hands hard to the left, then elbowed Denny's dead foot, pushing pedal to floor. The car leaped and, as the distance was short, built no killing momentum, but still it hit the killers' car on the oblique with a clanging charge of energy, enough to spin Bob himself almost backward against the seat.

But now he had a plan, and a man with a plan is a man with a chance. He reached up, pushing Denny's jacket aside, and plucked the Sig 229 from his hip holster, unsnapping it and making sure to pull it straight out, duplicating the draw angle so that the sights wouldn't get caught in the holster and no security device would pin it. Out it slid, and now he had a plan and a gun, and he had his opponents possibly in a daze from the unexpected smash of car one into car two. He squirmed back to his own off-driver's-side door, hit the latch, and tumbled out. Crawling madly down the length of the car, ripping knees and hands to shreds on the pavement, he emerged over the right front wheel well, putting tire and heavy axle and brake system as well as engine block between him and the killers, and saw the enemy car at an angle, slightly askew, its door caved and wearing his own car's left front as its new fashion accessory. A figure behind the wheel struggled with his seat belt, clumsy from the shock of the collision, mind a stew of confusions.

Bob found the Sig a blocky little piece of gun-craft that fit his hands glove-smooth and went to target hungrily; he locked his elbows as he put the front sight smack on the target twelve-odd feet away, fired four times on the angle and watched as the windshield fogged into quicksilver as the penetrating bullets left their legacy of fractured abstraction. Behind those smears, the dark figure kicked taut, then slumped sideways.

Bob withdrew, and a good thing too, as in seconds, maybe nanoseconds, a burst of automatic fire came hurtling his way to spall off the hood and spray randomly into the air, chewing up metallic debris, paint dust, and friction-driven sparks. He saw now what was so strange about all this—the absence of the other man's percussions, as his weapon was clearly suppressed. The bursts had a low, wet, rattly sound, as if made by a child playing at tommy gun with a throatful of phlegm.

Swagger started to rotate right, to get around the bumpers of both cars, flank the shooter, and take him down from the low defilade, even as he knew that if the guy was no idiot, he too would now be on the move, rotating also to the right. So he stopped, reversed his direction, and began a journey to the left, the long way around, to find and kill his man.

Rat watched the bullets take out the windshield and all behind them in a long sparkly rip, right to left, horizontal, but had a kind of inkling of disaster as the dancing web of punctures didn't seem to catch up quite to the rapidly disappearing number two target. He realized he should have gone left to right, goddamnit, and cursed himself for fearing the cop's handgun more than the agility and quickness of the unarmed but highly experienced man. He ate up the rest of the magazine—once you start shooting these things it's hard to stop, so seductive is the rhythm, the power of the recoil, the imagery of the world dissolving before the godlike reach of your bullet stream—shooting out more windshield glass, tearing up the hood, hoping to start a fire or send something through to take out the quick mover, but he knew: Houston, we have a problem.

The gun ran dry. If he'd more experience, he could have dumped the empty in a second and been back on target in the next, but he wasn't sure where the mag release was, and by the time he got it tripped to drop the empty box, found another, heavier box, got it inserted and locked into place, he raised his eyes just in time to experience astonishment.

The Impala piled into their car. The clang sent him thundering against the door, and the gun slipped from his grip. Holy fuck, where'd that come from? Spangles, fireworks, flashbulbs, all kinds of optic disturbance filled his tiny, concentrated mind, and he had to head-shake hard to get himself back to reality. He reached, felt for the gun, got it up, checked intelligently to see if the mag was still locked in place, checked again that the bolt was back and locked open, and came up to rejoin the fight just in time to blow his night vision on the four fast, bright muzzle flashes of his guy firing across both hoods through his front windshield, where dazed Tino struggled with seatbelt confusion. Too late for Tino; the bullets found him in chest and head, and Rat felt the hot spray of blood splattering from a high-velocity impact on flesh as Tino made some indecipherable sound of regret and slumped to the left like a sack of apples. Rat got the subgun—now it seemed so long—up and oriented in that direction and squeezed off a burst that ripped hell out of at least three panes of thick auto glass—his own right front, the guy's left front and, going through and out, what remained of the windshield; the bullets left a galaxy of spatter-pattern fissures as they flew, and many hit the hood where the other shooter had been but was no longer, spanging off in a spray of sparks and pulverized auto paint.

With his elbow he knocked the handle on the door behind him and spilled out. He hit the ground, gathered himself quickly into a shooter's crouch, and looked for targets. It was so quiet. All street sounds had died, all traffic had stopped, the many civilians had frozen or slunk away to let the players work out their gun drama on their own. For the first time in his life, Rat felt fear. His bowels almost came loose and the ice water that he'd thought filled his veins churned into his lower colon instead.

This guy was a pro. He was so fucking good. How could he get to guns so fast? Usually when the bullets flew, even the most hardened cops went into a kind of daze and it took seconds, sometimes minutes, before they were functioning efficiently, and it was in that gap that Rat made his living.

But not tonight.

Move! he ordered himself, rising slightly, again peering over the horizon of shattered glass, bullet-pierced vehicles, drifting smoke, and lights diffused in the drizzle for a target and saw none. He realized: he's coming to get me, meaning he'll be coming around the front of the locked cars, and when he gets to my bumper, he's got cover and I don't.

That got his ass moving. He scrambled left down the side of the car, dipped behind its tail, and felt vaguely secure, when the second brilliant idea hit him.

Shoot under the car.

He dropped to his knees, inserted the K under the car horizontally and squeezed out an arc of 9-mil, the gun spurting, the muzzle flaring, the bullets digging up dust and earth from the pavement as they swept right to left in search of the legs of the other man. Surely they'd take him down hard, and Rat could advance from the rear, put some finishers into him, and disappear down an alleyway. He wondered, Will I get Tino's ten long?

But the gunman wasn't crouched behind the car. His legs were not available for Rat's strategy. Instead, guessing it, he'd climbed upon his own hood, and in six agile steps bounded over his own roof to his trunk, where he stood above Rat, whose gun remained planted underneath the vehicle.

"Drop it," he said, though both were aware that Rat could no more drop it than he could drop his trousers, and as Rat pulled back to free his weapon, the tall cowboy shot him three times expertly in the chest so fast it sounded like he was the machine gunner.

The shots hit like hammer blows and scattered Rat's mind. He thought of all kinds of extraneous bullshit and had a kind of memory dump as half- or quarter-images from his twenty-six years fluttered through his brain like a fast shuffle of cards, and the next thing he knew he was choking on blood and looking into the close-up face of his slayer, who pressed the gun muzzle hard into his throat, to fire the spine breaker if that were necessary, though both realized by now it wasn't.

"Go to hell," said Rat.

"No doubt," Rat heard the reply, "but not before you."

Gunsmoke and silence hung in the air.

Swagger kicked the machine pistol further under the car, where the cops would find it.

He walked around the tilted Impala, looked in and saw Denny, ruined head back against the headrest, eyes unblinkingly open, blood like a broken bottle of wine down his shirt.

"I'm so sorry, Captain," he said to nobody. "You were the best; you deserved so much more. I swear to God there will be justice for this."

Then he reached into his pocket, made sure the plastic bag with Ward Bonson's coded letter to Ozzie Harris was still secure.

He stood. All along the street people were emerging from shadows.

Now what?

If I stay, I'm hung up in Chicago cop paperwork for a week, and these bad guys hunting my ass know exactly where I am. I have to give up the letter and wait for the Bureau to save my ass, assuming the Bureau, meaning Nick, *can* save my ass.

If I disappear, I have no resources, I am probably wanted as a witness, I am fleeing the scene of a crime, though I didn't commit it, and there will be questions to answer for months when and if we finally get this goddamn mess settled.

But there is one thing I can do on my own that I can't do in police custody.

I can hunt.

With that, he fired a shot in the air, to drive the peepers back to cover, turned down an alley, and was on the next block in total darkness before he heard the first siren.

29

Late night DC, traffic down, the city full of shadows, even parking available, most of the food joints that depended on lunch trade closed, few pedestrians. David Banjax found a space on the street, wandered around the buildings along Fifteenth Street between M and K, noted that the one on the southeast corner belonged to the competition. It was some seventies monstrosity, characteristic of the horrors of Big Paper architecture the world over. The places, even his own, all looked like midrange insurance agencies, both inside and out these days. At any rate, he kidded himself that they were working late at the *Washington Post*, maybe trying to keep up with him and the Sniper scandal. But they never would. He was so far ahead.

He walked around the corner, past a Radio Shack and a Korean lunch joint, and turned into a parking lot entrance, a wide, descending driveway, in the corner building, which adjoined the *Post*. It was deserted but not dark, and he wound down the spiral two levels, past a helter-skelter of the medium-price sedans that reporters and copy editors preferred, until he finally reached the bottom. He didn't like it: no escapes, not that there should be any danger. Still, his breath came hard, the air tasted icy, his lungs felt too small. He licked dry lips with a dry tongue. Are you sure this is how Bob Woodward got his start?

In a row of cars ahead of him, headlights winked

on and off. He made his way to that vehicle, a Kia, clearly a rental, and made out the figure of a man in the front seat, behind the wheel. David nodded, the figure nodded back, but at that moment, across the way, an elevator door opened, a blade of light penetrated the dimness, and a couple of people walked out, laughing. David dropped between cars and waited as the two made it to a nearby car—"He actually thought 'disinterested' meant 'uninterested'! He must be in his fifties! How stupid is that?" he heard—climbed in, started up, and pulled out. Copyreaders! The same everywhere!

When the car had disappeared, David approached the mystery vehicle and noted with both approval and a chortle that the man was wearing a fedora and a pair of Wayfarer sunglasses. He opened the off-side front door and heard a voice say, "Rear, please, that side. I will look at you in the mirror. You do not look back; keep your eyes down."

Now the convening literary master seemed to be John le Carré. It was turning into a spy novel. Wasn't this the part where the pawn gets murdered by a silenced .22? Or does the pawn miraculously escape the assassination, go on the run, and somehow still bring down the government and put the bad CIA cell in prison and win the Pulitzer Prize and write a best seller, all in 350 pages.

He obeyed.

"This is a little melodramatic, isn't it?"

"Look, pal, I don't need snark. I know you people like wisecracks, but stow the fucking wisecracks and be dead literal and we will get along a lot better. This isn't a fucking movie."

"I understand."

"Throw the tape recorder in the front seat."

"I—"

"Throw the tape recorder in the front seat."

Banjax threw the tape recorder in the front seat.

"Now throw the other tape recorder in the front seat."

"Hey, I—"

"Throw the *other* tape recorder in the front seat."

Banjax threw the other tape recorder in the front seat.

"I may have to prove this meeting took place, you know."

"I didn't turn 'em off. I'll return 'em if I conclude you're straight and that I didn't give something away I didn't mean to give away."

"Okay. Sensible. Now what have you got for me? And who are you?"

"Who I am is not relevant. I may be this, I may be that. I may be a courier or a controller or a rogue. You will never know. But I have a gift for you, as I said I did. It's amazing how successful you're about to be on my generosity."

"I'm sure you're getting something out of it. Nothing's free in this town."

"Hmm, fast learner," the spy guy said. Then, with a kind of practiced insouciance, as if he'd done this many times, he tossed a manila envelope over the seat to the rear, and it landed exactly in the space next to Banjax. Banjax noted the man was wearing gloves.

"Okay," he said. "Should I open?"

"Not here. What you have is Xeroxes of internal FN documents, from their South Carolina headquarters, recording their courtship of, their involvement with, their bribes to, their payoffs to, and finally their comments on Nick Memphis, FBI."

"How the hell—"

"We're good. We're not amateurs. You are not dealing with self-dramatizing whistle-blowers who are trying to get a segment on *60 Minutes*. You get to go on *60 Minutes*, not us."

"How can I authenticate? I have to authenticate."

"That's your problem. Our mole didn't have time to get affidavits."

"Well, there's a time thing here. I—"

"Jesus. Let's see, you might use Freedom of Information to get FN's original cover letter to the FBI seeking submission paperwork for the sniper rifle contract trials. Then run a typefont comparison. Or I'll tell you what, since time is a factor, find someone in the Bureau to leak those documents to you to shortcut the FOI process. You pick 'em, not us; that's your guarantee of integrity. Run the typefont comparison. If you get a match, you've proven that the FN official submission and the internal memorandum came from the same printer."

"There's only one printer in South Carolina?"

"In the FN USA headquarters, yeah. How big do you think it is? We're talking a gun company, not IBM."

"Okay," said Banjax, who had no picture in his mind for a thing called a "gun company."

"So you've made your guy. Hello, Mr. Pulitzer Prize. Why, good morning, Miss Senior Editor, Big New York Publisher. Do you know who I'm talking about?"

"Yes, I know. Woodward's—"

"David is a smart boy."

"You said you had a photo."

"I do. But it's not in the package."

"Why not? If you've got it—"

"I want you to authenticate this thing first. Then you contact me by, hmm, I don't know, wearing an orange toilet seat around your neck to work one day. That'll be a spy-type tip-off."

"I'm out of orange toilet seats. Will pink do?"

"Wear a hat one day. Guys your age never wear hats. It can be a baseball cap, a stocking cap, I don't care, a Sherlock Holmes cap. Wear it, we'll note it, and you'll get the photo by courier that afternoon, your bureau. If you're not an idiot, you'll figure out that the photo has to be vetted by top photo professionals, to make sure it's legit. Can your failing newspaper afford that?"

"If I can get it before they turn the bureau into a bowling alley, yes."

"Otherwise it goes to Drudge."

"I hear you."

"David, fast, fast, fast now. We can work fast. Can you dead-tree folks stay with us?"

"Yes, I can."

"Good. Now take your tape recorders—no lookee, see?—and get out of here. Go stand in the corner while I drive away. No peeking. And welcome to the big leagues, Woodstein."

30

Swagger awoke from ugly dreams with a start. The phone was ringing. Not his cell phone, the room phone. He blinked, trying to remember. Oh, yeah, Indianapolis. Near the Notre Dame campus, for its theoretical richness in wired coffeehouses. An Econo Lodge; it looked like the best room in Nowheresville, decorated in a nice shade of babyshit brown.

He stared at the ringing monster on the night-stand. This was not good. If it had been his cell, it could have been anybody, but if it was this phone, it meant someone was already on him. On the other hand, maybe it was housekeeping. He looked at his watch, saw that it was almost eleven. He'd sacked out here at 3 a.m. after a dreary bus ride.

He picked up the phone.

"Yeah."

"Bob?"

It was Nick.

"You figured out where I am."

"We are the FBI, you know. We do this kind of thing for a living."

"I—"

"No, you just listen to me. In words of two syllables, what the fuck is going on? I have some big gunfight in Chicago with a dead officer, two dead gangbangers, and a missing witness thought by many to be an FBI undercover. That sounds like a Bob Lee Swagger operation. I have the Chicago cops, I have the Cook County prosecutors, I have my own Chicago field office all screaming bloody hell at me, and of course I have my own director furious at me because he warned me Swagger couldn't be controlled and I assured him I could control Swagger and then I assured him I'd sent you home to rock on the porch. Oh, and I have the *New York Times* alleging on its front page that I'm dirty. Hmm, I think we could agree, it's kind of a mess."

"I sure wouldn't want to be in your shoes," said Bob. "Can't help with the papers. Never read 'em. I get my news from Fox."

"I need you in. I can have Indiana state troopers at that motel in ten minutes if it's an issue of security. I need you cooperating with the Chicago people, playing by all the rules. Maybe, just maybe, we can make fleeing the scene of a crime go away. And when we get all that straightened out, then maybe we can see where we are on the sniper. Oh, and I need Denny Washington's Sig back. For his widow."

"I will personally return it to her when this is over. Right now, I may need it, even if it's only got four rounds left. Maybe I can put 'em where they'll do some good."

"Swagger, listen to me."

"Nick, if I go to Chicago I'm stuck there for weeks. I have to move fast. These people now know I'm on to them, and they will go back over their tracks and wipe everything out and I'll be left with nothing but suspicions. And when it all dies down, they'll come to

Idaho, and just like Joan Flanders, they'll put a little cross on me from a long way out and put a 168er dead bang center into me."

"Chicago thinks this was a gang hit on Denny Washington, who had busted several Latin Kings leaders on big murder ones over the past few years. He was a very good cop and he did them a lot of damage. So they targeted him and took him out. The shooters were Kings; you just happened to be in the car."

"No way," said Bob. "That's how it was supposed to look, but the signature of this outfit is that it sets up its hits inside fraudulent narratives, which you guys get roped into every goddamn time. But tell me, did you see the piece? It was a submachine gun—"

"Bob, it's a mob town from way back. That doesn't prove a thing. Every Italian restaurant in the greater metro area probably has a Thompson hidden in the wine cellar."

"This was no Thompson. It was a suppressed Swedish K, an agency favorite in the 'Nam. I had an SOG tour, I saw the cowboys with them all over the place. That's a rare piece of spook hardware, probably aren't two hundred of them in the world, put together in the late sixties by company armorers at Tan Son Nhut. You don't get a subgun like that from the wine cellar or the local machine gun store. You have got to be wired into spookworld to pry one free, ex-spook, some kind of mercenary, some kind of spec ops professional, someone in the big game one way or the other. It's exactly what Graywolf would have in its arms vault, and it's just made for maximum firepower with minimum noise, exactly what's needed for street gun-downs."

"The report just said European machine pistol."

"The Chicagos didn't know what they had. I did, because I saw it up close after the shooting. Get your weapons people to look at it, and I guarantee you they will be impressed by the high quality of the workmanship, the genius of the engineering, and the absence of a serial number or any identifying marker. That baby's as black as the hubcaps of hell."

Nick was silent.

"Nick, I have a lead. Washington and I found something that points in a certain direction. We were headed to the station to enter it into evidence. But now that Washington is dead, I've broken the chain of custody, which means it can never be used as trial evidence. It can only be used by a rogue, someone unaffiliated. Let me follow it, and before I do anything stupid, I will clear with you. But if I come in now, all that is lost, Denny Washington's death is meaningless, and what we found goes away. I can't let that happen. I want to run the lead and lay it before you. It's only a matter of a few hours doing some basic research. You keep my involvement secret, you let me operate the way I have to operate, and I will clear with you before I jump. Just cover for me a little while longer."

"See, that's the other thing. There may not be 'a little while longer.' This reporter today published some bogus documents all across the front page of the *Times* alleging that I'm on the take from some gun company to get them a contract. I may be gone at any second. Then what happens to Swagger?"

"Swagger's been on his own before."

"Swagger's been lucky as hell before. That luck will turn; it's way overdue."

"Nick, I'm begging you. Let me hunt. I will bag you something big, I swear."

"You've got six hours," said Nick, and hung up.

It took nearly the full six hours. Bob called his broker in Boise, asked how he could obtain a copy of the final stock market report from—he checked the letter from Bonson to Ozzie, still wearing his rubber gloves— September 23, 1972.

His broker didn't know of an Internet archive, but he himself had a brother who worked in a big New York brokerage and would place that call. In the meantime, Bob checked the phone book, discovered a nearby place with computer rentals, and called. They delivered an Apple MacBook Pro, and he got online from his room, checked e-mail, news accounts, read the *Times* piece on Nick—*aghhhhh!*— and got a call finally from his broker, who said his brother had suggested he try the *Wall Street Journal*, which had its pages all archived online. The broker had another client who had, he knew, a son-in-law on the international accounting desk of the *Wall Street Journal*, so through that client and his son-in-law, a tenuous but impressive skein of fragile connections all beholden to or fond of the person next to them in line, an e-mail with an attachment containing those pages arrived in Bob's e-mail account a few minutes later.

And the son-in-law was as good as his word. There it was. Bob held his breath because getting things open wasn't his strong suit, but he managed to do just that. As a document it would be hard to manipulate, because he could only go through one long column at a time, to say nothing of the fact that he hadn't broken the code yet. That would be the first order of business.

It turned out to be the easiest thing he did that day. Bonson, all those years ago, was a very busy man and kept his professional espionage communiqués simple and the codes hiding them even simpler; he knew that was how far under the radar he was, even then. So what looked like a simple letter containing a list of stock recommendations was instead organized to yield a message, once the key was determined and the pattern figured out. It had to be simple, so that a man without training could piece it together.

It was. His pattern was a backward regression. Thus the first stock recommendation in the letter, ITGO PAK, yielded a *K*; the second, AMJWEL, an *E*, the third, KOMEST, another *E*, and the fourth, NOPINC, a *P*, for a first word of *keep*. This went on a few progressions, then, as the stock abbreviations were necessarily short, began again, usually on the fifth letter. Bonson, rushing, even made some mistakes. But three hours later, Swagger ended up with

> Keep item secure. It may prove useful later.
> Do nit share any hint of it with anybody,
> and don't not release to press, no matter
> how it clears clients.

The clients? "Clearing" them? Would that be Jack and Mitzi, and would "clearing" them have some reference to the bank robbery, with two guards shot dead, that they were suspected of committing? So did it mean they were *not* guilty of that? That proof would be a nice thing for them to have, even at this late date. It would open a lot of doors. The item? What could it be? He realized he'd have to go back and read more carefully about those days to even come up with a guess. But whatever it was, Ozzie Harris, in his travels through leftist America in the early seventies, somehow got hold of it. He held it. For years and years he held it. Possibly he contacted Bonson again over those long years, and Bonson could see no use for it and continued to order Ozzie to hold tight. Eventually, as Bonson joined the Agency and began his rise, and his career of careful betrayal, he may have forgotten about it. Or maybe he was saving it for some reason, with some great goal in mind. But then he ran into one Bob Lee Swagger and ended up looking all Jackson Pollock—except for his legs—on a metal warehouse wall, and if he'd been controlling Ozzie Harris all those years, he'd left that one thing undone. Ozzie, dying ten years later, knew all along that it had major bearing on the case of Jack Strong and Mitzi Reilly. In the end, only Jack and Mitzi had been there for him, and Bob saw how it would be of use to Ozzie in "clearing" them, and so he told them about it, maybe gave them the key to his apartment, and they'd gone to the place, looked under the bed, reached up into the structure, and Jack had yanked it free of the four yellowing strands of Scotch tape that had held it in place for so many years.

But when they realized what it was, they also realized it somehow had value. Great value. Somehow, it could be used to leverage millions of dollars to them, a lot more than "clearing" them ever could. That was the game they had tried to play, possibly seeing it as their reward for long years of service to the cause but not seeing how dangerous it was. Typical of the type: they love the violence of the game but can't believe it will ever turn, as it always does, monstrous and eat them alive. Whomever they had tried to leverage was such a monster and decided on a different course. He didn't want to give them the money; he gave them, instead, a bullet in the head in their broken-down Volvo in the alley behind their soon-to-be-foreclosed house. And this monster, whoever he was, found it so important to him that he not be connected to the case and that he obtain the whatever it was, the MacGuffin, the whoozie, the whatsit, that he buried that enterprise in a larger, camouflaging enterprise, a false narrative about an insane marine sniper, who'd snapped when he found that someone else had more kills in 'Nam. And he'd hired the best mercenaries in the world to make it go down just right. Joan Flanders and Mitch Greene were assholes, sure, but guess what, nobody's asshole enough to end up like that, with a 168er punching your guts or brains out to help someone keep his dirty little secrets buried. And Carl and Denny, even less did they deserve their parts in the drama; to this guy, they were just action-movie extras the hero blows away, without names or pasts or lives. He was protecting himself; he had money, he had juice, he had influence, he was part of this whole thing and always had been. There was only one man it could be, because there was only one player on the board big enough to make it all happen. And that would have its own set of terrible problems to solve, formidable obstacles to climb, penetrations to be made, confrontations to win. But Bob couldn't bring himself to say the name and face those challenges yet. It filled him with depression and it sucked his energy: so far to go, so hard a trek. Instead, he looked at his watch and saw that it was time to call Nick. He knew he had to do it fast or he'd decide against it and instead go hunting again, as in the old days.

He picked up the cell, dialed Nick's number. Not only was there no answer, there was no voice mail.

That was odd.

He tried again and found the same, tried three more times. Finally he called the general 1-800 FBI number, waited for a human to arrive after two minutes of robo-voices, got an operator and asked for Special Agent Memphis. He was transferred to what had to be a ten-year-old intern and told that Special Agent Memphis wasn't available. Would he care to leave a message? Bob thought a second; then he said, "Give me, uh"—what was the name?—"Special Agent, uh, Chandler, I think it's Jean Chandler."

Clicks, pops, silence, at least no Muzak.

"Chandler."

"Special Agent, this is Bob Lee Swagger—"

"Swagger! Where are you? Everybody's trying to find you."

Nick hadn't told anyone. Would she have time to set up a trace on the call? He guessed not, then second-guessed himself and started to hang up, then third-guessed himself and decided he had to know and he could bail out fast if it came to that.

"Ma'am, I'd prefer not to say."

"You have to come in. We need you here."

"I am not out of control. I told Nick I wouldn't do

a thing without his say-so. I will stick to that. May I please speak with him?"

"I'll call you back."

"I'd prefer to call you back. You're not tracking me? You're not setting me up or nothing?"

"We don't operate that way."

"Give me a number and a time. I'll call you tonight."

"I won't track you, Swagger. I have things to tell you and you have things to tell me. This is not a good place for a conversation."

Christ, she was stubborn!

He hated being at the cusp of the decision, but he remembered his earlier conversation with her and how she'd seemed to adore Nick. So maybe she was still on Nick's team.

He gave her his cell number, knowing that she'd already written it down from the caller ID feature.

He left the room, looked for a fire escape, found none. He went back to the room, went out on his balcony. The motel backed onto fencing and an alley, now deserted. Through trees, some kind of university structure was visible. But no one could see him. Groaning, remembering how the limberness had seemed to lessen with each day he aged, he pulled himself from the balcony railing by way of the gutter and got to the roof. His hip still ached a little from an old wound, then a bad cut in Japan, but he made it. No one saw him. He went to the front of the building, looking over the parking lot and the busy avenue. If cops came, he'd see them come and could maybe, somehow—

The cell rang, some absurd ringtone, out of vaudeville. Had to get a new one.

"Swagger."

"Nick's been benched," she said.

"Jesus."

"It's not formal. He didn't have to turn in his badge and gun. It's not a suspension. The director said he would appreciate it as a 'favor' if Nick went home while the *Times* story was the big news in town. The idea was he would not be suspended and have to turn in his things, nothing goes on the record, but at the same time, he would take no part in Bureau business until the situation clarified. He turned in his cell phone and the key to his office and went home at three; he is officially out of the loop for now, while Professional Responsibility investigates these charges the *Times* has raised. He will be interviewed sometime next week. So he can't be called, he can't be consulted, he is officially out of the game, and if you reach him somehow and try to talk, you compromise him, and I know you don't want to do that."

"No, of course not. He's not dirty. For God's sake, you know that. He's not dirty."

"I agree. However, the *Times* claims its experts have matched fonts on two letters, proving the incriminating one came from this FN outfit in South Carolina. That's why you have to come in. You may have to talk to our investigators and give a deposition on your arrangement with Nick and make them see that he can't be dirty. If you avoid that, you do him no good at all."

"Oh, Christ."

"You won't help?"

"It's not that. It's that I found a piece of evidence in Chicago that's very suggestive. Unfortunately, because of that gunfight, it got taken out of the chain-of-custody linkage. That means you folks can't never use it. I have to follow up on it, because only a rogue can do that, and I have to do it fast. This is a fluid situation, the people behind this are very clever, and now that they know I've made a connection to them, they will retrace their tracks, wipe them out, wipe the slate clean, make sure no evidence, no witnesses, no anything survives. I was trying to move against them before that could happen."

"You cannot 'move against' anybody, Mr. Swagger. You are not authorized, you have no arrest powers, you are not an FBI agent. I know you're a lone wolf type, but you will only screw things up. Please, for Nick's sake, come in here and make yourself accessible. You have friends here, people who knew about and remember Bristol. Take advantage of that goodwill; don't squander it on cowboy stuff."

"What happens to the investigation during all this headquarters bullshit?"

She hesitated for a second, her silence a harbinger of bad news.

"A new temporary supervisor to Task Force Sniper has come aboard. He's a headquarters guy, and his job is to smooth over things. We have been directed to prepare the report for release to the press. The report finding Carl Hitchcock and Carl Hitchcock alone responsible for the murders of Joan Flanders, Jack Strong and—"

Swagger felt the floor of his stomach give out. He had a dizzy flash, then a headache.

"I thought you'd agreed the baked paint debris on the weapon indicated—"

"There will be an appendix dealing with other possibilities. As yet, we've interviewed over seventy-five new persons of interest and come up with nothing concrete. We have Chicago and Ohio and now the New York State Police telling us to declare the case closed."

"So he wins?"

"Who wins?"

"You know who."

"No sir, I don't."

"Of course you do. Only one man connected to this thing has the power, the influence, the ruthlessness, the—"

"Swagger, listen to me very carefully. That kind of thinking has no place in modern law enforcement. We work from facts, not theories. We let the facts point to the guilty. If we have theories, they twist the way we see the facts. So far we have not turned up one fact indicating that someone else is behind this. No matter what you surmise or what seems conspiratorially logical to you by the rules of too many movies, we cannot and will not operate that way. Let me further warn you that any action you take to investigate or intimidate a private citizen, a rich one or a poor one, a violent one or a passive one, a professional or some Joe on the street, may well be viewed as assault, and it will be prosecuted extremely aggressively, if the Bureau has anything to do with it."

"There's a campaign to ruin Nick. You know it, I know it. To ruin him because he bought into my

read on the case and made time to run it out. Someone hated that, couldn't allow it, and set out to destroy
him. So right now, ma'am, it looks like his only chance
is me, not you. I don't know what you headquarters
people are doing. You're just letting somebody rail-
road your best man, and it ain't right. It is not right,
I don't care what the law says. Now tell me, please,
confirm for me, who is behind this campaign against
him? I know you've examined it."

"I am not able to share any investigative product
with you, Mr. Swagger. No names, no information.
It's for internal use only."

"I have—"

"You don't have anything, Swagger. The Bureau
will take care of Nick fairly, I guarantee you. If you
go off on some crusade, you lose our protection. As
it is now, Nick's last official act was to call the Cook
County prosecutor's office and inform them that the
missing witness was undercover FBI and therefore
should not be identified and pursued in alert bulle-
tins. You're a free man now because of that decision,
which frankly I think is a bad one. Don't do anything
to hurt Nick, to make him look bad."

"Someone's got to protect him. You guys aren't
doing a goddamn thing, it sounds like."

"Look, just be cool. If you won't come in, go to
ground. A week is going by with nothing happening.
It'll take that long for us to polish the report and for
Professional Responsibility to run checks on Nick and
the FN fonts to see if this holds water. On top of that,
you respect our rules, by which I mean you have no
information whatsoever that's actionable, no name

has popped up, you can identify no suspects, and anything you do is groundless and can only end by screwing things up. You stay put. Do I have your promise?"

"Same deal. You don't have me arrested, I won't jump without clearing it by you."

She moaned.

"Swagger, you are a bastard."

"I am, but I'm an honest one, Agent Chandler. If it comes to it, I will move aggressively to right this wrong, inside the law I hope, but outside it if necessary. I ain't telling you no fairy tales, young woman. I am a sniper and I will go about my business the sniper way."

"A week, or I cut papers now and make you number one on the hit parade."

"A week then. Dammit, you drive a hard bargain, young lady."

"A week," she said. "By the way, that gunfight? Great shooting, Sniper."

31

The hat seemed redundant as well as ridiculous. The story appeared today, featuring the confirmation from a bonded legal document master that the FN proposal and the FN internal notes came from the same printer, thus verifying the internal notes as being of FN origin, so what was the point of the hat? But the guy had said a hat, so Banjax wore a hat, an old Yankees cap. He had a moment of unease; the Redskins had just been creamed by the Giants, and maybe that idealized scrollwork *NY* on the blue cap would get him beaten up by an angry mob of notoriously volatile Redskins fans from, say, the hard guys at CNN or *USA Today*—he laughed at his own joke—but in seconds he saw that there was no particular brand loyalty on the streets of DC, as everyone wore a hat of his own choosing, from some kind of knit Afghan cap to stockings to baseball caps pledging allegiance to teams from all over the world. There was probably one from the Tehran Mud Hens.

He arrived late to the bureau, as befit a star. He actually didn't like big story days, because he was somewhat self-conscious; he preferred to not appear when he had a big one riding above the fold. But he had to be here, and so he made the most out of his victory lap, modestly accepting the congrats that came to him, the looks of admiration, the winks and thumbs-up. Still, he had to admit, it was pretty cool, though not quite as cool as when his editor told him the document master had confirmed that both docs had come from the same printer and that page one was taking the piece. He'd been so lucky; Will Rashnapur, who covered the Justice Department, had a Bureau source and had been able to get a Xerox of the original FN proposal quickly. That was the hang-up and it could have taken weeks, but whoever it was delivered within twenty-four hours, so the freight-train momentum of the scandal was maintained.

He sat at his desk and began his ritual. First, he turned on his monitor and onlined the *Post*, the *LA Times*, the *WSJ*, the *Tribune*, and none of them had caught up, although on its Web site the *Post* had rushed a denial from the FBI PIO and another no comment from FN, as if gun companies *ever* spoke with the press. He checked Drudge and was gratified to see "Paper—FBI Agent in Snipergate took free air, steaks and a night at Carousel from gun boys." He Googled "Sniper Nick" and got a thousand hits, the first fifty of which were simply repeats of an AP follow-up that some poor schmo had put together at 4 a.m. after the *Times*'s first edition broke on the Net.

Someone lurked. He looked up; it was Jenny Fiori, the TV liaison.

"Okay, hero," she said, "take your pick. Matthews, Olbermann, or O'Reilly. More audience at O'Reilly, but he'll just call you a commie and yell at you. More prestige at Matthews, but he won't let you finish your sentences. Olbermann will be the most fun, unless his leg starts twitching, at which point he turns nasty. Some dweebs at CNN also want you, but that doesn't look like much. I'd go with Matthews."

"I like Chris. He's okay. You can't get me off cable and onto one of the big networks? Katie? Brian, that guy—"

"The nets don't give you enough time and New York frowns on them. It's usually about making the anchor look smart. You can do any of the cable from here with our hookup, or just go over to Matthews, it isn't far."

"Okay, sure, Matthews."

"Great. I'll get it rolling. Hey, what's with the hat? Are we trying to be colorful now?"

"Uh, no, I forgot I had it on." He shucked it.

He checked his phone messages. Oh, so fun. His agent, "Call me." Two other agents, including a famous one. The local station, WRC, for a nooner, the girl should have gone through Jenny and could be safely ignored. Someone he knew at *Esquire*, someone at the *Atlantic*, someone at *TNR*. A couple of FBI-hating civilians. Someone calling him a rat.

Then he went to e-mail. Over seventy, not bad.

"Way to go," said Anthrax, of New Orleans.

"You the man," said Jefferson, of Florida.

"Did you discuss this with God first?" wondered a Mrs. Salatow, of Cape May.

"You red shit," observed ex-PFC, from North Carolina.

"Why are you tearing down the FBI?" wondered Gordon. "Do you want the terrorists to win?"

"You're doing a great job, David," said Bill Fedders. "Call me if you need any more help."

And on and on it went, the queue lengthening even as he tried to read through it all. Finally it was too much.

Time for lunch.

"Killer, join us?" said a colleague. "Thai, that little place on K."

"That'll be fun," he said, pulling on coat and hat.

"You're a Yankees fan? Never would have guessed."

"Yankees, baseball, right? Where they hit that thing with a club?"

Then they saw he was being ironic and laughed, and off they went and had a fine, merry lunch.

He got back late, again okay for a star. He ran the afternoon blogs, saw that he had heated up the boys at Power Line but was a god on Huffington, and the Daily Kos seemed close to declaring him a new religion. Calls from some tag-along foreign pressies—Australian, Japanese, Dutch, the Swedes and their pals the Danes—all wanting to do phoners. Ho-hum. Another call from WRC, a call from NPR, some woman who claimed she'd met him at a party.

It was almost time for the 4 p.m. meeting, and no, nothing had—

"Oh, David, this came for you, meant to drop it off earlier," said Judi Messing, who administered the office as its receptionist.

He took it. Big envelope, manila. He breathed hard.

Okay, maybe so.

He felt it; yes, there seemed to be a sheet of photo-thickness paper inside.

"David, the meeting. Don't be late," someone called, rushing past. "They'll be singing your praises."

"I can't come. Something just came in."

He saw all the reporters gathered in the confer-

ence room and the assistant bureau manager running the show, with the big man himself off to the
side, hiding behind those half-lens reading glasses
he'd affected for twenty-odd years. David watched
through the glass, as if observing a pantomime, while
each boy or girl self-promoted his or her own stories,
and the great man handed out nods of acceptance or
frowns of denial. There was a lot of laughing, as there
always was, as the very smart people who constituted
the office enjoyed each other's company, camaraderie,
shared values, sense of irony, dedication to professionalism, and, of course, ambition.

He felt above it.

I have transcended, he thought.

Now it was time. He looked around—nobody
nearby; someone taking dictation; someone on the
phone, too busy to attend the meet; Jack Sims, noto-
rious curmudgeon, boycotting as he had famously for
twenty years; researchers sitting at their screens still
grinding away; yadda yadda, the same old. God, he
loved it. It had taken most of his life to get here, and
it had seemed so far away for so long, but now he was
actually a member of the bureau in the biggest, fiercest
town of all, for the greatest newspaper that ever lived
and breathed, and he counted, he was one of them, he
was part of it, he moved, he shook, he influenced. Yet
for an empire it was a seedy palace: it looked, to continue with the customary metaphor, like a second-tier
insurance company branch office, decorated in early-
twentieth-century political posters. Some trophy front
pages also hung about, but mostly it had the industrial
cheeriness of the New Office Interior Design, littered
with piles of crap, stacks of crap, pieces of crap, little

doohickeys that reporters always got sent, for some odd reason, and a few morale-boosting quotations taped to the walls from men like Breslin, Mencken, Liebling, and Baker, the latter of which was the most helpful:

> Q: Mr. Baker, what do you do when you write a column and it's just not there, you know, you just haven't done it right, it's not very good, you know it's not your best?
>
> A: Publish it.

David always got a smile out of that truth. Anyway, now he opened the flap and slid the paper out, seeing that yes, it was a photograph, though upside down. He turned it around and his eyes drank up the details.

The first thing was the target. He thought it would have a black bull's-eye, but it was of a configuration he didn't understand: the predominant feature was a heavy black square about three by three inches in the upper quarter of the face. It lay across and occluded the top of a collection of circles within circles which seemed to form the nominal "target" of the thing. He looked at the printed label up top and made out "I.B.S. Official 300 Yard Bench Rest Target." Whatever. The sheet was mounted in a frame of some sort. The bullet holes actually weren't in the center of the circles or in the box either, but just off the box at about ten o'clock in the third ring. The cluster of shots had landed nowhere near the center, but the three men gathered about the target appeared joyous.

The one with the rifle was clearly Nick Memphis,

sleeves rolled up, tie loosened. He held a big gun, a rifle, with a tube along the top, an imposing-looking gadget with turrets and markings that sort of resembled a camera, if a camera were a tube instead of a box. The gun looked massive, and it wasn't the machine gun type of thing, with handles and bolts and cooling ventilation and curved magazines, but more like a hunting rifle, though somehow swollen, as if it had been ingesting steroids. It was black, like the scope, and lay against Nick's knee as Nick posed kneeling by the cluster of holes, five of them, a little constellation. Next to the cluster, as David bent and squinted to see, someone had written in magic marker, "Nick Memphis, 300 yards, FN Model PSR, .308 Black Hills 168, 1.751!, June 23, 2006, Columbia, S.C." David didn't know what the 1.751 referred to and why it bore an exclamation point. He didn't recognize the two men flanking Nick on each side, their sleeves also up, their ties loosened, each with an earphone pushed up on their heads, as were earphones pushed up on Nick's. In fact, it was like a glimpse into a strange world, maybe on a distant planet or a million years in the past or future, full of protocols that were mysterious, full of traditions that were meaningless, pride that seemed arbitrary, and most of all that big, immutable gun right in the middle, the center of it all, as if these three guys worshipped it. Very odd.

But the point was, here was visual, dramatic proof that Nicholas Memphis, Special Agent, Federal Bureau of Investigation, had journeyed to South Carolina in June of 2006 to examine FN's entry in the FBI Sniper Rifle Selection, against FBI regulations, especially, as the documents already obtained and proven authentic had revealed, at the expense of the Belgian arms manufacturing concern.

If it was real.

David leaned over as he opened his desk drawer and removed a magnifying glass bought two days earlier for exactly this purpose. Not knowing just what he was looking for, he ran his eye, through the magnified lens, over every square centimeter of the photo. He certainly saw nothing obviously fake, like a shadow going the wrong way or a subtly incorrect relationship of head to neck or a line around this or that figure or object. But who knew what they could do these days?

"Is that it?" Jack Sims asked, leaning over. Jack was of the old-professor type, usually a study in tweeds, jowls, horn-rims, rep-striped bow tie, blue Brooks Brothers button-down even though, regrettably, Brooks now had its shirts made in China, a man with whiskey breath and a memory for arcane political minutiae that was legendary in DC.

"Yeah. Jack, were you in the Army?"

"I was. A thousand years ago. No guns then, we used spears. I was in the 235th Spearchucking Regiment."

"Seriously, see where he's written '1.751' here, with an exclamation point and an arrow to the cluster of bullet holes. Any idea what that means? Is it a score or something?"

"No," said Jack, "it's not a score. Not with the decimal point."

"Could it be a caliber? Is the gun a 1.751 caliber?"

"Hmm, when I was in in the sixties, we shot

something that had millimeters. I don't know what the inch measure would be. Wait, I know a photographer who's a gun guy. For some reason photogs are gun nuts, more often than not. Maybe it's the love of small, well-machined little gizmos. Anyway, let me Rolodex his cell and see if I can get an answer."

Jack disappeared, not that David noticed, so absorbed was he in the drama of his examination, and it seemed that Jack came back in a second, when it was really twenty minutes.

"Okay," he said, "the 1.751 is a group size. In other words, the guy fired five rounds at the target and the five made up a group. They're trying to figure out the mechanical accuracy of the gun, not the shooter, and they get that from the group. So they use calipers to measure from center to center of the two farthest shots, and it comes out to be one and seven hundred fifty-one thousandths of an inch."

"Is that good?"

"At three hundred yards, that's magnificent. My guy says an inch per hundred yards is very good, so at three hundred it ought to be three inches. It's one and three-quarters of an inch. That's a wow."

"Okay," said David. "Thanks, Jack, big help. Now I get the exclamation point."

Just at that moment the bureau chief came over.

"I see you guys acting like teenage girls at the mall. Did it come?"

"It sure did," said Jack. "David's Pulitzer, gift-wrapped. He's taking the office to Morton's for dinner tonight, right, David?"

"It did come," said David, modestly.

"Okay, bring it in, we'll see what we've got."

David trekked into the chief's office, and just about everybody important in the bureau followed. He laid the photo out on the glass table as they crowded around.

"That's Memphis," somebody said.

"It sure is. Does anybody know who those other two guys are? David, was there any information with it?"

"No, Mel. It was just the—"

"Sir," came a voice; it had to be an intern. They were everywhere, ambitious little reptiles, incredibly smart and industrious, desperately wanting to eat the flesh of anyone who stood in their way. Little show-offy monsters.

This one's name was Fong, but his ethnicity wasn't Asian, it was ambition. David hated them, even though he realized he'd been one himself.

"I stopped at a gun store in Silver Spring. It's called Atlantic Guns. Anyhow, they were giving away catalogs of all the gun makers and I thought we needed the FN catalog, so I picked one up."

"Good, Fong."

"Let's fire David and give Fong his job," said Jack Sims, and everybody laughed.

"David, we don't need you anymore. Fong's here, he'll take care of things."

"Fong, you've just been appointed bureau chief in place of Mel," Janie Gold said. "Mel, can you be out of your office by five?"

When the laughter died down, they let Fong do his thing, and naturally he worked at a speed beyond the comprehension of everyone older.

"The guy on the left, see, that's a fellow named Jeff Palmyrie, head of operations, FN of America, and on the right, that's Pierre Bourre, President, FN International GMBh, Brussels. Here, look, make sure I'm right."

He put the slick paper catalog, opened to the executive page, down right next to the photograph, and yes, it was clear indeed that those were the two others in the picture.

"Did you call FN today?" asked Mel.

"No, not yet," said David. "But they'll have no comment. They've had no comment for eight days; I can't believe they'd change now."

"Still, you should do it."

"I will, Mel. Right after the meeting."

"What's the gun?" somebody asked.

"It's what they call their PSR," David said. "Police Special Rifle. I got that from the Web site. It's in the catalog too. It's a three-hundred-eight-caliber rifle. In the catalog you see the rack where they attach the telescope, yeah, but of course the one Nick is holding has a telescope. See, look, the stock, the handle, the trigger thing—it's all there just like in the picture, dead center. That's the one FN wants to get the sniper contract, and this proves they brought Nick in early, to get him on the team."

"He's not a very good shot," someone said. "I thought he was a sniper."

"No, he's a very good shot," David said. "See, he's shooting what they call a 'group,' meaning he aimed at one place and tried to put all the bullets as close together as possible. See, all of them went into a group at three hundred yards."

"Tell them what it is," said new friend Jack, setting him up with a smile.

"The point is to show off the accuracy of the gun. This one kept five shots inside two inches, and the standard is what they call angled minute or something, which means one inch per hundred yards. So if it's under three inches at three hundred yards, it's really good."

"Wow," somebody said, with the same enthusiasm with which he might have said, "My wife is divorcing me, but that's okay because I just totaled my car."

"Have you set up the photo examination?" Mel asked.

"Yes, by special courier. I'm sending it to Rochester, New York, to the Donex Photo Interpretation Laboratory, part of the Eastman Kodak system there. They're supposed to be the best commercial photo examiners in the country. We should know in a week."

"I don't want to know how much this is costing me," said Mel.

"To save some money," Jack said, "we could fire young Fong. Really, he's going to fire us when he gets the chance."

"I am not Young Fong," said Fong. "'Young' is Korean. I'm Chinese." He said it pure deadpan, and everyone laughed. The goddamned kid was funny too.

"Okay, so David, get busy on your calls. FN here, FN overseas, the Bureau, some governmental or law school ethics think tank. Hmm, Dershowitz ought to be good for a quote, maybe Schumer, anyone else?"

"GSA."

"No, they'll come in officially sometime later. Look for whistle-blowing pork barrel outfits. I've got some good numbers for you."

"What about gun people? Someone in the NRA who—"

"No, no, they'll just run your ears about the evil *Times* and how we use the Second Amendment for toilet paper," said Mel.

"I'll call Remington," said David. "They're the ones that stand to lose their cash cow. God, whoever realized there was so much money at stake? Anyhow, I've developed a relationship there and I think I can get to the president."

"Good, David, and check with Fong Young if you have any other ideas and he'll OK them," Mel said, again to great laughter and Fong's embarrassment. "Okay, meeting adjourned. Go, go, go, get away from me, I need to sneak a drink from the pint in my drawer."

Everybody filed off, and David trotted away to package the photo and begin his calls. A few people clapped him on the back, there was a punch on the arm, a thumbs-up and a wink, but best of all someone genuinely, and without irony, congratulated him.

It was Fong.

32

She was right, of course.

He sat in his motel room in Indianapolis, depressed.

Starling, the young FBI agent, seemed to have dealt him a mortal blow. You have imposed a meaning on these events. You have not discovered a meaning. And your imposed meaning stems from your anger at Tom Constable, billionaire lefty, business genius, owner of lefty networks, famous playboy and sportsman, above it all, husband to movie stars, friend of Castro, hero to millions, shit to millions of others, such as me.

The way you get Constable is simple: the man behind this thing has to be wealthy and powerful. He has connections in the government, he has immense resources, he knows everybody; in the end, he simply has the resources nobody else really does. Therefore you have assumed his involvement.

You have no proof.

It was true. Other than the marriage to one of the victims, there was not one single objective fact that connected the four deaths—five, counting Carl, six, counting Denny—to Tom Constable.

The guilty parties could have been some other players entirely—political, criminal, governmental, any entity with some power and some leverage in the spook world, and these days that could be just about anybody.

What do I know? he asked himself. Know as fact, know as reality, know as physical presence in the world?

I know somebody made very good shots to kill the four. Very good. Too good.

I know baked paint debris linked to the ceramic coating on the iSniper911 was found on Carl Hitchcock's rifle, and the iSniper911, in skilled hands, was capable of permitting the kind of shooting that took down the four.

Who knows? Maybe it was Carl. Maybe he secretly spent seven grand on an iSniper911, put it on his own rifle, did the deeds, then took it off, tossed it in the river, put his old Leupold back on, and blew his brains out. Maybe he was so titillated by the accuracy the unit offered, he wanted to claim that as part of his legacy too. If he was nuts enough to conceive of the plan in the first place, anything is possible.

Or maybe it was some other iSniper school grad, with the same anti-lefty agenda, and he just wanted to take out those bastards, but he didn't want to pay the price. So he put the thing together; he was one man; he was somehow able to do it and was just sitting in his trailer enjoying the big show. Meanwhile, as he said he was, Tom Constable was going crazy with all the speculation and he wanted to put it to an end, and being a big-foot asshole, he put a lot of pressure on poor Nick, and it had nothing to do with nothing. And again, it was just coincidence that he was in the shotgun chair with Denny Washington when the Latin Kings decided on payback for Denny's takedown of some Chi-town Two Four gangbanger now sitting in Joliet and getting cornholed each night by the Black Pagans or the White Aryans or maybe the crazy Salvadoran gang, MS-13. And the object that was in Ozzie Harris's hands was nothing of relevance to this case; and the look of Jack and Mitzi's house, its tidiness, which Denny picked up on, that was more coincidence; it was just that Jack happened to spend ten minutes straightening up that day. And the fluctuation in the mood of Jack and Mitzi? New meds, possibly?

Ach. Ugh. Oof.

He wished he were still a drinking man. The lure of the bottle was immense now. Boy, would it be nice to go for a fine dip in the bourbon pond, feel the world turn blurry and mellow, slide away greased by delight and optimism. Oh, it would be so nice now. The bottle was so tempting.

He shook his head. His hip hurt. He'd left his new painkillers in his room in Chicago, which, incidentally, he was still paying for. It was a dull buzz, not a throb so much as a grind. Somehow the sword blade—that fight seemed so long ago, in a Japan he hardly remembered—had ruptured the surface of the stainless steel ball joint, and that irregularity had cascading consequences of unexpected pain. That had to be taken care of. He was tired of the limp; he was tired of being on the wagon; he was tired of looking for conspiracies where only coincidence existed on top of bad luck and strange but not impossible occurrence.

Okay, he thought, train back to Chicago. Check out, settle up. Go to Denny's funeral. Give the Sig to the police and cooperate with them. I am guilty of nothing; it was righteous self-defense shooting and I wasn't even carrying illegally. Get your head out of the screwball conspiracy bag. Then fly back to Washington, clear it up with the FBI, and if they have made any progress, fine. If not, then that is the way of the world.

Then back to Idaho. Back to the porch. Back to the rocker. Back to my daughters, to my wife, to the world.

He called her.

"Okay," he said, "this one's over. Coming home. Standing down."

He explained brightly how he'd been mistaken and launched off on a fool's crusade, an old goat's dream. But his new plan would change all that. He told her about going to Chicago to somebody's funeral, then back to Washington to straighten things out with Nick and his people, and then he'd be coming home, for good. Gosh, it would be so great.

"Bob," she said, "I love you so and want you with me, but you are lying to me, and you are lying to yourself. I can hear it in your voice, and if you don't get it settled in a way that satisfies you, it will suck the pleasure out of the peace you've earned. I know you. You are samurai, dog soldier, marine fool, crazy bastard, marshal of Dodge, commando, the country-western Hector. You are all of those things. They are your nature. The girls and I are just where you park when you're not warring. You love us, yes you do, but war is your life, it's your destiny, it's your identity. My advice, old man, is win your war. Then come home. Or maybe you'll get killed. That would be a shame and a tragedy, and the girls and I will weep for years. But that is the way of the warrior and we have the curse upon us of loving the last of them."

"You're terrific," he said. "You help me see clearly."

"If you have a problem, solve it the old-fashioned way."

"And that would be?"

"The way your people and my people always solve problems. Hard work. Hard, hard work. Now hang up, have lunch, and get to work. Good-bye. Call me on DEROS."

All right.

It was clear now: he had to locate some kind of connection between Tom Constable and the deaths of Jack Strong and Mitzi Reilly. Something real, something palpable, something authentic.

What do I know?

I know that Strong and Reilly knew Tom Constable; I saw the picture of the four of them, Joan Flanders being the fourth, at some dinner. But that proved nothing. That proved only that in a glittery, jet-setty kind of life lived by minor celebrities, people whose pictures got in magazines, these two couples had known each other socially. That indicated nothing meaningful, mere acquaintanceship. They were both strong left; why shouldn't they have had a social relationship?

The question was, did Strong have a way of reaching Constable, an e-mail address, a special cell phone number, a contact? That would indicate something more than a casual relationship.

The second question was, how does a guy in a hotel room in Indianapolis with no powers, no contacts, no sponsorship, no authority, no resources, find that out—fast?

Impossible.

Can't be done.

It took him three minutes.

He went to the University of Illinois Chicago Circle Web site, clicked on the Department of Education, found that of course it hadn't been updated since the deaths; then he went to the departmental secretary, a Eustace Crawford, number given. He reasoned that secretaries know things, they see things, they get things. But nobody has talked to this one, because Jack Strong was never investigated; he was the victim of the obviously mad marine sniper who simply chose him for his symbolic value.

Bob made the call, thinking, concentrating, ordering himself: verb-subject agreement. No *ain't*, no *don't*, no profanity. You are some mealy little nobody who makes his living doing things for other people.

"Education, Ms. Crawford. May I help you?"

"Ms. Crawford, I wonder if you remember me," he lied. "My name is Daryl Nelson and I'm a special assistant to Mr. Tom Constable. I spoke to you many times in the last few weeks before the tragic passing of Jack Strong."

A pause indicated she didn't, but there is a certain something in people that makes them reluctant to disappoint strangers.

"Uhhh—Well, I suppose, Mr., uh, Nelson, you know it was so terrible around here, the deaths, they were such wonderful people."

"Yes ma'am, and I'm sorry to interrupt at this time of tragedy. Actually, I put this call off as long as I could."

"Yes sir. Well, I suppose, is it something I can—"

"Ms. Crawford, you know that Mr. Constable was

a friend of the Strongs, I'm sure; you've seen the picture in the house, the four of them, when Mr. Constable was married to the late Joan Flanders?"

"I have seen that picture, actually. I loved Mitzi. The Strongs knew so many people. There was something so magnetic about them."

"Yes ma'am. Well, here's the problem: Jack and Mr. Constable had a friendly e-mail relationship. Maybe too friendly. You know that Mr. Constable has a weakness for speaking his mind in public and he sometimes says unfortunate things."

"Yes. I remember that time he called George Bush a war criminal on Jay Leno."

"Yes, that sort of thing. Well, in private, it's even worse. Here's what he's afraid of—that somehow some of the private e-mails Mr. Constable sent to Jack could get into the newspapers or, worse, onto the Internet; you know all these terrible blog people. It would be very embarrassing and I don't think Mr. Strong would have wanted that."

"No, I'm sure he didn't."

"Now, I know his e-mail has a secret code, of course, a sign-in. Obviously, I don't know it. But I'm guessing, in the normal course of actions, someone such as yourself in daily contact with him might have noticed what that code was. He might have even called you and asked you to check for messages that came into that account."

"I have some idea."

"Of course I'm not at all suggesting you give it to me. What I am asking is a favor. If you could get into his e-mail account and run a quick scan or a search of some kind; you might search for 'Tom,' or you might try the name 'Ozzie' or 'O. Z. Harris,' he was a friend of theirs in bad health in Chicago over the last few months. If you come up with a batch of messages, again, don't open them."

"Do you want me to delete them?"

"No, I would prefer if you would change the entry code, to something of your own preference. Our firm will make an official petition to the university to recover them, but their existence right now is very troubling to us, and to know that the code had been changed would be a very good thing."

Don't let her say, Oh, I'll just forget the e-mails and change the code now. It's a very good idea irrespective of Mr. Constable's wishes.

But that seemed not to occur to her.

"I'll check," she said.

Two minutes passed, and then he heard the phone being picked up again.

"Well," she said, "if Mr. Constable was TomC@ Starcrostdotcom, then there were quite a few. They turned up when I searched for the Ozzie Harris name. Quite a few in fact, as if they'd been talking heatedly about Ozzie."

"This would have been in September, just around the time of Ozzie's death on September third?"

"Yes, exactly. Just to check, I did open the first. Mr. Strong was going to write a book about the seventies, and he'd found some items or relics that he thought might be of interest to TomC and he hoped they could continue their discussions, which he thought would have an excellent outcome for both of them. That was Mr. Strong, always trying to help. He had such a feeling for the underdog."

"Ms. Crawford, that's great. So you will change that code, and our conversation will be private, and I might say, you have earned Mr. Constable's appreciation. He will reach out in some way to show that appreciation; that's the kind of wonderful man he is."

"It was my pleasure, Mr. Nelson."

He put the phone down, exhausted at the effort of sounding so well-spoken for so long. But he had it. Tangible, objective proof of a contentious relationship between Tom Constable and the Strongs immediately prior to the killings. It wasn't something he'd made up, some "interpretation" that an old man who saw conspiracies in the choice of public restroom toilet paper had come up with. It was real.

Also real: "items" or "relics" of interest to TomC. That would be whatever it was that had been taped to the frame of Ozzie Harris's box spring for thirty-odd years, which now, in play, had the power to change lives and move mountains—of Tom Constable's money.

It was clear what had to happen next.

Whatever it is, Constable has it.

So I'll go get it.

33

It had been a quiet few days as David waited for the return of the photo and the report from the Rochester lab. He'd broken a minor item: his friend Bill Fedders—boy, was that guy wired or what?—had heard from somebody that Nick Memphis had a somewhat neurotic relationship with another sniper, a man named Bob Lee Swagger, who had, briefly, been the number one Most Wanted man in the country, fifteen or so years ago, and who, when the case against him for the murder of a Salvadoran archbishop was disproved, disappeared. Evidently this Swagger and Memphis had had adventures and engaged in some barely legal shenanigans, which somehow redounded with great credit to Memphis and got his career back on track.

But the point was that Swagger—"Bobby Lee Swagger," the name sounded like someone had run an algorithm on every NASCAR driver in history, Banjax joked—had somehow had a Svengali-like hold on Memphis, and maybe Nick's reluctance to push forward the case against Carl Hitchcock was some kind of psychological projection; he saw Hitchcock and Swagger as the same man, that tough-as-nails southern shooter marine NCO type so appealing to the immature mind.

"I mean, it seems funny on the face of it," Bill had told David at lunch at Morton's. "Memphis is an educated professional of great attainment, and evidently this Swagger is kind of a cowboy type, unlettered, cornball, barely a high school education, but possessing some magic charisma that certain types of people fall for every time."

"Weird," said David, who could make no sense of it at all. He hated the kind of man he sensed this Swagger to be, some kind of macho blowhard who radiated aggression and stared down every man in the room. Football captain, cop, jock, that kind of guy, hopelessly obsolete in America today, but too dinosaur to realize he was dinosaur. Dinosaurs: not too keen on self-awareness.

"But if you think about it, it makes a little sense," explained Bill. "Think of it as the puppy and the cat. The puppy comes into the household where the cat is a god. The cat can do anything—leap, fight, climb, race, hunt, kill—and he does it with utter disdain, ignoring the puppy, as if the puppy is too insignificant to notice and completely unable to ever impress him. And that is how the relationship is cemented in each mind, forever and ever. But what happens over time is that the cat grows old and feeble while the puppy grows into a sleek, magnificent animal that dominates every single transaction it enters. It has become the god. However, when it looks at the scrawny, desiccated, mangy old fleabag of a cat, with its rotted teeth and bloated stomach, it still sees deity. For him, the cat will always be the god, even if to the whole world, the cat is long past its prime and headed to the sharp end of the vet's needle."

"Maybe I could do a piece on that relationship. A holding story. To keep the scandal in the news."

"I'm sure there's not much on this Swagger. But there might be a little."

David worked it hard and came up with more myth than reality. No one had ever written a book about Swagger, and he'd never been the marine celebrity with the SNIPR-1 license plate that Carl Hitchcock had been, he was no gun show autograph seller and nobody had ever named rifles, ammo, or shooting matches after him, but it didn't take long to establish his bona fides as a war hero. He'd been a real mankiller in Vietnam, and two sources confirmed some ambush of a North Vietnamese unit heading toward a Green Beret camp. He'd won the Navy Cross for that. His kills were fewer than Carl's, to say nothing of that new guy, Chuck McKenzie, but still, he'd spent a long time in the boonies.

David shivered inwardly. These guys, where do they come from? They spend all that time alone, crawling through swamps and up mountains, just to snuff out another man's life. What was the point? What did you get out of it? It seemed somehow creepy. What was the difference, really, between them and the DC snipers, those two fruits who'd roamed the Beltway picking off people randomly while living in a car? Okay, the marine wore a uniform, but really it was the same thing—the same charge, that kick a fellow got from playing God and watching somebody else a long way out die of his own agency.

But after Vietnam the record got vague for this Bob Lee Swagger. There was a divorce on the record in South Carolina in 1975, and a few DWIs and minor scuffles with the law around the same time—drinking problem was written all over these years—and then silence, as if the guy had disappeared to re-invent himself. There was a *Soldier of Fortune* maga-zine story not available on the Internet now, because this Swagger was litigious; some Arkansas lawyer had beat the publishers of that magazine out of a substan-tial sum, and try as he could, David could never come up with the copy. Then there was that very odd busi-ness in 1993 with the Salvadoran. Again, it was hard to know what was real and what was fantasy. What was documented didn't make a lot of sense, and the way the case had disappeared without a trace gave the odd impression of some kind of government entity at work. Intelligence? The Bureau? Now it was said Swagger was retired and lived a quiet life as some kind of businessman in the West. But nobody really wanted to talk, and David kept running into a wall of silence, along the lines of, "Well, Bob Lee's not the sort who likes attention, and I love him too much to disappoint him. If you knew him, you'd know what I mean. So why don't we just agree to end this conversation right now."

As for Swagger, there was a listed phone number; he called it, got a frosty-sounding woman who would give him nothing at all and kind of frightened him, truth be told. His usual phone charm didn't cut him any slack with her.

In the end he turned out a little piece that page one wouldn't take, but it did keep the story alive on the From Washington page until the news from the lab arrived. His story simply pointed out that Memphis had a history of involvement with "sniper types," as this "Bob Lee Swagger" certainly was, and it didn't ask, there being no justification for pointed observations in a legitimate news story, whether an agent with known connections in the "sniper community," including a long-standing friendship with one of its legends, was an appropriate choice to investigate a series of sensational murders whose perpetrator was suspected to have come from that community. Maybe an editorial writer would pick up on it, and the next day, indeed, one had.

It wasn't the lead editorial, but even an off-lead got noticed in the *Times*.

> We wonder what is going on at the Federal Bureau of Investigation these days. The Bureau, charged with investigating the heinous deaths of four Americans whose only crime was that they used their constitutional rights to protest a war that was both a tragedy and a mockery, turned that investigation over to the stewardship of an agent whose experience put him more in sympathy with its alleged perpetrator than with its victims.
>
> As the Times reported yesterday, Special Agent in Charge Nicholas Memphis, who ran the investigation that quickly identified former marine sniper Carl Hitchcock as the primary, indeed only, suspect, has long enjoyed a relationship with another well-known marine sniper, Bob Lee Swagger, formerly of Blue Eye, Arkansas. One doesn't begrudge Memphis his choice of friends, but at the same time, perhaps one should begrudge the Bureau its choice of executives. In matters of such importance, it

would have been better for all concerned if
the Bureau had selected an agent in charge
whose connection to the act of sniping—
the cold murder of a human being, guilty or
innocent, at long range for something called
"military necessity," though too often neither military nor necessary in application—
was more distant and less inclined to be
tarnished with emotion.

Perhaps that is why the investigation has
apparently fallen off the tracks and a final
report, which all Americans must regard as
an act of closure to these final, horrible war
crimes, is nowhere in sight.

That got him the usual invites to the usual talking
head roundtables—he was getting pretty good at it—
but he passed that night because, well, because he too
felt some combat fatigue; it had been a nerve-rattling
few weeks, and he knew his career hung in the balance. It was still unclear whether he would ultimately
join, in Howell Raines's memorable phrases, the culture of complaint or the culture of achievement that
prevailed in any given newsroom.

I am so close, he thought.

And when his cell rang and he looked at the caller
ID and saw a Rochester area code, he thought he
might have a heart attack. It had to be the lab. He'd
appended a note with his number, asking for notifica-
tion. He knew he just couldn't face opening a FedEx
package with no idea in hell what it contained, especially as the whole office would be secretly watching.

"Banjax."

"Mr. Banjax, hi there, it's Jeremy Cleary up at Donex, in Rochester."

"Oh, hi" was what David came up with, so lame, his heart tripping off in his chest.

"Yes, you'd sent us a note; you'd asked for a call with our preliminary findings, before we sent out the final report?"

"Yes sir. Yes, I did. Do you have information for me?"

"I do."

"Well, gee, let's have it, Mr. Cleary." He felt his heart bounce into overdrive.

"We find nothing."

That was it?

What, *nothing?*

"I don't understand. I'm not sure of your nomenclature. Is that good or bad? Is it real or not? Is it authentic or what?"

"Oh, you don't know much about this, I see."

"No, not a thing. Is *nothing* good or bad? There's a lot riding on this." He had not told them he was with the *Times* because he didn't want that influencing their interpretation. Instead, he was just a David Banjax, of the given address of the bureau, Washington DC.

"Well, what we do is track fractal discrepancies. We examine by electron microscope, infrared scanner, spectroscope, even digitally break it down to sound waves and look for noise. That's what your money buys you."

"Okay, well, nothing would mean . . . authentic, right?"

He held his breath.

"We don't operate in terms of 'authentic' or 'inauthentic.' What you get from us is a report of a digital forensics inspection. We look at a number of things: the smoothness of the images, patterns of relationship between adjacent pixels in the images. Altered images have distinct differences between the edges of the images and the original area next to them. We look at the length of the shadows, the color consistency; we measure the lighting to see if it is consistent in various parts of the image. We look deeply in the eyes of the people to see the reflections that appear there and determine if they are consistent with the rest of the photo. We search for clone-stamped areas of an image—parts that are so similar to each other as to make them suspect of having been the same image from the original area. The lab also assumes that all original photographs have 'noise' to some extent, and the noise has a certain consistency. Introducing a piece of another photo will give a different noise level and pattern that cannot be detected by the naked eye. If we had the original neg, we would be able to analyze much more information."

"Did you have enough to make a call?"

"Well, our technicians don't make calls. They measure, they tabulate, and they issue a finding. In this case, the finding was nothing."

"So nothing is good?"

"Nothing means we can detect under various of our testings no indication of the presence of fractal discrepancies which would suggest photo manipulation techniques have been employed. Is it genuine? Well, that's the kind of contextual decision you have to make. That's about history, provenance, even trust.

Not our department. What I'm telling you is that we will issue a bonded statement, and defend it in court if so required, that we discovered no meaningful evidence of photo manipulation in the photo you sent us. If that's your definition of 'authentic,' then you have your 'authenticity,' Mr. Banjax."

"Nobody doctored it?"

"You'll never get me to say that. What you will get me to say is that at the level of detail of which our laboratory is capable—the best in the country in commercial use—there is no tangible evidence of fractal discrepancy."

"To me, that would be authentic."

And to the *Times*, that would be authentic too.

Suddenly the air was sweet and chilled, and oh so much fun to breathe.

I did it, he thought. I got him. I got Nick Memphis.

34

It was not a good day, but then there'd been few good days for Task Force Sniper since the suspension of Nick and the arrival of the Robot. The Robot had a name but no one ever said it; he was, it was alleged, human, just as they all were; he just never showed it. He was the director's designated enforcer, who was sent to trouble spots in the Bureau with instructions to make the trouble go away and make all the people who were making the trouble go away as well. His means were generally not pleasant. Like his namesake, he accomplished this task with mechanistic grinding and trampling; it was said that he could walk through walls and that heat rays burst from his fists when necessary.

It wasn't that the Robot was on the warpath. He was never not on the warpath, the warpath being the state of his life and career. It was that this particular day, he himself had gotten a prod in the butt from the director about the Task Force Sniper report, and since it fell to the team of Chandler and Fields to write it, and since Fields was a bum writer, it fell really to Chandler, and she felt everything grinding downward upon her.

"You can't move any faster?" the Robot demanded.

"Sir, it's writing. It's more nuanced; you have to find the best ways of saying things; you have troubles and problems and you have to reconcile conflicting evidence on nearly every page. It's not like something you can just *do*."

"It's not a novel. It doesn't need a style. It's not supposed to fly along. Nobody's publishing it except a Xerox machine."

"Yes sir, and I'm not Agatha Christie either, but it's got to make sense, be smooth, hang together, and give its readers a clear view of the case and our conclusions. That takes time."

"Is your support up to par?"

Of course it wasn't. The problem was Ron Fields, a brilliant operator, a former SWAT hero with more than a few gunfight wins to his credit, an up-and-comer of the Nick school, decent and true and modest and funny, but . . . he seemed kind of dumb. He was certainly no writer. A giant in the professional world, as her coauthor he became a kind of erratic junior member, lazy and mysteriously absent, and his warrior's reputation made it difficult for poor new girl Starling to cope.

On the other hand, she had a terrible crush on him, as she did on Nick, and she was never going to be one of those headquarters snitch bitches who rises on complaints of others' ineptitude.

"Agent Fields is a fine collaborator, sir."

"There are a lot of people in Washington who want this thing on their desks yesterday. I only tell you what you know, but I tell it in a loud voice in case you've forgotten it. If you need help, sing out. I'll get you interns, secretaries, typists, the works. I'll even hire John Grisham."

"I've just got to get it right."

"I know you liked Memphis. Everybody liked

Memphis. But you can't let any affection for him frost your efforts for me and your job on this assignment. I've heard it said that the task force agents are dawdling because they want to see Memphis cleared of these charges and are waiting to see if someone on the new suspect list takes the investigation in another direction. Tell me that's not true."

"Sir, I'm just working as hard as I can, that's all."

"Okay, okay, get back to it. Why are you wasting time on me?" And with that the Robot lurched onward, looking for another target to destroy, slightly frustrated because the girl had not crunched under as he'd thought she might.

And the other thing: he had her dead to rights. She had been stalling dreadfully, trying to keep from reaching the last page, and getting the sign-offs by the others. Because once the report—this report, with this conclusion—was issued, it became the narrative, the official version, even if she and most of the others weren't quite sold on it. But it seemed *everyone* in Washington wanted this poor guy Carl Hitchcock hung out to dry and all the evidence accepted as planned. The only way to halt that narrative was to halt the report that encapsulated it; that was its primary marketing tool. So she was in the absurd position of subverting her own biggest professional break because she didn't quite believe in what was being said. And because she felt something for Nick; he'd been decent to her and he always apologized when he called her Starling, even though everybody now did and would forever.

But there wasn't much more she could do. Wiggle room was down to zero.

The narrative, as they wanted, was all but done. It was exactly what everybody said was called for, a professional indictment of Carl Hitchcock, all i's dotted, all t's crossed, each bit of damning evidence assembled in its place, properly weighted, admirably described, the chain of events transparently clear: how this old warrior had cracked and gone off to reclaim the kill record.

She kept waiting for the day when one of the field agents working the list of new possibles that Swagger had turned up would deliver the key piece of dope that would smash the Hitchcock thesis, but it never happened. One by one the possibles became impossible: out of the country, dead, accounted for during that week, almost all of them, if not killing, off teaching. Jesus, far from being macho gung ho gun boys, professional snipers were like rabbis during the Middle Ages, heading from talmudic center to talmudic center, there to instruct, argue, dispute, spread reputation, enforce the orthodox, denounce the apostates, form and re-form cliques, network like young movie actors. Good Lord, who would have thought it?

But now—

Oh great, the cell in her purse. That was her private number and only her boyfriend had it and her boyfriend was in Kuwait this week going through some Al Jazeera tapes that might have been plants or might be the real McCoy. Only one other person had the number.

"Swagger, what?" she said.

"Agent Starling, hello. Consider this an anonymous tip—"

"Where are you?"

"If I'm anonymous, I ain't nowhere, am I? Here's your tip. You go to the University of Chicago, Department of Education, where Jack Strong was a professor. You subpoena the hard drive on his computer; you open his e-mail. Be sure to do it nice and legal-like so it can go into evidence."

"Swagger, what the hell—"

"Are you getting this, young lady? What you'll find is an amply documented relationship between him and a fellow named TomC, who you will certainly be able to identify as Tom Constable—"

"Swagger, I warned you—"

"You warned me that I had to have something real, not something that was my opinion. This is as real as it gets. Strong and TomC discussed an object which Strong had come up with that gave Strong leverage over TomC. Strong wanted dough, lots of it, tons of it. He wanted a new life in Switzerland, Armani suits, all that fine bullshit. He thought Tom would be oh so happy to give it to him. All this, by the way, was happening in the last few weeks before the killings."

She was writing it all down.

"That will prove that TomC had a motive to eliminate Jack and Mitzi, while hiding it behind the camouflage story of old man Carl having gone nuts."

"That's fine, but without formally verified evidence, we couldn't get a search warrant to impound. It has to be legal, don't you see? That's not legal."

"It is true, however."

"Unfortunately, there is a difference. I'll try to figure some way to justify it."

"Yes ma'am, I knew you would. Then there's the

boys he hired to make all this happen. I know where they are."

"Then you have to give them to us."

"If I do, them boys are gone so fast you won't see the blur. They's professionals, the very best operators in the world, way above all your pay grades down there. You'll never git 'em. Nope, if I give you them, I'm letting them git away, scot-free. A lot of people died on account of this and I mean to see the ancient law enforced the ancient way."

"Swagger, where are you?"

"Remember, I said same deal with you as with Nick. If I jumped, you'd know it."

"Swagger, I don't like the sound of that."

She swore she could hear the old man laugh from whatever twisted arroyo or stunted tree he now hid himself within and had an image of him in torch-light, gleaming with blades and rifles and bandoliers of ammunition and Molotov cocktails, some kind of coonskin cap on his head, a tommy gun in his left hand and a Winchester in his right, all frontier 24/7.

"Well, young lady, this is my courtesy call. Here's the news: I'm jumping."

35

Swagger snapped the folder shut and slipped it into the cargo pants. Then he went back to his Leicas and 15X'ed what lay at the bottom of the hill before him.

It was not Tom Constable's big, beautiful Wind River ranch house. That imposing structure, to all appearances manned only by a skeleton crew with its master somewhere else, lay a mile to the west, a strange accumulation of turrets and arbors and roofline nooks and crannies next to the most beautiful streambed in Wyoming, beneath the mountains and the wide blue sky.

This was the security compound. Tom wouldn't live way out here without a small army of protection; it wasn't his way. So Swagger reasoned: whatever he got off the Strongs, that's where it'll be. That's where I have to go.

He was unarmed. This wasn't a murder raid, even if the fucking *New York Times* had essentially decreed him a murderer yesterday. No sir. You could kick the door down way past midnight with an M4 and twenty magazines and try to kill all these boys flat, cold out, and what would it get you? A lot of return fire once they figured out what was going on, a running gun-fight on the way out, blood loss, and bleeding out in a ditch. You'd never recover what it was that was at the heart of this thing. You might shoot the right shoot-ers, but in the dark and the mayhem, who could tell?

No, the way you took this unit down was you got what they were here protecting. You got that and you made off. That got their attention. They had to get it back; that was why they existed, and if they didn't get it back, it wasn't just failure, it was something worse, some professional shame that only the best can feel, some place beyond shame. So they came looking for you somewhere out there—*out there* lay behind Bob, and it was the largest parcel of privately owned land in America, a wonderland of mountains and gulches and high meadows and glades and forests and mesas and canyons—you got them out there, hunting you, and like many a man before, they discovered you were hunting them. But to play that game the way Bob had set it up, he had to get the goddamned thing, and he didn't even know what it was, much less where it was. Probably in a safe. And how do you get the safe open? Maybe if you asked politely, they'd oblige.

He eyed the building, whose details were vanishing in the setting sun. It was the old ranch house, refurbished for this duty. Its barn was a garage that housed four jeeps and a dozen wheeled off-road buggies, ATVs. The house itself was an old piece of prairie design, familiar from a thousand and ten westerns, rewired, rewindowed, redoored, remade as a modern security vault. Bob saw cameras everywhere, and a network of lights, and some kind of bar code entry mechanism, and alarm circuits at all the windows, all seemingly high tech, maybe higher tech, maybe nowhere-near highest tech. Men—none of them Graywolf commandos, but all of them tough-looking townie cowpokes— hung about, all armed not with the ubiquitous M4s but with Ruger Mini-14s, which looked a little more ranch-like in the hands of boys in jeans and boots and hats. There was a regular patrol rotation, and every hour, three vehicles left to run perimeter; there was another complement of two after dark and one during daylight that staffed the entry gate, which was miles away. There was a big kitchen and a day room, and that was the downstairs. Who knew what was in the basement? Upstairs were sleeping quarters for the night shift. People came and went by a utility route that led off to the right and into an arroyo, because the grand people in the big house didn't want to be troubled by the sight of Johnny Lunchbucket showing up for work every morning.

Swagger had picked a zigzag approach, meaning a long night's crawl in the bulk of a ghillie suit. His entry point was the basement window, southeast corner. The building wasn't properly speaking patrolled or guarded, except by the presence of those living within. There seemed no steady, regular surveillance, no pattern of lights. He could pick out no motion detectors or Doppler radar screens. Security developmentwise, it was mid tech, definitely late twentieth century. Constable had laid out the bucks for it fifteen years ago, and that was that; maybe an upgrade was on his to-do list but he hadn't gotten to it yet.

The problem was the window. Kick it in? Noise, alarm. Cut the wires? Probably couldn't reach 'em. Set some sort of diversionary element—a charge, a fire, an alarm? Get too many cowboys awakened. Pick the lock? He had picked locks before and knew how to do it, and this lock was probably pretty easy; it was just wired.

No, the only way was to cut a hole in the glass, reach in, and cut the wire, then get through the lock.

Then he'd slide in and see what was what. He had no weapons, but he had five smoke grenades and five flashbang munitions, all of which would create considerable confusion if necessary. Here was the official version of the plan, the one he had to convince himself he'd believe in, the one they'd try to beat him away from, and he knew, if he gave it up, it was the first step toward losing this one. The idea seemed to be to find "it," booby-trap the place with smokers and flashbangs, disable most of the vehicles—not exactly high tech, he'd just pierce each tire with an icepick—and disappear with one. By the time they got the vehicles up and running, he'd be long gone and they'd have to call in the big boys, the trackers and the snipers, the Graywolf pros, to hunt him down.

But he knew that hope was a dream. The reality: this'll be a bad one.

There's going to be a lot of pain ahead, getting through this one.

You're going to pay for this one.

Then he thought, man, I am too old for this shit. I do not need this shit. I saw the six-zero a few years back and I ought to be rocking this way, then that, not putting gunk on my face and slithering in a suit that looks like a bush downhill a thousand yards to try to get in and out and away and gone, but instead probably getting my ass kicked hard and long until I ain't hardly human no more.

I do not want to do this.

But he looked around, and as usual, nobody else was there. If not him, who? Tell the feds. Telling the feds just opens a can of worms and lets lawyers and politicians and bullshit artists of all stripes into what is essentially clear-cut and demands action and justice.

So here I am and here I go.

His face blackened, he began the long crawl down.

It took six hours and he arrived at 0230. The temp had dropped, and a keening wind knifed down from the mountains. There was no moon, but tides and pinwheels of stars splattering the vault of dark threw off enough dim glow to let him navigate, and he'd committed the plan of the place, the location of the trees, the spotlights, the shadows, to memory. He slid between cones of light, riding the shadows, moving with a kind of slow swimmer's urgency as if through mud. You'd have to look hard at him to see movement at all, and he doubted the cameras were high-res enough to pick him out of the shadows in what was undoubtedly black-and-white. Every time he heard some odd noise, he froze, waiting to see if anything would develop, and of course it never did. At one point, around eleven, a couple of cowboys came out and smoked on the porch, had a good laugh at a supervisor's expense, and one took a nip from a secret flask. Then they ducked back in. At two-hour intervals, there was some clambering as a security shift climbed into vehicles, tested engines and lights, then left for a perimeter patrol, making a lot of noise as they went. Each circuit took four hours, so the first crew was back while the second and third were still out, prowling around inside the barbed wire in the dark in far distant places. It was a hell of a big spread.

Now he scooted the last few feet until he was flush

against the house. He lay, stifling his breathing, waiting for discovery. Why didn't they have dogs? A dog might pick up scent, where a man never would. But maybe Tom Constable, ever conscious of his image, didn't want the world to see him as guarded by baying howlers, long in teeth, red in fang; he was the modern billionaire, too cool and streamlined and ironic for that. So his muscle was hidden under down-home cowboy wardrobes, townies and locals in jeans just like in olden days. It made him more interesting for the celebrity magazine people whom he always had out for his big parties.

Bob touched the low-lying window. And what if he got through it and came across that drunken cowboy? Did he kill him? Choke the life out of him? Some nineteen-year-old townie punk who just needed a job and ended up on the night shift at Big Tom's. That wasn't right. Oh, "knock him out," that good one from the movies. Yeah, and brain-damage him forever, or siphon off IQ points the boy couldn't spare? What then? Cross that one when he came to it. He had a couple of Kimber pepper sprays aboard, which wouldn't put a man out but should put him down. But if it came to that, the whole thing had gone to hell anyway.

He slid out of the ghillie until he felt like he was lying next to a dead buffalo, a puffy weaving of silks and cottons configured to look like the great outdoors. With a good one you could go to ground and a hundred men could walk right by you and never catch on that you were the sniper, you were here to kill them. This one was very good. He hated to leave it behind, even if he had others.

The wind cut his cotton shirt, which was sweat-soaked after the long, hard creep, and the cold penetrated as he finally came free. He nestled next to the low window. He pulled a small waist pack around from his backside, unpeeled the Velcro fasteners to display a cache of small tools and one piece of Dubble Bubble bubble gum. He opened the gum and threw it in his mouth—it was cold and hard, dusted with sugar—and began to knead it to something malleable with his jaws. He took out a small SureFire and checked each corner for wires and went four for four. He went to the latch, saw that it snapped shut. He ran the cone of illumination across the room he was about to penetrate and saw that happily it didn't contain sleeping men but mostly housed stacked junk—some kind of storeroom. Very good.

He removed a glass cutter's tool from his pouch, tapped the glass to make certain it was no super security plastic, and was rewarded with the vibration of regular window pane. He turned the tool so that the auger installed at the other end of the grip was upmost and crudely drilled deep into the glass, feeling it yield to powder as he rotated, until finally he'd opened enough edge for the cutter to bite. Quickly he sliced a four-inch wound in the glass, cranked the thing horizontally and cut another. In short enough time, he'd cut a four-by-four square in the window. He plucked the gum from his mouth, applied it to the window gently, pressing hard enough to make it stick but not hard enough to break. Then he pulled, and the sixteen-square-inch glass rectangle plopped out. He gently set it down.

Wire cutters snipped the central wire to which each

of the corner devices was linked; then he popped the lock, opened the window, jimmied his body, and slid through. He closed the window behind him, though a breeze now pulsed through the open square in the glass. Nothing could be done about that; the cowboys wouldn't notice, or so the theory went.

He waited, his eyes adjusting to the quality of indoor darkness, with no starlight or far-off spotlights. It was clear he was in the kitchen supply depot, as industrial-sized plastic bottles of ketchup, mustard, and relish stood everywhere, as did other wrapped-in-plastic foodstuffs. A glowing stainless steel door admitted the cookie to the walk-in freezer where perishables were kept. Bob ignored it, slid to the door, unlocked it, and opened it a crack. Not much to see: institutional green walls, a few other closed doors probably giving admittance to other storage facilities, at the far end a hold tank, where drunks or paparazzi could be secured until LE came out from town to haul them away. At the close end he saw stairs, slipped quietly to them, eased halfway up—would there be a crack as the old wood adjusted to weight bearing? no, not this time—and slipped up a bit further.

He could see into the big room, well-lit but empty. Junky Walmart furniture mostly broken down from daily use, piles of magazines from *Guns & Ammo* to *Pussy & Juggs*. In other words, the debris and squalor of men living together. Coke cans, paper plates, candy bar wrappers, like any day room in any guard post anywhere in the world. The guys were upstairs, he guessed, having a feeling of dense sleep above him, hearing the wheeze of one, the fart of another, the dream-driven toss of a third.

He slid along the wall, peeked into the kitchen and saw the cookie hadn't arrived yet to throw the day shift breakfast on. Beyond it lay the security HQ office, he could tell, because although he did not see into that room directly, he saw the gray glow of security monitors on the wall through the doorway. A man or two would be in there; so would the arms safe and, he'd bet, in that would be the package, the whatever. Wouldn't that be the safest spot on the ranch: in a room guarded 24/7 by armed guys with orders to shoot to kill? It made sense, if anything made sense.

He didn't let rogue thoughts fly. He suppressed the notion that a) Tom Constable had simply destroyed the object (he wouldn't; holding it would thrill him too much; he would think there'd always be time to destroy it; it had some kind of meaning to him), or that b) he'd lock it in a safe in his bedroom, where his various wives and now visitors stored their jewels, or c) he had it with him, wherever he was, just to keep it near and dear, or d) he put it in a safe deposit box in the biggest vault in the world. Nope, none of those: couldn't be, wouldn't be, no way.

Bob stepped around the corner.

"Hello," he said.

"Huh?" said the security officer, rising from a soft chair where he'd been watching not the bank of monitors on the wall but a television showing some kind of spaceship thing.

Bob hit him in the face and eyes with the Kimber pepper and down he went, coughing spastically, and before he could reorient, Bob had him trussed in plastic cuffs pulled tight.

"You shut up, partner, or I'll have to hurt you harder."

The man spluttered, groaned, bucked, and Bob put a knee against the back of his neck.

"I can close you down the hard way if you don't do what I say."

The man went limp. But then he said, "Mister, do you have *any* idea what you're fucking with? You are going to be so messed up."

"Anyone else here? A partner, another patrolman? You alone, bub? Tell me or I'll hit you with two or three more shots of pepper, and son, you won't like that a bit."

"I'm alone," the man said. "Down here. But there are six very tough guys upstairs, so my advice to you is to run like hell and hope you get off the property before you get them pissed."

"I didn't come this far for the fun of it," Bob said.

Bob looked around the room, and yeah, there was the secure steel door of what had to be an arms vault, snug behind a combination lock the size of a dinner plate, very old-style.

"You keep the rifles in there, right? But because the guys go in and out, you only keep it day-locked, right? You don't want to fuck with the big combination six times a day, right?"

"I don't know what the fuck you're talking about."

"We'll see about that."

He raised the man to his feet and shoved him ahead.

"Key or more pepper?"

"Shit," the guy said, and gave it up. He nodded toward the desk drawer. Bob reached in, pulled out a big key ring. He went to the arms vault and inserted a key in the day lock and pulled on the heavy door. That easily, it swung open.

Bob pushed the guard in, then followed.

"Y'all planning for the invasion?" he asked.

Serious weaponry: not the Ruger Mini-14s but a rack of M4s, all with high-tech red-dot optics, several crates of 5.56 NATO and 12 gauge, four short-barreled pump shotguns, some chemical crowd control gimcracks, a rack of gas masks. On a metal shelf in the back, he found some papers, someone's copy of *Atlas Shrugged*, and a nice but well-beaten briefcase with the initials JTS, for John Terrence Strong, he guessed. He opened it, saw only a small cardboard package, four by four, white, that bore on its corners yellowed strands of old Scotch tape.

Got it, even as he realized the absurd ease with which all this had happened.

He grabbed the case, pulled the guard with him, closed the vault.

"Okay, here's the deal," he said to his captive. "If I had a brain in my head I'd snap your spine and be done with you, cowboy. But I'm a nice guy, see. So you and me, we's walking out the door like buddies, to the motor compound in the back. Then I'm popping tires on all the other vehicles, and you and I are going for a ride. I'll toss you out somewheres along the way, and tomorrow night you can have dinner with the wife and kids. You'll be out of a job but not out of the rest of your life."

"Mister, you are in so much trouble. You put that goddamn briefcase back or—"

"Let's go, bub."

He led the now cooperating man through the back entrance, and as he stepped through the door, someone hit him a perfect shot in the brachial plexus, the nerve group that ran from his shoulder to his neck, and his body went useless and puttylike on him. He fell, and the others were on him in seconds with their hard professional knowledge of leverage and application of force and pain. In another second, his own hands were snared in flex-cuffs. He was hauled roughly to his feet.

Whack! the man he'd taken hit him in the face, and for his troubles was shoved hard to the ground by another dark figure.

"You'll be minding your manners now, mate," said his persecutor.

Then he turned to Swagger, smiling. "Well, damn me eyes, look and see what the cat has brought in from the meadow."

It was Anto Grogan.

36

Nick was alone in the house, as he had been for much of the week. Sally was finishing up some big case and wouldn't be home until much later. Nick had read, watched DVDs, listened to music, and otherwise filled the time of his exile. But enough with the Lean Cuisines nuked, stirred, renuked, and stirred again. No more macaroni and cheese!

He looked out the window. Finally, they'd all gone away, the entourage of reporters who'd set up shop in the front yard to bedevil him. The weather had turned cold, it was late on a Friday night and nothing happened in Washington on a Friday night, so all the boys and girls of estate4.com had gone home early.

He should have shaved, but what the hell. He slipped on a sports coat, went into the garage, and pulled out. God, for just a few seconds the liberation was its own reward, the sense of being outside the house, away from the same four walls. He drove aimlessly through Fairfax and finally decided, since it was late and the line would be down, to head to Ray's the Steaks in Arlington. He slid through the Northern Virginia night without much difficulty, found parking on the street, and headed into the old house that had become one of the most popular restaurants in the area.

"Is the kitchen still open?" he asked the maître d'.

"You just made it, sir."

"I can eat in the bar if it's easier."

"No, we've got tables. This way, please."

He followed the man through the three-quarters-full room to a corner table for two, approved of its darkness and obscurity, and took a seat. In a bit, he ordered a drink, since he sure wasn't on duty and wasn't carrying anything except his credit cards.

"Bourbon and water."

"Preference, sir?"

"Sure, Knob Creek, if you don't mind."

"Yes sir."

He studied the menu and ended up with what he always ordered—house salad, filet, medium rare, mashed—and since Sally wasn't here, he allowed himself to enjoy the luxury of skipping the asparagus. He sat, meditating, enjoying the mellow power of the bourbon to confer its merciful blur on things, and tried to figure out what to do next but of course knew that whatever he decided would be preempted by the Bureau's next move.

Would he be formally terminated with cause? It might happen. More likely, he'd be demoted to some make-work job—hmm, had they closed out the who-really-fathered-Bristol-Palin's-baby investigation?—while the Office of Professional Responsibility put together a case against him; then he'd be advised of a hearing, he'd have to hire a lawyer, there'd be some back-and-forth, and what would happen would happen.

A shadow fell across the table.

He looked up.

"I figured it would be you. At least it's not Banjax," he said.

"Hi, Nick. I'm hoping you won't chase me away. We should talk," said Bill Fedders.

"Sure, Bill," said Nick. "Sit yourself down. Waiter, waiter, bring Mr. Fedders a drink, whatever he wants, on my tab."

"Well, aren't we feeling generous," Fedders said. "Better let me put it on my tab. It's the least I can do."

Fedders ordered a vodka martini, dry, Grey Goose, and explained that by "dry" he meant that the olive should be allowed to read the label on the vermouth and that was it for vermouth.

Nick thought it was actually kind of funny but suspected that it was a treasured Feddersism, famous all over DC. He was hearing it late because normally he was so distant from the fabulous Fedders orbit.

"So, Nick," said Bob.

"So, Bill," said Nick.

Fedders's drink came and Fedders toasted, "Nick, to you. I always liked you. None of this was because anybody disliked you. You're a hell of a guy, Nick, and a hell of an agent."

"Hear, hear," said Nick, drinking to himself.

"It's not too late, Nick. You can call the director, tell him in the time off your thinking has clarified on the case and you are one hundred percent behind resolution now and moving onward. Get that report issued, hang the case-closed tag on it, and sit back and relax. Then maybe some of the forces that seem to be conspiring to destroy you could conspire to help you."

"You can make it happen that fast?" said Nick. "You can stop the *Times* in mid hue and cry—or maybe that's full hue and only half cry—and turn it around to help me?"

"Well, Nick, you overestimate my power, sure. But I can make some things happen. I've been in this old town since the first Roosevelt. I used to date Alice Longworth, in fact. I've got a few favors owed me; I've sure done enough in my time."

"Impressive, Bill, I give you that. Impressive."

"Nick, really, what's the problem? The Big Guy doesn't want to spend the last years of his life reading how he hired aliens to murder his ex-wife because she was sleeping with some kid with too much mousse in his hair. Can you blame him? Once all you guys go to case-closed, the report is the record, the verdict, the official version. Nobody will have access to the evidence. No more nutcase articles, nobody getting rich on craptastic books and DVDs, no movie versions, no *Rushes to Judgment*. The whole circus dries up and dies."

"Wow, again, you can do that?"

"My pleasant voice, suave charm, brilliant instincts, and, oh yes, Tom Constable's six billion bucks. Money talks loud. He just wants this goddamn thing to go away."

"I'd think he'd want the guilty party drawn and quartered."

"Nick, I can't argue the case with you, but the crazy marine sniper thing made absolute sense to Tom and he bought it totally. Maybe he's deluding himself, because he also saw how quickly and neatly it ended things."

"Or maybe he did pay somebody to kill her and frame Hitchcock. Or maybe killing her wasn't even the point, maybe it was killing one of the others, like that, what was his name, the comic, Mitch Greene."

"Nick, believe me, nobody would go to that much trouble to kill Mitch Greene."

"Well, I'm sure you're right about it, but I can't see hanging it up until we've worked out all the possibilities, not just the most obvious ones. That's my obligation as a law enforcement officer. I can't walk away from that, no matter what."

"Nick, really, the news isn't good. Not tomorrow, but in a few days, the *Times* has another bombshell. It's bad, Nick. I don't think even your most ardent supporters in the Bureau will stand behind you after this one. I can't tell you what it is, but it'll leave a crater the size of Manhattan."

So that was it. That's why Bill was here, to deliver the news in person. Nick had no doubt that at some level Fedders was genuine in his affection for Nick and was probably going to some kind of extra exertion out of some kind of twisted nobility to deliver the news in person.

"You know, it's all crap," Nick said. "I never did a thing for FN, took one red cent, one lousy meatball. I didn't even know they'd bought Winchester. I have no brief for the Model 70 over the 700. I don't know anything about firearms acquisitions; that's handled at Quantico. I missed most of the meetings for the Sniper Rifle Committee."

"Nick, the evidence says different, and it's a hard one to talk your way out of. I'd get good counsel, if I were you, and I'll tell you what he'll say. He'll say, 'Let me cut a deal. You sign off on something else, maybe behavior detrimental to the Bureau, have a suspension, and when you come back, they'll move you someplace out of the mainstream. That way you keep your pension and it all looks rosy and cosy.' That's good advice, Nick. Don't try to play hardball with this thing. It's too big. It'll squash you. The more you fight it, the worse off you are."

"See, Bill, here's the funny thing. If you want to go after me, that's fine. I'm a big boy, I'm in a hot-seat job, it's what I wanted, it was the risk I ran to pay for my ambition. I can go down; it's the way of the wicked world. But you guys went after Swagger. Let me tell you, it takes a powerful kind of fool to go after Swagger. He never did anything but his duty, hard and straight, no bullshit, and he dodged enough lead in his time to sink an aircraft carrier. He did it for something he thought of as his country, and his country is a lot better off because of the risks he took and the wounds he bore and the responsibilities he embraced. Now you make him out to be some kind of cracker Svengali manipulating me into stupidity. I will tell you this: I've seen smart boys try to throw the rope around Swagger before and it always turns out the same. They think they're hunting him, and it turns out he's hunting them."

"Nick, it's nothing personal. It's just—"

"So when I talk to you, Bill, the truth is, one way or the other, it's like I'm talking to something that's already been hit and just doesn't know it yet. You and your rich boss and all the thugs he's hired? Baby, you're walking into bullet city."

37

They took him downstairs into a blank white room with a heavy lock. It was one of those zones of permanent noon. Two TV cameras monitored it, mounted on brackets in the corner. It had an antiseptic quality to it, and a drain in the floor, in the center of the cheesy linoleum. The lights were harsh and shadowless. A sink hung off one padded wall. He knew what it was for.

The search came first: it was hard and professional, a bunch of clapping and probing and rubbing. Jimmy, one of the hulking, muscle-knotted gym rat contractors, even peeled a bandage back on one of his fingers, looking to make sure it covered a bloody wound, and only picking at the scab to draw a drop of blood convinced him it was real enough. "Cut ourselves wanking, have we now?" he asked, as he squashed the thing back in place. Raymond, the scrawny one, went to it on his boots, probing the lasts for hidden blades or whatever, finding nothing.

Then they threw him in a chair, the four of them, three hulking men in desert tan battle dress and Raymond, who he now realized was Carl's doppelgänger during the week of shootings. Of course, there had to be a guy of Carl's size and coloring who, in grubby clothes with a three-day beard and a ballcap pulled low over the eyes, could pass as any grizzled loner.

But that was the past; in the present, he could feel

their weight and concentration of purpose palpably, filling the room. His tightly bound wrists, the plastic bindings deep in the flesh of his arms, sang in pain; his hands felt like blue gloves.

"I see Team Homo has formed up again," he said. "Shouldn't you boys be puking up green beer behind some dive in Boston?"

"Oh, Bobby," said Anto, "with the smart comments, as if he's reading from a movie script. He ain't scared, is he, Ginger?"

"He is not," said Ginger, "or if he is, the fellow controls it well. But we'll change that."

"We's in for a long night's journey, I'm afraid."

Two departed and returned with folders, and Anto Grogan sat across from Bob, taking off his ballcap, running a hand through his dark crew cut, smiling broadly; handsome fellow he was too, radiating charisma.

"Nicely handled in Chicago," he said. "Too bad we haven't it on film. *Counter-Ambush Tactical Improvisation.* A damn classic. Also too bad that damn kid was so slow on the gun. He liked filling up the black gentleman with lead, and by the time he came around for you, you was gone. And three seconds later, he was dead. Very nice. Who said this was no country for old men?"

"You killed a second good man that night," said Bob. "That goes on the list. When payback comes, I'll kill you twice for that alone."

Grogan and the fellas laughed.

"Him talking so big, all trussed like a pig," Grogan explained. "Still, it's the ego of the alpha. Even now, beaten and captured and in for who knows what ahead, he's bellowing insults and kicking up the dust. See, here's what I don't figure. Ginger, help me here; he's so damned good, the best, yet he comes in here like a clodhopping amateur and he's taken down easily as can be. Which Bobby would it be with us tonight, the tough operator or the clodhopper?"

"I wouldn't know, Anto," said Ginger. "Maybe it was overconfidence? Even the best make mistakes when they get overconfident."

"Possibly that's so, Ginger," said Anto. "Bobby, luv, here now, what's your interpretation? What explains the different levels of your warcraft?"

"Go fuck yourself," said Swagger.

"Now that's not helpful."

"I didn't think you boys would be here. I thought I was way ahead of you on the figuring-out. My idea was to get in and get out before you realized how much I knew. It was a recon, figure on what I'd need next time. I thought you'd still be at Graywolf HQ, going over intel, tracking me down, sending out other kill teams, better kill teams."

"Now, see, he is mixed up," said Anto. "He thinks Graywolf has a thing to do with this and it don't; this is private enterprise between us and his lordship Constable, who's making us all rich boys who won't be working no more teaching kids how to pop camel jiggers at a thousand meters out. Not that it ain't fun, now, but still, I'd rather live in Spain with seven gals and three pigs and a nice big potato patch. Give an Irishman his potatoes and you've made him happy."

He yawned and checked his watch.

"It's late, Anto, best get on with it," said Ginger.

"Yes, Ginger. You and the boys, fill them pails."

The three—Ginger, Jimmy, and Raymond—went to the sink, and with bangs and crashes and a lot of drama, they filled three pails with water, the water rushing hard into the tin confines, drumming like God's final rain upon the bogs, gurgling and seething.

"You know what's coming, Bobby boy, do you now?"

"Fuck you and the green horse you came in on, Grogan," said Bob. Yes, he knew what was coming.

"I will not lie to you, no sir. I respect you. I even love you, as soldier loves soldier in the pure and manly way, not like them camel shaggers love each other. You've been and done, I've been and done. We're mates of the rifle; we give out death and risk our own. Wish it could be easier."

He sighed, as if a tide of melancholy had rolled over him. He began to unbutton his sleeves and fold them back.

"You see how it has to be. Wish it didn't but it does. You're on to something. You've seen through the little rigged game the boys and I set up for Mr. Constable, as maybe no man on earth could have. Nobody knows enough about the things you and I know about to read the signs clearly. My bad luck you came along, your bad luck you came along. So what's a fellow to do?"

"Tell you what, Grogan. Surrender to me with a full confession and I'll get you life in a good joint, and you and Ginger can fuck each other three times a week. And Jimmy can have seconds."

Grogan laughed.

"What about poor Raymond, then?" asked Ginger.

"Hear that, mates? With them Yank wisecracks,

all Sergeant Rock style. Damn, the fellow's a prince."
Then he leaned forward. "Look hard in me eyes,
Swagger. I don't want to torture you, but torture
you I must and I will. Nothing you say means anything unless it's uttered by a man broken in spirit, all
his defenses crushed, his sense of doom large as this
room, him knowing that it's his last words and they
must be true, and that as a reward he gets to sleep and
there's not to be any more pain. Do you see that? I
have no choice."

"There's always choices, Grogan."

"Not for Anto there's not. All right, I'll give you
a chance. You tell me honest, maybe we won't go to
the waterboard. It'll just be a quick nine in the ear.
That's a fine bargain, isn't it? Why should a man like
you suffer? You've given so much. I know death don't
scare you a bit, you'll take the bullet like a man eating
a piece of toast. But the water in the lungs, the panic
it looses in your head, the fear of drowning as deep
as any ancient human thought, the joy when the air
comes back, and the crushing tragedy when the water
comes again. It takes your soul, it takes your dignity,
it eats your courage, and it dissolves your nobility. You
don't want to be where it leaves you. Believe me, I've
seen it. This is how we ran intel in Basra, until the
Clara Bartons got on us and ruined our fine game.
This is how we became Lord High Death with over
a hundred kills in a week. This is how we broke the
fucking back of their insurrection and put their leaders facedown in the sand with flies nibbling on the
brains all over the wall. I know it, I've seen it. Nobody
can work the board better than I, and I'll kill you dead

a hundred times and you'll believe it each time. Ready for a hundred deaths, Bobby Lee Swagger?"

"All right," said Swagger. "You get an Oscar for the speech. What do you want to know?"

"Who are you working for? What have you told them? What is the state of their intel? What are your callback protocols? How far have you gotten? How far into it are you, and do they believe you or are you here as some kind of prelim, as a way to snatch evidence to convince them? Do they expect a callback by a certain time? Do you have a control in a motel a few miles away? Or is there a team there, a big SWAT thing, ready to jump? What will their next move be?"

"Jesus, you think I'm some kind of FBI undercover, don't you? You poor fool, you better watch the paranoia. I'm pure freelance on this one. Like you, I'm mercenary. I want the money, the gals in Spain, and the patch, only mine'll be full of peas, not potatoes."

Grogan looked at him.

"Do you believe him, Ginger?"

"Not a bit of it," said Ginger. "Let's wet him a bit and see how the tune changes."

"I was asked by the feds to look over their case, because I'm such a smart guy," said Bob. "I realized whoever done the shooting couldn't have done it with the scope on Carl's rifle. I do know someone at the FBI, and I got a chance to look at the evidence. They got me in your school. But I told 'em the bad guys had to be one of your clients and when you gave me the client list—brilliant, someone smarter than you figured it out, right—"

"That was me," said Ginger.

"Someone around here has to have some brains. Anyhow, they've been out wasting time on those names. I knew it was you on the trigger, Anto, when I saw you nail those beachballs. You know how? You hit 'em dead center. That was your mistake, you shot too well."

"I told you that," said Ginger.

"Go on," said Anto. "I'm listening hard."

"So I realized all the sniper bullshit was camouflage to run a mission on the Strongs. I used a cop connection I had to get into their house and I found evidence that their mood had suddenly gotten real good. They were going to get big money just ahead. It tracked back to the death of a guy named Ozzie Harris. They got something from Ozzie Harris, and as I reasoned and later proved, it gave them leverage over Tom Constable. They thought he was going to move a chunk of dough into their Swiss account and they could live happily ever after in the land of chocolates and ski bunnies. Instead, they got 168ers through the central medulla, courtesy of one Anto Grogan, along with two other poor souls, including the babe Constable once was married to, and her presence emptied tons of irrelevant bullshit into the case so thick you need a pitchfork. I knew that underneath it, under all the crap about movie stars and stand-up comics, all that yellow smoke, there was something, I don't know what it was, but some little object, maybe a photo or a letter, whatever, that was worth billions to Constable. I thought it had to be here at this ranch, in this house once I saw it. My deal was I'll crack that place, I'll recon, I'll see what I need, for next time. Then I'll blow and put a team of professionals together. When we come back, we'll take whatever it was and we'll leave a yardful of dead Irishmen, payback for Carl and Denny. Then I'll run the deal with Constable, and because I'm a professional and have been around the block a bit, I won't end up with my brains on the windshield. My guess was it's here. So I'm here."

"Don't believe him, Anto," said Ginger. "I smell the constabulary all over him. Them FBI fellas would never have pulled no strings to get him into our tutorial if he weren't working for them. He's with them, they're waiting for a callback, and if he don't give it to 'em soon, they'll hit this place and we'll have a gunfight on our hands, twenty dead garda and the Americans after us till forever turns to cheese."

"I think Ginger sees through you, Bobby Lee, friend. I don't for a second believe you'd go for money. Your kind doesn't need money. Your type gives it all to king and country, no matter who's king. You're rotten with honor, that's you, sniper. You stink of the shit. I always hated your type because the bloody smell of virtue just made you stronger, and the more pain you racked up, the more you loved it."

"I say, work him hard now," said Ginger. "Get his callback and get him to use it, and make sure we don't get the SWAT boys in their little Johnny Ninja outfits tossing them bangers in and trying to be all herolike."

"That's good advice," said feral Raymond. "Anto, Ginger's got the point. He'll be tough, but we have to snap him now."

"Wonder if he'll go as long as the lieutenant colonel," said Jimmy, contributing for the first time.

"Good question, Jimbo. Bobby, the lieutenant colonel rode the board for close to three hours. He was a believer, head boy in al-Sadr's militia. Strong and tough he was, hard inside as he was outside. Lord, the man fought us. Remember, fellas? But in the end, even Lieutenant Colonel Abu Sha-heed broke, and he gave us a coupla caches and we set up upside and dropped them sand niggers for a day and a half before we called in sappers to blow the joints. Got me nineteen in the first hour alone, great sniper shooting it was too."

Swagger said nothing while the Irishman recalled his day of killing, probably the episode that got him nicknamed Lord High Death.

"All right, sniper," Anto finally said. "I hate to do this, but I only half believe what you said. I have to know the other half. It's time for the water."

38

Constable was precise, organized, immaculate. He left little to chance. He knew what was important: that was his talent. He cut to the core, acted swiftly and decisively, and made endless preparations.

Now the thing was coming to a climax. The forces he had set in motion were brewing and would explode. He had to be at his best, he had to be ready. Two days hence, the Cold Water Cowboy Action Shoot, at Cold Water, Colorado, would commence and he would— there was no doubt in his mind—win the Senior Black Powder Duelist Shooter championship.

To that end, he sat at a table in the rear of his gigantic rec-V and tested cartridges. They were .44-40s, for his two Clell Rush–tuned six guns, painstakingly assembled by Custom Cartridges of Roswell, New Mexico, 14.5 grains of Goex FFFg over 250-grain semi-wads from Ten-X. CC was the best in the business, and they'd weighed each and every piece of brass (from Starline), reamed the primer holes, squared the primer pockets, measured the rim thickness, and segregated the two thousand rounds by that thickness into four lots, so that he'd always be shooting cartridges in the same lot together, for continuity of point of impact.

But that wasn't enough. Constable now sat with the two thousand cartridges and a Wilson .44-40 cartridge gauge—that is, a replica chamber precise to the

nanomeasurement—and now he inserted each cartridge into that chamber, making sure that it fit, that
it slid in easily, that no rogue burrs or lead smears in
any way defiled the circumference of the shells. When
he loaded, over the next few days, he'd load fast, and
he didn't want some unseen microscopic chip of metal
screwing him up.

He worked intently, some might say insanely.
When he was done he would do the same with the
.44-40s for his rifle and 12-gauges for his 1897 Winchester pump, just like the fellows in *The Wild Bunch*
had carried. Everything would be tested; any shell that
was in the slightest out of spec would be discarded. He
would have the best and it would be up to him to be
the best.

He loved the way the cartridges slid neatly into
the chamber; that was one of the joys of guns, the
way parts fit, meshed, clicked, moved in syncopation,
smoothly and efficiently. He had a gift for the mechanics of it and saw the big picture, the way the rods and
pins all worked together, powered by the mechanical energy of the springs. It was such genius old Sam
Colt had rendered onto earth all those decades ago
when he ushered the modern revolver into existence
in 1836, and in that way, Tom Constable felt a part of a
great American tradition, totally and completely.

Totally and completely could have been his creed.
Tom never did things halfway. He was a creature
of obsessions, and when he discovered a new one,
whether it was sailing, radical politics, billions
making, movie star courting, book writing, network starting, old movie colorizing, whatever, he

hammered it with the full force of will and intelligence until it became his, he beat it into the shape he desired. This cowboy gunfighter business: stupid, sure, with the aliases—"Texas Red"—the costumes, his being jeans, leather vest, red placket shirt, and ten-gallon Stetson, as he was of the realistic school, whereas some were of the fanciful school and still others of the character school (Hoppy was big, and so were Marshal Dillon and Paladin) and some of the *Wild Bunch* school. Yet the culture, the challenges, the guns—all of it was incredibly satisfying.

He loved being Texas Red. Wild as a pony, fast, loose, beautiful, proud, dangerous, all the things that Tom himself had once aspired to be and that, even though he was a buccaneer of business, he felt he'd never really let out. He'd always played by their rules, and somehow Texas Red, the twenty-four-year-old gunman with twenty notches, was his way of imagining a life, of touching a life, lived by his own rules.

Where did Tom end and Red begin? He got into character and he got out of character by simple act of will. It wasn't some horror-movie freak show of him turning into Texas Red, and there being no Tom Constable to turn back into. Maybe he'd caught an acting bug—he'd caught several others!—from Joan, maybe the TV images had poured into his unresisting head in a torrent of unfiltered power when he was a defenseless seven, maybe it was his quest for the outlaw ideal that had moved millions of men, only he, in his T. T. Constable way, had let it go too far, as was his tendency. Whatever, like no one else in his life, from a father dead early to business associates to women to smooth operators to whomever, Texas Red made him happy. He would not let Texas Red down.

If he could just hold together on the multiple target scenarios, especially the last one Sunday night, just before he flew to Seattle for a speech as Tom "T. T." Constable. But he worried about his hands.

He'd worked for a year to strengthen them, developing forearm muscles, relentlessly squeezing rubber balls, finger-cruncher gizmos, rolling up weights at the end of ropes, anything. The problem was he was cursed with fast-twitch muscles, and the strength simply would not adhere. Someone like Clell had large, strong fingers and abnormally shaped and defined forearm muscles and off-the-charts natural dexterity that would have made him a superb pianist, watchmaker, blackjack dealer, or surgeon; his fingers were living organisms, each with a seeming brain to keep it on mission. Goddamn it, Tom's were not so gifted; his strength stayed level, his grip stayed at the same measure, and he simply was not dextrous enough to manipulate the gun, even with Colonel Colt's great imagination for ergonomics, with efficiency. So Tom had substituted labor and repetitions for genius and had been practicing six hours a day for the last few weeks.

He could shoot fast. He could shoot accurately through three targets. And then that goddamned fourth target came up and he missed. Or he stopped, readjusted his grip, and fired again, this time hitting but hopelessly blowing his time. He'd even hired a numbers cruncher to examine the course from an arithmetical point of view and answer definitively the question of priority: speed or accuracy. Which was more important? After hours on a mainframe computer, the fellow came up with an answer: both.

Agggh. The problem was that the gun shifted with each report, as it took a long stretch of his short, weak thumb to reach the hammer spur, ratchet it back, then resettle thumb on frame, then fire again. Each time, the gun shifted incrementally, and by the time it had been fired three times, it had cranked around to such a degree that it no longer aligned with his wrist and held true; thus, misses.

What on earth can I do? He'd tried an orthotic brace, adjustments to the gun (such as lowering the hammer spur, which was technically illegal, but even a few unspottable hundredths of an inch might help), and ammunition selection (the last three rounds being a load that tended to shoot, compensatingly, to the right), and nothing worked consistently.

I am so afraid of that goddamned Mendoza, where I go against the five Mexican brothers I—

His cell rang, his very private cell. Only one person had the number.

"Yes, Bill."

"Well, Tom, tomorrow's the day. The *Times* has verified that photo. It runs, page one, with a dynamite piece by our friend Banjax, and I don't see how the Bureau can do anything but make Memphis's suspension official, make the Robot the new head of Task Force Sniper, and get the report out by the end of next week. Then it'll go to the judge and everything's sealed up forever. No 'Did Tom kill Joan' books or articles, not without any access to evidence."

"Good, Bill. Boy, that's good news. Bill Fedders

comes through again. You know that town, I give it to you, pal."

"Tom, for what you're paying me, I'd better."

"I think you'll be pleased with a little bonus that comes your way when all this settles down."

"Why, *thank* you, Tom."

"The pleasure is mine, Bill."

Yet the victory over the FBI didn't delight Tom as much as it ought to. Such manipulations were a part of his way of doing business, and he hired expensive experts, such as Bill Fedders, to get them done—fixers, nudgers, influence peddlers. He never expected a different outcome. This one just took a little longer than—

The phone again. No, the other phone, the encrypted satellite phone, entrusted only to those who handled Tom's special business. He checked the number, knew in a flash what it was, felt a spasm attack his heart.

"Yes." He was breathing heavily.

"Mr. Constable, his self-same?"

"Of course. I hope this isn't an emergency. I told you, only in cases of dire emergency."

"I have that instruction learned, sir, that I do, and no, this ain't no emergency. Still, I do believe you'd care to hear what's been happening, if only to set your mind at ease."

"Go on."

"'Tis himself that came, that annoying fellow I've been telling you about. He presented himself to us as predicted. No miscues as in the unfortunate business in Chicago. The fellow all but surrendered himself."

"No problems?"

"It's him I've got for certain, sir. Presently we'll learn what secrets he's carrying and what he's after and what his knowledge would be. We'll know what authorities he's told and how much. He won't wish to tell us, but then that's the nature of the game he and I chose to play many years ago. We'll know all his secrets and see then where we stand. As for him, he'll be gone forever and a long day, sir, if that's still what it is you desire. I'm only checking so there's no misunderstanding, this being strong stuff."

"It is, Grogan. That's why I chose strong men. You do this thing as you said you would, and it's over and gone, and the little taste you've had of life at the topmost level is only a start. I'll settle on each of you enough for an estate in the aulde sod."

"That's a right fair thing, sir, and me and all the boys be thanking you, though if you don't mind, I think we'll choose Spain instead. It don't rain there so much and the taxes are lower."

39

Anto had many interesting observations and thoughts to share. He commented on the events transpiring before him as if the man were a learned don at Trinity College, Dublin, a barroom poet known for his loquaciousness, an epiphany-rich critic of the art in the great days of the Irish belles lettres tradition, say around the 1920s, when revolution made for murder and brilliant prose.

"Now," he explained to Bob, "there are to be found several kinds of torturers. First there's the sex torturer. He is deeply miswired. In his fetid little atmosphere, he's got pain and pleasure not only entwined but hopelessly confused. He's not the one to take pleasure in the suck of nipple, the lap of cunt, the piquancy of the anus, the zoom of the first wet plunge; no, no, more likely he gets his member heavy with blood at the sight of the welt, at the tightness of the buckle, the way it imprints so deep, down to bone itself, in the flesh. He is all monster, and any sane society would cull him early, put the nine just behind the ear, and throw him by the pathway for the trashman. But no, that rigor has left the formerly Christian nations of the West; only the barbarians have the strength of will and the confidence to execute the perverse on sight, though it is said that they themselves lean toward perversity behind the casbah's closed byways."

Raymond and Jimmy wrapped heavy rope around

Bob, binding him tightly from shoulder to wrist to the chair. Then, each taking a side, they carefully tilted the bound man backwards, not fully to the floor but to a crate nested where it was to give the chair support while putting Bob's head at precisely the right downward angle, which all the boys knew from long experience.

"Now your second type," Anto continued, "your second type is driven by stupidity. He is of slothful demeanor and mental habit. He's after knowing nothing of the torturer's trade and art, of the subtle progressions in debasement, the delicacy of psychology, the nuance of pain. He's pure brute, usually a fat boy whom all the wee ones picked on when he himself was wee and wan. So he grew in pain, he hated his own fat self for its immensity, for how slow it made him at games, for the way it drove the girlies far away, as who'd cuddle with a fat one, who was probably moist in odd ways too, and breathed also through his mouth. This fella takes all the pain and he simply inverts it; after fifteen years or so of torment, he decides he will himself be the dispenser of torment. By this time, the fat that exiled him has turned to muscle via the alchemy of rage and he learns that size has its virtues: he is the crusher, the stomper, the basher, the giant atop the beanstalk, chanting, 'Fee-fi-fo-fum, I smell the blood of an Englishman.' His empathy has been burned out of him, spent all on himself. He feels nothing for what he does to you. It does not register. He is relentless, energetic, unstoppable. Alas, he has no finesse. Be glad it's not him who's your guide through the land of torture, but someone a filigree wiser. For the crusher would crush; he'd have broken all them ribs by now, knocked out all them teeth, crushed all them fingers. Your nose would be a lamb patty, and if your lips locked shut in seizure, you'd drown in your own blood and puke before they could be pried open, as he'd have no idea which nerve was the button to pop the lock. It would be a banjax and a half, I'll tell you, and I'd be breathin' hard as if at sport, and the boys would be drenched in sweat and blood and vomit—messy, messy, and worst of all, so inefficient. For if I put my strength against yours, I put your ego into the equation and you see a way to beat me. No matter how I pound you, no matter how my sharp knuckles rend your flesh, your ego keeps your hate alive, which anesthetizes you. Give you hope of victory, and it's victory that comes your way."

Next came the towel. It was wrapped heavily around Swagger's face, flattening his nose, clogging his breathing passages, taking his vision from him. Why imprison the body when one could imprison the head? It was the same thing. Claustrophobia, most men's scourge, was set free by these powerful folds encasing the face, making the air itself a labor to obtain, sowing seeds of fear meant to blossom in the coming minutes.

"Then there's the regretful torturer," said Anto. "Him I despise the most. He's too good for his line of work, and what got him here in the dungeon with the animals unleashing debasement and humiliation and filth upon another human being, that is such a complex story, and he'd love nothing better than to tell it to you in all its ironies and comic macabres, straight out of our minor Irish writers, but alas he hasn't the time, because he's got to crank the telephone wires full of juice to fry your man parts. 'So sorry. Don't think ill of me. I'm as much victim as you are. I feel your pain. My heart is with you. We should bond and somehow, if you'd but break, you can spare us both the torment of the next hours. It's in your power. Don't make me do it. I don't want to do it and it's only your intransigence that forces it upon me. Is it not manifest that, morally and intellectually, I am so far in advance of such behavior?' Do you not see the play of narcissism in the fellow's maunderings? Your torture isn't about you, it's about him. He's the secret hero and victim of the transaction. The first bucket, fellows. Bobby Lee, try not to fight it, me friend. If you fight it, it goes far worse, and it ruins your heroism. Accept it, go with it a bit, and then you'll have done your duty. You'll probably beat the lieutenant colonel and that's enough, but no man can stand more than two buckets. You'll go three, that's an hour. You're the hero type, I'm knowing. He's a right bucko, eh, Ginger?"

"I don't know, Anto. Possibly he's a shitter. Many are, you know."

"Indeed, many are. The lieutenant colonel, I remember, he was a shitter, finally, at the end."

"He was."

"Still, I doubt Sniper Bob will be a shitter, Ginger. His head is on too tight and it's far too full of chary notions like honor and dignity. He'll keep his bottom plugged hard, you'll see."

Swagger felt the water, first as weight, then as damp, then as wet, then as drench, finally as death. It came as infiltrators arrive, from all points, without a lot of commotion or hubbub, glimpsed from far away and then somehow suddenly gigantic and everywhere, the world was water.

The water rose through the towel and clamped itself upon his face. He tried to hold his face tight to fight it, keep it from tunneling into his systems, but that defense lasted only a second. It unleashed fear. Swagger was not a fearful man and had learned over long, hard years how to separate himself from the rat teeth of what little fear he felt, how to objectify the agony and examine it as if it were the product of some other mind, a scientific phenomenon to be studied. That worked for a bit, and then that defense too was overwhelmed.

He felt his body jack and spasm as the Irishmen leaned into it and all his strength went against all theirs and since there were more of them, they prevailed, leaving him alone, finally, with the water.

Water, water, everywhere. Funny little rhyme from somewhere lost, it was nevertheless the hard truth of this moment, as his mind now spasmed, just as his body did and lost control against the totality of death and wet that clamped upon his face, until he blew hard against the towel, expelling some small portion of what had come in, and then he reflexively inhaled and there was no air, only a rushing wall of water, coded with cold and death, and here it was at last, he'd dealt enough of it to men the world over, turning Panther Battalion's legions to anonymous grave markers in a foreign land, blowing Payne's arm off and Shreck's lungs out, outsniping the general in the bitter woods of Arkansas, taking down the Cubans on the high road in the mountains, oh so many, sending the fat Jap's head spinning through space as he was about to dispatch Susan, then upstroking Kondo, the man stunned that his own blow had bounced off a steel hip, him driving the sword so hard to spine, God, the blood, a man had so much blood inside him, and those four Grumley fucks, in store and parking lot, each thinking himself such a gunman and finding out no, I'm not much of a gunman next to Swagger, and finally those two gangbangers in the car fight, so many of them, and now he'd join them, they'd saved him a place in hell right among them—

The air rushed in. He breathed it hard as the towel was torn off, sucking it in, pure elixir of ambrosia, cold and life-sustaining, his lungs inflating greedily.

"Did I not tell you, boys, did I not? A strong fellow, sure, so he is. Almost a minute in the universe of the drowning and not a word for it."

"And no shit at all," said Jimmy. "His buttocks got a cork a'tween 'em."

"He is tough," said Ginger. "Give the poor beggar that. Impressive start. A right bucko, as you said, Anto. Maybe 'twill be a long night's work."

"On the other hand," said Jimmy, "maybe that was it for the fella. Now he's spent. He gave it a good go, but he isn't holding it today, not now that he knows what it's like and how far beyond deciding it is."

Anto took the opportunity to continue the lecture.

"Finally," he said, "there's my kind of torturer. I am what is called the duty torturer. I ask no understanding, and if caught out by the Clara Bartons of the news, then I go to me fate with dignity, sure in the conviction that what I done was in the right, no matter how them lady-fellows spun it round and made it seem evil. Because of Anto Grogan and his three leprechauns, there's a hundred-odd British squaddies back in Blighty, drinking Mr. Guinness's black velvet and enjoying their fine plowman's lunch. We won't comment on the fact that the fookin' Brits always make their pet Irish their torturers, because they know we have the strength, which they themselves do not, and at the same time will take our ultimate fate, our dismissal and disgrace, with dignity befitting our proud race. So when the four of us are found out and called beasts and driven from the service we have given our lives to, then that's fine by us, it is. We seen the duty, we done the duty. We take the crap that comes afterwards, the shit the Clara Bartons bring to us. You may ask the boys, perhaps they differ, but because of what we done in the night in the cellar of the jail with the buckets and buckets of lovely snotgreen water—because of that we knew in the day where the camel jiggers would be, and we put them down. Lord God, Sniper Swagger, you alone of men would know how godly that was, how Christian civilization was what we defended with our manly trigger fingers. Remember that wolfish Yank in the movie and his speech about standing on the wall? That was us, boyo, on the wall, doing the duty that had to be done. Or do you read Orwell? You've heard the one I loves so, about the comfort and warmth of many fine people in England, which I extend to Christian civilization, because rough men do dark deeds by night. We here in this room, all of us, are mates, having done the dark deeds, having been the rough men. Sniper, are you ready for more?"

Who could outspeak a poet? Not Swagger.

"Fuck you, Mr. Potatohead."

Anto sighed, as if disappointed in the lame zinger that Swagger had improvised, and more disappointed that his hero was no Oscar Wilde, answering in honed epigrams.

"A comment bespeaking futility. No better than the sod carrier's curse. Are yis not finished yet?" he wondered and stared into Swagger's twisted, drenched face, and answered his own question. "You are not. Still, I think you'll be before I have my breakfast eaten. Second bucket, buckos."

"You talk too much."

"I do, I do. The Irishman's curse."

The second bucket was a creature. It hunted him through the towel and he squirmed and struggled, trying to fight for a last wisp of oxygen trapped in the fibers of the towel, but then it had him. He thought of some kind of wet squid, something monstrous from the dark, dark well of human fear, some glistening, tentacled, boneless crusher from the deep that wrapped its wet strong arms about him and buried his face in the nexus where all those legs formed some kind of hideous, pink, cold, horror-movie sucking mask. Wet and cold and slimy, oceanic and ancient, it fought to snatch his soul from him, and he felt his body bucking against its grip, his bound knees trying to rip free, his hands trying to claw away from their plastic wires, and he had an image of ripping the thing off his face and throwing it to the floor and stomping it, smashing it with his boots, feeling it squirm in endless pain as it died spewing green greasy guts across the floor and then it all went black—

"You said he'd be a fighter, and a fighter he is,"

Ginger said, as Bob came back to consciousness through a sense of dislocation. Air, there was air.

"Almost nobody lasts long enough to actually pass out," said Jimmy, with just a hint of awe showing in his voice. "I don't recall any man ever passing out. They panic and beg for release, but no one can consciously hold their breath long enough to simply make themselves faint like that."

"Agh," said Anto, "he does have the fight in him, for such a string bean of a fellow. You'd have thought a bruiser might have a bigger lung capacity and do well under the towel, but this fella's nothing but skin and bones, yet he's got a lot of battle in them scrawny pants of his. And again, Ginger, not a shitter, is he? I should have bet you, Ginger, on that. Give it to me. I *knew* he wasn't a shitter."

Anto leaned into Bob's face, peering intently, seeking answers.

"Sniper, you're a lot of trouble."

"Begging your pardon, Anto," said a new voice— it had to be the one called Raymond, who hardly ever spoke—"but maybe it's best if yis don't be calling him 'Sniper.' It reminds him of who he is, and in that perhaps he's finding his bloody strength."

"Hmm," said Anto, "good point, Raymond. Should I try the reverse then?"

"I should," said Raymond. "Don't build him up, tear the fellow down. Make him see how little he is, how he cannot win, how we hold all the cards, we are the power. This man here is a man being tortured in a cellar, the lowest form of life there is, at the whim and mercy of them that has him."

"Did you hear that, you bloody bastard?" Anto

asked Bob. "Raymond thinks I'm all wrong, I'm building you up when it's tearing you down that should be my pathway. All right then, I'll try it. Nobody can say I don't listen to suggestions. Hero! What tripe! What rotten spew! What yellow runny shit! You'd be nothing. Do you hear? You're a man who's killed boys and women in your time, as have we all. You ain't no hero, you're a bloody killer, with your fancy rifle, lyin' up in the grass, waiting for the poor sods to come out and then taking all from them with but the three ounces you put into the trigger, and it's nothing to you, but somewhere there's a widow cryin', a baby or two starvin', a mate grievin', a father disconsolate, a mother ruined. But that's nothing to the bastard in them bushes calmly and without a scratch on him looking for his next voyager and hoping to get back while the scoff's still hot. Aye, looking at him makes me sick, boys. Douse him again. Get this bastard done so I don't have to truck with the gobshite."

The next bucket was pain. That's all. Through all Swagger, the pain was general. It had nothing to do with concepts such as "water" or "torture" or with who he was and what he knew and who he was responsible to; it had no meaning whatsoever. It was just pure, harsh, absolute pain, radiating outward from his lungs as his discipline gave and he took water deep inside all his channels, and yet through it all, he noticed that a little pain in his backward-bent wrist, where the flexcuff's sharp plastic edge cut him enough to penetrate the general blanket of agony, and in need of something to control his mind, some servomechanism on panic, he twisted that wrist harder, feeling the goddamned plastic edge bite deeper and deeper, and he tried to imagine how it sawed through the muscle fibers, rawly separating them, and how of their own volition they peeled upward, away from each other, emitting a thin penmanship of blood from the subcutaneous network of capillaries in his skin, not a gush of blood, just a scrawl of it, but he concentrated on the pain, the sharp, biting pain of that tiny wound against the larger insult to body and mind and—

"Goddamn the fellow, will he not give!" screamed Anto. "The bastard is getting on me nerves. We're all knackered hard, sure we is. What, how many buckets now, Jimmy?"

Three, thought Bob, I've lasted three buckets on these motherfuckers.

"That would be seven now, Anto," said Ginger.

Seven! He'd lost track, his mind was falling in and out of gear. Seven. He must have been there for hours. He had no idea.

Someone slapped him hard in the face. His eyes opened, revealing nothing but blur and sparkle behind which figures moved, and then someone wiped them clear of water, and he saw now the four had stripped off their shirts and were down to undershirts, the bulky ones, tattooed muscles glistening with either sweat or splash from their labor, and scrawny Raymond like a wet rat. They were breathing hard, and all had hair pasted down flat and damp.

Seven buckets on you motherfuckers, he thought, even though it was hard to remember who, exactly, he was, and why he was here or what this was all about. That had vanished somewhere along with the untracked buckets.

"Jaysus Janey Mac, he's hard of head," said Anto.

"All right, goddamn your black heart, Swagger, now I'm giving it to you straight. You listen hard. I'm bloody tired of you acting the maggot. This time, we kill you. If you'd any to tell, you'd have told, I'm sure. Your silence makes its point: you've told no one of your findings, because if you had, you'd give them up. You'd put them between you and the horror of the water. Remember Winston in Room 101, when finally he gave up Julia out of fear of the rats lunching on his nose. If you had a Julia to give us, you'd have given us she long before. So there is no Julia—"

What was this asshole ranting about?

"—there is no Bureau, there is no report protocol nor coded words, there is no waiting SWAT team. You're on your own, Sniper, and I should have known because us snipers is lonely bastards, out beyond, doing the dark thing solitarylike and crawling back then where all the boys pretend they don't see you because you're naked death, whilst they's battle-killin', a whole different kettle of shad, unless of course Johnny Muhammad has snipers, and then it's your ass sure they be lovin'. But you're alone in this one, and that means that in the way things are, you're no better at all than I. You're not a holy warrior fighting for some holy cause like the goddamned rug weavers, you're a bloody mercenary. You take your wages and you'll soon be dead, and heaven ain't suspended and earth's foundations ain't fled. You're just dead. Okay boys, this is it, I'm done fooling with this one. Swagger, 'tis a shame to end up drownded dead in a bucket like a *Titanic* rat after all ye've been and done, but there it lies."

Again the towel was clamped and the hard muscled limbs pressed against his bound body to hold against the spasms of the drowning man, and again he felt the dread infiltration of the water, its first mild licks, its rising chill, its fingers somehow clawing to rip at his mouth and nose and tear them wide open to fill them and kill him dead drowning.

This bucket was blue. That is to say, as the water rushed through the towel and clamped its intensity across his face, he was taken back in memory close on fifty years, and he remembered a day at the public pool in Little Rock, sometime in the fifties, a bright, hot summer, he and a thousand other kids flapping and jostling and splashing in that vast blue wetness, and he was trying to swim on his own and somehow his thin boy's arms propelled him a certain blind distance in a certain blind direction and for just a second he actually was flat in the water propelling himself along on the rhythm of his muscles and then he ran out of strength and settled to the bottom, and that was when he realized he had swum too far in the wrong direction and was now in over his head. This is how children drown; caught in the grip of panic, he opened his mouth to scream but it didn't happen and instead the cold, chlorinated brew of the pool raced in torrents into lungs and gut, and the lack of oxygen tripped off a flare of fear and he flappity-flap-flapped and he sank yet further and he had a moment when he knew he was dead and he saw blue blue blue shot with bubbles arising as if he were dying in Alka-Seltzer or some terrible thing, and suddenly someone strong had him, and the sun burst above him as if it were some kind of skyrocket, and the air rushed him, sucked with all the hunger of the young, and he was propelled this way in the strong hands of his savior, who of course was no one less than his father.

"Whoa, Bobby, you almost went to Davy Jones on your old dad, would have upset Mommy for days!" his father sang as he brought the boy to safety. "Yes sir, she'd never give me a moment's peace!"

The man laughed, and Bob saw his father's face clearly for just a second, a great man, a good man, a brave man, the best who ever lived for this among a million other reasons, all much better than this one, and it occurred to him that if he died, who on earth would remember his father? No one. He was the last who'd shared time on earth with Earl Swagger, of Blue Eye, Arkansas, the son of Sheriff Charles Swagger, Earl who'd gone off to war with the Marines and won the Medal of Honor on Iwo Jima and come home for ten good years as a state trooper in the Arkansas Highway Patrol before he was taken from the world for nothing, really, nothing that counted. And Bob felt some kind of sudden strength: if you kill me, if I die in this water, it is of little interest to the world, but it means Earl Swagger's memory dies too, and I cannot let that happen.

Time passed.

His father aged.

It was a few years later. Daddy left in the late afternoon, knowing without looking that his son watched him go, and he raised a hand. So long, little boy. See you soon, little fellow. Daddy'll be back and we'll play some catch or walk in the woods or something, yes sir.

But his father didn't come back again, ever. Instead, late at night, the colonel showed up, and then Sam and then some newspaper people and then some neighbors, and then some Negroes from the other side of town. They were all silent, except for his mother's sobbing, and in time, the colonel came up and told him that his father was dead. Compared to that pain, that long, hard trek through wasteland and jungle, this shit was nothing.

"Goddamn him," screamed Anto, in lost and wild fury, as the towels came off in what seemed like only three hours. "Look at the bastard. He just looks at us, him growing stronger, with them mad sniper eyes. Does he like it, do you think? Has he grown gills to live in water? Has he evolved himself backwards to some fishy lurker? The bastard, the bastard," and he let fly, smashing Bob hard in the face with a muscle-clotted palm, driving him to the floor with a clatter.

There was silence in the room, except for the heavy breathing of the torturers. Finally Anto spoke.

"Get him cleaned up. Rinse him down. Get him some food. Let him piss and finally shit. I've got to try something else. The bloody fooker. He must be Irish to have a head or heart that much of steel."

40

Nick had, for the first time in his life, taken to sleeping in. And why not? He had nowhere to go or be; he was just home, besieged by press, waiting for various accusations and investigations to reach some kind of clarity or resolution.

But that morning, Sally nudged him awake at 7 a.m.

"*Umm. Ummphh.* Yeah, what?"

"Sweetie, sweetie, wake up. Something's happened."

He blinked, rubbed shellac out of his eyes so that they finally cracked open to admit the dawn, and sat up.

"Whattya mean?" he mumbled, his tongue still stuck to the roof of his dry mouth.

She stood by the window, trim in her blue business suit, her horn-rim glasses glinting.

"The vultures," she said, hooking a thumb to indicate the alien gathering on the lawn, "they've tripled. Maybe quadrupled."

"Kill some of 'em when you back out, will you?" he said.

"I just want to break the foot of that prissy little bitch Jamie whatever. She's out there, the wan, pale little zombie. She nailed me on the Mason thing with an ambush on the courthouse steps. I still owe her."

"Really," Nick said, "it's much cheaper to kill them.

If you just maim them, you have to support them for years. If you kill them, their buddies lose interest in a couple of weeks."

"Okay, sweetie, have to run. Summary's at ten thirty. Have a good day."

"Doubtful."

She turned and left, hustling with efficiency and purpose. She hadn't let this thing throw her off one iota and believed that Nick would, as usual, triumph in the end.

He lay there, heard the door slam, the garage door rise, her Volvo ease out as the reporters reluctantly made room, and then she sped off.

Lord God, thought Nick, looking at the now swollen mass camped in the front yard of his home, where they crushed grass to mud, left McDonald's cups and wrappings everywhere, and annoyed the hell out of the neighbors, though nothing was said, as all of them worked themselves for the gov and knew this sort of thing happened every once in a while. It was what you got for pursuing a career in the town of power.

Nick stumbled into the bathroom, decided to shave for the first time in three days, showered, then climbed into blue jeans, New Balance hikers, and his favorite University of Virginia hoodie. His glasses were where he'd left them, which happened about twice a month; usually the strange men who came in and moved his clothes around in the dark did the same for his glasses. He made it downstairs, turned on the pot she always left prepared, and in a few seconds had himself a nice cup of joe, dead black and steaming, while he watched the news, which didn't, for once, picture him and bring out breathless updates. These guys outside, they were ahead of the curve then, while local TV was behind or couldn't get its stand-ups into position quickly enough.

He thought he might let 'em stew; he thought he might go online and read the papers and get the info that way, but after a while, it seemed sort of pointless. He got up, went to the front door—no jog today, too many morons on the front steps—and opened up.

"Nick, Nick, what do you have to say about the *Times*'s photo?"

"Nick, were you there? Did you let them pay your way? Why didn't you tell us?"

"Nick, did you just forget about the photo somehow? It slipped your mind or something?"

"Nick, are you going to resign today? Save the Bureau the trouble of putting together charges against you, going through the whole charade, a hearing, that kind of thing?"

"Nick, have you talked to your lawyer yet?"

"Nick, is this like the classic Greek thing, where a mighty hero makes some errors in judgment out of a sense of entitlement and—"

Nick held up his hands, and near-silence briefly alighted on the mob.

"You guys, I can't comment, I don't know what the hell you're even talking about. And no, I haven't talked to my lawyer because I don't have one."

"You're going to need one now," it seemed a dozen people said at once, and somehow a copy of the morning's *Times* was located, expressed hand-by-hand through the mob, and presented to Nick, who looked into his own face, kneeling, surrounded by two guys said to be FN reps, holding a rifle and looking at a group he'd just shot. It had a terrible familiarity to it but it touched nothing coherent enough to be called a memory.

PHOTO SHOWS FBI AGENT AT GUN COMPANY, said the headline.

There was—it was the *Times*, after all—a sub-head: "Evidence disputes Memphis' claim to 'no prior involvement' with Belgian firm."

The byline, of course, was that of David Banjax. The story began,

> The New York Times has obtained and authenticated by laboratory examination a photograph showing beleaguered FBI special agent Nicholas M. Memphis at a shooting range owned by a Belgian armsmaker after having tested a new rifle for consideration by the Bureau's SWAT teams, in contravention of Bureau rules.
>
> Charges have been raised that Memphis, whose stewardship of the famous "Peacenik Sniper" investigation has been called into question, inappropriately attended gun firm functions as the federal investigative agency prepares to decide on a multimillion-dollar sniper rifle contract.
>
> The photograph, which was obtained by the Times's Washington Bureau, depicts Memphis kneeling with two executives of FN, an international arms company headquartered in Brussels, Belgium. Memphis is displaying a target he has just tested the rifle on, the new FN PSR model, which is

to be included in upcoming FBI sniper rifle trials, the winner of which stands to gain not only the agency contract but commercial advantages throughout the world.

"Whoever wins that contract," said Milton Fieldbrou of EyeOnGovernment.com, a think tank that keeps track of government procurement and its commercial implications beyond the actual monies, "will have a PR bonanza that could spell survival in the troubled firearms industry."

FBI regulations specifically forbid employees to attend industry sales events, particularly at industry expense, and despite documents that seemed to suggest Mr. Memphis had traveled to the Columbia, S.C., headquarters of FN USA, he has denied any involvement with the company.

Oh Christ, he thought. This is what my good pal and drinking buddy Bill Fedders was warning me about. Not warning. Just telling me to hang on, I was about to get creamed.

He looked at the photo and half-believed he'd been in Columbia, South Carolina, for a second. Who wouldn't believe it? And how do you prove a negative, in the face of visual evidence so compelling? And who were the two grinners on either side of him? And how the hell had he shot such a great group at three hundred yards?

"Nick, Nick, what do you say?"

"I have no comment at this time," Nick said, and ducked indoors.

Oh Christ. He sat on the sofa, stared at the photo so long he began to believe it was real. He tried to straighten it out in his mind: did I forget?

But that was insane. Amnesia was for bad movies from the fifties.

It *was* phony. Yet the goddamn thing had a familiarity to it that haunted him, that rooted it in some sort of previous experience, though he could not place it. The two other men were utter strangers. Then there was the rifle: there was something peculiar about it too, but again his brain couldn't find the file and yielded no information. He knew one thing: it was a suit day.

He poured himself a cup of coffee, went upstairs, and opened his closet to his festive collection of workplace garments. Hmm, which shade of gray? Okay, he decided, plucking a middle-toned, somewhere-between-destroyer-and-sweatshirt hue, a brilliantly colored white shirt and a tie that was more toward the *R* than the *O* of the Roy G. Biv spectrum, and oxfords that were shined up too gleamy to show off that nice shade of black suggesting death, taxes, and cervical cancer. He had the pants on and was buttoning the shirt when the phone rang.

"Memphis," he said, having recognized the caller ID as the director's office.

"Special Agent Memphis, hold for the director, please."

"All right."

He waited, and then the man himself wished him a brusque good morning.

"Good morning, sir," he said.

"Nick, I suppose you've seen the *Times*."

"Yes sir."

"Are you lawyered up?"

"No sir, not yet. I'd hoped this would go away when the full forensics report on the documents came in and the suspension remained unofficial. Has that changed, sir?"

"Well, Nick, we have to discuss it, I'm afraid. Can you come in today for that discussion?"

"It's not as if I had anything else to do," Nick said.

"Okay, I have to restructure my whole morning, and I've got a lunch I can't avoid, so let's say three p.m."

"Yes sir."

"Nick, I'd like to send a car. You don't sound upset, but I'd prefer not to take any chances."

"That would be an excellent idea. I might lose control backing out and crush nineteen reporters to death."

"That would probably make you America's hero. Okay, Nick, I'll have it there at two."

"Thank you, sir."

Nick continued dressing, and then, feeling rebellious, tore off the white shirt, dumped it in the hamper, and put on a nice blue one. Now that was sending a message! he thought as he tightened the tie.

41

They cut the flex-cuffs off after clamping on walking manacles that allowed him mobility and slightly more freedom of movement. He was allowed time in the bathroom. Food followed, served carefully—protein bars, a frozen meal thawed by microwave, a diet Coke. He ate it down, astounded at how hungry he was and how desperate for sleep. He began to feel slightly civilized again until a blindfold was plastered over his eyes.

Then Jimmy and Raymond marched him in the small-step shuffle of the bound man along a hallway, their bulks marshaled against his, turned him through a door, and sat him down on a folding chair. He sat for five minutes, hearing mechanical things being manipulated behind him, some small appliance of some sort, he guessed, wondering if the water phase was over and now came the telephone electrical generator for applications of voltage to delicate areas. But why coddle him first?

"All right, Sniper," Anto said, having slipped silently into the room and sidled up close, "God help me, but I love you. I've fallen hopelessly into a man-crush. What a bucko you'd be. Lord, wish I was as much man."

"Anto, have you joined the fairies now?" asked Ginger.

"Sounds like it, don't it, boyos. No, I don't want to fuck the fellow, I just want to pay him what he's due, even as I struggle with the problem of putting him down. That won't be a fun task, but it has to happen then, doesn't it?"

"It does," said Raymond.

"But look what he's done. He's made us sniper fellas look good, brave, tough, the best. He's made us the chivalric heroes of the land, instead of the screwball creepy killer dogs we've been so many years. He's stood up against the water over what was left of night, the whole morning, even into the afternoon. He is a dead-on lad, no man can deny it. Game, yes he is."

"You think he can't be broken, Anto?" Raymond asked.

"Maybe still." He addressed Bob. "We found, the boys and I, that a respite, a rest, some new information, even a hope can have an immense effect on the subject. He realizes the comforts of the normal life and suddenly yet another session with the buckets don't seem so sporting. And he realizes he can't get his little dick hard for it again, and so he folds easylike, and there's no need for any more water drama. We's all knackered, we'd all like sleep, and that would be the best for all. But you're tougher than that, I know. So here's what it is. I'm going to show you what this little caper's been all about. You'll see it, you'll know it, and to a fellow like you who's killed near three hundred poor souls, you'll see it ain't, by your standards and mine, no big deal. And you'll wonder, why on earth am I going through the tortures of wet gagging vomit-hell over this wee thing? And that too will have its way with your mind, and then we'll have a nice little discussion and see if we can't settle this matter amicably and make it all coolaboola, so?"

The blindfold was pried off. Bob blinked, dazzled at first, and as his vision settled in, he saw that he was in another small institutional room, linoleum-floored, bland and neutral. Before him was an actual movie screen of the old kind, not a plasma flat-screened monster television monitor, but an old white screen impregnated with glittery stone for better refraction, a true relic of the fifties. It was mounted on a rickety tripod, the sort of thing Ozzie showed Harriet and the boys the home movies on.

"Had a time finding such an antiquated piece of hardware," said Anto. "But it's the old things that contain the treasure. Now, Sniper, you've probably thought this caper was about some forgotten atrocity, no? Hmm, let's see, the villagers didn't want to move for the pipeline, so the contractors genocided their black heathen asses, something like that? Or some huge business deal his lordship Constable put together with the Russky mafia, Al-Qaeda, and the Home Guard? Stolen warheads for the Moluccans, heavy water for the Albanians, poisoned bird poo for the Lakota? No, it's nothing like that, it's merely a man trying to hide a long-ago mistake and get away with a thing you and I and all the boys and any man who's fought for his king and country has done as well. Collateral damage. Something happened that needn't, there was tragic loss of life, but then that's the way of the wicked world, then and now, forever. That's the cost of operating; it's a crime, a shame, a tragedy, but now, do we really want to destroy so much to pursue a thing called pure justice, when a more appropriate behavior might be forgiving, followed by forgetting? I've had a talk with the man on the subject, as I had to know before I committed my team to this enterprise. I had to settle in me own mind the righteousness of what I was about to undertake, at such risk to meself and mine. He had to sell me and I had to buy. So I will convince you as he convinced me, and when it's over, you'll see what has to be done, of that I'm confident. Ginger, turn on the picture show."

The lights came down. From behind came the electric grind of an old, small projector, also vintage, and that bright beam of light splashing against the screen before it disappeared in the opaqueness of the leader, which sprocketed through the aperture between lens and light displaying only scratches and smudges and trapped pieces of lint while that eerie movie-projector sound, familiar to anyone who'd been in a western world school anytime between 1945 and 1985, a kind of 24-frames-per-second clicking hidden in greasy grinding and turning, filled the dark air of the little room and its cargo of watchers.

Swagger put eyes to screen, saw a black-and-white, herky-jerky, grainy, badly lit, artless, dead-hand image of some kind of room full of some kind of people in the costume of a long-ago period called the early seventies. Swagger saw bushy hair covering ears, bell-bottom jeans, lots of army surplus, no baseball caps, and through all of that divined from the listless lines of customers at two counters, waiting to get to a teller, that he was in a bank and that this was some kind of security camera, exactly like the one that immortalized Patty Hearst. He could see a tall, beardless but mustached hippie kid up at the window. Bank? That meant he was watching a robbery, and he knew at once that it was that fabled day in counterculture history, February 10, 1971, when, or so it was alleged by their haters, Jack Strong and Mitzi Reilly pulled off the Nyackett Federal Bank and Trust robbery, leaving the realms of amateur radical criminals and joining the ranks of professional killers forever. Somehow it had been stolen from the police evidence room and somehow, through the political complexities of the radical underground in those days, it had been stored with Ozzie Harris, known for his probity, his toughness, his loyalty to the cause. He would be an earnest protector of the fates of Jack and Mitzi.

Except that, Swagger saw now, as the action began and two strangers came in and suddenly, from postures both too influenced by movies and too freighted with uncertainty, drew guns, it wasn't Jack and Mitzi. Not at all. Oh, they were radical hippies, yes, in Army surplus, watch caps, a droopy mustache on the fella, the gal with her hair all frizzed up as if electrified and a watch cap to encapsulate it, both wearing shades, but both not Jack or Mitzi, by body type, by coloring, by gracelessness, by the clutch of fear that enveloped them as they screamed at the poor girl behind the counter, as the other customers backed away in their own fear, the tall boy last, and the camera watched numbly from its perch above it all.

So *that's* why old Ozzie Harris, on his deathbed, wanted to will the thing to Jack and Mitzi; it proved undisputedly that they were not the perps of the bank holdup, who were some other, not this particular radical couple. That would take the cloud of interpersonal violence off the necks of Jack and Mitzi, remove the taint of murder for money. It was, in the way the imagination of the public sometimes works, possible that it would end their hated exile to the left and gain them readmittance to the parade of Normal Life. So it was a great gift old Ozzie thought he was bestowing on his friends, the only people who attended him as he neared death.

What Ozzie couldn't have guessed, however, was that for a reason not yet clear, the tape had a bigger importance to Jack and Mitzi, represented some kind of opportunity they could not turn down, a temptation they could not ignore. So that was the road they chose to follow, not to redemption but, like so many a tarnished pilgrim before them, to the bucks. Their final creed had not been Revolution Now or Give Peace a Chance but Show Me the Money. They tried to go big time and, like many a rat with ambition, ended up with brains on the windshield and cops eating doughnuts over their body bags.

As for the true brigands in the scene, Bob knew that if he spent a few minutes on the Internet going through the radical rogues' gallery that some Web sites had accumulated, he could tease out the names. But then Anto saved him the trouble.

"I'm told by himself that the couple with the peashooters is Miles Goldfarb and his girlfriend, Amanda Higgins, soon to be dead in a shootout in San Francisco with FBI and police types. They'd fled the East for the West, and on unrelated charges were sought, betrayed, required to surrender, and shot to pieces when they refused. So is justice sometimes served."

Bob watched the drama unspool in the haunted,

blurred silent imagery of a film that was nearly forty years old. It continued; the girl behind the counter got ahold of her senses and began to shovel money across the teller's counter before her, as Amanda leaped forward to scrape it into a bag so movielike it should have had the helpful $ imprinted on it. Meanwhile Miles, with a long-barreled .38, stood behind nervously, waved the gun, shouted contradictory orders, stomped his feet, tried to control bladder and colon and hyperventilation difficulties, and waited for the bag to get heavy enough to signal success.

It was such a different time and place. The two-handed shooting thing, invented in the sixties and seventies in the far West and popularized on *Starsky and Hutch*, hadn't caught on yet, so all the gun handling was one-handed, and on the film it looked childish, particularly that big thing in the right hand of bandit Miles, and he seemed as scared of it as the others were. He kept waving it this way and that, hopping up and down like a clown with a cold pickle up his ass, very nearly out of control. Meanwhile, slightly higher up the coordination tree, Amanda scooped the bills into the bag, even stooping to retrieve a crumple that had fallen to the floor.

A rule of the world: when the shit happens, it happens fast. And so it was in suburban Boston in the Nyackett Federal Bank and Trust, February 10, 1971. A blur suddenly exploded behind very-nervous Miles, as the men involved moved faster than 24 frames per second, and when stopped, they revealed themselves to be two Boston armored car guards, who had been alerted by passers-by. They too were one-handed revolver gunners, in their Ruritanian Elite Guard uniforms, complete to braiding and double-breasted tunics; they too were scared and excited; they too gestured foolishly with their weapons, but they did, or so it seemed, have the drop.

As if he anticipated failure, Miles gave up without a twitch and yielded to the momentum of the transaction. His hands shot up before he even turned to see if the adversaries were armed, and that probably saved his life, for had he turned, almost certainly the very nervous truck guards would have fired away and dropped him, Amanda, the clerk, and any other poor soul whose body came to be in the line of their twelve-shot panic fusillade. Then Amanda turned, dropping the bag; her hands came up. And for just a second, the blurry frenzy turned to tableau: downward forty-five-degree angle freezing five human beings—clerk, two robbers, two guards—in perfect stillness while the moment downticked, or so it seemed, from violence. The poor clerk didn't even have the thought to now duck, as her presence in that same line of fire was no longer required.

Then it all changed.

More blur, more craziness, more seventies mayhem. A person separated himself from the herd of frightened customers who'd fallen back to form a clot at the bank's wall, his one hand out in some unusual fashion that one didn't usually see in bank customers. That was because it held a gun, another revolver, surely a Colt or a Smith from right there in New England. It was the tall hippie boy first glimpsed at the teller's window, now in the shape of pure counterculture wraith—a Prince Valiant hank of hair that flopped over ears, an out-of-place Zapata mustache—and he was himself in the costume of the day, the tight jeans, the Army field jacket, the crunching black of Navy blue watch cap pulled low. He looked like any kid in those days, except that now he held a revolver. He held it low, cowboy style, clearly an untrained shooter, but he was so close—less than six feet from the furthest of the uniformed men—he couldn't miss. He fired six times in a second, discharging all his ammo, and he shot faster than the film itself ran through the camera, so that shots three, four, and five were not seen between frames, and only one, two, and six were documented. The powder was clearly smokeless, but it still produced a great fog of gun haze by today's standards, and the muzzle flash illuminated itself as blades of sheer incandescence against the otherwise grainy texture of the filmed reality, as it spurted, then vanished. The guards, blindsided from the right, never had a chance, and Bob knew from reports that five of the six .38 bullets struck them, moving right to left, through biceps into chest cavity and blood-bearing organs. One simply yielded to death like a sack falling off a truck and went down graceless and stupefied, dead before he hit the floor. The other tried to respond and was halfway into turning to return fire when his knees pointed out to him that he was dead by giving way, and he went down to ass on floor, though still upright, then curled over in the fetal and died.

Another moment of stillness, though in the back you could see the knot of terrified customers recoiling further into themselves; the clerk put her hands to her ears, because the gunfire was so loud. Miles hopped up and down in feckless panic; Amanda stood still, frozen by the eruption of killing violence so close. Then, again almost too fast, Miles and Amanda leaped over the fallen guards and bolted out the door, presumably to the getaway car. It was the new shooter who had the brains to dash to the counter and pick up the fallen sack of money, turn, command the customers to remain rigid; he did so by pointing a now-empty gun at them, although they didn't seem to notice. Then he knelt, picked up Miles's dropped revolver, and instead of fleeing in panic, backed out coolly, keeping the gun on the crowd. He pivoted and was gone.

"Did you recognize him?" asked Anto, as the film ended in more opacity and scratches. "Yes, it was himself. He was twenty-one, had just been kicked out of his fancy university. He knew he had to return south, where his daddy would await with opprobrium and disappointment and put him to work in some dreadful department of his advertising agency. Little Tommy wasn't yet ready for that life, so instead he floated about in the Boston underground in them days, grew the pile of hair and the guardsman's furry brush. Too bad he didn't have the hormones in him yet for a beard. He smoked pot, he got laid, he went to the demonstrations, he drank cheap wine, he met people, and he met other people. Somehow he volunteered to go along as tail gunner on a robbery attempt for some radical heroes of the moment. They never knew him as anything but Tommy, and he only realized later who they actually was, as all those boys and girls liked to play at IRA tricks like noms de guerre and suchlike. They was Nick and Nora to him, revolutionary pseudonyms. They gave him bus money and he left town that night for Atlanta—where you can bloody bet he shaved mustache and cut hair and became Mr. Neat n'

Trim, which appearance he clings to until this day—
and ain't been back to Boston ever since. The film was
somehow stolen from the development laboratory by
some kind of radical affiliate, and being hot was stored
with a man who was loved and trusted by all them
boys and girls of the time, the saintly commie journo
O. Z. Harris. There it sat for thirty-odd years while
Tom Constable built a life, enjoyed the lucky break of
a father dying young and rich, and took that nice gift
and expanded it into something gigantic and world
famous.

"So there you have it, Sniper. Are you going to take
him down for a second's madness all them years back?
Are you going to make a mockery of the name? And
what about the good? What about the thousands of
employees, dependent upon his lordship for their sus-
tenance in businesses that will surely collapse when the
news comes of his fall? What about the more than two
hundred million in philanthropy over all them years,
perhaps driven by guilt over the lives of them two fellas
he gunned down? That's a lot of good in this bad world
to outweigh the moment of craziness. And you're being
the one sittin' in judgment? You, who's killed and killed
and killed, mainly poor men doing what they seen as
duty to country and cause in their own land. And for
that, the mighty Bob Lee snuffed them from a mile
out. Some of them sure never killed nobody nor would
have, as you know most private soldiers is just marking time till they're homeward bound. You must have
killed your share of peasants without a hint of politics or
patriotism on the mind, just working-class slobbos on
patrol against their will when the mighty sniper took it
all from them with but three ounces of pull in one fin-

ger. You're going to judge another fella who pulled a trigger, and he in hot blood, not our sniper way of cold execution?"

Bob said nothing. He had not spoken since, "You talk too much," which seemed from the Jurassic but was only from the Triassic BT—Before Torture.

"You haven't reached him, Anto," said Jimmy.

"I haven't," said Anto. "He won't speak. He just looks off, his eyes going to hard little kernels of hate, like pieces of black corn. Give him a pistol at this second, and we're all dead in the next. He's a hard man. Unforgiving, like a bloody IRA gunman."

"I'll cuff him about a bit," said Ginger. "Loosen some teeth, maybe it'll loosen some words."

"I'm not having that, Ginger. We're the gentlemen sort of torturers, not the mad brutes bruisin' our fists up. All right, Swagger, play it hard down the line. But I'm laying something on you now that may keep the sleep away, even if we leave you alone in the dark for some hours. You listen now: no better offer will you ever get, ever, never, no way in the whole black parade of a life full of so many wanton killings. Call it professional courtesy, call it sniper's honor, call it me own damned sentimental weakness, but listen and then sleep, and then we'll see if you can keep your silence."

Anto took a deep breath and sat back, peering intently at Bob.

"It's this. Here's an offer you never thought you'd hear. Your life."

"Anto," said Ginger. "Have you cleared this with his lordship?"

"Hush now, Ginger. His lordship is off playing cowboy. So it's on me, if you're worried, but I tell you his lordship is no Clara Barton. So yes, boys, we'll let him walk. We require only his cooperation, then his word. He can walk, go back to them daughters and that handsome woman and that farm or whatever piece of paradise it is. Think of it, Sniper. Put it in your mind: home, hearth, love. You'd bade 'em good-bye, but maybe prematurely."

The silence in the room grew uncomfortable. Bob simply looked off into nothingness, as if what Anto had said didn't matter.

"Next you'll be offering him swag," said Jimmy.

"He would spit on swag, am I right, Sniper? He's the ideal, of which us four are only poor third-gen copies. Swag would tarnish the holiness of his cause. No, not swag but something else will buy him for us. We need to pay him in honor."

"What are you talking about, Anto? Honor's not a coin to be handed out."

"It is. Here's the offer, Sniper. You agree to walk away from all this. Being a man of your word, I know you will. And for us, the issue is finished. We've done our mercenary mission for his lordship. But a rub's coming and here it is: I then move not to Spain but to some other, nastier place, and I blow the caper from there. I give you his lordship on a platter by way of a confession to the federals, with copies to all the papers and nets. I put it on the bloody Internet. I offer up some specific pieces of hard evidence, so there can be no denying. Thus is brother Hitchcock cleared and reelevated to his rightful spot. Thus is his lordship felled. Thus I blaspheme the mercenary code, and I do it the coward's way, in some land that lacks an extradition treaty with America. I live in decadence and guilt, go to drugs, kill meself in five years on an overdose of pleasure. I don't expect his lordship goes on trial or to prison, but I am most certain that the done thing equates to the ruin of his reputation and the hounding of him over his last few years, perhaps even hastening that end. So, Sniper, there you go: right has been restored to the world, and you yourself are alive to see it happen. A better offer no man was ever given."

Swagger said nothing.

"In his eyes, though," said Ginger, "I seen the reflection of thought. They widened, narrowed, and looked to sky, signifying recognition and cognition. It's in his brain. That's a hell of a break you're cutting the man, Anto, and he knows it. I'd never do it. Sniper, I'd put a Browning bullet through your head, I would. You're lucky Anto's running things here; he's so much smarter than we are." Then he turned back to Anto. "He ain't ready to talk yet, but let him sleep upon it, and when he wakes up and faces either the water eating his lungs permanently or a world with more justice than he ever dreamed, maybe he'll make the right choice."

"Maybe he's just tired, Ginger," said Raymond. "After all, he's been up longer than we have, and I know I'm tired."

"All right, boyos," said Anto, "get him trussed tight in flex-cuffs again, wrists and ankles; he's got too much movement in them manacles. Take him to his cell; we'll give him some sack time and take some for ourselves. Then we'll get this thing finished, one way or the other."

42

It was like being a movie star, only without the fun part. When the car pulled into the driveway, Nick was swarmed as he walked to it, amid a whirring buzz of digital Nikons, lit up by the flashbulbs and the Sony Steadicam lights, as if they expected him to wave and bow and escort a goddess to the car. Instead the bright blades of light cut at him and he winced and hunched furtively like a felon. The questions hung in the air, and though he pretended not to hear them, how could he not?

"Nick, how much gun company money did you take?"

"Nick, will you resign today?"

"Nick, was it worth it?"

"Nick, will this ruin your wife's career as well as your own?"

"Nick, do you regret your love affair with guns? Has it ruined your life?"

"Nick, are you in the NRA?"

Nick ducked, bobbed, wove, sidestepped, and ultimately got into the limo with no dignity intact.

"Go on," he said to the driver, "back out, kill 'em all, I don't care."

But the driver, a decent guy from the Federal Protective Service, just laughed and handled the issue coolly enough, and soon had Nick hurtling downtown along the parkwayed banks of the federal river amid the usual assortment of inspirational marble monuments, arching white bridges decorated with valiant steeds, and Greek-styled buildings that were designed, on such broad avenues, to glow white with the fervor of democracy. Yeah, well, whoever thought up democracy never heard of the *Times*, he thought.

The driver got him there a little early and in by an obscure entrance on H Street, so when he dipped into the fortress of the Hoover Building, he was spared the Evil Clark Gable treatment. With a little time to kill before the meet with the director, he headed up to the Major Case Section, curious to see if his various IDs with their computer chips still admitted him or he'd already been classified a nonperson by the hall watchers, who had their ear to the ground as stealthily and efficiently as anyone. Yet all doors opened, the elevator stopped at all floors, and in another surprisingly quick transit, he stepped into what had been the work area he commanded, and before they saw him, he saw them, Fields and Starling talking at her computer monitor, a dozen others on phone or monitor, all intently absorbed in their tasks, as if this huge cloud weren't whirling about them. He looked, saw his own glass-enclosed office with its glory wall still intact— the photos of his career, all the stops in hick towns and taco circuit cities, the triumphs, the setbacks, the pics of himself and Sally at this vacation spot or that, the pics of himself and the four men who'd served as director in his time, a couple of grateful senators and other DC lizard species, so forth, so on. The Robot sat erect at his desk, and though Nick should have despised the Robot, he really didn't, as a man did what a man did to keep a career running hard, and the

Robot hadn't made a fetish of clearing out all traces of disgraced former team leader Nick Memphis.

Fields finally saw him.

"Nick, hey!" said the big guy, and a dozen faces snapped toward his. It wasn't like he'd been in a POW camp or anything and his unofficial exile had only run a week, but still there seemed to be a sense of welcome, as people rose and came forward to wish him luck.

"Good to see you back, Nicky," said Fields warmly, his eyes brilliant but not with brainpower. "I know you'll beat this shit. We all know who's behind it."

Starling smiled. He smiled back, and then others clustered about, so he uttered banalities like, "Oh, nice to see you guys. Hey, how's it going? Great haircut. New tie, huh? How's Mary?"

Finally he asked, "So can anyone tell me what's going on?"

"Well," Starling said after a pause, "I'm working on a case narrative, and we've gone through most of the names on the new list and are trying to close that out. Maybe one of the last few will break it open, but even that seems—"

But she trailed off as the Robot came over, leaned in, and said, "Nick, if you want to use your office, go ahead, I'll take a hike. I tried not to disturb anything; most of my stuff's in the corner."

"Nah, thanks," he said.

The quasi-reunion, strained as it was by the necessity of avoiding commenting directly on what had appeared in the *Times* and what brought Nick here today, went on for a bit and then, when Nick glanced at his watch and saw that it was now five till, had to end. He joshed a bit, then by body language indicated it was time to slide and began to make his way to the door.

He was somewhat surprised to see a lurker in the hall, someone clearly waiting to escort him to the elevator to the Seventh Floor. It was Ray Case, of Arson-Robbery, a legendary gunfighter who with Nick served on the oversight board to the Sniper Rifle Committee. He'd actually taken it seriously. What was *he* doing here? Was it just coincidence?

But no, it wasn't, because Ray made eye contact aggressively, followed by a little nod signifying a need for a quick chat.

Nick pulled away, gave a last broad good-bye to the team he had assembled, proud of them that they had done such a totally professional job and stayed on task despite all the political bullshit and the flamboyant crash-and-burn scenario enacted by their leader, and then headed to the door, the hallway, the elevators, and his fate.

Ray Case slid next to him.

"Baby, we've got to talk," said Ray.

So Nick was a few minutes late to his beheading. Still, the director, who wasn't the sort of man who cared about little stuff like that, welcomed him with warmth, considering the situation. They stood in the director's office making idiotic small talk, then the director led him to his private conference room.

"Nick, I asked Jeff Neely and Rob Harris of Professional Integrity to drop by. Their report isn't due yet, but I wanted them to give us their preliminary findings before you and I try to figure this thing out, so we'll know just what's going on here and I have

something to say at this press conference I'm scheduled to address in"—he checked his watch—"fifty-
one minutes."

"Sure," said Nick, nodding to the two headhunt-
ers, who nodded back behind tight, professional, non-
committal office smiles.

Everyone sat, the director at the head of the table,
Jeff and Rob on one side, Nick on the other.

"Okay, fellows," said the director, "you're handling
the forensic document examination of the items the
Times ran."

"That's right, sir."

"Now, Nick, just for the record, although you
aren't under oath, this meeting is being tape-recorded,
and I want it acknowledged that you've so far forgone
legal representation and are here without counsel or
professional advice."

"Yes sir," said Nick, loudly, as if to help the tape
recorders do their job.

"And, although I hate to say this to a special agent
of your seniority and brilliant record, you understand
that any misrepresentations can be considered perjury,
and if in the opinion of prosecutors it is necessary and
appropriate, you will be charged under statutes blah
blah and yadda yadda if it can be shown you've will-
ingly misrepresented."

"Yes sir," said Nick.

"So, for the record, you deny any trips whatsoever,
either under your own expense or at their expense, to
Columbia, South Carolina, and the headquarters of
FN USA, is that correct?"

"Yes sir."

"And you maintain that these documents, which

the *Times* uncovered and published, are some sort of fraud?"

"They'd have to be. Other than that I have no opinion on them."

"So we asked Professional Integrity to run forensic document tests on them, to try to ascertain their authenticity. I'm speaking for the tape recorder: these are documents allegedly showing FN USA's transcribed notes on Nick's alleged trip to Columbia, as compared, for authenticity's sake, to the proposal on their official stationery that accompanied their formal submission of their rifle to the sniper competition and was already logged in our files. You have compared them, to establish the authenticity of the notes, assuming the baseline authenticity of the submission. I'm about to learn their results. Okay, Nick?"

"Yes sir."

"Okay, guys," said the director, turning to the two internal affairs specialists. "Are they authentic or not?"

Jeff looked at Rob, who looked back at Jeff, who looked at the director.

"We have been able to ascertain that both documents were, as the *Times* reported, prepared on the same word-processing system and printed by the same printer. That is, we find corresponding letter eccentricities, imperfections, spacing issues, and misalignments in each document consistent with the same in the other document. I can show you our courtroom presentation exhibits if you want, Mr. Director."

"I'll take your word for it. So that means they're authentic?"

A brief look passed between Rob and Jeff, which then fluttered to Nick, then back to the director.

"That's what the evidence suggests, sir."

"*Suggests?* Interesting choice of word."

"Yes sir."

"What would *suggests* mean, as opposed to *proves*?"

"Sir, it means that wherever that word processor/printer is, that specific one, a Hewlett Packard 960 with the capacity to print in a font called MacPhearson Business 3, that is the origin of the letter and the copied-over notes and comments. As for the receipts, all are photocopies in various hands, which might be authenticated later on, assuming there is a later on."

"Hmm," said the director. "So if I get this right, what you're saying is that the two key documents were from the same typewriter?"

"Word-processing system software, printer hardware, sir."

"But the same machine. The same physical object, right?"

"Yes sir."

"I see. And the fact that one of the documents was an officially notarized and authenticated submission from the factory headquarters itself—you wouldn't regard that as proof? I don't understand."

"Well, I hate to say this, sir, but it depends on the meaning of *is*. Yes, the documents are—present participle collective declination of *is*—from the machine. Yes, that machine printed out a document located in our files and thereby officially designated as having come from the gun company. However—"

"However?" said the director. "I hate *however*."

"Yes sir."

"Okay, let's have the however."

"However, as the document was kept in the files of

the Sniper Rifle Oversight Committee, which is held under extremely loose security in Admin and Logistics—after all, remember, someone leaked a copy of it to the *Times*—there's no way of authenticating that document. I should say, no way accessible to us at this point in the investigation."

"Our next step, sir," said the one called Rob, or maybe it was the one called Jeff, "would be to obtain search warrants from the federal district court in Columbia, and examine each word-processing system on FN property, and determine if one of them— presumably in the CEO's office—matches up. Then you'd have a good case that the origin of both documents was the CEO office in Columbia, South Carolina. But absent locating that machine, and given the lax security in Admin and Logistics—"

"I think I saw a memo on that," said the director glumly. "But if the documents aren't from Columbia, South Carolina, then that would lead to a highly implausible scenario, right? I mean, what are the odds on it being fake? Pretty remote, right? I mean, for it to be fake, one of our own people would have had to sneak into the files, filch the submission document, take it out of here, reprint the company letterhead in some convincing way, recopy the submission letter, then type up the commentary, replace the faked submission document in our files where it could later be found, and leak the commentary to the *Times* reporter. Then the reporter would have to find somebody to leak him a copy of the submission document. Pretty elaborate hoax. Is that logical to assume?"

"Sir, we can't comment on odds. We don't investigate odds. We can only prove that the docs came from the one machine. We need authorization to proceed, and while we have requested it, it is not forthcoming."

"So basically, we have . . . nothing."

"Not until we get that subpoena, find that machine. People think documents are magic, but the truth is, in cases of law their application is usually surprisingly limited. We need that application approved to get that subpoena."

"I'll see if I can't shake it out of the tree for you," said the director. "Okay, fellows, you can go. Good job."

They smiled drily at Nick, collected their undisplayed exhibit, and trundled out.

"Well, guy," said the director, "you dodged that bullet for a little while at least. I must say, I thought the *Times* had made a pretty convincing case, even without the photo."

Nick nodded.

"Hmm," said the director. "Well, let's see what we can make of the photo itself. All right, Nick?"

"Yes sir."

"All right, for the record, can I ask you to state categorically your position on the photo, which appeared today on the front page of the *Times*."

"Yes sir. I have no recollection of ever having traveled to Columbia, South Carolina, and visiting the corporate headquarters of FN USA, not in 2006, not ever. I have no recollection of shooting a one-point-seven-inch three-hundred-yard group with what the caption identifies as an FN PSR .308 rifle at their firing range and no recollection of posing for a picture with any executives of that company."

"Yet this photo exists that shows you doing exactly

that. The photo has been authenticated by the newspaper."

"Sir, let me point out, the photo hasn't been 'authenticated.' It has been characterized by a photo lab as having 'no fractal discrepancies suggestive of photo manipulation.' It's the same difference as the previous document situation. Lack of evidence doesn't prove anything except lack of evidence. Photo interpreters and analysts, like document interpreters and analysts, don't 'authenticate' in the pure sense; they only testify to the presence or absence of discrepancies and from that come to an inference, a best professional guess."

"Noted. But again, for a photo to pass muster without discrepancies, it would either have to be authentic as stated or it would have to have been manipulated by technicians of such skill and with access to such sophisticated, not to say expensive, equipment that it is highly unlikely to be found in the private sector, right?"

"Sir, I have no opinion on that. I haven't looked into what equipment is or isn't available. It's beyond my area of expertise. You'd have to get expert opinion."

"Yes, I agree, and in fact, I've already started the process to obtain the original from the *Times* by subpoena and place it with top people in the field for a confirmation. I've also examined the reputation of the *Times*'s investigating entity, Donex Photo Interpretations, and it is top-rate. It's bonded, gives frequent expert testimony in legal cases, and has a worldwide reputation."

"Yes sir."

"Nick, is there anything about this photo you

want to tell me? This is the killer, you understand. I don't know what I can do about this situation with this photo on the front page of the *Times* and leading every network news show tonight. The presence of the photo is pushing the action, and for the sake of the Bureau, I have to be ahead of the action, not behind it. If there's anything, tell me now. If, for God's sake, you made a mistake, tell me now. We can deal with it. A quiet resignation, a saved pension, recommendation to positions in the private sector. If I have to formally suspend you and Professional Responsibility files a complaint and it goes to formal hearing, there's nothing I can do for you. Your record is so damned good, I'd hate to see it end like this."

"Sir, I can only say, I have no opinion on the photo, and I have no recollection of ever traveling to Columbia, South Carolina. I didn't do it."

The director sighed.

"Okay, Nick," he said, "then I have no choice but to— Nick, I have to say, you seem to be enjoying this. That's what I don't quite understand. I see, well, not quite a smirk, but a kind of look. Ace up the sleeve, I know something you don't know, nonny-nonny-boo-boo, my class wins the Bible, that kind of look. A shoe waiting to drop look. Am I wrong?"

"No sir," said Nick and then he couldn't hold it anymore and started to laugh. The more he laughed, the more he had to laugh, until the laugh became a fit, almost a seizure.

The director adopted a look of benign condescension, let Nick go on and on.

"Okay," he finally said, "you've enjoyed your joke at my expense, and I've heard you are a very funny fellow. But it's time for the punch line. I'm due at a press conference very shortly and I've got to tell them more than 'Special Agent Memphis is upstairs having a good yuk.'"

"I'm sorry, sir."

"Go ahead."

Nick thought.

"I just don't see how I can be suspended for a picture of me at the FN USA shooting range in 2006 with a rifle that doesn't exist."

"I don't know what—"

"It's not even an FN rifle. It's from their arch competitor, Remington. But not only is it a Remington rifle in my hand, it's a Remington rifle that didn't exist until 2008."

"I don't—"

"That rifle hadn't even been designed in 2006. It's in their current catalog, but in 2006, it wasn't even a dream in an engineer's eye. So the picture's a fake. It's manifestly, self-evidently a fraud. I don't know who did it, or why, or how. But not only that, whoever did it understood exactly what the *Times* knew nothing about and he took advantage of their congenital weakness, and the upshot is, he got them to publish a photo that twenty million people will instantly know is phony!"

The director looked at the picture.

"Well," he said, "it looks like the joke's on them, doesn't it?"

"Yes sir."

"Do they know yet?"

"If they don't, they will soon enough."

"Boy, would I likc to see *that*."

43

David Banjax decided to award himself the morning off. He knew no one would mind. He was the hero. He wanted to savor it. So instead of going to the bureau, he slept later, just wandered a bit on the streets of Washington, past the *Post* on Fifteenth and the garage where he'd gotten the original pack of documents, down K, past McCormick & Schmick's, which had become a lunchtime favorite, down to Connecticut, then up it, past the square, past the Mayflower, past Burberry's, up still further to Dupont Circle, then a deviation down embassy row on Massachusetts, all the great old houses from the gilded age converted to little bits of sacred ground of other nations, behind walls and hedges and largely Mediterranean architecture, giving this arcade in the capital city a Roman Way look to it.

I am Spartacus, thought David with a bit of a grin.

He felt as he always did of late when he'd landed the big one, the talker. He felt painfully self-conscious, aware that everybody was aware of him, that his few fans admired his success, that his competitors in the bureau resented it, as they hated it when someone stepped away from the pack and became an individual, a star, and got on TV and had calls from editors at S & S and Knopf and Chris at MSNBC and Bill at Fox and Larry at CNN and Scott at NPR and Charlie at PBS, even Jon at Comedy Central. He wanted to stretch it out, settle himself down, enjoy the day and the exquisite anticipation.

It was chilly but bright. The brisk wind blew his raincoat against his sports coat, fluffed his hair, blew tears into his eyes. Everywhere people looked hearty and happy, absorbed in the narcissism of their time and place, consumed by scandal, a soon-due report, an upcoming meeting, a conference, a screening, an opening, a reception, a recital. It was a town of meetings. Everyone except David seemed to have one that morning; his wouldn't arrive until four, and as he planned it, he'd wander casually into the office about, say, hmm, 3:43, just enough time to deal with any invitations, take the begrudging congrats of peers and admirers, nod at those who weren't moved to offer their congrats, and make a quick run-through of his e-mail to see if the congrats from his liberal friends outnumbered—they usually did, these days—the hate mail from his conservative enemies. He figured, I bet I set a new record today. I bet I get over a hundred e-mails.

He had a solitary lunch, late, after the lunch crowd had left, across from the Motion Picture Association of America on I Street at BLT Steak, a quiet, sleek new beef house in town. He chose it because it was out of the way, a good seven blocks from the bureau and from the *Post*, and nine blocks in another direction from the National Press Building, so it was unlikely he'd run into any journos there. And he was right: nobody he knew entered, and he spent the time sipping a nice midrange merlot while eating his steak salad and reading his own paper, the *Post*, *USA Today*, the *LA Times*, and the *Boston Globe*, to assure himself that nobody else had anything, that he was out front, that the scoop was his. Tomorrow they'd catch up, and he knew right now that in various newsrooms around town, the scramble was on.

He paid, left the papers, ambled out and down the street toward his shop, enjoying every second, every atom, every nanophenomenon, every twitch of unmeasurable black energy that comprised the wonder of his life until at last he reached the lobby of his own building.

"There's the champ!"

It was that hoary old legend Jack Sims, looking like he'd just stepped out of a confab with FDR himself, all tweeds and oxford cloth, with that square, ruddy, Washington face. Jack, on his way out for the late lunch or an early martini, still wore a belted, buckled Burberry trenchcoat foreign correspondent style, and with a fedora low over his eyes looked like Mitchum in a film noir, but he had the gravitas to bring it off and seemed authentic in the role, not affected.

"You know," he said in his booming voice, "at my age, my only pleasure is watching one of you young kids kick ass and take no goddamn prisoners. Congrats, Dave. You ought to be so goddamn proud!"

"Thank you, Mr. Sims," he said modestly, not even bothering to correct the old guy for calling him Dave, which he hated. It was his ambition to be admired by all the players in the office, no matter the generation, not just his immediate peers.

"Go get 'em, Tiger," said the old legend, eyes twinkling, with a last clap on the shoulder.

David rode the elevator in silence, aware that

everyone in it realized from the Sims greeting that he was somebody special.

Yet when he got to the office, there was a different vibe ahum in the air than the one he expected. He hung his coat, slid down the aisles between the desks, and was aware of just some kind of . . . difference. Usually he felt love, hatred, admiration, begrudging respect, a whole palette of emotions. Today it was, hmm, what? Embarrassment? Shame? Hostility, even anger? What was this all about? It seemed that people squirmed not to make eye contact, that his appearance carried with it the power of silence. All the office chit-chat dried up; the place went silent.

What could that— Was it— Why was— All very strange. He looked, and backlit against his window, Mel the bureau chief was huddled in conference with some others, and they spoke tensely, even urgently. His secretary was even in there with him.

David didn't like the feeling.

He got to his desk, sat down.

Everything seemed the same, everything seemed fine. So what was the big deal? Maybe it was just his nerves.

He looked at his watch. It was 3:50, ten until the 4 p.m. news meeting. Just enough time to get the lay of the land.

He clicked on his computer, waited for it to warm up just like a fifties TV, until the code prompt came on and warned him he had to change codes in nine days but he could do it now if he wanted, and he didn't, and he waited till his icons came on, little cartoony emblems against the field of deep blue, and he decided to skip the Net—Drudge, Huffington, Power Line, TNR, NRO, and the others—and instead moused straight to Lotus Notes, double-clicked, waited again until the e-mail index came up, checked to see how many he'd gotten, good Lord, it was over 200 and—

Wait, it wasn't over 200.

He looked carefully.

It was over 8,000.

8,456!

David felt his respiratory system ice over in that moment; it just solidified into something heavy with cold and death, immovable and gargantuan, something not him.

He flicked away from the page to refresh it, and when it came back, the e-mail count was up to 8,761.

He looked around, convinced that everyone in the office was staring at him but would make no eye contact, as if his colleagues were turning away exactly as his eyes rose to meet theirs.

That many e-mails could mean but one thing: the Big Mistake.

He glanced at the displayed topic lines of the e-mails in the column that ran the length of the screen.

ASSHOLE

Times commie

ignoramus

Should have called NRA

Fool

what about seven-day waiting period for YOU!

Can't tell Winchester from Rem

Not a PSR, clown

DUH

And on and on it went.

He picked one that seemed less incendiary than the others, its topic line reading "Visual vocabulary insufficient." At least this guy might understand punctuation and capitalization.

> Dear Mr. Banjax,
>
> I suppose by now you have been notified you ran a four-column photograph on the front of your newspaper claiming that you had a picture of a crooked FBI agent firing an FN PSR at the FN range in 2006, when what he is actually holding is a Remington VTR 700, a model not introduced until late 2008. You must also realize that the photograph completely invalidates the premise of your story and your investigation, reveals itself to be a fraud, and suggests that the integrity of the *Times* has been tarnished beyond recovery. All in all, a smashing performance. Congratulations! You couldn't have done more harm to your cause if you actually TRIED to harm your cause.
>
> This represents a distressing tendency on the part of Mainstream Media. You all are so opinionated on gun matters, gun policies, gun politics, yet you lack even the most fundamental gun knowledge to buttress your implicit claims of expertise. Quite the opposite, you oh so frequently expose your woeful ignorance

and laughable grasp of reality. But even by
that standard, this morning's blooper is quite
spectacular.

You represent the media assumption that a
gun is just a gun. Any gun is any other gun and
therefore you of the enlightened, educated ironic
classes needn't trouble yourself with actual facts
about it. The facts don't matter, only something
you're sure you see, called "the truth." But if
there are no facts, there is no truth. It's a pattern
we see repeated over and over again. Someone
once defined a newspaper gun story as "something with a mistake in it."

You idiot. You were incapable of looking at
one rifle and distinguishing its differences from
another rifle. It's not rocket science, chum. Thus
you publish a picture misidentified that literally
millions of people—not all redneck neanderthals
listenin' to CW n' drinkin' moonshine in trailer
parks, neither, Snuffy—will see through in a
second.

The FN PSR is a refined version of the
Winchester Model 70 and still bears the
hallmarks of that VERY FAMOUS weapon.
The most obvious of these is the trigger guard;
the Winchester designers of the early 30s who
created that piece of metallic (later alloy) genius
had a sense of streamline and grace and they
managed to come up with a classic interpretation
of the oval. That Winchester oval is part of the
visual vocabulary of our times, and any hunter
recognizes it instantaneously; it carries with it a
trace of art moderne, reflecting the fashions of

the period of its creation, and, serendipitously or not, it was so slick and eye-appealing and perfectly scaled and brilliantly machined and blued that even now, over 70 years later, its inheritors in South Carolina can't bear to part with it. That is why all the new FN rifles bear approximations of it, and any rifle claiming to be FN bolt action would feature such an emblem. The rifle you identify as an FN SPR does not.

It contains another equally vivid symbol of an American classic. Remington had a different, though just as distinctive, interpretation of the trigger guard. They knew that their rifle, the Model 700, had to have an immediately apparent visual signature that marked its difference from their main competition, the 70 (do you get the 70/700 dynamic?). They were coming into the market 30-odd years later (1962) and at that time, the Model 70 was the baseline, but they saw an opening because they knew that Winchester was planning an upgrade that would ease manufacture but coarsen the product. So they had to deliver something distinctive. Their trigger guard has a kind of bow to it, an expansive exaggeration that takes it out of the oval, opens it up, out, and downward (some say the function is to allow a gloved finger easier access to the trigger), but again with a harmony and grace that is instantly recognizable to anyone who knows even the slightest thing about firearms.

Evidently, you and your confreres at the *Times* missed this OBVIOUS distinction, as you missed several other unique hallmarks of the VTR that make it all but impossible to confuse with the PSR.

I could go on to various differences in the nuance of stock and bolt design. I could point out that the scope on the rifle is a Leupold 9X and unlikely to possess the refinement for the kind of shooting (less than MOA at 300 yards) the picture and the story attribute to Mr. Memphis and the "PSR."

But you get the point: all in all, pathetic, ignorant, transparent. Quite ugly. You think we're so stupid, while you're the one who's stupid. You should be ashamed.

> *Sincerely,*
> *Neanderthal P. Country-Music*
> *Redneck*
> *3d Trailer on Right*
> *Passel O' Toads, NC*
> *aka*
> *Lawrence M. Fisher, MD, PhD*
> *Director of Oncology*
> *Methodist Hospital*
> *Kansas City, MO*

Banjax realized he had been had. He had been faked and ruined and he'd walked right into it.

"David?"

It was the bureau chief's secretary.

"David, Mel would like to see you."

"Well, I—"

"David, right away," she said in a voice that communicated the secret meaning *David, right away.*

44

Swagger lay in darkness, too focused to sleep. He was curled on the cot, facing the wall under a thin blanket, aware of the TV camera in the corner of the dark room, its red eye signaling its activity. He waited for time to pass, for his torturers to select a guard, then bed down for the night.

His wrists were bound together by the tough plastic of the flex-cuff, impervious to most blades; it took a pair of clippers and a great deal of force to cut through them. Thus, by the configuration of wrist on wrist, his fingers were closely intertwined. With the fingers of his right hand, he went to his index finger, left hand, and began to carefully peel the Band-aid around the base of the finger—"Cut ourselves wanking, have we now?" It was a process made more arduous by its taking place behind him, in the dark, and inside out, with the left to the right and the right to the left, with numb, swollen fingers. But by picking at the edge of the Band-aid, he got it loosened, and by stretching, sliding, manipulating with great focus and energy, he got the Band-aid removed from the base of the finger. There, buried in scab from the skin-cutting tightness with which it had been wound about the finger, a few inches of hard cutting wire used in certain surgical applications rested, coiled tightly. He got the coil off the finger, ran it through his hands to open it and clean off the dried blood, then—again straining at the awkward angles, the stretch of joint, the numbness in his fingertips—he looped the cutting wire over the plastic of the flex-cuff, caught an end in thumb and forefinger of each hand, and began to saw.

It was not easy. He felt the sweat rising, slicking his body in the dark little chamber, and he tried to lie quietly, as a man asleep might lie. Meanwhile, the wire would not bite into the plastic and kept slipping. It would snake out of one hand and was tense with inbred circularity, having been wrapped around his finger for such a long time. He focused everything he had on the ordeal, trying to get his fingers to obey, trying to get the cutting wire to bite into the plastic, trying to hold it taut, trying to keep his whole body still for whoever was watching the television monitor, and it seemed for the longest, the most frustrating time not to be happening, it was not happening *goddamnit to hell* it was not happening he could not get the wire to catch to—

And then it happened. Why then and not a minute earlier or a minute later he'd never know. Somehow he scored enough into the flex-cuff for the wire to catch and bite, found some leverage in his hands (though they cramped as if being crushed in vises) and, emboldened by his tiny taste of success, began to saw away. On that surge of energy, he got the flex-cuffs cut in less than twenty minutes.

The trick then was not to give in to the temptation to throw out and stretch his cramped arms, to flex and satisfy his tightened fingers, to rub his raw wrists. He lay still, breathing, waiting.

Time passed.

No one rushed in, beat him senseless, and clapped the iron manacles about his limbs.

He squirmed, turned, and still keeping his hands, though now free, behind his back, twisted downward and got the wire looped over the flex-cuffs about his ankles. With free hands, he had better leverage this time and was able to wrap the wire about his fingers instead of pinching it between them; he was done in five minutes.

He flicked his ankles, and each shoelace in his left hiking boot presented itself to him, as if specially weighted. It was weighted; from each he withdrew a two-inch-long piece of titanium needle, extremely strong and unbendable, a millimeter wide. Again, he waited for the sound of footsteps, the crash of the door opening, the arrival of the Irish goons with fists and truncheons to beat him to pulp for his audacity. Nothing happened.

Now, tricky. Was the fellow on the monitor asleep? Was he just drowsing? Was he watching an episode of *Star Trek* on TV or jerking off to an old copy of *Juggs*? Or was he enjoying Swagger's struggle and letting it build in hope until it was time to crush it?

Swagger's hard combat mind banished doubt and speculation. No purpose was served, except to slow his directness, and he needed speed, decisiveness, surprise for what lay ahead.

Easily, he slid off the cot, coming to rest on the floor. He was aware of the red light as if it were a red eye, a dragon's eye, staring at him. But he pressed on, snaking his way across the dark floor to the door, where he slid upward, leaning against the hard metal, and found the key hole. He probed, a pick in the fingers of each hand. The job required delicacy, and after thirty-six hours of bound torture, he had none; his fingers felt like stone, when they weren't atremble like the wings of a butterfly. The process seemed to devour time. It seemed hours, as he probed, felt the give of levers inside, the weight of tumblers, the dense cylinder that was the core of the lock, whose flanges had to be manipulated properly, while he held a spring down by pressing hard against it with strength he no longer had. Hours passed, then days and nights, then months. Somehow the years changed, and decades later, the door at last yielded, not with a click but with a whisper. He eased it open, stepped into the well-lit hallway, blinked for focus and clarity, looked each way for a weapon, saw none. He did exactly what he'd done earlier when he'd first entered the house, but he did it more artfully this time, using the sniper's gift for silent movement, the sniper's patience for goals reached surely but without rushing, and he came at last to the steps and then to the doorway atop the steps, and he slid through, hearing heavy snoring. His trip took him through the kitchen; he quietly pulled a drawer, then another, and finally a third until he located a butcher's crude blade with enough point and length to reach blood-bearing organs in a single cut.

He eased around a corner into the security office and there saw on a screen his own empty cot and the door of his own cell half ajar. Alas, no one was awake to notice, for Ginger, the smartest of the Irishmen, lay sound asleep in a chair, his feet up on a desk under the TV monitor. No time for deliberation now, as Swagger's trembly, weakened muscles were pumped by the pressure of adrenaline foaming into his bloodstream, and in three swift steps he was upon Ginger, had the man's neck wrapped in the crook of his elbow, securing it, and with the other hand, drove the knife point into the delicate skin of the neck just tenths of an inch from the river of red blood known as the carotid.

"Wake up, you Irish fuck," he said sharply, jerking on the neck as if to break it, for that was another of his options, given the leverage he had attained.

"*Ggggg—kkk,*" was all his crushed passages allowed Ginger to mutter.

"You listen to me, I'd just as soon cut you open"—he put pressure so that the tip of the butcher's tool sank another tenth of an inch or so into skin entirely too fragile to offer it anything of an impediment—"and watch you bleed dry on the floor, but what's going to happen is I'm going to roll you to the vault just like this and you're going to open it. And if you pretend you don't know the combination, I'm cutting your carotid clean through and you die vomiting blood and shitting and pissing, while I go upstairs and get myself another Irish artery to split. I will kill all night if I have to. I'm only letting you live because I want some dough, and you're the messenger."

The softness of surrender flashed through Ginger's big body, and Bob rolled him on the strength of his shoulders, and in a few seconds they'd arrived at the heavy door. This time it was locked, but Ginger got his hands to the dial, a silver disk the size of a destroyer day-room clock, and spun and clicked the knob back and forth half a dozen times, and a vibration announced that he'd opened it, and then the door, of its own volition, unlinked and opened an inch.

Bob rode Ginger to his feet, not wanting to give

the bigger, younger, stronger man any space to acquire leverage; Bob could not afford a fight now, even if he won it. When Ginger was upright, Swagger said, "Open it," and the door flew wide, and Bob pushed Ginger in. He saw stacks of rifles, bins of ammo, and just where it had been, the film, safe in its cardboard package on the shelf.

"Knees," said Bob, and Ginger went down.

Kill him, Bob thought. One fewer of the bastards. Murder his ass and send the message that this is to the death.

But cutting a half-strangled thug's throat was not a thing he could do; instead, he released the clamp on the neck, quickly seized a rifle—it was a Remington 700—inserted the butt into the cleft between skull and shoulder against the neck, and forced Ginger facedown.

"Tell Anto I'm too old to give a fuck about honor. I want dough and lots of it. I'm sick of being poor and noble. But I want to be in control, not him. I want to get paid for my trouble. I want to get paid for that war in something other than nightmares. This is my chance and I won't let him fuck me like everyone else. I'll contact him tomorrow and we'll rig an exchange somehow in the wilderness. And I want dough up front so they best get on the phone to Constable and get a big pile of cash here. You can remember that? Oh, and I hope you don't suffocate."

With that he withdrew the buttstock a few inches, then drove it hard into the back of Ginger's skull, knocking the fellow either out or, more likely, into a grogginess so intense and a pain so heavy he could do nothing for minutes.

Swagger wished he had time to disable the rifles or at least twist all the knobs to hell and gone, but he didn't. Instead, he snatched the film, slid out, and locked the heavy door behind him. Whether Ginger lived or died did not at this point seem an issue to ponder.

He went quickly to the shelf, plucked off a radio unit next to the blinking receiver by which the professional security people stayed in contact. He looked around until he saw a heavy ring of keys. Then he slipped out the door.

Piles of stars filled the western sky. A wind pushed cold air across the plains, fresh out of the mountains close by, whose darker bulk obliterated the low starlight. Vegetation, moved by that cascade of air from above, filled the sky with the sound of its own rustling. Far off, a coyote howled, and his mate responded.

Swagger sucked the cold air, glad of its plentitude, hoping for energy. Then his adrenaline took over.

He set out on a course to the vehicle compound next to the barn, stopped to retrieve a knapsack he had wedged into a culvert on the way down. He opened it, removed an ice pick.

At the compound, it took a second to find the right key, and then he unlocked the padlock and lifted the gate back. He walked past each vehicle—five four-wheeled all-terrain vehicles, two jeeps, a pickup truck, and a Cherokee—and thrust the penetrating needle of the ice pick into each tire. It sank without difficulty into the tires, and it produced in him a reverie of vengeance as he fantasized it was going into the thoracic cavities of his captors. In a very few seconds he had disabled all the vehicles save one of the ATVs.

He knelt, used the grip of the tool to shatter the plastic housing of the ignition, found the wires tangled beneath, did some pulling and jiggling before he freed the leads up, then sparked the vehicle to life. Maybe it was loud enough to awaken the sleeping Irishmen, maybe not. It didn't matter by now.

Throwing the ice pick in the knapsack, he threw the whole thing on his back and his leg over the saddle of the ATV, a thing built by Honda called a Foreman. It was essentially a broader, slower, but more agile four-wheel motorcycle, its broad base giving it stability, designed to negotiate the back country, the vehicle that made hunting fields accessible to lazy, out-of-shape suburbanites. He kicked it into gear and twisted the throttle at the handlebar's end and peeled out of the compound, turned, and headed out into the wilderness. No noise arose behind him, and he roared onward in the dark, his pains forgotten, his angers quelled, his righteousness unstoked. He was only thinking one thing: time to get my rifle.

45

At five, Raymond's alarm woke him and told him it was time to relieve Ginger. He rose, dressed, brushed his teeth, ran a wet comb through his hair, smiled at his cheeky beauty in the mirror, and thought of the many gals he'd had and the many more, with all that swag, that awaited. Then down he went, whistling and calling, "Is the coffee hot still, Ginger, or must I make it meself?" and first discovered that Ginger was missing, then saw the empty cell and open door on the security monitor, turned quick to check the vault, saw it locked, then heard the pounding from inside.

Things happened in a blur after that. Raymond pulled Anto and the others from sleep. They got the vault open in time to save the gasping Ginger's life, though the man was cross-eyed with a skull as bloody as if the red Indians had taken his hair from the pounding the sniper had administered.

The team made quick checks, discovered the useless vehicles, the stolen radio set, got Swagger's message as relayed by the slow-of-wit Ginger, and realized they'd just inherited a new game.

"Do you see?" said Anto, the first to figure it out. "This was the bastard's plan from the start. Remember how daft I thought it, him coming in all clumsy and stupid, him giving up without much fight, him just a sponge in our hands? Give it to the bold bastard, his plan was canny—to let us work him hard, him believing it was in him to last us out, and last us out he did. Then, knowing where the film was, he became himself again and ceased with the stupid and the slow. He got out, took down poor, unsuspecting Ginger, and now he's the one with the cards."

"The bloody magician," said Raymond, a little awestruck, "but a hard man he'd be to know what was coming and ride it through."

"Hard he is," said Anto, "hard and smart, but he'll be dead, I swear. It's Twenty-two he's fighting here, not some ragtop A-rab boy petters."

"What now, Anto? Do we track him? I'm thinking them tire tracks would make the job easy."

"We do not. He has a rifle cached, I'm sure of it. We track him, he puts us down one at a time, from way out. I'll not have that."

"Then what is left for us to do?"

"Well," said Anto, "what we must do is figure where he'll set up and be ahead of his thinking, not behind it."

"Anto, yis cannot read minds. That's a hell of a spread out there in all directions. He could be anywhere. Guess wrong and you're the dead one."

"Yeah, Anto, Ginger's got a point. The smart move, I'm thinking—"

"Jimmy, don't wrinkle your brow with thinking now. It ain't becoming. And no, I don't read minds, and yes, it's a hell of a big spread and he could be anywhere. But think of him, think of us. Snipers all. He fears us; what's he want? Where does he seek safety? How would he feel at his most comfortable? And who would know of such a place?"

"Anto, I—"

"That fellow who manages the ranch operation for his lordship. He must know the land like his wife's wrinkly arse. Get him by phone, please, Jimmy. He'll have an answer."

Jimmy searched the database—the task normally would have fallen to the brighter Ginger, but Ginger's head was a little messy—and in time, the phone was handed to Anto.

"Mr. McSorley, it's Anto, of Mr. Constable's security team, sir, and I do apologize for the early nature of the call."

Anto listened to the old grump pretend to be undisturbed, fight for time to clear the grogginess, remind Anto that he, Anto, had told him to clear the property of working men for a few days, and then settled in to listen.

"Sir, I've heard from Mr. Constable this very morning and he's asked me to set up a security exercise to keep the boys sharp and for him to watch when he returns. Thus I wonder if I might explore the knowledge ye'd be havin', livin' here your whole life, and help us find a chunk of land out there suitable. Yes, thanks, Mr. McSorley, what I need is distance, space, a long way for the eye to see and no place to hide in nature. Not glades and trees and rocks and foothills but an open valley, short grass, and it would be helpful if it weren't too far out, because transpo's an issue as well. Oh, I see. Yes, that's right. 'The Goggles,' you say. Perfect, you say. I'd have looked at the map a hundred years and not have known, but you've got me right to it, and I'm thanking you kindly, sir, and will tell Mr. Constable of your cooperation. Good day to you, sir."

He hung up.

"What would 'the Goggles' be, Anto?"

"Look to the map, boys."

The geodesic survey chart was quickly pulled from a drawer and unrolled.

"He says there's a couple of broad valleys about, twenty mile out, the first one, the second another four mile along. He guessed a compass radial from security HQ to be around two-fifty, not quite true west, but a little shaded to the south, over rough territory, foothills and the like. He thinks they was formed by comets striking the earth a million years ago. A double tap, you might put it."

"There, Anto," said Raymond, pointing out the irregularity on the map, "and can you not see why they're called the Goggles?"

Indeed, the broadness, the circularity, and the separation of the elevation lines to convey gentleness of slope appeared to the naked eye like two broad, clear lenses against the density of marking that expressed rougher ground. Squint and you were looking into the eyes of an aviator from the open-cockpit days.

"He'll be able to see a long way coming," said Ginger, as if his head had cleared, "and having set up, and alone knowing the site and having a chance to examine it with his fine eye, he'd have no fear of hidden shooters."

"Moreover," said Raymond, "the land right on the approach is rugged, craggy, with lots of dips and arroyos and valleys, then it crests up, you cross over, and there's a big emptiness. He'll bounce you through them valleys on the approach."

"He will indeed," said Anto. "Then this is where it'll play out. He'll call late afternoon. He's got to sleep the day away; he's not slept in three and he's had that bout with the water, which would break all other men. So this I'll tell you: he's in a fog now. He'll know that and not want to make mistakes. He's found a fine bog and and he'll sleep like a bear. Then he'll call, and the game begins."

"And we arrive at the crest once he's exposed himself, you're thinking, Anto," said Raymond.

"Then with iSniper we write The End to this story," added Ginger.

"No, fellows, too many slips could occur. This is how it must happen. This is the fulcrum, the key. *It's that you're already there.* You moved in at night—tonight, that is—you set up a hide so good it can't be spotted, because when he gets to the place after the long game he's run, he'll pass his shrewd eyes over it. That's where your snipercraft must be as I taught you, and I won't be there to check and improve. It's on Team Irish, not on Anto. It must be perfect, and your patience and your stalker's stillness and your shooting ability with iSniper911 and Mr. 168-grain Black Hills must be at the top of the heap, because you'll only get one chance. You put the beam on him, let the magic bean do its trick and solve your jumble of numbers and designate your point of aim, and then you hold, control breathing, press to surprise, break, and put the man down."

"Anto, suppose we search the body and the MacGuffin ain't upon him? Should we then shoot for hip, smash it up, and leave him still breathing for further interview?"

"You will not. Shoot him dead. I don't want him wounded, I want him belly up, the Sniper nailed. He'll have it on him, as it's fragile and can't be left in nature, and if he's hit or takes a fall, or the play blows him this way or that across the land, that makes picking it up afterward a consideration he'd rather not face. He'll have it upon him, that I know."

"I'd like the shot, Anto," said Ginger, "if it can be arranged. It was my head he thumped, enjoying the blow, and it was my lungs that would've come up empty if Raymond hadn't needed his cup of coffee, so with me, it's taken on the personal."

"You'll understand, then, Ginger, why I'm placing you low, with a carbine, for close-in if it must be, because I don't want you brooding in your hide and getting anxious and bumbling on the delicacy of the trigger. I'll let Raymond take the shot from above, with Jimmy spotting, and you're my security, down close. I'm putting you in a ghillie where I think he'll make the play and you'll be closest to him. If Raymond misses, you'll have but a second to dump a magazine into him, or it's poor Anto among the angels, what a mighty tragedy that would be. So Raymond, the shot you'll take will be through the moving stuff, and that's why it's yours, because you are the best wind reader and through shooter on the team, as I know the fellows would agree."

"It's true," said Jimmy. "Raymond's a genius in the breeze. Otherwise, the poor man's the dullest blade in the drawer, but fluff up the weeds and set the leaves to rustle, and Raymond's the man you want."

Everybody laughed, even Raymond, who was known to be a sensitive type.

"Then, mates," said Anto, "we're done with this bloody job and this bloody country with its thin beer and bad poetry, and it's off to castles in Spain where his lordship has set up our fine lives for us."

46

Swagger awoke from dark sleep that felt drugged, shook his head to drive out memories too grotesque to be recorded, wished hard for a cup of coffee. He didn't feel refreshed or enlivened a bit; he wanted to go back to unconsciousness and escape his reality: in a dirty-smelling nook in the rocks, heaped with the crap he'd brought along, faced with a mission he felt too old for. Have to get my combat mind back, he told himself: *have to!*

He crawled out of his sleeping bag, crawled up the incline to the mouth of the cave, and went to his Leicas for a good five-minute examination of landscape. It looked fine—a drift of low hills and sparse forestry, a glimpse of green-yellow valley floors, a haze of far-off peaks. At one point he thought he saw a line that seemed a little too straight for anything in nature, and he put down the binoculars to take up the rifle. Through the Leupold Mark IV's 10X, he studied hard and realized it was a length of birch trunk 240 yards out.

He glanced at his watch, saw that it was nearly 5 p.m., meaning it was 8 p.m. in the East and he was already behind schedule.

He ate three protein bars because he'd need the energy for the long night ahead, and stuffed a couple in his cargo pants pocket. Then he crawled to the mouth of the cave, checked again, crawled out, and pulled out his ccll and punched in a number.

Come on, goddamn it, work, goddamn you, and in a bit he heard ringing.

"Where the hell are you?" said Nick Memphis.

"Never you mind," said Swagger. "Are you back, are you out of the woods, are you the boss?"

"I'm back. Long story. Forget me. You said to Starling, 'Jump time,' and then you went incommunicado for three long days. What the hell is happening? What the hell are you doing? What is your situation? What are your plans?"

"Here's what's important. I have to get you something. No point describing it. Hmm, don't see no FedEx offices around this neighborhood, so tomorrow I'll find a way to get it sent FedEx; tomorrow being Saturday, I'll pay for Sunday delivery. I want you ready for it, expecting it, set up to receive it, protect it, and understand it."

"Where's the nearest big city?"

"Lord, it ain't that near, probably Missoula."

"Too far? Give me a town then. I'll have a team there tomorrow."

"Place called Indian Rapids, Montana, downstate and east a bit from Missoula."

"I'll fly a team in. Bring it to the Indian Rapids airfield or airport. Anytime after noon. Go to the American Eagle desk, tell 'em it's for Mr. Memphis. An agent will take it from you."

"And take me too, no doubt. Well, I don't think it'll matter none by tomorrow. Tomorrow's going to be a very damned interesting day, Special Agent Nick, that I guaran-fucking-tee you."

He broke the connection, put the phone away, then reached in and pulled out the radio unit he'd taken from the charger in security headquarters. It was a Motorola CP 185 VHF two-way, set to MAINT DIRECT. He turned the unit on, then snapped a selector switch to VOX, which automatically voice-activated transmission on the preset frequency.

"Mr. Potatohead. Calling Mr. Potatohead."

"Is it you, Swagger?"

"It's me, Potatohead."

"Tricky bastard, yis screwed all me plans," came the voice, clear against some marginal static. "We needed them machines to get into Indian Rapids before the bank closed at noon, so's I could access an operational account with more cash than a scoundrel like yis ever seen. Now it's all buggered."

"Then rob it tonight, I don't care. If I don't see a ton of cash tomorrow, you get nothing but a bullet between the eyes. The film goes to the feds. Your boss goes to prison. Then I bring some friends in, boys who know a thing or two, and we hunt down the other three O'Flanagans and take heads. I don't have an Irishman over my mantel yet."

"Him with the big talking. What's the game, Sniper? You've got a game."

"Tomorrow you're up at oh-five-hundred. Oh, and you're naked. Buck-ass, jaybird nude. That's so you don't have a shiv or a .45 slickered away in some dark place."

"For God's sake, what about me dignity, man?"

"Not my department. You get aboard an ATV, also stripped, except for that big bag of money, and you set out on the Water Hole Road, and you make tracks to the hole. At the hole, you take High Ridge Trace and you make tracks down it. I'm guessing you'll hit Big Bend Creek at oh-six-thirty just as the light's beginning to come across the valley. I'll call you on this radio, this frequency, so you better have a headphone set. Then you can guess the drill. I'm going to give you GPS headings and bounce you up hills and down valleys and over streams. Sometimes I'll be watching, sometimes I won't, but you'll never know. You move straight and fast to where I tell you. You're alone, you're unarmed, you're naked. When I satisfy myself that your goddamn boys aren't following you and that you aren't in communication with them, I'll take you to me, someplace wide open where nobody gets close. I take the dough. I give you the first half or so of the film. I leave you naked, I take your radio and your ATV and I'm gone. Again, when I'm satisfied I'm not being followed and your boys aren't around, I'll call them and give them the coordinates of your spot and they come get you. The first part of the deal is over."

"You're a bastard, Swagger. Do you know who you're dealing with?"

"Yeah, a naked Irishman hoping a grizzly doesn't decide he's lunch. Sometime in the future, when I'm feeling secure and have thought out the angles, I'll make contact again. This time there'll be an exchange not of cash but of account numbers. When mine's full up, I'll turn over the last of the film to the naked Irishman. You'll never see or hear of me again unless you come after me, and if you do, I go after the big guy, and since you know how good I am, you'll sell him on the proposition that if he wants his legacy clear and to live out his years in peace, he stays the hell away from me. Have you got that?"

"I have."

"And no one else goes out either. I'll be watching the house tonight, and if I hear motors on those ATVs as you send the boys out, I'll sneak down and cut your throat and head into town. They'll have a long wait tomorrow, and when they get back, they can watch the FBI arrest the boss on the TV."

"They's not going nowhere. Where would they go?"

"Tomorrow, oh-five-hundred. Tonight you better hope I don't have nightmares of you guys holding me down while the water crushed my lungs, because I might decide to take it personally and put a bullet in the potatohead." He clicked off.

The call finished, Bob knew he had to check kit while it was still light. Though it was probably an unnecessary precaution, he didn't want to be throwing flashlight beams into the darkness.

Weapons: He wore Denny Washington's Sig 229 in a Mitch Rosen horizontal leather holster under his left shoulder. It was loaded with twelve .40 Corbon +P hollow points, and he had two more twelve-round mags hanging vertically under his right shoulder, to balance the weight of the automatic on the other side of the harness. That gave him thirty-six; if he needed more, he should have had an M4 along.

The rifle was a stainless steel Remington 700 Sendero with a gray-green camo McMillan stock, more hunting rig than dedicated sniper, but accurate as hell way out there with its 7mm Remington Ultra Magnum 150-grain cartridges loading Swift Scirocco polycarbonate-tipped bullets, of which he had four boxes of twenty. The only tactical flourish was the Leupold Mark IV 4–15X scope with the old mil-dot range-finding system built into its reticle, secured in heavy Badger Ordnance tactical rings and bases. The barrel, which he had taped black to mute the dull silver gleam, was fluted, which theoretically meant it cooled faster and empirically made it lighter, and it wore a Blackhawk black canvas cheek pad lashed to the stock to provide the higher stockweld necessary from the prone.

He had an SOG black steel Bowie with seven inches of razor-sharp death taped to the ankle of his right 5.11 assault boot. He had a Colt .380 Pocket Automatic 1908 in his right cargo pocket, with eight Corbon 95-grainers aboard.

Wish I had an M4. Wish I had that Swedish K. Wish I had the best weapon of all, which is two thousand marines.

Food and drink: He had a hydro-pack on his back, a water bladder slung flat against his spine and sustained by shoulder straps, with a tube that curled around his neck, so he could hydrate anytime he needed to without the excess motion of unlimbering, then unscrewing a canteen, then reversing the motion. He also had a Depends on, for obvious reasons. He had six energy bars. He had insect repellent, lip balm, alcohol swabs, and a trauma kit strapped to his lower left calf, with scissors, bandages, a couple of packs of clotting agents, disinfectant, and morphine Syrettes.

Communications: He had the radio unit from the ranch, freshly empowered with new batteries. He had his Nokia folder, freshly charged.

Camouflage: He had his best ghillie, a cumbersome exoskin made largely of heavy gauze secured to a one-piece reinforced tactical unit and woven cleverly with six-by-one-inch strips of cloth in the green-brown-gray dispersal pattern of the natural world in autumn, an abstraction so dazzlingly authentic that it all but disappeared when inserted into nature and further camouflaged by its wearer's willingness to endure the ordeal of complete stillness. He had a boonie hat, soft and floppy-brimmed, itself multihued but more importantly also woven with tufts of the nature-toned material. He had three sticks of face paint—green, tan, brown—that would fold the whiteness of his face into the blur of natural color. The only odd color visible would be the lenses of his Maui Jim prescription shades, tear-shaped, brown, sprayed with lacquer to counteract their tendency to reflect the light. All in all, he looked like a bush.

He geared up. An observer, though of course there was none, might have thought of a samurai preparing for a duel at a temple against a hated enemy, or a knight strapping on the armor for a joust to the death with the forces of darkness. Swagger, no romantic, thought of none of this, only the careful placement of gear, the protection of the film reel inside a nesting of bubble wrap inside a thickness of duct tape, in his left cargo pocket, the buttons well closed and checked; he thought of the ordeal of the night and the different ordeal of the day. He put on his war face, smearing alternating abstractions of the green, tan, and brown face paint this way and that, until all his pink flesh was hidden and only the absolutism of war camouflage showed. He thought of the long shot, of the short, quick encounter, all of it shooting for blood. He thought of his plan and how many ways it could fall apart and leave him alone surrounded by enemies; he thought of his age, which was way beyond the limit for this kind of mission; he thought of the soreness in his joints, particularly in his right hip from both a bullet and a sword cut, and six or so operations; he thought of his wife and two daughters and how he missed them; and finally he thought of Carl Hitchcock, head shot open, his legacy tarnished into CRAZED MARINE SNIPER, and all other thoughts, memories, dreams, hopes, and fears disappeared. Now the advantage was his. No more recon, no more recovery, no more negotiation. It was straight killing time, at last.

It was time to hunt.

47

The boys, heavily geared up, left at 2100, when the last smear of sun disappeared. Theirs was a hard thing: they had to cover the miles on foot, hung with weapons, ammo, ghillies, knives, water, and protein bars; night-navigate off their GPSs, shortcutting over foothills and down draws to achieve crow-flight directness; arrive in the dark still, low crawl a thousand yards, dig in, camo up, and settle into perfect stillness for four or so hours of perfect snipercraft awaiting the shot. It was more ordeal than job, just barely doable by war athletes at the peak of operational perfection with two hours in the gym and a five-mile run per day behind them for years. But then, this is what you trained for.

Anto was left alone in the house. He didn't fancy his own agonies: he'd be naked to the elements in harsh weather for a barely survivable length of time, and riding the goddamned ATV fast over rough territory, his bollocks bouncing and squishing, the brutal cold—in the thirties, sure—turning fingers blue and bum white, and when he got there, there being the goal at the end, then a new game started and he'd be thrown this way and that on the radio or the mobile, all of which was getting him into a delicate shooting situation where he'd be so close to the target, a hair's width of mistake in hold or press would dress him in a 7.62 forever, which might only last the eight seconds it took to bleed him out.

He'd smear his flesh, particularly his feet and hands, with thick grease to fight the cold; he'd wear gloves and socks, surely the bastard wouldn't complain about that; and he'd stoke on amphetamines, the soldier's little chemical buddy, that would keep aggression, alertness, and quick thinking at the highest pitch until the natural juices of combat took over.

He tried to sleep but couldn't; he jacked off to a dirty book, but that didn't calm him; he didn't want to mix booze with the recipe of pills he'd take on leaving, so he just tried to sit there, soothing himself with memories of kills.

The best: a squaddie of fellas setting up an ambush in deepest slum Basra, the hide given away by waterboarding that Iraqi lieutenant colonel. So he sets up to the east with Ginger spotting, and Raymond's shooting from the west with Jimmy on the tube. It's pure sniper pleasure. He got nineteen in about two minutes, firing, finding a new target, firing again, throwing the bolt in a blur, watching them boys pivot when hit, then go slack as death sent them to paradise, them falling with the thud of jointless collections of bones and meat. The bastards had no place to run that day, because that was their plan, to blow a Coalition Humvee at a place where all the exits was blocked, and shoot down the survivors. Ha! Hoisted on their own petards, was they.

Now that was a goddamn day a sniper lives for. He doubted even Swagger at his finest hit so many so fast. Maybe Swagger did more in a day, but 'twas over time and involved moving about, staying ahead of his hunters, a different game altogether. But he'd never had the intensity of taking that many that fast. A machine gunner might get it, but again, different: blurred, rushed, the working of the gun, the spray of empties flying, the muzzle blast and noise. His was *pop, pop, pop*, the suppressed AI taking them down, but each image against the reticle was memorable.

Was they all insurgents? He was shooting so fast and Ginger was changing magazines so fast, Anto couldn't tell if indeed each had a giveaway AK on his back; did it matter? Not really, and what dif could it make if the Rockies howled "atrocity" or "massacre" or "murder" or whatever? The point was to give 'em a taste of obliteration in the boldest of ways, so it would haunt them, and maybe that was the beginning of the turnaround in Basra, even though his teams never got no credit, and soon enough the Clara Bartons had turned on them.

He glanced at his watch. He'd eaten enough time. It was 0430, time to grease up.

Nobody was blown, but Ginger, still fighting the concussion, wasn't in the best of shape. He breathed raggedly, held his guts in, crouched low. A bit groggy, he swore he was fine, but Jimmy didn't quite believe it. Eighteen miles is a long haul on the double time with all the stuff aboard, as well as the extra load of Anto's rifle and pack with clothes, even though they were at acme shape. They'd made the crest, hidden Anto's stuff where he'd designated, and now crouched just under the ridgeline, looking down on the broad, dark valley. Because he was cautious, Jimmy checked the GPS again and confirmed for himself that this was indeed the valley Anto had selected, the more southern of the two goggle lenses on the map.

Ginger gulped some water from the tube running out from his backpack.

"Easy, mate," said Raymond. "You may be needing that around noon."

"I'm fine," said Ginger. "It's me goddamned head, hurts so much. That fucker done a fine job on me."

"He's a grand one, he is," said Raymond.

"We'll see his corpse lying still in the grass tomorrow."

"For sure we will."

"Okay, lads, time for a last piss, then to camo up."

They turned for modesty to hasten a last urination, pulled their own Depends adult diapers tight afterwards, and zipped and buckled up. Then came the squishing of the face paint, easy enough, for all had experience in this theatrical craft. Their features gone gray-green-brown, the next thing on the list was the wretched crawl-squirm-tug-wrestle into their ghillie suits and the button-up that followed as the heavy garment closed, heated, and tightened about them. This was followed by the labor of arising and pulling on packs and hats, and finally seizing rifles.

Each, of course, looked like an animated fluff of greenery, some cartoon-factory creation. It got worse when, three large beasts of war, caparisoned in the texture of the natural world itself, with packs of gear and mean implements of death strapped on, they began the long crawl down. At the halfway point they separated, partners Jimmy and Raymond heading for a shooting site and Ginger veering directly downward, to place himself and his M4 close to the creek and therefore, by design, close to the action.

A chill wind bit. He wore slippers at least to the bike. Above, moonglow but no moon lit a sector of sky, and in others the stars lay out in their millions. He could barely make out landforms, though some of the drugs he'd taken were said to enhance night vision. He felt revved, twitchy, intense. His ears were closed off by the headset leading to the radio, which was affixed to his one garment, a Wilderness belt about his gut.

"Potatohead?"

"Go ahead, bastard," he said.

A scrambled crackle of mixed syllables responded.

"What?"

"I said, ta——socks off."

"You bastard. Me feet'll freeze."

"An——gloves."

"What again? I can hardly hear you, this radio transmission sucks. Can we switch to me mobile? It'll be so much clearer and—"

"No. *Gloves.* Take off——*loves.*"

"*Ach,*" complained the Irishman, and complied. "See, nothing."

"Ho——ight leg up."

Anto did. "See, nothing."

"Ok——going."

The radio went dead.

"Bastard," said Anto.

Anto threw his leg over the Honda Foreman, turned the key. At least he didn't have to kick-start it, as in the old days. The little engine turned over, and with his bare right foot, he threw the gears, slipping once, tearing some skin, but he was so drugged up and so charged with uppers he barely felt it. He settled it, throttled up, and the four-wheeler's tires, roughly nubbed for backcountry treks, bit into the earth and the thing lurched ahead.

It was easy going, though the wind bit at him, even through the drugged haze, and now and then a pebble or twig flew up and took off a chunk of skin. His bollocks were undisturbed as long as the road was more or less smooth, and in no time he'd gotten it up to forty, which was top speed on the Honda. He roared through the starglow, through the dark forms of mountains, following the directions he'd been given.

The water hole came up, and he circled it, looking for another track that was the High Ridge Trace, found it, and headed along. Here the going was rougher, as this wasn't a road shared with pickups and Jeeps, but more of a bouncer, and it also took him so close to trees and brush that the limbs and leaves whipped him hard, sometimes very hard, as he rushed along. By now his hands were all but numb and controlling the brake and the throttle was getting harder. His feet, being close to the motor's warmth, were surprisingly comfortable still and hadn't begun to edge toward nothingness. He bent at another lash, saw some fine open road, ginned the throttle, and leapt ahead. As he flew, he checked his watch. It was only 0545 and he knew he'd make his destination in plenty of time.

Jimmy and Raymond, breathless and ragged and clotted with bits of grass, burrs, a slathering of dust stuck to sweat after the long crawl, set up about three hundred yards from the center of the valley flat, with a great overlook on the creek below, with no undulations or folds between them and the presumed target zone. It would be easy shooting, especially with the iSniper911 to solve the shot.

They got down in the prone, and rather than exactly digging in against the slight cant of the land, more or less insinuated their way into it, as if it were a crowd, not the planet Earth itself, squirming, adjusting, kicking now and then, trying to do all this without raising telltale signs like clots of thrown earth and dead weeds about themselves. Finally they had enough room to scootch down flat and not at the tilt, and Raymond took up the rifle, unfolded the bipod legs and had a time on the adjustments, getting the height just right, digging into the earth so that the legs of the support would be even, which would make the traverse easier, if indeed that's what was called for. Meanwhile, Jimmy set up the spotter on its baby tripod, adjusting it for the same presumed target zone three hundred yards and fifteen degrees beneath horizontal out. It was still too dark for him to focus, though in fact a satiny glow had begun to light the eastern horizon across from them. After a bit of busyness, both were as set as they could get, and it was then that Jimmy unfurled a camo tarpaulin, a sheet of canvas threaded heavily with the strips of nature's-coloring fabric as well as the odd twig or piece of thatch, so that it enveloped them, leaving only a peep slot at the farthest extreme, which left them barely enough room to observe and shoot. They settled in for the long, slow wait in abject stillness, a zen beyond death that was the sniper's hardest discipline.

*   *   *

As Anto had predicted, it was much harder on Ginger. He was alone, and after breaking contact with his colleagues, he was *really* alone, seemingly on the face of the Earth. He continued his downward slither, swimming against the soil. It ate his energy and got him dirty, sweaty, and breathless in a hurry, exactly as he stayed throughout the downward progress. He persevered, reaching the valley floor, and before venturing out on the flat, tried to pick the best spot. Certainly dead center, right? But then his mind grew confused: he tried to imagine which way to orient himself; Anto hadn't specified.

Did he want to be on his belly, looking forward to the action, able to haul himself up to his knees, throw the rifle to shoulder, and open up? Or was the best posture on his back, flat, his soles to the action, by which he could simply sit upright as he drew his legs in and fire from that situation? That would be faster by a second, involving less movement and adjustment on his part. On the other hand, he could only see straight up in that position, and he'd be bereft of visual keys. Suppose Raymond hit dirt, to clear the way for his fusillade, and he was just lying there watching the clouds roll by.

But if he were on an incline with his head lower than his feet, sure he might see, but just as sure, with the blood collecting in his damaged skull, he might pass out or endure so much pain that he would begin to involuntarily twitch. Thinking it over, he decided on a compromise and would lie on his left side, facing the creek bed. He could push himself to his knees off his left arm and get to firing almost instantly—full auto, safety off, his finger in the guard housing, resting on the curve of the trigger—yet watch the action as well, and best of all, his head wouldn't be a collection point for all the bad blood that still cruised his veins.

He chose the middle, as near as he could find it, and slid himself down among the higher grass, the knots of brush and bristle, the gnarly little twisted stems of the strange things that grew upon the plains. He settled in possibly twenty-five yards out, with a good view of a hundred yards either way. He felt for comfort and finally achieved what little he could arrange. That done, he threw the camo tarp over himself, like a blanket, so that he only peeped out from the smallest of cracks at the edge, which itself was concealed largely from view by two knots of brush. The matting of fabric strips and leaf clusters stitched to the outside of the tarp vibrated slightly in a soft, predawn wind. His diaper secure, his water source a lick away, his fingers on grip and forearm, the rifle cinched by combat sling close, twenty-eight Corbon 5.56s in the PMAG, and another PMAG so loaded secured to it by a Magpul link for the fastest reload in the game, he allowed himself to settle in and try to relax. As the sun began to paint the limits of his vision, it caught on the tips of trees and the upper reaches of the valley slope across the way.

Ninety hard minutes had passed, and Anto's balls were now turning blue and his hands no longer belonged to him. An uncontrollable chill racked his body. The amphetamines seemed to have worn off as well. He felt pain everywhere, the numbness of the cold, the bite of the wind, the sting of all the particles and branches that had pelted and whipped him.

Jaysus, he hated this evil bastard Swagger like the devil hisself. Him a fine strong man, the sniper's sniper, an NCO in 22, the finest of all units on earth, reduced to nude messenger boy in forty-degree morning, cold and shot through with pain. *Aghhhhh,* such pleasure ahead, in seeing the man take Raymond's 168er and ride it hard to ground, not believing it had finally happened to him. Anto hoped for a bit of eye contact there at the extreme moment, so Swagger would know who'd nailed him. But he'd pass that up for a simple sure death, and if this ordeal, by Jaysus, were the price, he'd pay it in hard, cold cash.

At last he rolled into a grove of trees in a narrow valley that announced the presence of a creek; it had to be Big Bend. He pulled up, turned the motor off, and watched as the sun began to light up the higher bits of elevation, turning the tips of the trees bright with warmth and hope. His machine ticked as it cooled; he sat, immobile, waiting, enjoying the cessation of the vibration against his bollocks, the cut of the wind and the branches against his shoulders and arms. Only his feet were warm, and he put his hands down and opened and shut them against the numbness in the soothing radiation from the engine.

"Potato!"

He responded into the microphone held on a strut just beyond his frozen lips.

"You bastard, Swagger, this being one hairy fooking bitch of a tumble. Man, I'd wring your god-damned neck if I had the chance."

"Not——day," Swagger said, the transmission just a little clearer. "Set your GPS on a radial two-sixty-five an——distance indicator for one-point-seven miles. When the b——ings for one-point-seven, turn to .109. Go. Fast. Now." Then of course the radio went to nothing but static.

Anto struggled to get his GPS out of the bag with the money—actually, old magazines and TV dinner packaging—and with his clumsy fingers found the proper buttons and set the heading, then switched modes and set the distance. It was the Garmin trail-marking model, set to ring when he went the 1.7. Looking at the route, it looked as if he was going straight over the foothills, not around them, and that would be a lot of jostling, a lot of barefoot shifting, a lot of diddling with the throttle and the brake for leverage and control.

Fooking bastard.

He set the GPS onto its neat little bracket affixed to the handlebars for that purpose exactly, gunned the engine to life, and set out, cursing all the way.

Nothing. It was nearly ten now, and the sun was bright and hot. Under the tarpaulin the sniper team did what ninety-nine percent of sniping is: they waited. In the flashy books and movies, the waiting part is always skipped. Alas, for Jimmy and Raymond it could not be. They just felt the numbness spread through their bodies, the warmth of the morning meeting the chill from the ground beneath, and were soon enough miserable, too cold from below, too hot from above. They knew: best not to think of time or check watches, best not to anticipate action, contemplate the future, make plans, hope it would end soon. Best to concentrate on the now, confront the suck in its pristine suckiness, attempt to engage it without letting it destroy the mind, not fret, whine, think of what could have been, refight old fights, discuss anything with meaning, comment on the situation in their adult diapers, profess either hunger to kill or fear of death. Just endure, as snipers had since the first Chinaman threw charcoal, saltpeter, and stinky sulfur together in a bowl and mashed them up.

"Think I'll light a nice cigar, have a piss, open a bottle of stout, and go for a little stretch-it-out walk," said Jimmy, the joker.

"You will not," said Raymond, who was cursed with an earnest, literal mind, "that would completely blow our—" and then he saw it was Jimmy's joking and pulled up.

"Had you, boyo," said Jimmy.

"That you did," said Raymond.

"You poor sod, believing everything that's said. That's why you shouldn't buy nothing till you run it by me, 'cause you're such a gentle, trusting fool, you'll be taken ad of every time."

"I wasn't raised to no fast ways in a city like," said Raymond. "Out in the country, all was what was said, and all you city lads, you play these damned games on me."

"If yis wasn't the best shot in Ireland, what woulda become of ya, I'll never know."

They settled down again, for their spurts of conversation came about every twenty minutes and lasted but a few seconds.

Each rode the optics before him. On the spotting scope, Jimmy's was by far the wider view, and he patrolled the valley floor, then up and down the opposing slope in calm, orderly fashion, as he had been trained, never rushing, never tiring, never blinking, apprehending each and every detail, hunting for some kind of change—the straight line, the shadow falling in the wrong direction, a quick movement, a puff of dust where there was no wind, a dead branch amid bright green sprigs. But there was no change at all, only the lapping of the grass under the pressure of the steady, slight wind and, above the horizon of the valley, the slow, magnificent rush of the clouds, boiling cumulus that looked like frozen explosions with utterly detailed fretwork in their tumbles.

"Look," said Raymond, who'd seen them first.

A flock of strange beasts had moseyed in, with white tails and throats, the size of goats, their horns like the arms of a lyre for a Greek god to pluck a melody on.

"Jaysus, what craytures them be?" wondered Jimmy.

"Did we take a wrong turn and go to Africa, I'm wondering, Jimmy," said Raymond.

"We did, sure of it. No, we did not. Them's antelopes of the American type. Good eating, so I'm told. Hunted hard, the more you kill, the more they breed."

"Who could kill a beauty thing like that?" wondered Raymond.

Agh. How much longer? And how had it gotten so hot so fast? And where did the left half of me butt go?

Ginger lay, like any sniper, hard and calm in the

hide. But this was no ordinary hide. In all the fighting he'd been in—considerable, what with Gulf I,
Gulf II, the odd secret tiff in times of alleged peace,
the long hard pull at Basra during the insurrection,
all the security jobs for Graywolf after the fall—the
hides offered a bit more comfort and movement. An
apartment, an arroyo, a station on an outpost sand-
bag wall looking across a valley of heathen for movement. He'd never been asked before to pretend to be
the earth itself, silent, abiding, unmoving.

Not an easy role to play. Thank God for the water,
he could not stop drinking it, and what happened if it
went too soon, by midafternoon say? He was out here
till well after dark if nothing happened.

And of course his head. The Yank had battered
him good. Hit him hard; you could understand it, the
fellow paying him back for the water procedure. But
still. A doctor would have put stitches in and given
him light duty for a week, as well as the best painkillers Irish medicine could produce. But no such niceties
existed here in wild America. No stitches, so under
the bandages, he could feel the wet of blood seep-
age. The painkillers were over-the-counter, and any
more Advil and he'd be a walking Advil himself, all
brown and bluntlike, a six-three, 240-pound pill of
ache medicine.

Worse, at least Jimmy and Raymond had visuals
to amuse them. His vision was locked on to a spread
of a few dozen yards about the creek, and even when
the strange craytures came down to drink, he hadn't a
good look at them because they never quite came into
his zone of vision. *Ach,* what was they? Some kind of—

He heard something.

Low and far off at first, then it rose. He waited for it to clarify, and presently it did. His heart leapt in actual joy, a rare thing for a man so stoic and duty-bred as he. He knew it to be the sound of the ATV Anto was driving.

His hands tightened on the pistol grip of his M4, he said a quick Hail Mary; he wished he had time to pop another upper for a jolt of energy and concentration; he flexed what he could flex and got ready for the action.

The ATV climbed a ridge and a bell sounded and Anto was happy to see from the GPS that this was where, according to previous radioed instruction, he turned from radial 265 to 109, that is, along the rim of this ridge. He had been worried at first, with all the this-way and that-way until he was confused, but he had a general idea he was trending away from the valley he'd designated as the spot for the final play, toward which he'd bet Swagger would guide him, and where, obedient to his wishes, the Spartans Jimmy, Raymond, and Ginger now lay concealed in ambush.

That sense of despair increased as the game progressed and the clock wound its way onward, but now, finally, he was oriented correctly, or so he believed.

He felt like he was on the moon, as on each side of his ridge, a wide-to-forever stretch of undulating hills, dips, crescents of shadow, outcrops of rock yielded spectacle but little information. Beyond in a distance too far to be measured, he saw snaggled peaks arise, some even snowcapped. But here in the high grasslands, it was all dips and humps, a frozen sea of waves dappled in shadow.

He followed the heading and might have gone to eternity or at least dark when he heard the buzz of the radio signal. He dropped to idle, twisted, got the radio out. Of his clothes, now that he'd adjusted to nakedness, what he missed most was pockets.

"Potato?"

"I am here, goddamnit," he said.

"Stop. Re——ent to heading zero-nine-six, go for one——iles and stop. It'll be—"

"How many miles, goddamnit?"

"One-point-six. Stop. Stay on the scooter—— isappear on me. Ro——r?"

"Roger that, ye slabber."

As usual, the voice didn't rise to any provocations but merely disappeared. Anto reset the GPS and followed its guidance, pleased to see that now indeed it seemed to be taking him where he thought his designated valley ought to be.

The 1.6 passed quickly over bare ground and slopes that weren't quite hills until, at 1.5, he found himself on a steep upgrade, rising to a rim that, examined from a distance, seemed larger than the others. The machine chugged stubbornly against the incline, and in a few more minutes he halted.

The promised land. The valley was vast and he saw in it the same features that had been represented pictorially on the geodesic survey map. It took him a second to orient himself, then he realized he was at the south edge, which meant that of the slopes before him, the right hid his ambushers, and the left would in time present Swagger for the killing.

He was certain that at this moment he was under observation, and so he fought the impulse to show emotion at the success of his strategy, and he fought the instinct to double-check his placements by looking for signs of his hiding men. He kept his face impassive and registered no excitement, no recognition, nothing but the sullen war face of his breed.

He knew he'd wait a bit. Wherever he was, Swagger himself had just arrived, for just as certainly as Anto had been moved about, Swagger, monitoring him, had to be moving too, to get from place to place and watch for followers. But now Swagger would study the valley, for perhaps as much as an hour, examining every tuft, every rill, every knoll, every bush, every rise, every fall, looking for signs that Anto had somehow done exactly what Anto had indeed done—that is, guess the spot and place men there. So this was where the boys' snipercraft had to be at its highest.

The day seemed to disconnect from time. The only noise was the persistence of the wind; otherwise the surface of the earth seemed devoid of life except for the naked, now red-shouldered man on the odd four-wheeled vehicle, which looked more like a toy than anything of serious purpose. A bird rode wind funnels in circles, hunting for prey—another sniper, in his way. Some kind of yowl rose briefly and disappeared as briefly, as something ate something else. The time passed, second by second. Anto sat alone on the bike seat, straddling the engine, buck nekkid as the day he was born but now used to it and not feeling shame at all.

Finally a voice crackled through the earphones.

"See the creek running through the valley?"

"I do."

"Aim for its center. Bisect it——fectly. Within

fifty feet, halt. Climb off——ike on the right side.
——ands are up, you sidestep ten feet, and stop
——n grass. Any sudden mo——ullet in the brain.
Whe——dy, I come out of hide."

"I read."

"Now do it."

Anto turned the ignition key.

As the vehicle jumped to life, he tried to fight the grin that split his face, but he was thinking, *Dead bang center.*

48

Like all western boomtowns, Cold Water had a raw quality to it. Money brought in commerce, which required construction, and soon enough a Main Street sprang up—a bank, a general store, a saloon, a restaurant, a bathhouse, a hotel, all slatternly and crudely constructed of fresh wood, wearing coats of bright paint. The shoppers and watchers and townies, the pioneers, the travelers, the dance hall gals, the town sheriff, all trod back and forth along the dusty street, while above in bright sun the mythic clouds rose and tumbled, and much happiness was felt by all present, for all belonged, just as all adored. All, that is, except Texas Red.

Because Cold Water, for its acquisition of capital, its possible destiny as a railhead, its array of vices and pleasures, had also attracted scum, crude and violent men, for whom civilization meant only one thing: banquet.

Texas Red was one of them.

Wild gun boy, fine dancer, quick to shoot, quickest from the leather, holder of grudges, kisser of gals, he was the whirlwind. His reputation was made in blood and lead. He shed the former, he dealt in the latter. He was the devil to the good citizens of Cold Water, who had formed a posse to take him down. He faced sixteen men.

The first five were to be engaged by rifle, through

the window of the hotel. His .44-40 1892, loaded, would be lying at a table to the right of the window. He'd seize it, throw the lever closed, and fire. Then, having put them down, he would set down the rifle and move fast to the window of the saloon, where seven more waited. Seven meant of course he'd have to use both his handguns, the down-loaded .44-40s from Colt, one at his hip, one on his other hip in the reversed and tilted holster. Done with that, he'd move to the next window in the hotel, to see where four more fellows awaited just down the street, and by that time, his smokepoles empty, he'd go to shot-gun and slide two 12-gauge red boys into the load-ing gate of his supremely polished and finished Model 97 Winchester—by way of the Harbin Industrial Fab-rication Plant No. 6, Hwang Province, China—and quickly pump and shoot and pump and shoot. Then a reload from the leather bandolier he wore across his red placket front, and two more blasts of justice, and he'd be finished with the first stage of this year's Cold Water Cowboy Action Shoot. After that, until late tomorrow afternoon, eleven more stages would determine if Texas Red was indeed the best gun in the Senior Cowboy Black Powder Duelist category, and if all his work was worth it. He just had to be fin-ished—to win!—in time to be airborne by six for his eight o'clock in Seattle.

Now, finally, it had begun.

He reached the loading area, and when the shooter ahead had finished and cleared, and the targets had reset, he was approached by the lead range officer.

"Load 'em up, Red."

"Yes sir," said Red. He walked to the lever gun,

slipped ten .44-40s into the chute on the '92 receiver, leaving the lever down to show empty chamber, and laid the rifle where designated. He returned, drew each Colt, threaded five robin's-egg-heavy cartridges—"cah-ti-ges" the Duke had called them as Ethan Edwards in *The Searchers*—into each chamber as accessed by the popped-open loading gate of Sam's marvelous, intricate machine, an orchestration of lines and symmetries and streamlines and densities like no other. One in, he spun the cylinder past the next, then sliding in four more, then cocking under control to rotate the cylinder one last time, then closing the gate and restoring the masterpiece to its leather. That ritual was to assure that no live cartridge nested under the firing pin's pressure, a design weakness in the old gun so grave nobody noticed it for over 110 years. Then, finally, he took his shotgun from his guncart, its pump racked backward to expose empty chamber and empty magazine as well as all the spring-driven, leverage-turned ingenuity of its interior, and moved to set it on the table next to the far window.

He readied himself at the starting line, shivering a little, pianoing his fingers to get them loose and ready, tensing and relaxing his upper-body muscles. He put his earplugs in, then his hands came to his waist and he put on his grimace-tight gunman's face.

"Shooter ready?" came the question, muffled by the ear protection.

He nodded.

He heard the three-beat timer ticking down, *ding, ding,* and *dong,* and on *dong*—more precisely on the *d-* so that he was halfway to the first station by the *-ong*— he raced forward, seized the '92 in a liquid, practiced choreography, slid it to shoulder, keeping muzzle level and downrange even as he was closing the lever, and fired the first shot as the sight came into focus over the blurred image of the bad guy, in this case a black metal plate, and the trigger came back and the gun shuddered gently as it sent its hunk of lead on its way at a little over six hundred feet per second.

The trick here was not to wait for the clang of the hit and the sight of the plate toppling on its hinge but to be already into the leverwork and already moving the gun by that time, and he fired again and again and again and againagainagain, only aware at the unfocused edge of the drama of the ejected shell casings flipping through the air but most attuned to the great spurt of white, a billow at each report that rivaled the clouds above. And when the last plate fell, he left the action open, set the rifle down, and *moved his ass fast* to the next window.

This was the killer. The subtlety of cowboy action was that it wasn't an athletic contest of speed of foot and dexterity, but of course it was, and that it wasn't a fast-draw contest, but of course it was. You had to calibrate effort versus grace, for to seem to hurry could be called "against the spirit," a ten-second time penalty; at the same time if you loafed, you lost.

Red had it today; the gods had been kind, and in his last practice, he had suddenly felt the gun rock solid all the way through the string. He'd hit plate after plate yesterday, watched them prang and fall, and felt oddly accomplished. All that practice. He'd done it. He'd mastered the goddamned thing. He was a gunfighter.

He came to the window, turned, drew, and in the same fluidity the gun was in his hand, thumbing back as it rode up, and he saw the sights against the black blur, and axiomatically the gun discharged, and again he thumbed a new cartridge home, rotating up from the next-in-line position in the cylinder, perfectly sustained and perfectly timed by Sam's engineering genius all those frosty years ago, and each time the gun popped, and he was moving it and thumbing back the hammer and restoring the grip just as Clell had taught him before the just-hit plate fell. Five and he was done with gun number one, holstered smooth as butter. He rotated to the left for the next snatch and brought that beauty in line, cocking as he got it there. Five soft pops, five spurts of glorious white fume; they stood for America, for liberty, for the West, for patriotism, for old movies and TV, for growing old with grace and still winning every goddamn thing. He was done, slipped number two back into its leather den, and was halfway to shotgunland before the last plate fell.

This was pretty easy for Red because in another life, as a southern billionaire playboy, pheasant and dove hunts with $14,000 Perazzis had been a Sunday necessity in the fall, if the Falcons weren't playing at home, and he had no problem with the four inserts, the four pumps, and the four shots, each of which delivered a handful of spattering birdshot to the larger, heavier plates, and down they went *ker-plunk*.

"Good shooting, Red," said the range officer, reading off the time—29.2—to the scorekeeper, adding, "all targets down, no penalties."

Red sat back, smelling the gunsmoke, watching the white gas drift and seethe until a light breeze took it and it dissipated.

Soon enough Clell would be there to tell him how well he'd done, urge him to stay cool and collected— no rush, no sweat, no nerves, no expectations, just there, in the zone—and a nice round of applause rose to congratulate his efforts, some of it from people who surely recognized him and were sucking up as if he'd give a clapper a mil just for kicks, but much of it genuine, from those who didn't know.

But he knew it best of all: Texas Red has it.

49

Anto slowly revved the ATV, then slipped into gear and took it down the gentle slope of the valley toward the center. He had a black-comic thought of accidentally running over the heads of his own sniper team as he progressed, and had to fight a grin in case Swagger, from his own hide, was eyeballing him.

He switched back, left then right, eating up the distance, came in out of the high grass onto shorter, where ugly prairie things—they looked like turds but were some kind of cancerous vegetation—littered the ground, along with the odd low scrub of bush, the scraggily unspectacular cacti, stones, smallish boulders, what have you. He was a man who'd spent many days in action and had taken more fire than even the many professional soldiers of his culture, with the scars to prove it, and he wore that time in hell well. In fact it was not even hell to him, as it is to most men. The truth is, high-level professionals like Anto and his mates from 22 SAS and most commandos in the forces and SEALs and various foreign alphabet-soup high-contact teams don't fear battle at all; they relish it. To them it's an exhilaration like a drug high, and they truly savor the act of taking life, at close range or by rifle through optics; it's like scoring baskets or goals in the sports-driven youths that most had.

So Anto was far from scared, far from choked with dread, far from concerned with his own death, which, through many wounds and much recovery time, had nevertheless only seemed like a final joke. He was pure alpha, the war dog in its most distilled form. Oh, this one would be so damned much fun!

He got to the creek where advised, eased down the throttle to an idle, came out of gear, and slipped into neutral. He let the motor run on general principle. Although unlikely, a mechanized getaway would be a lot more efficient than a barefoot one, running uphill nude for nine hundred yards among prickers and buffalo shit.

As instructed, he scissors-stepped off the vehicle, moving ten feet away. At that spot, he assumed the position, faced east, hands up, legs spread. Now where was that bad boy Swagger? Would he come over the hill on an ATV and take his time, letting Anto bake even redder in the sun as he trekked down for the exchange? Raymond knew: don't shoot until he's still, and he and I have had a chat. That was the sign. Then take him, because of course Anto wanted to watch him die from as close as possible, possibly even having a word or two with the mortally stricken man.

Jimmy had gone to binoculars, so much easier to manipulate than the tripod-mounted spotter's scope, if somewhat less steady. He fixed on Anto as he came down the hill, watched him course this way and that, detected no nervousness. And what happened if Swagger simply killed Anto, shot him dead on the spot? Then he, Jimmy, would find the sniper's hide and give the site to Raymond and talk Raymond into the shot, and Raymond, steady as an ingot, would put the man down.

Then they'd bring their fallen Michael Collins back and give him a burial Irish style that he'd deserve. There'd be drinking and keening and piping, with the banshees howlin' of a great man's death on the glens and in the bogs. But it would be all right: that was Anto, giving himself up for the team and the mission, without even a thought to the sadness of it all.

"Would you see anything?" asked Ray, stuck in the smaller field of vision of the iSniper911 atop the AI.

"I do not," said Jimmy, "only fat Anto's fat arse scrunched up on the bike's seat. Not a pretty vision, I'm telling yis."

"No man should have to look on Anto's great ass, sure," said Raymond, and Jimmy couldn't tell if it was Raymond's first joke or if he meant that with his customary earnestness.

Anto arrived at his designated location, stilled his machine, and slid off. He moved to the side in odd steps, keeping his hands high. From the site of the boys, he was on a slight oblique.

Raymond, as practiced on the iSniper as any of them, shot the distance and reported it to be 297 yards in 0-5 wind, a downward angle of 13 degrees over the yardage, not enough to require any correction. The device then told him three down, .5 to left, and so he went back to the scope, traced three lines down the axis of the center of the reticle from the larger reticle, adjusted the rifle ever so slightly until the fat, slightly angled, red-dappled shape that was Anto's naked back rested exactly in the space between the third hashmark of the vertical axis of the crosshair and the first small + to its left, and there he rested. He could kill Anto easy enough, but that wasn't the point then, was it?

Jimmy ran the binoculars over the known world fast enough to make time, slow enough to see what he was looking at. He was just on the edge of blur. It should be happening soon enough now.

Suddenly he saw Anto jump, not as if hit, but startled. All of Anto's muscles became tense, even his buttocks, clenching in the drama, and he turned, stopped as if commanded, and began to speak.

"What the fuck," said Jimmy, shifting his binocs after concluding from the evidence that somehow the sniper was close to but behind Anto. "Raymond, Raymond, look at where the bastard is!"

Ginger didn't jump when Anto appeared at the edge of his vision; nor did he twitch, tighten, or kick. He was professional. He just let the scene unfold. He saw Anto arrive at the creek, not thirty yards away.

So it begins, it does, he thought.

He double-checked his weapon under the camo tarpaulin, ran his thumb up to the safety to see it was indeed swung all the way around to full-auto, then broke contact with the grip to crawl his fingers up the receiver to test the cocking handle, pulling it back toward the butt to find it loose, which signified the weapon was cocked fully with a round in the chamber. He slid his hand up higher on the receiver to the face of the Eotech holographic sight, a clever tactical enhancement that looked like a small TV set mounted in a smooth plastic streamline bolted tight on the receiver's Picatinny rail. Activated—Ginger did that, pushing a button first for power-up, then pushing it a dozen more times to elevate the brightness— it beamed a holographic circle on its screen of glass, a powerful icon glowing red against the clear, so perfect for close-quarter battle because you didn't even have to look for it, it was just there to your eye, and you put it on target and squeezed and sent a fleet of 5.56s off to do the job right and proper. Now he was ready and sure that what might happen to need his assistance in settling would be occurring soon enough, and he said a brief prayer to Jesus to grant him the favor of putting a mag into the Yank, to pay him back for the fooking cracked skull he took and the embarrassment of being the fella to let the team down.

That done, he screwed up his focus, his concentration, his war persona, and watched as poor naked Anto just stood there, his bollocks all loose, his shoulders red, waiting for whatever.

Surely soon the American would appear, coming on down the far hill, approaching for the exchange, and it would all—

What the—?

Jaysus, will you look at that?

Who'd have guessed? Not a man among them.

The earth moved.

It did, it did. Twenty yards behind naked Anto, a smallish knot of brush and grass quivered and gave and transmogrified itself as beneath it rose, like a prehistoric beast coming out of a millennium or more's sleep, a shape that soon enough took on the damned image of a man in ghillie, black pistol in hand, face a green-black-brown silent killer's mask. He rose to both legs and extended the pistol toward Anto, as if to shoot.

Ginger had a moment of panic: should he rise himself now and fire the killing burst? But before he could commit, it appeared that the enemy sniper was not about to fire. He too, it appeared, wanted a little chat.

Anto seemed to wait forever and almost put his arms down out of sheer fatigue, ready to throw them up again at any sign of the approach, but then he heard a voice from too close to be real but real indeed say, "All right, Potatohead, you stay frozen," and felt himself jump in surprise.

What in God's name?

He turned halfway and saw in his peripheral the man himself, or rather a man disguised as planet, all fronds and frills and floppy hat, as ghillied up to perfection as any sniper could be, a Sig pistol in his grip, the camo smock falling away. He wasn't a mile away, he wasn't a half, a quarter, a hundred yards, a hundred feet. He was right there, almost in spit's distance.

"Move another inch, Irishman, you're dead as shit."

Anto froze. The fellow was there, unseen by Jimmy and Raymond and even close-in Ginger. He'd been there all along. He had to have gotten there ahead of them. He'd planted himself in the earth and outwaited the stillest, best men in the business!

Anto's mind hurried then to another ramification; who'd been on the radio, who'd been guiding him in?

"Is it Ginger?" asked Raymond.

"No, no, get on the damned gun, man, put the bastard down. It's him, it's him, can't you goddamn see how dif his camo is from ours? Do it, do it now."

Raymond didn't panic, professional that he was,

but reacquainted the rifle butt with his shoulder, settled microscopically, tried to quell a heart rush, took
a breath or so. Then he reshot the iSniper911 laser
ranger to initiate the target acquisition sequence,
committed to screen, and saw that it was 281 yards
off, and the angle had risen to 16 degrees, still too little
for a cosine correction, and the new shooting determination was still three down, but now without the .5
left adjustment, so he found stock-weld, acquired reticle, acquired new target—large man in grassy ghillie
suit—tracked downward on the central vertical axis
of the reticle to the same third hashmark but this time
didn't need to make the same .5 to left, let the rifle
settle, let his breathing settle, and began to take slack
out of the trigger.

"How much did you get, Anto?" asked Bob mildly.

"'Tis over two hundred thousand for the sniper's
pleasure," said Anto with a merry, comic lilt to his
voice. "Oh, sure yis be having some wicked pleasures
on that swag. It's yours, Sniper. Want me to bring her
to ye, or will yis grab it yourself?" him thinking, *now,*
prang the boyo, finish him with Mr. .308, blow lungs
and heart out, Raymond, don't let your old sarge here
down.

"Won't that be fun?" said Bob.

"It's good craic you'll be having with that—"

The shot sounded from above and away and far
out, not an eardrum-snapping whack, but more a soft
report as if muted by distance.

Anto flinched and turned, thinking to hell with
the position, and was surprised to see Swagger standing, unhit. He saw then why the radio was decreed

instead of the mobile: it distorted voice and made recognition impossible. He'd been talking to another fellow while Swagger lay in his ghillie still as death in
this valley.

There was another damned sniper.

Goddamn him!

"My boy just tagged yours," Swagger said.

A second shot followed, Anto flinching.

"And now he's done the spotter."

Raymond felt the slack giving, he was on the cusp of
the shot, his finger's steady press against trigger, the
crossed lines of the reticle steady upon the ghillie-
suited man who held the pistol and

Lightning lightning lightning.

A storm suddenly blowing in, the sky full of jagged illumination.

The green glow of the countryside.

Over a hundred kills.

The taste of Guinness.

And that was all.

Nine hundred and thirty-four yards away, Chuck
McKenzie watched as his first shot splashed the
shooter hard in a jet of crimson at the left quadrant
of what, before destruction, had been skull, and the
ruined fellow went limp in supertime, giving it all up
as he became instant meat, the upper half of his body
falling hard at gravity's insistence, but then Chuck
was so quick into his throw and correction he lost his
first target, knowing he'd killed it, and came across
to the second. Number two had dumped the binocs
and was tugging the rifle from his dead pal's hands,

driven even now to finish the mission, even though
his face wore splatter everywhere, as did his shirt-
sleeve and hand. Brave guy: it never occurred to him
to chuck the rifle and go to hands up, which might
have saved his life, as Chuck wouldn't shoot a sur-
rendering man. But number two was all warrior and
actually had the rifle half in play and was setting up,
albeit in panic time, for his shot, when Chuck snuffed
him with another head shot, even as he heard a spray
of gunshots and automatic weapon fire from down in
the valley.

Anto's speed surprised even Bob and the speed was
more efficient for the decisiveness driving it, but even
if Bob had the shot, he let it go, because even before
Anto was yelling, "Kill him, Ginger," Ginger was rising from the dead. Bob was surprised Ginger was so
close, though he knew him to be about from the noise
the fellow'd made just before dawn as he put himself
into the earth.

Still, it was long for a pistol shot, and Bob went to
a knee to take up the two-hand supported and put two
fast ones into the rising man close to fifty yards away,
and missed once, seeing a puff flick off the earth next
to Ginger, who, though shuddering upon the strike
of the second round, evidently a low lung shot, still
got his M4 up. He fired at Bob but Bob was not there,
having rolled like a crazy man to the right. Ginger's
nine-round burst tore up a smoky stitch of dust and
grassy fragments and cactus shrapnel in the space
where Bob had been.

Ginger, bleeding badly, tracked the gun right
through the glowworm incandescence of the Eotech

sight and brought the gun right to bear on what of Bob he could see or sense, even while rising to his feet. A normal man would have yielded to collapse by this time, but Ginger was all bristly, insane beast, a charging boar, a crazed wildebeest, a here-comes-death buffalo, and would not check out without vengeance, and he willed himself to fire again.

Bob had by this time gone further to prone for the calming influence of the ground in support of his arms, though he was so deep in the loam, he could only see Ginger's upper third. A fleet of 5.56s rocketed overhead, inches from ending it forever, but he didn't flinch as most will do but instead fired twice again, the front sight bold and sharp as death in the notch of the rear, and was sure the bullets had gone home. But Ginger didn't show any ill health and fired another burst, which tore up the ground in ragged spurts as it vectored toward Bob, seeking him.

And then Ginger was down.

Clearly Chuck had finished what Bob couldn't, putting a .308 home from his perch on the hill, not a head shot but the heartbreaker, and the big Irishman slid sideways, face slack as a misbegotten moon, and toppled, though as he fell his finger tightened on his trigger and he emptied the 5.56s into the turf just before him, setting off spasms of geysering dust. Then it was quiet.

Except for the sound of Anto's departing ATV.

Bob came around, saw the nude man at full throttle, bent as low as he could get, more than two hundred yards out, and he fired from prone, aiming high, dumping what remained of his own mag, but the distance was too far for a handgun, Anto was too deft in zigzagging the little bike, and when he achieved slide lock-back, Bob knew he hadn't hit him.

He jumped up madly, gesturing to Chuck, pointing with one wild arm while he screamed—probably the sound didn't reach Chuck—"Kill him, kill him!"

Chuck took his time setting up the shot, but as far as he was from Bob, he was even further from Anto, who was almost to the crest and had the bold man's luck with him, for he veered just as Chuck fired, and Bob saw the bullet punch up a gout of shredded vegetation just as Anto disappeared.

Fuck, he thought. That bastard made it out alive.

It's not over. I didn't get him.

He turned, shedding himself finally of the heavy ghillie, dropped the spent clip and thrust in a new one, released the slide to jab forward with a *clack!*, dropped the hammer, and replaced the Sig in its shoulder holster. Then he picked up his as-yet-unfired rifle and headed up the crest to meet up with Chuck, only to see that Chuck was roaring down to him on his own ATV.

They met in another two hundred yards.

"Great shooting, Sniper," Bob said, clapping the other man on the arm. "Jesus, you got three of them and all I did was put bullets in the ground."

"Sorry I couldn't take that fourth guy. Do we go after him?"

"No, he's picking up a rifle and some pants just now. Nothing he'd like more than to see us crossing a field. Take me to my own ATV."

He jumped on behind Chuck and they headed back up the slope, followed a creek down the gap in the ridge, down into an arroyo, and finally to a little glade where Bob had left his vehicle.

*   *   *

Anto had been hit by one of Bob's long pistol shots but not badly. It was a burning groove in his left arm above elbow, below biceps, and it oozed the red stuff and hurt like bloody hell. He looked at it without interest. He'd been hit enough times to know this was nothing.

Then he concentrated on the fact that he was alone. That fooking bastard had done them all, the great boys of Basra and SAS sniper element blue, with over three hundred kills among them, to say nothing of all the other jobs for king and country in places that still couldn't be divulged.

Black Irish grief collapsed upon him, a nude man with serious sun poisoning in bright light in the middle of the savage, featureless high plains. He went to the bag and reached through the crap that filled it out until he found his amphetamines, and he gulped six of them. Get me concentration back, me energy, numb me out from the pain, that's what I've got to do.

Then he climbed aboard the bike, oriented himself, and began a big curl around the eastern rim of the valley to a certain designated tree, where the boys had left him kit and rifle.

He knew exactly where Swagger was going next, and he'd play his own self's little trick on the fellow and be the one getting there first this time.

Swagger reached into his cargo pocket.

"Here it is," he said to Chuck. "I want you out of here fast, before Anto gets geared up. You go hard west for an hour; don't stop for anything. Then you call your buddy with the chopper and bring him in to you.

Have him fly you to the Indian Rapids airfield—there should be some kind of airline terminal there—go to the American Eagle desk, and tell whoever's there you have something for Mr. Memphis. Either he will take the package, or he'll get someone to take the package."

"And then?"

"And then get a beer with your pilot. Wait for my call. If it doesn't come, then get another beer and drink it for me, and remember me for a few years. Tell my wife I died snipered up all the way."

"Come on, Gunny. Come with me. We'll both give 'em the package, we'll both get the beer, followed by a steak. Then we'll start in on the hard stuff. How much bourbon can a town called Indian Rapids have, anyway? We'll drink it all and wake up in three days. The feds can pick up that last Irishman. He's not going anywhere for a while."

"No, he is. And I know where. And I'm going too."

"Then let me come along. This time I'll be the bait and you can do the shooting."

"No, Chuck, that film has to reach the FBI, and the sooner the better. Constable will hear about this shit somehow, and once that happens, he'll bolt. With his dough, he'll be long gone before the feds can pick him up. That's why you've got to get the film to them. So I want Anto Grogan after me, not you. Long as I'm alive, he'll come after me."

"Christ, Gunny. You're going to set yourself up for this motherfucker, aren't you? You're going to gull him into taking the shot and pray that he misses, and then you'll shoot back. With that scope on top, he isn't going to miss. You think you can get a killing shot off from seven hundred yards with 168 grains of lead in your chest, while you're bleeding out? It doesn't have to happen. You don't have to be the last man to die in a long-ago lost war. You call me up and invite me on this little war party and now I have to leave before the end and I don't get to cover the hero but have to just let him sit out there on his lonesome? That ain't no bargain, Gunny."

"For me it's the best bargain. I lost my spotter, Chuck. I couldn't bring him back from the war. So you have to get out of here now, and fast. Only two things count. Getting the film to the FBI and getting Chuck home in time for his daughter's graduation. Go, Chuck. DEROS, Chuck. Now."

"You goddamned Marine Corps bad-ass gunnery sergeant retired. Jesus, you are all old-fashioned man, that's all I can say. I thought you guys had all died off, but dammit, you're too salty to die."

"Go on, get out of here, Lance Corporal."

Chuck clapped Swagger on the shoulder and gunned up his ATV and headed west.

50

Texas Red celebrated his success with a very fine buffalo steak—low in fats, low in sodium, low in calories—and a 2001 Château Sociando-Mallet, served in his motor home by Chin, his chef. It was still midafternoon: he hadn't breakfasted because he hated to shoot on a full stomach, and so his first order of business after finishing his four events—four more tomorrow and four on Sunday—was to eat. His second order of business was business: calls to stockbrokers, vice presidents, PR folks, and so forth, pleased to note he was recovering from the meltdown well enough. He noted with pleasure no incoming from either Bill Fedders in DC or by satellite from the Irishmen at his main ranch.

That done, he summoned the ever-plain Ms. Jantz and had her take dictation for an hour, then got his daily blow job, surprisingly intense for a non-Viagrafied event. The shooting had gotten juices all astir in a way that was unusual. Then he dismissed her, with the admonition, "Get me Clell."

Clell appeared shortly thereafter, all rangy gun pro, with the big hands, the smoothness of encoded neural pathways, the data bank beyond measure.

"So," he said, "no bullshit. Critique. Forget I'm paying you three times what you charge. Give me the truth, as if I'm a little punk trying to hang out with the great Clell Rush."

"Yes sir."

"Yes, *Tom.*"

"Yes, Tom. First thing is, congrats. You shot well today. Dynamite. I think you've beaten the grip slippage that seems to screw you up sometimes. You were hard and tight and the gun stayed set. Even on the exchange, when you holstered the righthand piece and cross-drew from the left holster, even that was tight. It was a good chance to screw up, and happily, you evaded it."

"I'm liking what I'm hearing. Sure you're not just trying to pick up a bonus?"

"It ain't just suck-up, Tom. Look at the standings. You're number four. You've never been that high in the standings at this point before. Last year, as I recall, you's about number fifteen. There's no way of coming back from fifteen. You're still in the hunt."

"How about rifle and shotgun?"

"You plan to save handgun mistakes on rifle and shotgun, and that's fine, but I thought you ran too hard on the rifle. That's a sophisticated motion, throwing the lever but not so hard you pull the muzzle out of control, keeping that left hand in good command, closing up and touching off, then throwing even while you're moving to the next target. You done well, I'm not saying that, but I thought you's a little overexcited. It was the first event, you had adrenaline, so you brought it off. Don't know how tomorrow will be, or the next day, if you don't drop back into second gear, particularly on the last few rounds."

"Good advice," said Tom.

"As for the shotgun, maybe the same thing, but since there's only four reloads, it's not likely you'll turn to fumblethumbs that quickly. Though by the time you get to shotgun, your hands are tired from all the shooting you've just completed. But your fingers are so happy when they're on the shotguns, even a trumpet gun like the ninety-seven, I don't think that's going to be your problem."

"Hmm, I've got a problem? I thought you were telling me how damn good I was."

"Well, it's a problem most men have. Called pride. It goeth before a tumble, or so the book says."

"I'm listening."

"I feel you pushing too hard. It almost means too much to you. I'm worried that late, tired, your hands all beat to hell, you'll face a challenge where you need your best. And you won't be able to find it, Texas Red. Because you are a man of accomplishment, you cannot conceive of failure. Yet even the Kid hisself failed; he went out unarmed, and along come Pat Garrett and put a jujube of lead into his gut. The Kid was proud; in his pride he got away from his greatness, and his greatness was doing all them little things right, like always sitting with his back to the wall and forswearing that fourth drink, because it was the fourth one that slowed him, and always carrying a gun. That night in Fort Sumner, he's feeling so Kid, so invulnerable, he gets cocky, he gets sloppy, and he can't conceive of a man coming into his own space and facing him. He's unarmed, except for a butcher knife. He steps into his bedroom, *quien está?* he asks, who's there, he *knows* someone's there, he's holding that knife, and it's still in him to make it through the night, all he has to do is be the Kid and lunge, and he lives till two and twenty. But his mind freezes, and old Pat, slower, grumpier, used up, old Pat gets big iron whipped out fast and puts a forty-four into him. And down goes the Kid."

"You see that in me?"

"You ain't no Kid, Mr. Constable, not by a long shot. But I'm worried there'll come a time when you think you is. And as the Kid found out, thinking you're the Kid can get a man killed."

51

There wasn't much point in stealth, not at this point. No reason to wear the ghillie. He even poured some water from his bottle and washed the paint off, so that he'd get through this last on his own face, not the jungle's.

He steered a wide circle on his ATV and came into Lone Tree Valley from the west, wondering if Anto was already there. Anto, driven by anger and fear and vengeance, had to take a more direct route, which was in length about four miles; this more circuitous journey was almost seven. Coming over the crest, he saw the lone tree itself, surprisingly dense for fall, its leaves vibrating in the low wind and, as they did, seeming to shimmer as first the dull and then the bright side showed itself to the sun.

He rumbled down the slope, acknowledging the featurelessness of the place. It was all epic space in a shallow bowl of undulating grass, capped by the frosty marble of the western clouds against the bluest blue of all. No animal life was visible, and the push of wind filled the air with the sound of air and the stalks of grass leaning against each other.

He drove to the tree but left the ATV well short of it. He got off, feeling the Sig bang under his left arm, holding the 7-mil Ultra Mag in his right. It was Chuck's, a hunting rifle for knocking down big animals at long ranges with a cartridge case the size of a

cigar, something new cooked up more by the marketing department than the true ballisticians. The industry needed new products. This one was a lulu: kicked
like a mule, but it shot fast and flat as anything on
the planet, and when it arrived, it had excess power.
Chuck said he'd hit an antelope at over five hundred
yards, and the poor thing had cartwheeled, it was
slapped with such energy.

He squatted, going into a sniper's stillness, flat out
in the open, though in shade, maybe a little to the east
of the tree. He presented his back to Anto. He pulled
his khaki hat down over his sunglassed eyes.

What would happen next would all come down
to character: Anto's. A true sniper would creep close,
take and make the shot. That was duty, that was mission, that was job, even to a merc. He thought of that
merc poem: "followed their mercenary calling, took
their wages, and are dead." Which war? Oh, yeah, the
first big one. The boys who stopped the Germans for
pay. And for professionalism: no vanity, no wasted
motion, no ceremony, no self-celebration, no self-pity.

But Anto? Anto had that manic streak in him, that
desperate need for approval and attention. His personality might be too big for standard military and
then even for a genius outfit like 22 SAS. Maybe it
was a death wish. Take the fall from grace in Basra:
he'd had to have seen it coming, read the signs,
and had plenty of time to back down or readjust—
that's the way the military worked, after all—but he
insisted on his way with the aggressive interrogations
and the ever-climbing kill count. So the Brits ultimately destroyed him, and you could blame them for
their unwillingness to sustain the man who was, ever

so distastefully, winning the war, but that was the way of the modern world, and of general staffs and politicians with the guts of puppies. Still, you had to blame Anto too, since a more modest professional, committed to his cause, would have found a way to keep operating, only under a lower profile. Not Anto. He wanted somehow to burn at the stake and give interviews from the flames.

Bob sat and sat and then, finally, Anto spoke through the radio.

"You bastard, you killed me mates!" said the Irishman, and the connect was loud and clear.

Anto cursed and ranted and vented a bit. When he stopped to catch his breath, Bob said, "You left out the part about them set up to kill me. We only shot men about to shoot us. You decided to put them in place; it's on you, Colour Sergeant, not me."

"You're a bastard," Anto said.

"But Anto still wants the film. Anto *has* to get the film."

Anto said nothing for a while.

Finally he asked, "You didn't send it out with that other fellow?"

"Nope," said Bob. "Because Bob still wants the money. Bob *has* to get the money."

"You're as mercenary as himself," said Anto. "When all the flags been put away, and all the speeches done, and all the warriors locked up in mental homes, the only thing left is the money, no?"

"The only thing left is the money."

"Ha," said Anto, enjoying his little jest.

"Where are you?" asked Swagger.

"I'm still at the goddamned site of the atrocity. I

had to bury me boys proper. You think I'd leave 'em for the jackals?"

Bob knew he had left them for the jackals.

"Where are you? I'll bring you the money, now I'm confident shooter number two ain't lurking."

"Then you know he's long gone."

"He broke a crest and I got glass on him. He didn't have the film, did he?"

"No. He's an old friend. He did his job. I didn't want you picking him off, I wanted him out of here. And I wanted it as it should be, you and me."

"Right and proper," said Anto.

"You set a course on your GPS roughly radial one-thirty-four east, for four miles. That will put you on the rim of another valley, called Lone Tree. When you look over the rim, you'll see the tree. There's only one. I'll be under it, rifle ready. You radio me, notify me of your position. You're still naked, by the way?"

"I am not," said Anto. "Have some bloody decency."

"When you get to the rim, you're naked. You're naked and unarmed all the way in and I'm watching you all the way in. You get here, you pull up fifty yards out, and this time you're not ten feet from your bike, you're a hundred feet."

"You're so smart; that was a big mistake, Sniper. I got to it in a second, and off in another."

"Easier with the late Ginger there to cover for you. But yeah, sure, I made a stupid mistake. I'm old, do it all the time. This time, you go flat spread-eagled in the grass. I'll take the money."

"And leave the film."

"No."

"Bastard."

"I'll take the film and I'll go out to the east. You'll see a tree on the horizon at roughly one-twenty-two from the lone tree. I'll leave the film there. By the time you get there, I'm long gone."

"And suppose there's no film?"

"You think I want you dogging me? I'm as sick of this shit as you. I want my dough and I want a vacation. I'll disappear and be in contact in two or three months while I set up the big exchange. Take it or leave it."

Anto paused.

Then he said, "Okay, I'll be taking it."

"Buzz me then when you're on the rim, though I'll probably see you first."

The radio went silent.

Now it was waiting time. How long? Maybe an hour. No, it couldn't be an hour. Swagger knew Anto was close. Now was the question of character: shoot or chatter? Smart or stupid? Professional or self-indulgent?

Can I make the shot from here? Anto wondered.

He was at the rim, in a good prone, almost directly behind the position Swagger had taken. He could see the man crouched down, working his binocs in the wrong direction but not too intensely. The poor sod thought he had at least an hour before the play resumed. He had no idea he was sitting on the bloody bull's-eye.

Anto was in a good shooting position. He was relaxed, the Accuracy International .308, on its bipod, solid into the earth. As a kind of prelim, he drew it to him, took up almost exactly the position from which he'd fire, though keeping his finger indexed along its green plastic stock, put the complex iSniper reticle on Bob's blue-shirted back, and fired—fired the range-finding function, that is.

He read the answer on the screen: 927.

He'd made 927-yard shots before, and many longer. But he'd missed a few too. He waited for the target acquisition solution to run through the chip-driven computer and got his instructions: nine down, three to the right.

He went back to scope, counting out the nine hash-marks notched on the central vertical axis, then the three to the right. There it was. A tiny reticle, about the size of the + on a word-processing program, lay athwart the prick of blue just barely recognizable as a man at this range, despite the 15X magnification.

He felt his muscles begin to tighten, his tremors to cease, his breathing to shallow out; he felt the soft curve of the trigger, and then it began to slide almost of its own desire.

B-R-A-S-S, the from-time-immemorial shooter's mantra.

Breathe.

Relax.

Aim.

Slack.

Squeeze.

He didn't fire.

Nine-twenty-seven was way too far out there. A puff of wind, even a twitch by Swagger *after* the bullet was launched—its time in flight at this range would be over a second—would compute to a miss, and then he'd be in a duel at over nine hundred yards with a man who was still maybe the best, or second- or third-best, in the world. No percentage in that.

He'd shoot from five hundred.

Five hundred would minimize wind, minimize trajectory, minimize time in flight. From five hundred he could make the shot on iron sights; with the iSniper911 he could make it a hundred times out of a hundred, in one second if need be.

Next question: How long will it take to low-crawl over the 427 yards to his shooting position? The answer was close to an hour, and none of it much fun, unless you liked crawling, and almost no one did. He sure didn't. Also, everything in him said, Get it done. Finish it. You have the advantage, press it.

He looked at Bob all that way off, steadily gazing at the wrong horizon.

I could walk up to him and shoot him behind the ear with me Browning.

Well, probably I could not. But I could walk five hundred yards and quite possibly he'd never see me, looking as he is to the east, convinced as he is that I'm still miles away, bouncing naked across the plains.

He rose. He felt liberated. He did a rifle check for about the thousandth time, opening the bolt to see the glint of the Black Hills 168-grain Sierra match HPBT cartridge nested snugly just where it should be, re-pressed the bolt to lock up, then touched the safety, making triple certain it was off so he could fire the fast one if needed. He looped his forearm through the cinch of the sling, tightened it so that it tugged against his arm and body and left just enough play so that, when he dropped to prone or sitting, it would be held firm against him and, by virtue of the position, against the solidity of earth itself. With his right hand, he performed a battery check on the iSniper911, reassuring himself he was all fired up with power to spare.

That done, he adjusted his boonie cap, his tear-shaped Wiley X shooting glasses, and began the big walk toward Bob Lee Swagger.

Swagger waited, still as a rock. Some living thing finally came, a white moth, flitting in this and that direction. Eventually it moved off.

He felt ticks of sweat running down his face from under his hat. His ears, encased in the radio pads, itched. His breathing came shallowly. He yearned to turn, to see if the Irishman was there, but the longer he waited, the closer Anto got, and the closer he got, the easier the shot that took him down would be. If he was stuck shooting it out at nine hundred yards, he'd lose. Anto's technology trumped his more powerful rifle. He wouldn't have time to lase the range, figure the clicks, crank the scope, assume the position. Anto would kill him. He'd have to guess at the range, and that wasn't a talent he had, as some did. So if he guessed wrong, read the wind wrong, so easy to do at the extended ranges, Anto would kill him.

Tick tock, tick tock, tick tock, the big clock in his head spun its second hand, draining time from the world, while somewhere people laughed and drank and flirted and fucked and dug ditches or wrote poetry or flew planes. He was a sniper. He sat still, waiting to take or receive the shot. It was what he did. He'd snipered-up young and really lived his whole life that way, taking on the responsibility of doing the state's dirtiest work and coming back tainted with the smell of murder about him. That was it, that was the way it went. You chose it, asshole. It—what was the god-damned word?—*expressed* you. Count yourself lucky, blankethead. You got to do what you was born to do. How many can—

"Boyo," Anto said over the radio.

"I don't see you."

"Maybe you're looking in the wrong direction, Sniper."

He stood up, began to scan the far horizon.

"See me yet? Maybe look behind you."

He did. Anto stood, fully dressed at some indeterminate spot in the slope of the featureless plain. He held his rifle cocked against his hip, supported in one hand, the radio earphones and microphone obscuring his face, his shades tight to eyes, his boonie cap low on his brow. He looked like war or death.

"Surprised, mate? Thought you'd see a naked man on a bike putt-putting his way to you and hoping that you showed mercy and knowing you wouldn't, Sniper?"

Bob was silent.

"Cat's got his tongue, does it now? We're in a new game, mate. Here it is. I'm walking at you. You can sit there or not. I was you, I'd walk to me; lessens the range. When you think you got the shot, my advice is, take it. But on that move I take mine. Seeing as how my tech is better than yours, Sniper, I've a funny feeling I'm going to be faster and better. This is the beach-ball game we once played, only we're the beachballs."

"You're a sick motherfucker," said Bob.

Anto laughed.

"You could surrender. You could toss rifle one way, bolt the second, and handgun still another. Then I'll have you strip naked and assume the position. Who knows, once I get in there and get the film, I may let you live. I'll shoot both kneecaps to pulp so I'll know you'll never track me, and maybe I'll blind you so you won't be scoping me, but you'll have some kind of life. How's that for an offer, Sniper?"

Bob threw his radio headphones and mike away.

Anto held all the cards and knew it. His ego thrilled at the sheer theater of the moment he had so shrewdly engineered. He was the best. He'd outthought Swagger, he'd nailed the Nailer, and he'd leave the sniper sniped and the jackals would tussle over his bones. He walked toward his target. It was like *High Noon* at six hundred yards, snipers in a face-off, approaching each other on the emptiness of prairie until they knew they couldn't miss, and then it just came down to who was faster on his gear, and Anto knew he was faster.

The wind pressed against his face, and the uppers had him radiating concentration and sense of self, even if, absentmindedly, he felt the sun on his exposed back of neck.

Swagger was oddly quiet. He didn't move a step. He was just waiting. The fool. The closer he got, the less chance of missing he'd have. It was as if he'd given up already and was just waiting for the dispatch.

Anto guessed, 550? No, maybe closer, maybe 530. I am so close, I am, to my 500, oh, this is the pinnacle, the highest, the best.

And then an odd thing. He noted it first on his

face, a difference, and then on his bare arms, another difference. What was it?

The wind. For some damned reason it had dropped to zero.

That was a present from God. That was also a message. God was saying, Anto, dear boy—for some reason God had always been English to Anto—here's a gift. A still moment. It will only last a bit, but take it, old chap, as my endorsement of you and my thanks for all the mullahs and their camel buggers you've sent over.

Now, he thought.

With a fluidity that seemed odd given his bulk but was in fact greased by countless thousands of repetitions until burned into muscle memory, Anto dropped to one knee, the other leg bent stoutly in support underneath him, simultaneously bringing the rifle to his shoulder, feeling the adjusted sling put exactly the right pressure to tighten the whole construction into a perfect support structure, while his finger flew to the iSniper unit, hit the button, and the little genius inside worked the numbers, solved distance and humidity and atmospheric density and what little whiffs of wind might remain, and came back almost instantly with the information 534, 5 down, 1 right, and as his hand closed around the grip and he tugged it back solid as an anvil into the pocket of his shoulder, even as his trigger finger found and began to press the soft curve of that lever, his elbow solid on his planted leg two inches behind the knee in a bone-to-bone lockup, he tracked the hashmarks on the vertical axis properly down, then right and—

He saw that Swagger was still upright but that

he was in the standing shooting position, elbow out, head perfectly steady, knees locked like steel bolts, but before he could even process that information, he saw the bright spurt of muzzle flash—

Swagger watched him come, holding steady, feeling the wind lick a little at his face, then go away. He had adjusted his stance slightly and was standing bladed to the approaching man, still such a long way out, though enlarging steadily as he came. He tried to shake his mind free of the past and not put any thought into Carl, with his brains blown out in his underwear, going underground in the rain as witnessed by seven people, or Denny Washington, that good man, his head blown open so that he'd never return to his wife and daughters. He wanted the past to go away but it wouldn't and then it did, and a mercy came to him, as it came to all snipers great and small, who put themselves not at the point of the spear but way out there beyond it, lonesome and duty-driven but also—what was that word again, goddamnit—expressing themselves, and he felt a wave of peace and from that a confidence rocketing skyward as the palsy fell from his limbs and the pressure from his heart and he wound down in his mind until he was nothing but rifle.

He saw Anto pause, even if Anto himself didn't feel the pause, and he knew that this was the moment, and he drew the rifle up to him and tight, but not cinched because a stander doesn't cinch, since he's linked to nothing solid but instead holds the beauty thing in a light command, as if it's alive in his hands. The reticle was there before him exactly as his heart seemed to stop pumping and the universe itself froze between instants, and the crosshairs exactly trapped the man far off, who was now himself moving into a kneeling position, and without his telling it to, his trigger finger decided, the rifle somehow *was* fired by it, and Bob held the head still—it takes years to learn this—in follow-through and held the trigger squished flat back, and waited as the scope came down from its hop, neither hearing report nor feeling recoil.

—somewhere in his mind *howisthispossible?* seemed to emerge at light speed as the question of the day, and the next thing Anto'd been hit by a shovel and sent pinwheeling through the air.

He landed in a stunned jumble, blinking, thinking to get back to the rifle, but he didn't see the rifle. He felt no pain at all but his body was somehow not right, and he looked and saw that his left arm had been split away from his body at the root. It hung grotesquely and rivers of blood rushed in black, ceaseless torrent from the astonishing tear that progressed from clavicle down deep into chest. He rolled, instinctively, to his still-whole side, with the inborn mandate in his brain to crawl to safety but, with only one arm to pull him along, made no progress at all, and he tucked his boots up close to his ruptured torso, rolling sideways to the final fetal position.

How the fuck did he make that shot? he wondered as he died.

Swagger got out his cell and punched a key in his menu.

In a bit, Chuck McKenzie answered.

"Gunny? You're okay?"

"I seem to be. Don't see no blood. Let me give you my coordinates."

He looked at his GPS and read them off.

"We're leaving right now."

"Did you give that package—"

"Yep. It's gone now. The jet took off an hour ago. How are you?"

"Tired. I'm too old for this shit."

"That last Irishman?"

"What's the Irish word for *toast*?"

"I think it's *toast*," said Chuck.

When that was done, Bob put in a call to Nick.

"The package is on the way."

"I know. And we are all set up here. I've got a film restoration team to supervise the process, but they're sure we can get good clear images off it without damage. I've got search warrant teams laid on in three states to hit Constable's headquarters after we get warrants and subpoenas, and I've got a team in Chicago to take possession of the hard drive of Jack Strong's office computer and the safe in Strong's office. And I've got the Cook County state's attorney people here; they can issue warrants and we can serve them. I've got a guy from the Nyackett, Massachusetts, prosecutor's office to issue his warrant. If this is everything you say it is, we'll be all legaled up sometime tomorrow and pick him up at a speech he's going to give tomorrow night in Seattle."

"Cool," said Bob.

"You don't sound excited."

"I'm just tired as hell," said Bob. "Are you sending people here to the ranch?"

"Yes."

"Make sure to hit the security team headquarters. That's where his sniper team was based. They all had laptops and were very professional. I'm sure there's a lot of stuff there, and if you track back to wherever they lived privately, there's even more."

"Got it."

"And you should send some people out into the wilderness area. I'll give you the coordinates tomorrow. There's some bodies to be bagged and pickled. Long story."

"Jesus Christ. No wonder you're tired. Get some sleep. Then get in here by—this is Saturday—by, say Tuesday?"

"Sure. Out."

Bob rested a while but then gathered up his rifle and dragged his weariness to the ATV. He climbed on and gunned it to life and covered the yardage to Anto.

There lay his foe. The 150-grain Scirocco would be banned in land warfare because of course the point that kept it so accurate was only black polycarbonate and meant for streamline and accuracy, but it hid a hollow point and a lethally blossoming design. When it struck flesh, the polycarbonate tip was driven back into the bullet body itself, and that dynamic intrusion, plus the self-destructing design of the bullet, caused the missile, traveling through flesh at about 2,500 feet per second, to open like a flower, its petals yawing wide. They yawed, they sawed. They went through meat like a butcher's keenest blade, opening a temporary cavity on the power of velocity that was the size of a football. Even when, by the elasticity of the flesh, that cavity closed up some, it closed up on organs that had been gelatinized, literally turned to viscosity. At the same time, the bullet's impact shattered bone and sundered skin along predictable fault lines, which is how the splitting effect came to be.

Anto lay curled up on his right side, his left body half so damaged it made no anatomical sense. It didn't even look real.

You stupid Irish bastard, Bob thought, remembering the long evenings at the Mustang Bar in Wyoming and what a happy time that had been. So much talent, so much guts, so much charm, and you end up in the high grass with your body blown in two, and for nothing but some rich asshole's benefit, and he's going down too.

By this time, the helicopter Chuck had hired was closing in. He raised a hand, not that it was necessary, as he stood out on the slope in a vastness of nothing. The chopper, a familiar old Huey, set down a hundred yards away, flattening the grass, lifting small stones and a haze of prairie dust, seeming inappropriate in a place otherwise so still. Its racket drowned all sound and made chatter impossible. Chuck ran over and gave Bob a nice thump on the shoulder, grabbed the gear, including the ghillie and his own Remington Sendero, while Bob carried Anto's AI. They made it to the chopper, tumbled in, but not before Bob pulled his friend close and whispered, "Man, do I need to change my goddamned diapers."

52

Washington DC, like any cosmopolitan city, has wife restaurants and mistress restaurants. If you're with your spouse, your partner for life, your better half, your ball and chain, the mother of your children, and you have a hankering for steak, then you go to Morton's, subdued and swanky at the corner of Connecticut and K, right in the center of lobbyland. It's wonderful, it's tasteful, it's perfect, it's dull. If, however, you're with your "mentee," your walking, talking, quivering fountain of youth, your single-evening Viagra-consumption record, your "niece," your lambchop, and the next Mrs. Whoeveryouare, then it's off to the Palm, on Nineteenth, for your slab of protein.

The Palm has swagger, bravado, a New York gangster dive ambience. The waiters all look like they made their bones in Newark in '67, with those walnutty faces, thick pomades of rich Mediterranean hair, and little khaki waiter's coats, with all kinds of odd bric-a-brac pinned across the belly. The place is dark and, even in the decreed absence of cigarettes and cigars, still *feels* smoky; the walls are festooned with somebody's dim idea of celebrity caricature (unrecognizable); the potatoes look like they could be called the myocardial infarction facilitation kit—pancakes fried in diesel grease, possibly?—and the meat is stark, primordial, and bleeding.

Thus on his one mistress dinner night of the month (his wife of thirty-five years and mother of his four children was *so* understanding), Bill Fedders sat with current flame Jessica Delph, in his usual booth on the left side of the dim room, sipping a powerful vodka martini while admiring the young woman's aquiline features, drawn-back blond hair, and hooded eyes. God, she was beautiful! Too bad he was going to dump her soon.

"Jessie, when I look at you, I wonder why you haven't given your heart away to some twenty-five-year-old linebacker."

"Possibly it's because all the linebackers in this town are Redskins, that is, losers," she said, with a smile that concealed the fact that she had in fact given her heart away—and some other goodies, as well—to a thirty-one-year-old stockbroker, because she didn't want to have that conversation until Bill had gotten her, as promised early in the relationship, a job with a really fine lobbying shop.

"I love a gal who knows that she's as beautiful as she is smart and as smart as she is beautiful," he said. It was a treasured line, but he didn't think he'd used it on this one, and besides it didn't matter, because he knew about the stockbroker.

"So are we celebrating something, Bill?" she asked.

"Actually, we're in mourning."

"Ohhh, death. I hate it when that happens."

"It's not death, just massive frontal trauma, a coma, the patient in the oxygen tent out like a light, but I think it'll come out of it."

"*It?*"

"Not a person, a campaign. My oldest and dearest

client had me running a campaign to hurry a certain federal policy toward implementation."

"Details boring or classified?"

"Details unnecessary. Long story shortened: I had a young guy on the team, he seemed so promising, and I let him develop something on his own and it proved to be a hoax. A fraud. He was caught. Disaster."

"You let him go?"

"He wasn't really in my employ. I was helping him in his career. Anyhow, he's been placed on probation, as I understand it, and now he's covering New Jersey sewer commissions."

"Bummer."

"Indeed. I do think we'll be okay. It's just that Monday I have to make a phone call I'm not looking forward to. But it'll work out, I'm sure, just not quite as quickly as we had hoped. But that's why I'm a little down for now."

"Poor guy," she said, reaching across the table to touch his hand. "Jessie will try to make you feel better."

"Excellent. Now let's order and—"

But a shadow fell across the table.

Bill looked up and was surprised to see Nick Memphis of the FBI. He almost did a double take.

"Nick, I—"

"Bill, imagine running into you here. Gosh, what a surprise."

Was that mockery in his voice?

"Uh, Jessica, may I present Nick Memphis, Special Agent, Federal Bureau of Investigation. Nick, this is Jessica Delph, a friend of mine."

Nick bowed.

"Ms. Delph, a pleasure," he said.

Then he turned to Bill and smilingly said, "Bill, you know, I think it would be a good idea if you gave Ms. Delph carfare and sent her home. I think it's going to be a long evening."

Bill swallowed, dammit, and looked for the joke in the agent's face but saw no humor.

"Ms. Delph, sorry, but I think your evening with Bill here is over."

"Bill, is anything the matter?"

"Uhhh," Bill stumbled, at a loss for words for the first time in his life. Then he said, "I don't know. Is anything the matter, Nick?"

"Well, Bill, that depends on how well you do over the next few minutes as we have our little chat. I'm trying desperately to find out why I shouldn't touch this button on my pager and stand back as our crack apprehension team—this is five guys who were all tackles or guards at Nebraska—come through that door in full SWAT gear, guns drawn, and throw you to the ground, mace you, slam on the cuffs, and drag you out by your ears, your Allen Edmonds shoes dragging in the sawdust. Imagine how quickly that would get all over town. We don't want that, do we?"

Bill had no desire to find out if Nick was bluffing.

"Jessie, here's a twenty, honey. I'll call tomorrow."

Quickly, she scurried out, and Nick slipped in.

Bill took a sip of his martini, then another, and ate the olive.

"Am I allowed to order another?"

"Sure."

"And you're not drinking, I'm guessing."

"You got that right."

Bill gestured Vito Corleone over and sent for another vodka martini.

"Okay, Nick, I'm all yours."

"I want to know why I shouldn't arrest you on seven counts of aiding and abetting a felony crime, namely murder, the first-degree kind."

Bill's lower jaw not merely hit the table top but fell clean through the floor to the wine cellar beneath. When he got his breath back and his jaw reinserted in its hinges, he spoke with a weak, phlegm-choked voice.

"I—I—"

It was not much of an argument.

"We recovered a 1971 bank camera film of a robbery in Nyackett, Massachusetts. It clearly shows the young Thomas T. Constable shooting and killing two security guards from behind."

"I—uh— Are you joking?"

"Not at all. Then we recovered very solid information linking him to four Irish contractors—professional snipers—who murdered Joan Flanders, Jack Strong, Mitzi Reilly, Mitch Greene, and Carl Hitchcock, and I'm betting we can pin the murder of a Chicago cop named Dennis Washington on him too. Tomorrow when we serve warrants, we'll have a lot more evidence. Now, Bill, here's where we are. You are either part of the solution or part of the problem. My bet is that you'll want to get ahead of this thing, because you know if you don't, it'll crush you. You'll do very hard time in a very bad joint."

"Nick, I knew nothing—"

"Save that for your own lawyer. I don't have time. Mr. Fedders, either you come with me tonight and start making like a tweety-bird, or you are looking at a grim end to a very pleasant life. Somehow I don't think Ms. Delph is going to make the long trip to Marion every Sunday to hear your sad stories of gang rape. And maybe Mrs. Fedders won't either."

Bill threw down his martini, signaled Vito for another one.

Then he turned to Nick and gave him a solemn, sincere look, rather fatherly, one of his most persuasive tools, and in his rich mahogany voice, he said, "Nick, you're asking me to turn on a man who's supported me my whole life. Because of Tom Constable's belief in me, I wear fine shoes—Aldens, not Allen Edmonds—and suits, am married to a beautiful, understanding woman, have four extraordinary children, well educated and prospering in their careers, and as you can see, I do still get out on the town once in a while, old dog that I am. All because of Tom. I make over five million dollars a year, have a fine estate in Potomac, a beautiful house in Naples, and another on the Eastern Shore, right near Dick Cheney's. I have horses, Perazzi shotguns; I have a two handicap and am noted as one of the best poker and bridge players in town. *Everyone* returns my calls. All that because of the generosity, the support, the belief, even the love of Tom Constable, whom you now accuse of horrific crimes. And you say to me, will you betray this man? Will you turn on this man? Will you do harm to this great American?"

"That's the sixty-four-year-in-prison question."

"Well, Nick, I can answer you very quickly, in words of one syllable: *of course I will.* In a second. In half a second. And have I got stuff to give you. Now let's get out of here. I hope you've got stenographers and typists ready, because it's going to be a very long night."

53

Two hours later they sat in a diner across from Indian Rapids's only motel, an Econo Lodge, showered and changed into clothes they'd bought in the town's only store, a beat-up old joint featuring everything from guns to butter. The two men were eating nothing great but a lot of it.

"Didn't know I was so hungry," said Bob.

"I can tell you're gassed. Best get some sleep now. I think you've got an advanced case of what I'd call combat stress syndrome."

"Umph," said Bob. "Maybe so. Felt better. Called my wife, told her I'd be home in a few days. She wasn't real sure who I was, and when I finally got her to remember me, she told me my daughters are all grown up and married and have kids."

"You need to chill for a long, calm year."

"I wish. Maybe later. I have to go to DC one last time on Tuesday to get this thing straightened out. Then I want to stop in Chicago. I have a gun that belongs to a police officer that I'd like to give to his widow."

"No rest for the weary," said Chuck. Then he said, "Look, Bob, nobody's going to say this, so you're stuck with me and I'm not any kind of speech maker. Too bad for you. But you wouldn't let 'em do that to Carl Hitchcock, and by extension to *us*, the snipers, the mankillers, the bastards way out there with a rifle that never make it into the history books even if they make it back to their own lines. So sniper to sniper, the only thing I can say is—hell, I don't know—Gee, Roy Rogers, you made all the little buckeroos happy."

Swagger smiled. That was good enough for him. Then he suddenly felt a wave of fatigue. Time to go.

"Brother Chuck, I've got to crash."

"Got it."

"You'll wake me in the morning and we'll figure out where to go and what to do next."

"Good."

"See you then."

"Gunny, one last thing. I won't sleep. How in hell did you make that shot? You were what, six hundred yards out, with a mil-dot, and he had that super-computer-driven thing. But you beat him and put him down before he even got a shot off. How? For God's sake, that was the greatest shot I ever heard of."

"Oh, that," said Bob, as if *that* were something like picking up a sock. "He thought he was hunting me, but I was hunting him. I knew if it came to Lone Tree, the shooting would be fast and far and it'd be a one-round war. I spent a night in Lone Tree before you came in and even before I went in. I walked it, I studied it on the maps, I tried to learn it good. I figured out where he'd start in if he came on a beeline from the first valley, 'cause he knew where the games would be played. That was the whole point. From there, I tried to figure where he'd shoot from. I discovered that there was a spot he'd move through, either on foot or low crawl, where there wasn't no wind. That's because you can't hardly see it, but about two hundred yards to the right, there's a knoll, about twenty foot tall, a natural windbreak. So if Anto's coming down that slope, when he gets to that dead spot, that's where he'll shoot. Any sniper would. Why fight the wind at the muzzle if you don't have to? I lased the range from the spot back to the tree. It was five hundred thirty-seven yards. When I got your rifle, I zeroed it to point of aim, dead bang center, no holdover, right at five thirty-seven. Then I just watched, and when he felt the wind stop, he halted, just for an instant, to process it; then he went to shoot. But I was maybe a half second ahead of him, and I put it on the money, though a little to the right. I was five inches off my center chest hold. Blew his arm out at the root. Wasn't pretty, but then little in this game is.

"Now, you know what? I'm going to drink some goddamned whiskey tonight, with Chuck McKenzie, Chuck-Chuck-Chuckity-Chuck, the great marine sniper, my friend, the fella who shot three Irish gooney birds off my ass and saved my worthless drunk's life three times in three seconds. Can you stay up with the old guy, Chuckity-Chuck, you goddamned sniping mankiller, you?"

"Gunny, I will drink to your mankilling ways and my own, and to all the snipers, and we will have ourselves a toot!"

54

Nick's apprehension plan was brilliant, and he cleared a major obstacle that Sunday morning, after a long night with his team listening to the confessions and accusations of Bob Fedders, by obtaining a federal warrant against Thomas T. Constable for murder by way of hired hitmen who crossed state lines to execute their crimes. That made it a legal federal pinch, and even if that charge ultimately proved hard to make in court—much of the information, in the form of e-mails in various laptops, had yet to be collected—it would stand until Massachusetts authorities were able to file murder charges against Constable for the 1971 killings, of which photographic evidence now existed.

Given that arrest warrant, Nick was also able to get his search warrants, which were eight in number: three for Constable offices in New York, Atlanta, and Los Angeles; one for the ranch property in Wyoming (especially the security team headquarters); one for Constable himself, including any possessions with which he might be traveling; one for the hard drive on Jack Strong's computer; one for all e-mails exchanged prior to the murders of Jack and Mitzi between Bill and Tom; and finally one for all properties belonging to the late Jack Strong and Mitzi Reilly.

All this had to be delicately coordinated, as all agreed that Constable had revealed himself a borderline sociopath given to violence and flight, and with his enormous resources he would have plenty of places to flee to, including homes in Costa Rica, the South of France, Switzerland, the moors of Scotland, and Bali. It was further thought that the governments of Cuba, Venezuela, China, Libya, and Indonesia would give him refuge if necessary. Therefore, all the searches were timed for 7 p.m., at which time Constable would be on the ground and ideally on the runway from his flight to Seattle to address the annual Amazon.com employees banquet. An FBI apprehension team was laid on, heavily armed, not because they expected trouble from Constable's three Graywolf bodyguards, who were after all sworn to obey civil law as a condition for their firearms permits, but Constable himself; who knew, who could predict how he might act when confronted and cornered? He might prefer a gun battle as a way of suicide by cop. Nick wanted him in custody with no difficulty, quietly and carefully before he realized the totality of the charges against him. Nick sure didn't want him shooting up the Amazon .com banquet; that would be a bad career move of epic proportions.

Like all brilliant plans, it began brilliantly, and like all brilliant plans, it failed brilliantly. Someone in the New York office got mixed up on time and thought the 7 p.m. jump-off was western time; to compound this error, it turned out that the New York AIC misunderstood the concept of time zones and thought that 7 p.m. in Seattle was 3 p.m. in New York.

"Oh, Christ," said Nick when he got the news. Heads would have to roll on this one, but that was for later. Now a real problem: would Constable hear? If he heard, he could bolt. If he got to his jet, he could head to Costa Rica or wherever, and what would the Bureau do then?

"Hmm," said Ron Fields, with his usual subtlety and political acumen, "I think I'd launch some F-18s, intercept over water, go to air-to-air, and do the shoot-down where it'll do the least damage."

"Thanks, Ron. Helpful as usual," Nick said grumpily, even though everyone else had laughed. "Okay, we go. We go now, we make the arrest wherever he is, before he gets word. Where is he?"

That's when it occurred to brilliant Nick that he'd made a brilliant mistake himself. He had purposely turned down the option of locating Constable and tailing him, because such a move, to a paranoid like Constable, might spook him into early flight. And the Seattle date was so solid that of all options, the Seattle airport takedown, well staffed, well planned by top tactical people, seemed absolutely the best.

"Where is he?" he asked again.

"We could do an NRO satellite interception of his cell phone notifications," said the ever-bright Starling.

"We need his number."

"Fedders would have it."

But Fedders was in a safe house in Roanoke, Virginia, and Bureau policy was never to call, because you never knew who was listening in, and if Constable somehow got away, Fedders's life would be at risk, to say the least. His security was not only mandated by regulation but paramount to Task Force Sniper's enterprise.

"Oh, shit," said Nick, sitting back.

"Nick, we can get FAA, we can find out the flight

plan of his Gulfstream, and we can move an apprehension team there ASAP."

"Good. Get going on it, Starling. I'll call the director and get his authorization to assemble apprehension teams at all field offices so that when we find out, we can move them fast."

Nick looked at his watch. It was now well after three. He felt like he was going to have a heart attack. All the shit they'd gone through and now it was beginning to topple—

"Wait a second," he said.

He took out his cell and called a number.

The phone on the other end rang and rang and rang.

"Swagger."

"Hey. How do you feel?"

"Better. Did some drinking last night, nothing much, I'm happy to say. Had a good time with a good pal. Is something up?"

"I'm afraid so. The good news is I've got a fed indictment on Constable, I've got search teams ready to—well, I told you all that."

"Yep."

"Okay, short version. We fucked up somewhere along the line and one of the search teams jumped early. It's possible—it would depend on who, if anybody, was staffing that New York office—the upshot is that it's possible someone could notify Constable that he was the subject of a federal operation. You know the guy has access to a jet. He could bolt overseas, we might never get him. He'd just end up more famous and admired by the world's assholes than he is now."

"Yeah," said Bob.

"So we need to bust him now, not in four hours when I had it set. But we've lost contact. We don't know where he is. I've got people tracking his plane; I may violate a regulation by calling someone I shouldn't to get his cell phone number so we can satellite-locate on him. I'm thinking . . . I don't know, just a shot: you were on his property, whatever, maybe you overheard something that would give us a tip."

"Well," said Bob, "I can give you a general location."

"Great! Oh, great!" said Nick.

"Yeah," said Bob. "He's in Colorado—"

"Alert Denver!" Nick shouted to his people.

"And he's, um, he's somewhere between, I would say, now this is just a guess, a rough one, one-sixty, one-sixty-five feet from me right now."

"What?"

"Yep. And here's the funny thing. He's dressed like a cowboy. And here's another funny thing. So am I."

55

Last stage, the Mendozas. The hard one. Oh, he was so close. He now sat in second, because Marshall Tilghman had screwed up his reload in the Buffalo Gulch thing, and Two-Gun Jack had had a couple of misfires—his own handloads!—on the last stage, Ambush on the Overland.

So only Tequila Dawn stood between Texas Red and the seniors championship. Tequila had been at this a long time, had won championships in other divisions, had even quit for a while and licensed his name for use on holsters, an Uberti Colt clone, boots, run a cowboy action shooting camp, but had finally come back to the game. He was good, but like Red, he was old, and he made the old-guy mistakes that Red had heretofore avoided, like dropping a cartridge in reloading or missing a target and having to come back to it, breaking his rhythm. That's why Red, so much slower, was still close. But now they were at Tequila's best event—straight pure pistolero artistry—and Red's worst one: the Mendozas.

Five into five Mendozas, shift guns, five into five more; then move through the saloon doors, reloading one, then the other gun as you went, and in fifty feet or so, you were in a corral where ten more Mendozas waited. Sure were a lot of Mendoza boys; well, maybe some weren't brothers but cousins or in-laws or something. And of course by the rules of political correctness, they were no longer identified as Mendozas, as that might be considered disrespectful to Latino Americans, more and more of whom were coming to the cowboy action world. They were just bad guys, but since the stage was a classic and had been around a long time, most people still called it by its original and now memory-holed name.

He was in the standby circle, alone, gathering. His hands felt good, and he'd only raised one cut—the front sight of his left gun had nicked and drawn a little blood—but no bandages were allowed in cowboy action, as there hadn't been bandages in Deadwood in 1883. But the cut wasn't deep and only hurt a bit when a drop of salty sweat fell into it. He wiggled his fingers, occasionally bent forward to stretch out his calves and thighs, or reached overhead with one hand to touch the other shoulder, stretching bi- and triceps. He tried not to pay any attention to Tequila. It was best if he didn't know. He didn't want to watch and psych himself out of his best per—

Tequila's first gun rang a quick staccato, and each shot banged home with a clang as the plate fell. Then came the switch of guns; it was fast, and again the five shots were fast but—he missed one! The agonizing seconds ticked by as Tequila reloaded one round, spun the cylinder, and fired, taking down the last target. Then he was on the run, reloading each gun as he went. He got to the corral, and Red heard the shots, lickety-split, each completed by the *Gong Show* sound of the plate struck at six hundred feet per second by a large lump of lead and—God, he missed another. Quickly the old gunslinger finished the string and decided to reload and fire rather than accept a ten-second penalty for a missed target, and he probably got the reload in and the shot off (*clang!*) in seven seconds.

Oh God, thought Red, I have a chance. I just can't miss a target. Slow, calm, collected, the gun reset just right. It's there. It's for me. I can do it.

He took a deep breath, trying to keep himself calm as he stepped into the loading area. He showed guns empty to the range officer running the stage, then, one at a time, slipped the cartridges in—one, skip one, four more—then cocked and gently lowered the hammer, keeping the muzzle downrange. Did it twice.

Turned to face the reset plates.

"Do you understand the course, shooter?"

"I do."

"Are you ready, shooter?"

"Yes."

"All right then—"

"Mr. Constable! Mr. Constable!"

Aghhhh! There went his concentration. It was Susan Jantz, his secretary. What could she want? *Aghh,* he could get disqualified.

He turned and saw the range officer trying to push her gently back to the cordoned crowd area. But Susan was persistent, slipped by him, and raced to her boss with his cell phone.

"What on earth—"

"You *have* to take this call."

"Shooter," said the range officer, "I'm going to have to call a 'spirit of game' infraction if you don't—"

Red put the phone to his ear.

"Constable."

"Mr. Constable, you don't know me. My name is

Randall Jeffords. I'm an accountant in your New York office."

"Why the hell are y—"

"Sir, I came in to catch up and the place was being torn apart by federal agents. I asked, and they wouldn't say, but there were some cops with them, and one of them said—I know you won't believe this—felony murder one. I just can't believe it. Against *you*, sir. I've been trying for hours to get your number. I thought you ought to know."

"You did the right thing," Texas Red said, clicking the cell closed.

He had a moment of disbelief, of stunned nothingness. His first cogent thought: where the fuck is Bill Fedders? He's supposed to be wired into that system. I'm supposed to know in advance when—

But quickly enough he saw the pointlessness of that line of inquiry. He realized a decision had just been made for him; he had to instantly accept its reality and deal with it first and fastest. There was but one answer: he had to get clear of the country, now. Nothing else mattered. From Costa Rica, he could sort things out, but the deal now was to avoid custody—the circus, the humiliation—and to see what they knew and didn't.

"Okay," he said to his number one bodyguard, who had by this time bullied his way forward, violating the rules, and stood waiting near him, "we've got to get out of here. Call the plane, tell them we'll be there in ten minutes."

"Yes sir."

"Thanks, Susan, you're the best," he said to his loyal secretary and daily sex servant.

He started to walk off the event stage.

"Shooter, you *cannot* leave without showing empty, you *cannot* leave, I will DQ you if you do not *immediately* return to the loading area and make your weapons safe."

Tom turned.

"Fuck you," he said, and walked off.

"DQ! DQ! Shooter is DQed!" shouted the range officer but made no step forward as the three beefy guards closed in behind Texas Red and the crowd parted in the thrust of the armed man and his armed bodyguards as they headed down the main street of the town of Cold Water, through the corridor of stunned competitors and fans.

And then a tall gunman stepped into the empty street ahead of him, raising one hand.

"A cowboy!" said Nick. "What the hell are you talking about?"

"It's the Cold Water Cowboy Action Shoot, Cold Water, Colorado. I saw something on CNN about it this morning and realized I'd heard the Irishmen talk about the boss being off playing cowboy. So being Sherlock Holmes, I put one and one together and came up with Cold Water. It was only a hundred miles from where we was. I had my pal Chuck drive me hell-for-leather over here, but since it was a gun crowd and I wanted to fit in, we stopped off. Chuck's an ex-lawman; he could buy a gun without no wait. We picked up a nice used Colt in a pawnshop. At a gas station I bought a hat, and when I got here, I picked up a holster and some black powder forty-fours. I wanted to see this guy face to face."

"You haven't called him out or something insane like that?"

"Of course not. I only look stupid. I just wanted to see him. He don't know nothing about me."

"Boy, was that ever the right decision. I am one lucky little federal flunky today. Just a second."

Bob waited as he assumed Nick was shouting orders to his people to get the information to the closest field office to Cold Water, Colorado, and get a SWAT team gunned up and on the way by helicopter.

Nick came back, sounding breathless.

"Okay," he said, "I've gotten Denver. They're on the way. They were on the runway because of an earlier alert. I'm told it'll be less than half an hour. Just stand by and—"

"Oh, shit," said Bob. "Something's going on. He's up there to shoot but all of a sudden his gal comes over, hands him a phone. He talks real urgent into it. Now he's breaking away, his mob of boys. They're getting out of town, Nick. He's going to his plane."

"Oh, Christ," said Nick. "How many?"

"It's him, three bodyguards, heavy guys. I don't see no guns but I'm guessing they're carrying."

"Oh, shit," said Nick.

"I can stop them," said Bob.

"Oh, God," said Nick, as if envisioning details of a terrible shoot-out in a huge crowded area, dozens dead, the whole thing a complete fuck-up, his career, just saved, trashed beyond redemption.

But then he thought, I rode this far with the gunman. Might as well go all the way.

"Okay," he said, "use your best judgment. If you think following them is the way to go, then—"

"You better give me some kind of verbal authorization to shoot damn quick, 'cause they's a hundred feet away and coming toward me."

He heard Nick whisper to others, "Witness this and record it," then he said loudly, "Do it. Take him down."

It took a second for the situation to dawn on the crowd, but then they all seemed to get it at once. Two gunslingers facing each other in a western town under a blaze of sun, shooting for blood. They backed off—not away, but off, cordoning themselves along the streets of Cold Water, witnesses to that which had not been seen for real in a century. Nobody was going to get them to look away.

"Kill him," said Texas Red to his bodyguard.

"Sir," said the man, "I am a bonded employee of Graywolf Security, and I am not empowered to open fire unless fired upon. I cannot engage unknown civilians, particularly in a crowded area. I have no idea who this guy is."

"Who are you?" yelled Red.

He saw the man start to answer, but someone else from the crowd yelled, "He's an Arizona Ranger," for some odd reason.

A moment of silence creaked by, then the bodyguard said, "Possible law enforcement agent. Cannot engage. Graywolf rules." He stepped away from Texas Red and led his colleagues to the sidelines. They wanted to watch too. That left Clell Rush.

"Don't do this, Red," Clell said quietly. "He's got a big iron on his hip."

Red looked, recognized from the top view exactly

what he himself was carrying, only his Colt wore the gunfighter's 4¾ inch barrel, while the Arizona Ranger's iron was indeed big; it was the 7½ inch model, which gave him a lot of metal to clear from leather.

In an instant, something ticked off in Red, or was he back to being Tom? Whatever, something flashed vaingloriously before his eyes. He imagined himself killing this "Arizona Ranger" in a fair gunfight—who, after all, could stay up with him?—then making the getaway. He knew that by the twisted currents loose in American culture, such an act would make him not merely famous but legendary. It would take away the onus of the murders he'd committed or ordered, all of which could be called cowardly. Facing and slaying an enemy old-style, in the oldest of Old West styles, as captured on a thousand cell phone videos, would make him perversely admired. He was a bastard, but he was a brave bastard, they'd say.

"I warn you," he called to the Ranger, "these guns are loaded."

His adversary cracked a dry smile.

"Mine too," he said. "Never saw no use for an unloaded gun."

It was quiet. How could it not be? Of all the audiences in the world, this was the one that appreciated the ceremony of the gunfight more than any other and had worshipped its warriors like the old gods. And all were in the garb, some slightly theatricalized, of the 1880s, so as a tableau, it looked as if it belonged captured in the sepia of the best photo Mathew Brady ever took or in Remington's or Russell's brushstrokes. Everyone understood the dynamism, the thunder, the flash and pain that was about to be released for real.

The two men began the slow walk toward each other, by now oblivious to crowd and setting. Their boots sloughed dust; their neckerchiefs were tight. One wore red and one wore blue. Texas Red slipped out of the stylish black leather vest he was wearing, in case its tightness proved an impediment. He set his white hat lower on his eyes, to shade the sun.

The stranger wore jeans and a denim shirt; he was a rhapsody in worn blue. His handkerchief was black; his hat was crushed and bent, and you'd have thought it was one of those ridiculous Richard Petty imitation hats that gas stations sold, but of course a man so elegant and brave would never wear such a thing. His gun was in a Galco Texas Ranger rig, heavily figured with floral motifs, on an equally figured belt, which also supported a row of twenty more robin's-egg-big .44 cartridges. But all present, having seen Red shoot, thought this handsome stranger was about to meet his death.

There was forty feet between them when they came to make their play. No words, no smiles, just deadfaced gunfighter's harshly focused concentration, eyes slitted, mouths tight and grim, no visible breathing, no visible emotion, and as if on silent agreement they went to leather.

Red was fast and loose and strong, and the truckload of adrenaline in his bloodstream turned his gunhand into a blur as it flew to grip, thumb to hammer, driven by an ideal unspooling in his mind, as if from the myth-pure western that no man had made, the one where the hands flash and the guns jackhammer a bolt of flame and a blast of smoke and it's the other man who's spavined to the ground, oozing blood and sorrow. That did not happen.

The Ranger's hand abandoned time and physics as it seemed to pass into invisibility, and in the next nanosecond, when it returned to the known universe, it had somehow already oriented the old revolver, cocked it, busted cap with spurt of muzzle flame and white cannonade of rocketing gas, and launched a fat .44 on its track across space.

Red had not cleared leather before the bullet fairly ripped, hit, mutilated, and exited. He went down hard, kicking up a puff of dust, which the wind took, just as it took the gunsmoke of the Ranger's speedier Colt. Red curled as he fell, gun flying away in a twisted angle, the sound of the shot lost to all, so intent were all in the essence of the age-old drama.

The moment was utter antique. Not a single thing spoke of later times that any man or woman or child could see. The white smoke and dust, teased to action by the relentless wind, seemed to lie over all for just a second, glazing and blurring all surfaces, suggesting again that this was ancient times.

But then the applause broke out. Well, who could blame them? And the chants, "Ran-ger, Ran-ger, Ran-ger!"

One might think, how terrible to cheer a mankill-ing, no matter the circumstances. However, it became instantly clear that Texas Red may have been fairly ripped by the bullet's progress, but he was not dead by a long shot. Instead the Ranger had brought off that trope of fifties cowboy TV—shooting the gun out of the hand, as Gene and Roy and Hoppy had done countless times, so that the bad guys gripped their sore mitts and shook them as if experiencing something akin to bees in the bat.

Red rolled, screaming for help, and it then became obvious what was different about this particular variation on the theme: the Ranger had not quite shot the gun out of his hand but had shot the hand out from his gun. The bullet had struck him in the wrist bone and deflected downward, knocking the gun this way and three fingers of his right hand that way. The mangled paw now spurted a crimson jet unseen in fifties tube time.

The Ranger slipped his gun back into its holster and walked to the fallen man. Texas Red gripped his destroyed hand as if with finger pressure he could stop the blood flow, but as his eyes came up to his victor, he tried to slither backward, caught in a vise of fear. The man waited until at last eye contact was made.

"I don't know who you are," Red said, squinting into a sun that turned his opponent to a black silhouette.

"Oh yes you do. I am the sniper."

Then he turned and walked clear, hearing someone scream, "Get him a doctor," but before that was accomplished, the whole nineteenth-century illusion was devastated by an updraft of dust, a sudden density of shadow that announced a helicopter was settling out of the sky, right there in Cold Water. It was the FBI apprehension team, and as the bird settled, its rotors beat up a mighty wind, filling the air with a hurricane of dust, driving folks this way and that. The Arizona Ranger seemed to disappear in the drifting grit just as mysteriously as he had arrived.

56

The Constable revelations rocked the nation, as might be imagined, and the story of the trials and the sentencing, the appeals, the retrials, and an account of the whole surrealistic Fellini movie that came in its wake—the television shows, the circus of sensational journalism, blogism, essayism, talking headism, and schadenfreudeism—is best left for elsewhere.

For those involved, however, the trials and interviews and think pieces et al were really signifiers of nothing. It was just the assholes in the world catching up to what the people on the point of the spear had already done in their names. All that media crap wasn't much for real endings. But there were real endings, possibly too many to choose from.

One came after the first trial and halfway through the second, when in all the ruckus, Nick Memphis found Special Agent Ron Fields sitting in the Nyackett, Massachusetts, courthouse cafeteria, waiting to testify. He had not been able to catch the fellow alone since the day it all went down.

"Hi ya," he said, slipping in across from the big guy.

"Hi, Nick," Fields said. "You got my note. Thanks for the commendation. It looks like I will get the sniper program," Fields said.

"I hope so," said Nick. "You deserve it."

"Ah, Nick," said Fields with his sloppy grin, "I'm

just a dumbbell gunfighter and gofer. I'm best suited for Quantico and teaching SWAT. That Starling, she's the bright one. She'll be a star."

"I bet you're right on that one," Nick said. "I wrote her up too."

"Great."

"But I'm glad you mentioned her. I wanted to ask you something."

"Sure, Nick. But don't expect subtlety. I'm the grind-it-up type."

"You know what they're saying?"

"Hmm," said Fields. "Well, I've heard some stuff."

"As I understand the story, it goes something like this. There's this young special agent who's pissed at the hosing her boss is getting in the press. And guess what, the fiancé of this young agent happens to work for a certain outfit located in Langley, V-A. He's in photo intelligence. Anyhow, when this agent's boss is in trouble and everyone's calling him a crook, she and boyfriend come to the rescue. Boyfriend uses agency tech to dummy up a photo; this is, of course, after both put their heads together and figure out what a certain great newspaper knows nothing about. But first, they snitch a document out of an unguarded file, retype it on their own processor and replace it. Then they pass a reporter a document typed on the same word processor, and for a while, it looks as if the reporter has got a real scoop on his hands. Well, I'm telling the story all wrong, out of sequence, but you can figure it out, I'll bet. The famous newspaper goes to press with its picture and gets *slaughtered*. Just gets massacred. Pretty damn funny, if you ask me. And the campaign the newspaper was running curls up and dies, and old Nick goes back to work, same as it ever was, and we even end up putting a bad guy away and who knows what might have happened if the guy in charge didn't have this naive faith in some outlier named Bob Lee Swagger. Boy, would we be in a different world, I'll tell you."

"I've heard that story, yeah," said Fields. "As I said, she's a smart one. And that reputation should help her in her career. People look at her and say, don't mess with Starling. It's a ticket up."

"It is. And try as I might, I can't see that a crime has been committed. I mean other than misuse of government resources, but that's not my bailiwick. If someone chooses to play a prank on a newspaper, what crime has been committed?"

"I can't think of one either, Nick."

"So, I'm going to let that drop. That's my decision. But I look at Fields and I think, I'll run it by him, just get his take on it; he's a salty old dog."

"The salty old dog says, sometimes it's best to let things drop."

Nick smiled.

"Then it's dropped. She'll be a star. You get Sniper SWAT at Quantico. Maybe I get assistant director."

"If there's any justice—"

"And the important thing is the bad guys go down or away. Let's not forget that."

"Never forget that. It makes me feel all warm and fuzzy."

"Cool," said Nick, rising. "Okay, that's a big help. I'll let you concentrate on your testimony now. I've got to get back to DC and— Oh," he said, "one other thing."

"Sure, Nick."

"How do you suppose she got it down?"

Fields smiled but his eyes showed bafflement.

"What're you—"

"You know, my picture. The fake photo used info from a real picture. It was hanging on my glory wall. Sally and I in Hawaii on vacation, about four years ago. They needed a real photo so their computers could transfer and manipulate the information. That's why it seemed familiar."

"Gee, I hadn't thought of that," said Fields. "I mean, I guess she just wandered into your office one day and slipped it off the wall."

"I suppose," said Nick. "But she's only five-two. She can't reach any higher than six feet, much less manipulate something. That photo was in the top row, close to seven feet off the ground. And my office has a glass wall. So she'd have to do it in plain sight of the office, and she'd have to move a chair over to get up to it, and she'd have to have another photo to hang in its place, and all that would take time and anyone would notice it."

"I guess she did it after hours."

"But she's only an SA. Special agents aren't allowed in after hours unless they're with an assistant special agent in charge; of course an ASAIC can come in any-time."

"Huh," said Fields. "Interesting. So you're say-ing—"

"I'm not saying anything. The facts are saying that if someone took down that pic and replaced it with something else, it was done after hours, meaning by an ASAIC or higher, six-two or taller. Know anybody like that? Oh, and he'd have to be familiar with that wall."

"Maybe she—"

"Maybe. But I did some checking. It's interesting, yeah, her fiancé's a CIA guy and might have had access to that lab. But did you know there's a guy on Taskforce Sniper who partnered up early with a guy named Jerry Lally? Five years, a few gunfights, that sort of thing. And of course Jerry took a leave of absence, went back to school, got a master's in chem and a PhD in physics and came back to work science for us. He's now head of *our* photo interp. And let's not forget that although CIA has the best photo lab in Washington, we have the second-best photo lab in Washington. Really, not one floor and a hundred feet from our office. And whoever did this little thing, he really knew our building forward and back, much better, I'm guessing, than a new special agent. No, this guy'd be an old salty dog."

"Pretty interesting," said Fields.

"And see, here's the funny thing. Everybody thinks this guy is a big, lovable, loyal lunkhead, but if you look at his tests, his IQ maxes out, as do all his other tests. See, everybody thinks he's a jovial door kicker, but maybe he's the smartest of them all, smarter than his own boss, because he figures getting known as an egghead isn't going to get him Sniper at Quantico."

"Nick, you have some imagination. You ought to write a book."

"Nah," said Nick. "Nobody'd believe it. As I say, it's dropped now."

Then a bailiff came and called Fields as next to testify, and he rose, and Nick reached out to shake his hand and said, "You are the best, big guy, the very best," and Fields smiled and was off.

Here's another possible ending: a notice that appeared on page A-2 of a recent issue of the *Times* in the Corrections Box.

> On October 29 of last year, a photograph appeared on page one of this newspaper purporting to show a federal agent in the company of executives from a firearms company attempting to land a federal contract with the agent's employer, the Federal Bureau of Investigation. The Times has since learned that the photo was a fraud and its publication was in violation of the newspaper's own code of professional ethics. The Times regrets the error.

Still another ending could have been the marriage of Bill Fedders to Jessica Delph, who was younger than his youngest child. Bill had quite a run on the strength of his multiple testimonies against Tom Constable and emerged as some kind of media hero. He was also smart enough to make phone calls to a half dozen or so representatives and senators at his earliest convenience and warn them ahead of the curve that Constable was going down hard and that they ought to begin this second to distance themselves from the sordid spectacle. All were grateful, all did favors in return, and Bill prospered beyond belief. He finally decided that, for some reason or other, it was time to retire the first wife and be seen about town with the trophy more than once a month. It just shows that in Washington, you can't keep a bad man down. Perhaps God will punish him by giving him a few more children.

But maybe the best ending was the reinterment of the marine sniper Gny. Sgt. Carl Hitchcock (Ret.) in the consecrated ground of the USMC Cemetery at Camp Lejeune, North Carolina. Unlike his first interment, it didn't take place in a heavy rain and it wasn't sparsely attended. In fact, among the two-thousand-odd attendees, almost the entire shooting community turned out, from writers like Ayoob and Bane and Huntington and Taffin to editors like Brennan and Venola and Hutchcroft and Keefe; to the sniper researchers Peter Senich and Maj. John L. Plaster; to shooters like Tubb and Leatham and Enos and Wigger; to dozens of aging grunts who made it back from 'Nam because of Carl and the few men like him; to some of those men themselves, such as Chuck McKenzie and the other great marine sniper who never sought fame or recognition, Chuck Mawhinney, likewise the Army sniper Bert Waldron, even the widows of posthumous Medal of Honor winners the Delta snipers Randy Shughart and Gary Gordon; to gun rights authors and advocates like Cates and Gott-lieb and Kopel and LaPierre; to SWAT sharpshooters from all over the nation; to the FBI team of Task Force Sniper, who in the end labored so hard and risked so much to bring this moment to life; to Marine officers and NCOs from the commandant on down; and finally to ordinary people who happened to be lovers of courage. And because reality is often trite and doesn't acknowledge that thing the intellectuals call "the pathetic fallacy," it followed that the sun was bright, the leaves green, the wind fragrant, and not a dry eye remained, no matter how battered and grizzled the warrior, especially when the ceremony closed down and that last, mournful note of taps hung in the air. It was sad, it was sad, it was so sad, but at the same time it was, for all of them, a happy time.

There was one other difference between this ceremony and the first one.

Swagger was not there.

And where was he?

It is known that after a week of depositions and debriefings in Washington, he took a train to Chicago and presented Detective Sergeant Dennis Washington's widow with her husband's firearm. It was all he could do after missing the funeral. He and Susanna and the three girls had a good time together and it was kind of all right but not nearly as good as it would have been if the big guy was there. They all promised to keep in touch.

Then, all presumed, he retired to his place in Idaho. But no one knows for sure, because he stopped answering his phones.

After all, he is the sniper. You're not supposed to know where he is.

ACKNOWLEDGMENTS

To begin with, two confessions of literary license: There is no such thing, yet, as iSniper911. I'm anticipating developments by a few years, as all the components exist and have been proven in the field, but no one has figured out quite how to pack them into one instrument, at least as I write now. Perhaps as you read that next step will have been taken.

Second, I am aware that the FBI's marksmen's rifles are built by H-S Precision; I chose to attribute them to Remington because it saved me the effort of explaining to readers who and what H-S was and because Big Green, as Remington is known, has provided the world with such weapons for 25 years, through its brilliantly engineered 700 bolt action.

On to thanks: Gary Goldberg, of course, was my majordomo throughout the writing of the book. If I had to know how a Garmin GPS worked or where the possessions of the intestate are taken in Cook County, Gary was the go-to guy. Through Gary, I reached the following: Amy Jo Lyons, Special Agent in Charge of the Baltimore office of the FBI; Jennifer Haggerty of the Cook County Public Administrator's Office; John Stephens, for technical information on photo forgeries; Dr. John Matthews, founder of SureFire LLC, the great flashlight manufacturers, for information on modern suppressors; and Lew Merletti, former Director of the U.S. Secret Service, for fast, accurate feedback on equipment and tactics. I'm grateful to all and of course all errors of fact and judgment are mine and mine alone.

My readers' circle provided helpful ideas and suggestions: Jay Carr, the former great film critic of the *Boston Globe*; Lenne Miller, my solid good friend since 1966; Bill Smart, late of the *Washington Post*, now of Montana, for info on Cowboy Action; John Bainbridge for skillful proofreading; Roger Troup, a great gun guy; and in L.A., my good friend Jeff Weber.

Kathy Lally, now of the *Washington Post* and the editor who invented me at the *Baltimore Sun*, introduced me to her cousin, the Irish actor Mick Lally, for a long discussion of the Irish accent in Dublin. Hmm, I think some drinking was done.

Weyman Swagger, now in ill health, for unflagging enthusiasm; and also, thanks for the use of the name, guy.

My wife, the journalist Jean Marbella, who rolls her eyes when the books on arcane subjects begin to pile up in the bedroom and announce the arrival of a new Swagger adventure, but hangs in through it all. Hey, at least they weren't swords this time!

Otto Penzler provided me with *le mot juste* at *le moment juste*.

Michael Bane, for his enthusiasm and support via his great blog.

The professional researcher Dan Starer who set me up with Special Agent Royden R. Rice of the Chicago office of the FBI.

In the professional realm, my agent Esther Newberg, my publisher David Rosenthal, and my editor Colin Fox stood foursquare behind me all the way through this one. That makes it so much easier.

And of course the great Marty Robbins, for providing the Ur-text to Chapter 55.

And for the record: I love Turner Classic Movies!

Read on for a sneak peek
at the next riveting novel

DEAD ZERO

from *New York Times* bestselling author

Stephen Hunter

Coming soon in hardcover from Touchstone

WHISKEY 2-2
Zabul Province, SE Afghanistan
0934

Consciousness came and went; the pain was constant. It was the day after the ambush. The flesh wound in Cruz's left thigh still oozed blood and the entire left side of his body was a purple-yellow smear of bruise. It hurt so bad he could hardly stay conscious, much less move across the raw landscape that strobed in and out of focus all round him, harshly bright in the sun. But Cruz, a gunnery sergeant in the United States Marine Corps, was one of those rare men with a personality of hard metal, unmalleable, unpenetrable, unstoppable. It's why back at Bravo/3/4 Forward Operating Base he was called The Cruise Missile. Once fired, he kept moving until he hit the target. He was the go-to guy on patrol security, Agency snatch-and-grabs, and various counter-sniper and IED problems. He was always there, in the shadows on the ridgeline or the village roof, sometimes spotted-up, sometimes not, depending, with his SR-25, a beast of a .308 semi-auto with a yard of optics up top, paying out survival for his people at long range in packages that weighed 175 grains apiece. He never missed, he never counted or cared about the kills.

Yet now, no one would confuse him for what he was. He was dressed in the loose-fitting, easy flowing tribal garments of the Pashtun, the people of the mountains. He looked like Lawrence of Afghanistan. His olive face was crusty with beard and filth, his lips cracked. He wore sandals and a burnoose, obscuring his face and not one item of government-issue clothing. He was also among goats.

There were fourteen of them left. It was fine to love animals until you try to herd goats. The goats weren't into team spirit. They free-ranged, depending on need or whim, somewhat raggedly, and Cruz was able to keep them coherent and moving roughly forward only by constant screaming and beating with his staff, and when he swatted at them with the staff, the weight went to his violated leg and a new prong of pain thrust up into his guts. They shit everywhere, without apparent effort or notice. They attracted flies in clouds. They smelled of feces and blood and meat. They babbled constantly, not so much a classic bah-bah-bah but more of a whiney singsong, some bleating like kids on a long bus ride. He hated them. He wanted to kill them with the SR-25 under his robes, eat them, and go home. But he had a goddamned job to do and he could not make himself quit on that job. It wasn't will or habit, it certainly wasn't out of any notion of the heroic or Semper Fi or memories of Iwo and Chosin and Belleau Wood. It was just what he did and his mind wasn't organized in such a way as to consider alternatives.

The rifle shifted uncomfortably under his swirl of robes. Its strap bit into his shoulder and its rough surfaces gouged him as it slipped this way or that. It was like a BAR, a heavy piece of complexly machined moving parts, mostly metal with knobs, angles, bolts, all sorts of things sticking out of it, including a Schmidt & Bender 10X cinched atop. He hated it. Yet he was lucky to have it. And one magazine of 20 Black Hills 175-grain match cartridges.

It was all he had left; he'd started with a spotter, an ample supply of food and water, and no bullet having blown a quart of flesh off his leg. The trek the long way around to Quait would be only three days in; after the shot, maybe a day of escape and evasion. Then they'd go to green, his spotter would put in the call, and a Nightstalker would helo them out and they'd be back at the FOB in time for beer and steak. And the Beheader, as they called Ibrihim Zarzi, warlord of the southeastern Pashtun tribes, opium merchant, prince, spy, charmer, betrayer, Taliban senior commander, and Al Qaeda liaison, would be sucking poppy from the root end first.

But it didn't happen that way; reality seldom follows mission op outlines.

"Why send men, Major," Ray had asked S-4—the intelligence officer—in the S-4 bunker, where the audience included Colonel Laidlaw, his exec, and his own section lieutenant. "Can't our agency friends send a missile? Isn't that what they do? They have some zen master pinball kid sitting in a trailer in Vegas flying a joystick take him out with a Hellfire?"

"Ray, I shouldn't tell you this," Colonel Laidlaw said, "but it's your ass on the line so you have a right to know. The Administration has tightened up on the missile hits. Too much collateral. This guy's complex is in heavy urban. You go all Hellfire on his ass, yes, you probably send him to his God. But you send two hundred other rug-monkeys along with him and you've got the *New York Times* squawking. These folks don't like that."

"Okay, sir. I can take him. I'm just worried about the E&E from Quait. I want to get my people out. Can we have Warthogs standing by to cowboy up the place if it gets tight? We won't have enough firepower to shoot our way out of anything."

"I can get you Apaches ASAP. Our Apaches. I don't want to lay on air force Warthogs because I've got to go through too many chains of command and too many people have to sign off on it. It's not all that secure."

The marines didn't like the air force guys because they thought the pilots should always get lower, down to marine level, before they started blowing shit up and killing people. But the pilots, on strict orders from above, were constrained from nose-in-the-dirt flying. They launched smart bombs, then toggled them in, then went home and slept between clean sheets after martinis in the officers' club. Some even had girlfriends, it was rumored.

That was it and it never occurred to Ray to come up with a turn-down. If he didn't do it, somebody else would, and whoever that somebody was, he wouldn't be as good as Ray.

It had to be done. The Beheader—the nickname came because it was rumored he was the mastermind behind the kidnapping of a journalist who'd suffered the fate when he'd gone off on his own in Quait to get the Taliban side of the story—was an eternal problem for marines in the southeastern operating area. When IEDs went off only as command vehicles passed in resupply convoys, it was because the Beheader's spies had infiltrated and knew how to ID the one Humvee out of 25 that carried brass. When patrols were ambushed, and major ops had to be launched to get them out of the trouble they'd gotten into, and the shooters had mysteriously vanished into nothingness, it was suspected they had simply ducked into the off-limits Beheader compound. When a sniper dinged a CIA operations officer, when a mortar shell or a rocket-propelled grenade detonated with far too much accuracy to be a random shot, when an Afghan liaison officer was found with throat cut, all the signs pointed to the Beheader, who was in all other respects a wonderful man, a handsome, well-educated fellow (Oxford, University of Iowa) with impeccable table manners who, when he allowed Americans, including high-ranking marine officers, into his home, boldly violated Islamic taboo by designating a liquor room, where a superb bartender made any drink you could imagine served under little paper umbrellas.

"I want this guy deadr'n shit," said the Colonel. "I had to fight command and the agency all the way to the top to get a kill authorized. Ray, I'd love to push the button and watch the computer kids whack him, but it's not going to happen. You've got to walk in, drop him with a rifle shot, and walk out."

"Got it," said Ray.

The shooting site had to be the roof of the Many Pleasures Hotel, across the street from the Beheader's compound. Once a week, the man was predictable. At twilight on Tuesday—it was always Tuesday—he left the compound by armored Humvee and went into the District, and visited a nice young prostitute named Mindi, with eyes like almonds, hair the color of night and ways and means beyond imagination. And why didn't he just move her in? Well, concubine politics. He already had three wives and twenty-one kids, and already wives No. 1 and No. 3 hated each other; his second concubine was plotting against his first concubine, all the women were lobbying incessantly for a trip to Beverly Hills and what little domestic tranquility could be had would be shattered by adding Mindi to the mix. Thus it was felt that not only her sexual skills but the fact that she was deaf and dumb gave the Great Man a peace and serenity unavailable in his own hectic home.

In any event, Tuesday at twilight, he predictably strode from his house to the vehicle, a distance of some ten yards. It was then and only then he was vulnerable to a shot. Shooting suppressed from a little over two hundred yards out, with just enough angle to clear the wall but still access the target, Ray could easily put a 175-grain package of peace and love into the Beheader in his five-second window of opportunity. Chaos would ensue, the militiamen in the bodyguard squad would have no idea where the shot came from and would certainly begin firing wildly, driving people to cover. Ray and his spotter would fall back from the Many Pleasures Hotel, rappelling off the roof and making their way into the crowded slum district of Jamal, just a few blocks away, where they would go to ground. They'd just be two more faceless Muslims in a city full to bursting with them. The next night, they'd exfiltrate the city, make it to a certain hill about five miles to the south, and wait for the Nightstalker to pick them up.

"It sounds easy," said S-4. "It won't be."

It got hard the second day. On the first, he and Skelton had passed a couple of Taliban patrols on the high road but attracted no interest from those wary fighters, whose gimlet eyes were used to piercing the distance for the sand-and-spinach digital camo of marine warfighters. They saw goatherds all the time and if these two were a little more raggedy-ass than most they saw, it didn't register. They moved at goat pace, without urgency, without apparent direction, letting the wiry little animals eat, shit, and fuck as their goat-brains saw fit, but generally moseying in the direction of the big market at Quait where their fifteen treasures could be sold for slaughter.

As part of security procedure, Whiskey 2-2 avoided villages, slept without campfires, ate riceballs and unleavened sheaves of dry bread, wiped their hands on their pants, and shat without toilet paper.

"It's just like the Sigma Chi house," said Skelton as they came to the top of a rise and found a tricky path down the other side.

"Except you don't jack off as much," said Ray.

"I don't know about you, Ray, but I don't need to jack off much. I had a real nice time with that blond goat last night. She's a princess."

"Next time, keep it down. May be bad guys in the vicinity."

"She sure does moan, doesn't she? Boy, do I know how to please a gal or what?"

The two men laughed. Lance Corporal Skelton didn't have an SR-25 under his caftan, but he did have fourteen pounds of PRC-104 High Frequency radio, an M4 with an Advanced Combat Optical Gunsight—ACOG—twenty-six magazines, and a case containing a Schmidt and Bender 35X spotting scope. All that shit: he moved like an old lady.

They were in high plains country, trending north. The Paki mountains rose ahead, over the unseen border, mantled in snow and sometimes fog, more tribal territory where white guys couldn't go for fear of execution upon apprehension. The land they negotiated was rocky and hardscrabble, clotted with waxy, tough, gray vegetation. Rocks lay everywhere, and each hill revealed a new landscape of secret inclines and defilades, and it was all brown-gray, coated with dust or grit, about as hospitable as hell's outhouse. They were right on the border between the rising plains and the actual foothills, and out here it was desolate. Except of course they knew they were being watched and always assumed some Taliban was gazing their way through the scope of a Dragunov or a nice pair of Russian binoculars. So no American jock crap as young athletic fellas are wont to do, no air basketball or long, deep fantasy passes, no scooping up the hot grounder and firing to first. No middle fingers, no mock comic "fuck yous," no hyper attention to hygiene, no acknowledgment that such things as germs existed or that Allah was less than supreme. Prayer mats, five times a day on the knees to Mecca; you never knew who was watching.

And, of course, somewhere up above lurked either a satellite or more likely a Predator drone configured for recon as it rode the breezes back and forth behind a tiny piston engine. They were probably on monitors in living color in every intelligence agency in the free world. It was like being on *The Tonight Show with Jay Leno*, except for the Afghanistan part. So another sniper discipline was: don't look up. Don't look at the sky, as if to acknowledge that somebody was up there to watch over them.

FOB WINCHESTER
Zabul Province, Afghanistan
1556

"I didn't think it would take all this time," said the Colonel.

"Sir," said his exec, "that's rough land. That's really rough land. And the goats. They seem to be having trouble with the goats. Maybe the goats were a mistake."

"S-4, are they on schedule?"

"More or less," said the intelligence officer. "That goat market has been there for 3,000 years and I don't think it's going anywhere soon."

The Colonel rolled his eyes to his exec. What was it with intelligence people? They always had a little bit of an

I-wouldn't-be-in-intelligence-if-I-weren't-intelligent deal going on. This one, even worse, was an Annapolis grad and convinced he was on a straight run to become the next commandant.

"It's not the market, S-4. It's the Tuesday shot. If they miss that, they have to hang out there in goat city undercover for another full week. They'll make a mistake and get nabbed and the Beheader will get to practice his specialty."

"Yes, sir," said S-4, "I only meant—"

"I know, S-4. I'm just ragging on you because if I don't pick on somebody I'll have an anxiety attack."

Colonel Laidlaw stood in the S-4 bunker behind the base's many miles of concertina wire and sandbags. He had three patrols out, and word was brewing that the whole battalion was up for a major assault sometime in the next month and he had too many men down with malaria, too many in psych wards, and too many on leave. Battalion strength was about 60 percent, nothing worked, one of his officers was showing disturbing signs of depression, and replacing him would be a political nightmare. The intel that came through the Agency was always late and bad, and now he had two of his best guys way, way out on a limb. In other words, things were just about normal for combat operations.

He lit up what felt like his 315th cigarette. It tasted just as shitty as cigs 233 through 314.

He looked at what was before him on the monitor screen. It was Whiskey 2-2, from an altitude of about 2,000 feet, except that altitude was a magnification. Actually the bird was close to twelve miles in the sky, rotating in a slow low-earth orbit, under the control of the geniuses at Langley, and it had cameras with lenses capable of resolutions considered nearly unbelievable only a few years before. If they wanted, they could probably tell if the Beheader had his eggs over easy or poached.

What Laidlaw and his staff saw, through the drifting smoke and the hum of tiny jihadi insects that buzzed and bit and were otherwise invisible, was the dark ripple running diagonally across the screen—the crest of a ridge. On it, a tiny, almost antlike movement that signified ambulatory life was held under the white, glowing cruciform of a center lens indicator. A whole lot of meaningless numbers—Laidlaw wasn't good on tech stuff—ran along the border of the image, and it took some getting used to. With practice, you got adjusted to the stylizations of the system, the brown-to-black-to-gray color scheme, the foreshortening, the scuts of dust that blew this way and that, and learned to determine the difference between the two marines and the longer, squirmier form of the goats spilling this way and that.

"How much longer?" asked the Colonel, meaning how long before the satellite continued its way around the earth and Whiskey 2-2 passed from view for another twenty-four.

"Only about ten minutes, sir," S-4 said. "Then they go bye-bye."

They knew that these semiabstract forms trekking across the opaque screen of the large monitor were Whiskey 2-2 and not some group of actual goatherders by virtue of the cruciform that kept the camera nailed. It signified the origin of a GPS chip in the grip of Cruz's SR-25, a security concept S-4 hadn't bothered to explain to the guys. But it simplified the problematic issue of target acquisition and identification and meant that when the satellite was in range, it could eyeball the guys the whole way. Still, both S-4 and Colonel Laidlaw felt a little uneasy about it; it was spying on their own men without permission, as if an issue of trust were involved. The Colonel justified it by telling himself it was necessary in the case of emergency evac, if Lance Coporal Skelton, hurt or killed, couldn't get to his radio and sing out coordinates. They could call in air force Warthogs and ventilate the area with frags and 30-millimeter while guiding in marine aviation for the extract. That is, if Whiskey 2-2 found itself in a firefight.

"Who's that?" someone said.

"Hmmm," said S-4.

"Where, what, info, please," said Colonel Laidlaw.

"Sir, ahead of them on the same axis, on the hilltop a little back, I'm guessing maybe a half mile out to the west, that is, to the right."

To spare the Colonel the agony of translating the directions into an actual location on the gray wilderness of map, S-4 ran up to the screen and touched what the Exec had seen first. No goats, that's for sure. No, it was a group of guys, slightly whiter against the dull sage of the land-form, only they were lengthier than goats and not moving, which meant they were prone. If they were facing in the right direction, they were on line to intercept Whiskey 2-2's line of route.

"Taliban?"

"Probably."

"Is that a problem?"

"Shouldn't be. They ran into Taliban patrols twice yesterday and once earlier today. To the Tallys, they just look like goatherders. Unless they get close enough to see Cruz is part Filipino. And even then, he's so scruffy—"

"Yeah, but those guys were on their feet, standing, eyeballing, lollygagging, moving in their own direction. These guys are setting up. This could be an intercept."

The group of men continued to watch the monitor as the drama played out in real time before them. Laidlaw lit another cigarette. S-4 didn't say anything snarky. Exec didn't suck up. It just happened.

The group ahead of Whiskey 2-2 seemed to squirm, then settle. Damn, why hadn't the staff seen them come in; maybe their direction of origin would have been an indicator.

"How much time?" asked Colonel Laidlaw.

"Two minutes."

"Sir, I can reach Whiskey on the PRC-104. Give 'em a heads up." That was Exec.

"Sir, all respect, but if you do that, Skelton has to hunker down, peel off his caftan, unstrap the radio, and talk into the phone. All those are tells. If these guys are bad or there are some other bad actors, say in caves, we're not picking up on, that gives Whiskey away for sure. The mission goes down. They get whacked for sure, or end up in a running gunfight."

"Shit," said the Colonel.

"I don't like the orientation. Those guys are prone, they're setting up to shoot. Could the agency have a team in there?" said Exec.

"I got negative from liaison on that not an hour ago," said S-4. "This is the only area op."

"Let it play out," said the Colonel. "Goddammit."

They watched. The two small forces drew inexorably together, the raggedy fleet of goats spilling across the landscape on the ancient track in the hills, and the six interlopers set up orthodox Lejeune style for a shoot, legs neatly splayed, maybe one up on his knees working binocs, the others bending into scope.

"I don't like this one fucking bit," said the Colonel. "Where's our goddamned Hellfire when we need it? I'd like to punch those bastards out, whoever they are."

"They're probably birdwatchers from National Geographic Channel," said S-4. "Or maybe missionaries from the World Orphan Relief League. Or—"

But the question was answered. Whiskey had reached its point of maximum closure with the unknown force on the hilltop and lay exposed to them. Spurts of incandescence flicked out from the prone team with speed that has no place in time, signifying the muzzle flashes of high rate-of-fire weapons.

"Ambush," said the Colonel.

WHISKEY 2-2
Zabul Province
1605

It was raining goats. They flew through the air amid blasts of earth debris, some whole and bleating, some sundered and spraying blood, some atomized. The weather had become 100 percent chance of goat guts, red mist, gobbits of blasted flesh, the unself-conscious screams of animals suddenly sentient to the prospect of their own extinction.

Then Skelton launched. He pinwheeled fifteen feet through the air, his face a study in wonder, spinning, legs and arms extended, defying gravity as he sailed.

Ray lurched in that moment, saving his own life, for surely the gunner was shooting right to left, semi-auto. He had missed twice, hitting goat flesh, the huge .50 caliber detonations unleashing waves of energy that flipped other goats airward, then scoring a hard one that took Skelton solid, and then pivoted the huge weapon on the bipod another half a millimeter to plant one in Ray. But aiming for center mass, he was behind Ray on the action curve, and time in flight from half a mile out didn't help either. The express train hit Ray on the outer surface of the left thigh. It hit no bones, broke nothing full of coursing fluids, and delivered nothing but energy.

Ray flew. He left the earth behind. He'd seen—and hit—enough guys with a .50 to know what the phenomenon looked like. Usually the delivered energy is so high—in the 5,000 foot-pound range—that a frail sack of blood and struts like a human being will flip through the air, sometimes as far as thirty feet, limbs askew, and land like a pile of wreckage. So it was with Ray and he seemed to be in midair for a long while, and had a full measure of time to miss his mother and father, those good people dead since '01, who had given him exactly what he wanted and needed, love and support and belief, and enough time as well to miss the Marine Corps, which took over when his parents were called away, which had given him so many opportunities to do that at which he excelled, and then he hit the ground in a concussion of dust and stones and sprigs of leaf and twig. He spat out a missile of phlegm and grit, thanked god he hadn't landed on his back where such an impact would have driven his SR-25 into his flesh, possibly breaking some ribs and bruising his spine.

The surviving goats bleated pitifully, flicking this way and that in utter panic, not even stopping to shit.

"Oh God, Ray," he heard Skelton scream, "I am hit so bad, oh, Ray, he killed me."

"Stay there," he yelled back, "I'll get to you."

"No, Ray, get the fuck outta Dodge, I am checking out on this one. Fuck, he blew a hole clear through my guts and I can't move, Ray, go, go, go."

Another burst of .50s lit up the ridgeline, delivering more theater of destruction. Goats flew, dust exploded from the earth, angry chips of stone and metal sang through the air. Ray was just a bit out of the beaten zone, as he'd been deposited by the whimsy of physics off the crestline, maybe a little below it, while poor Skelton was exposed for a second delivery of the heavy packages.

Ray squirmed left, pushed himself down and wished he could get a good visual on his pard. If the boy was dead, no point in hanging around. If he was wounded . . . well, that was a different story, as he had his rifle and if he played it cool and those motherfuckers came to examine their kill, he could take a bunch of them down before they closed. Ray low-crawled a few feet back up, slipped behind the carcass of a dead animal and peered over the top. Neither part of Skelton appeared to be alive.

Cocksuckers, he thought, and swore there'd come a time when he put the dead zero on these operators and watch them sag to stillness under the entreaties of his .308 hollowpoints.